SHOW BUSINESS

Show Business

A NOVEL BY

Shashi Tharoor

ARCADE PUBLISHING • NEW YORK

FIRST NORTH AMERICAN EDITION

This is a work of fiction. Names, characters, places, and incidents either are the product of the author's imagination or, if real, are used fictitiously.

LIBRARY OF CONGRESS CATALOGING-IN-PUBLICATION DATA

Tharoor, Shashi, 1956–
    Show business : a novel / by Shashi Tharoor.—1st North American ed.
      p. cm.
    ISBN 1-55970-181-1
    I. Title.
    PR9499.3.T535S5   1992
    823—dc20   91-41791

Published in the United States by Arcade Publishing, New York
Distributed by Little, Brown and Company

10 9 8 7 6 5 4 3 2

RRD VA

Designed by Barbara Werden

PRINTED IN THE UNITED STATES OF AMERICA

For my sisters
Shobha and Smita
in fulfillment of a twenty-year-old promise
to take them to the movies

Contents

Interior: Day

I can't believe I'm doing this.

Me, Ashok Banjara, product of the finest public school in independent India, secretary of the Shakespeare Society at St. Francis' College, no less, not to mention son of the Minister of State for Minor Textiles, chasing an aging actress around a papier-mâché tree in an artificial drizzle, lip-synching to the tinny inanities of an aspiring (and highly aspiring) playback-singer. But it *is* me, it's my mouth that's moving in soundless ardor, it's my feet that are scudding treeward in faithful obeisance to the unlikely choreography of the dance director. Move, step, turn, as sari-clad Abha, yesterday's heartthrob, old enough to be my mother and just about beginning to show it, nimbly evades my practiced lunge and runs, famous bust outthrust, to the temporary shelter of an improbably leafy branch. I follow, head tilted back, arms outstretched, pretending to sing:

> *I shall always chase you*
> *To the ends of the earth,*
> *I want to embrace you*
> *From Pahelgaon to Perth,*
> *My love!*

My arms encircle her, but, as my fingertips meet, she ducks, dancing, and slips out of my clutches, pirouetting gaily away.

Drenched chiffon clings to the pointed cones of her blouse, but she raises one end of the soaked sari *pallav* to half cover her face, holding the edge across the bridge of her perfect nose in practiced coyness. Her large eyes imprison me, then blink in release. Despite myself, I marvel. She has done this for twenty years; it is my first attempt.

> *I shall always chase you*
> *From now 'til my rebirth*
> *And it's only when I face you*
> *That I feel I know my worth,*
> *My love!*
>
> *I shall always chase you,*
> *I'll never feel the dearth*
> *Of my desire to lace you*
> *Around my —*

"Cut!" I am caught in midgesture, midmovement, midword. The playback track screeches to a stop. I freeze, feeling as foolish as I imagine I must look. Abha snaps her irritation, turns away.

"No, no, no!" The dance director is waddling furiously toward me. He is fat and dark, but nothing if not expressive: his hands are trembling, his kohl-lined eyes are trembling, the layers and folds of flesh on his bare torso are trembling. "How many times I am telling you! Like this!" Hands, feet, and trunk describe arabesques of motion. "Not this!" He does a passable imitation of a stiff-necked paraplegic having a seizure. The technicians laugh. I smile nervously, looking furtively at my costar. Abha stands apart from us, hands on hips in a posture of fury. But am I imagining it, or is there something softer around her eyes as she looks at me?

I open hapless hands to the dance director, palms facing him in a gesture of concession. "OK, OK, Masterji. Sorry."

"Sorry? Is *my* good name you will be ruining. What all is this, they will be saying. Gopi Master has forgotten what is dance." His pectorals quiver in indignation. "For you maybe doesn't matter. You are *bachcha*. I am having fifteen years in this business. What they will say about me, hanh?"

I shrug my embarrassment. I thought I'd done what I had been told to do, but that doesn't seem the right thing to say. Gopi Master

4

stamps his feet, one oily ringlet of black hair falling over a flashing red eye. He tosses his curls and strides off.

"OK, OK." This is the director, Mohanlal. Mohanlal looks like a lower divisional clerk. He wears a fraying white cotton shirt, black trousers, thick glasses, and a perpetually harassed expression. Right now it is even more harassed than usual. I am evolving a Mohanlal Scale of High Anxiety, ranging from the pained visage with which he embarks on any second take (one on the scale) to the extreme angst that furrows his face when the producer-sahib visits and wants to know why the film isn't finished yet (ten). My terpsichorean incompetence has him up to about five, but he is teetering on the edge of six. I try to look earnest and willing.

"OK," says Mohanlal for the third time. "Let's get back to this. Abhaji, I am sorry. Just once more, please, I promise you. Right, Ashokji? We'll get it right this time."

"Right," I respond, without confidence.

"OK, clear the stage." Mohanlal's instructions emerge in the mildest tone, and one of the producer's sidekicks, standing beyond the arc lights, claps his hands like a manual relay station to reinforce them. The clapper boy holds his board up for the start of the take. I grin at Abha, hoping for sympathy. She averts her gaze.

"Lights! Camera! Action!"

Ah, the magic of those words! I suppose that's what brought me into this business in the first place. Years of amateur theater, from college productions of *Charley's Aunt* and *The Importance of Being Earnest* to postdegree forays into Pinter and Beckett, had given me an irrevocable taste for greasepaint and footlights. Except, of course, that there was no money in it, and not much recognition either — unless you count the occasional notice in the *Hindustan Times,* sandwiched between a dance recital and an account of a Rotary Club speech. I spent months rehearsing foreign plays after work with other similarly afflicted ex-collegians and four evenings at a stretch putting them on for audiences of a few hundred Anglophile Delhiites, all for no reward other than a mildly bibulous cast party at which ignorant well-wishers poured pretentious praise into my rum. After half a dozen of these productions I decided I had had enough. But I couldn't stop wanting to act, and when I discovered that I could no longer face going to the office without the prospect of rehearsals afterward, I realized what I had to do. I had to take the advice of my classmate Tool Dwivedi, as avid a cinephile as ever queued in dirty *chappals* and torn *kurta* for black market tickets to the latest releases. I had to go into films.

"Only real world there is, *yaar,*" Tool had said between lengthy drags on his chillum, before disappearing to Benares to study Hindu philosophy. I had not heard from him since, but his enthusiasm lingered. I decided to act on his idea.

"But it's all so artificial," Malini had protested when I told her of my plans. Malini was an afterwork thespian too — an account executive in an advertising firm in whom I was moderately interested.

"Artificial?" I asked incredulously. "What do you mean, artificial? Isn't all acting artificial?"

"You know, all that running around trees, chasing heroines. Singing songs as you waltz through parks. You know what I mean."

"That isn't artificial, that's mass entertainment." She raised her untrimmed eyebrows and I decided to let her have it. "You want artificial, I'll tell you what's artificial. What we're doing is artificial. Here, in Delhi, putting on English plays written for English actors, in a language the majority of our fellow Indians don't even understand. What's more artificial than that?"

"Are you telling me," Malini bridled, "that our work in the theater, in the *theater,* is artificial, and what you want to do in" — she uttered the phrase with distaste — "Bombay films, is not?"

She was beginning to get angry, and this was a bad sign: I had had hopes of a farewell kiss, if not more. But I was in too deep now to pull back. "Yes," I said firmly. "We're an irrelevant minority performing for an irrelevant minority in a language and a medium that guarantee both irrelevance and minorityhood. I mean, how many people watch the English-language theater in this country? And how many of those watch us?"

"Numbers? Is that all that matters to you?" Malini was scathing. "We're reaching a far more important audience here, a far more aware audience. We're in the front line of what's happening in world theater. We're doing plays that have taken Broadway and the West End by storm."

"Yeah, ten years ago," I retorted. "Look, Malini, English-language theater in India has no place to go but in circles, and you know it.

6

The same old plays rehashed for the same ignorant crowd. Who cares? Films are for real."

"Hindi films? Real? Give me a break." She got up then; she was always fond of matching movements to words, to the despair of our directors. "Look, Ashok, if you want to go off and make a fool of yourself in Bombay, do what you like. But don't give me this kind of crap about it, OK?"

That was my cue, and for the sake of fond farewells I should have taken it and recanted, if only to mutter "nevertheless it does move" under my breath. But no, I had to stand up for my choice, didn't I? "It's not crap," I asserted. "Hindi films are real, much more real in India than anything we're doing. They even constitute a profession, an industry, which is more than anyone can say for us, for Chrissake. And if all goes reasonably well," I added hastily, because Malini seemed either about to explode or exit, "the film business will bring in some real money." One hit, I thought, one hit, and I'd be raking in more than I could hope to earn in several years in the Hindustanized multinational I had predictably joined after college. Without tax deductions at source either. Wage payers in movieland were notoriously less finicky about the tax laws than the paisa-pinching accountants who remunerated me for marketing detergents.

"And if all doesn't go reasonably well?" Malini was angrier than she needed to be. It suddenly struck me that the woman cared. And I'd never noticed it before. "You're chucking up a good job, decent prospects, a pleasant enough life here and serious theater to knock on the doors of the manufacturers of mass escapism. What happens if they don't answer?"

"They will," I said defiantly.

"Drop me a postcard when they do." And she walked out, slamming the door behind her. Theatrical, that's what she was, in a word. Theatrical. I didn't try to go after her. There would be no going back to theater.

So here I am, in Bombay, filmi capital of India, shooting my first starring role at S. T. Studios, which has seen many a hero cavort his way to cinematic immortality. And in Choubey Productions' *Musafir,* alongside the legendary Abha Patel, who has had a fair stab at cinematic immortality herself. Me, Ashok Banjara, sharing celluloid with the star whose bust, vividly painted by a proletarian social-

7

realist on a cinema billboard, once caused a celebrated traffic jam. The magic words "Lights! Camera! Action!" are ringing in my ears, the bulbs are beaming in my face and likewise Abha, if only in her screen persona. So why am I so desperately unhappy?

Of course I shouldn't be. After all, I've scored one in the eye of the dreaded Radha Sabnis, alias Cheetah of "Cheetah's Chatter" in *Showbiz* magazine and author of the one and only reference to me in the filmi print media to date. That wasn't too long ago, and every line is burned into my memory.

> Darlings, Cheetah has been asking herself for weeks who is that tall, not-too-dark and none-too-handsome type who has been hanging around all the filmi parties of late? From his hungry expression and anxiety to please, I thought he might be a new caterer. Not an actor, surely? But yes, my dears, surprises will never cease in Bollywood. Actor he is, or rather wants to be. One glance at him, and Dharmendra and Rajesh Khanna can continue to sleep soundly: this soulful type with the looks of a garage mechanic isn't going very far. Hardly surprising, then, that producers aren't exactly falling over themselves to sign him. But then why, Cheetah asks herself, does he keep getting invited to the fun soirees of filmland? Simple reason, darlings: he's a minister's son. Our mystery man turns out to be none other than Anil, elder son of the Minister of State for Minor Textiles, Kulbhushan Banjara. Our canny filmwallahs seem to have adopted the maxim, if you don't need him, at least feed him—no point offending a minister, after all. Who says our filmi crowd are out of touch with modern Indian realities, eh? Grrrowl!

Anil, indeed. The witch couldn't even get my name right.

But here I am, anyway, Cheetah's grrowls notwithstanding.

And in the teeth, I might add, of familial opposition, indeed disbelief. My father's jaw actually dropped when I told him; even at home I couldn't escape the theatrical. My younger brother, Ashwin, who had grown up attached to my shirttails like a surplus shadow, should have been pleased that he would now have a filmi hero to worship instead of a mere Brother Who Could Do No Wrong. None of it: he just looked at me, large eyes limpid in disappointment, as if I'd been fooling around with his girlfriend (which, in point of fact, I had, though he didn't know it). "Films, Ashok-bhai?" he asked incredulously. "Bombay? You?" And he shook his head slowly, as if wanting to believe I knew what I was doing, but failing in the attempt to convince himself. Only my mother, as usual, was nonjudgmental. But all she could bring herself to say to me were the standard words of blessing, "*jeeté raho*" ("may you go on living"), which hardly qualified as active encouragement. Pity Tool Dwivedi wasn't around to buck me up and cheer me on, but then he was contemplating his navel and his dirty toenails somewhere on the banks of the Ganges, beyond the reach of the Franciscan old boy network. In my great adventure I was, it seemed, completely alone.

But alone or not, I'm in the middle of a film set now and there's no time for existential self-indulgence. The playback song starts again, I lip-synch my melodic vow of eternal pursuit, the rain falls through holed buckets, my feet move as they have been taught, but I am terrified they will trip over each other. I am acutely aware of the ridiculousness of what I am doing, even more aware of the incompetence with which I am doing it. Double embarrassment here, to be doing the ridiculous incompetently. I am so petrified with fear of failure that I do not sense the tickle in my nose until I reach for Abha in midcavort, my back impossibly bent in choreographical adulation, one hand behind my rump like a bureaucrat seeking a discreet bribe, the other stretching up to her chin, lips moving to the playback lyric. I am hardly aware of it as I look into her eyes, my nostrils flaring in desire, and sneeze.

"Cut!"

"Oh, Christ," I mutter under my breath, reaching for my handkerchief. I am not Christian, but fourteen years of a Catholic education have taught me a fine line in blasphemy.

All hell breaks loose. As I sneeze again, I see Gopi Master, beside himself, launching into a paroxysmal frenzy that could easily be set to music in his next film. I see Abha throwing up her hands and stalking off toward her dressing room. There is the crash of a door: I seem to have this effect on women. I see angry faces, laughing faces, exasperated faces, black and brown and red faces, all animated and contorted in their urgent need for self-expression. I sneeze again, hearing voices raised, announcing how many takes have been taken, recording how many hours have been lost, recalling how overdue the next meal break is. Mohanlal nears me, reproach written in every furrowed line on his brow. His anxiety is eight on the Scale, and climbing.

"Sorry, Mohanlalji," I sniff. "Couldn't help it. Must be all this rain. I'm very wet. Achoo." I dab at my offending proboscis, and my handkerchief turns an alarming color. It's even more serious than I'd thought! No, I've just taken some makeup off.

Mohanlal looks decidedly unsympathetic. "Abhaji is being wet, too," he says. "So also half the technicians, with perspiration if not with this water. How is it that you are only one who is catching cold?"

I am completely taken aback by this evidence of directorial heartlessness. "It's hardly my fault, is it, if I — *achoo!*"

Mohanlal is spared the task of apportioning relative blame for the uncommon cold by the arrival of one of Abha's *chamchas*. He is a lower grade of hanger-on in that he doesn't travel with her, but shows up at the studio to run odd errands and generally gratify her sense of self-importance. Mohanlal turns to him, his anxiousness clearly heading from eight to nine. When Abha sends her sidekick to him, there are obvious grounds for fearing the worst.

"Memsahib not coming," the *chamcha* announces importantly, confirming Mohanlal's apprehensions. "Too tired."

"Wh-a-at?" The director is up to nine now. "What do you mean?"

The sidekick switches to Hindi. "Abhaji says she is not coming back today for any more shooting. She is very tired after all those takes." He looks meaningfully at me.

"But she can't do this to me!" Mohanlal begins, quite literally, to tear out his hair, his long fingers running through the thinning strands like refugees fleeing in despair, taking with them what they can. "We're behind schedule as it is."

"That," said the *chamcha* pointedly, "is not *her* fault."

Mohanlal turns to me, murder in his ineffectual eyes. "This is your doing," he breathes in a furious bleat, switching back to Hinglish for my benefit. "You are not being able to dance, you are not being able to move, you are not being able to do one song picturization right. No wonder Abhaji has had enough." He reaches out for the *chamcha,* who is sidling away from this sordid domestic scene. "Where is she?" He returns to Hindi. "I'll go and talk to her."

"It won't do any good," the sidekick replies, with a knowing shake of the head. "And it might just have the opposite effect." Mo-hanlal nods wearily. Abha's rages are legendary: she is efficient and professional and even occasionally pleasant, but once her temper is aroused, flames leap from her tongue, singeing wigs at sixty paces.

"OK." Mohanlal's favorite two syllables emerge reluctantly, like air from a deflating radial. "We'll take a break now," he tells the technicians, who have begun to throng around us in the manner of the traditional Hindi movie crowd scene. He says this with a groan, a man at the end of his tether.

"Look," I suggest helpfully in conciliatory Hindi, "while you all take a break, why don't I try and have an extra rehearsal with Gopi Master?"

"Because he'd kill you, that's all," Mohanlal says with a sudden passion. "Which mightn't be such a bad idea. Where is he?" He looks around, and spots the dance master in a corner, face buried in his hands in a mournful sulk of great intensity.

"Just trying to be helpful, that's all," I say, backing off. "You're right, I don't think we should disturb him. Maybe I could use a rest after all."

"*Rest?*" Mohanlal is almost screaming. "If I were the producer, I'd give you permanent rest." He must be upset; he has never spoken to me like this before. I will have to redraw the Scale. By the stan-dards of everything that has gone before, this is practically an eleven.

But high anxiety has suddenly metamorphosed in my director into aggression. "You are not going to rest, Mr. Hero," Mohanlal adds, jabbing his forefinger into my chest to punctuate his return to English. "I am telling you what you are going to do. You are going to get Abhaji back here. Is your fault she is not here, isn't it, is your fault this picture is not having shooting now, is all your fault. So you get it going again. You were wanting to be filmi hero?" he demands rhetorically, taking me by the upper arm and propelling me toward Abha's dressing room. "I am giving you your big chance. Enter the tigress's den and bring her out. I am not caring if you are in her jaws and bleeding when she comes out, but you get her here."

He might have put it a little less colorfully, I think, as I shuffle to the door. My diffident knock elicits no response. I try again.

"What is it?"

"Abhaji, it's me. Ashok."

"What do you want? I'm changing."

"Just to talk, Abhaji. When you've changed."

"There's nothing to talk about. I'm going home."

"I know, Abhaji. But I must talk to you. I need your advice."

"Advice?" She laughs, but the tone seems to soften. "I can think of other words for what you need."

"Please?"

There is a pause behind the closed door. Then the famously girlish voice, still undulled by age, responds, "All right, give me a minute while I get dry."

"Take your time," I agree, looking back at Mohanlal to make sure my progress thus far has been noted. He catches my glance, snorts, and looks away. Around him reigns the amiable anarchy of a studio set during a break: a confusion of wires, a diffusion of lights, a profusion of grips moving reflectors, stools, and power boxes. Not to mention a steady infusion of teacups, lubricating both activity and idleness. In a corner, oblivious to the clatter and the clutter, sits Gopi Master, palms on temples, red-eyed in mourning. Red- and black-eyed, actually, because emotion has smudged his kohl. I turn hastily back to Abha's dressing room and knock again.

The door opens and a mousy little face peers out. It is Celestine, Abha's dresser, a girl who contrives to be even smaller than her famously petite mistress. She has undoubtedly been chosen for that, as well as for her bridgeless snub nose, frightened black eyes, and downy lip, all of which give the star nothing to worry about in her mirror while being dressed. What the hell, we all need reassurance; there's nothing better than being able to employ it.

"Memsahib says you can come in now," Celestine whispers, respectfully or conspiratorially, I am not sure. I step in, and she closes the door behind me. Abha is seated at the dressing table, her head tilted as she tries to insert a gold teardrop into a perfect earlobe. She has changed out of the wet sari she was acting in into a splendid *churidar-kameez* in blue silk. She is looking pleased with the result, as well she might. My eyes linger on her exquisite face, seen so many times larger than life on so many movie screens in my childhood, on the sweep of black hair that flows to one side with the tilt of her head, on the creamy feet half slipped into tiny high-heeled black sandals. And inevitably — for in Agra you can't help noticing the Taj — at the most famous bust in India, iconically displayed on so many cinema posters across the country, rising taut and firm against the silk of her *kameez*. For years her breasts had been Abha's trademark, like Monroe's legs or Bardot's derriere, though, unlike these actresses, she was never called upon to reveal as much of her assets. Indian screenplays did not require it, and even if they did, our Indian censors would not permit it. Nudity is a commonplace in our countryside, of course, where many women cannot afford much to wear, but it is banned on our screens; whereas fisticuffs and homicide, which are illegal, are energetically portrayed. I must get someone to explain it to me sometime.

No time for idle musings on the senses of our censors, though, as I take my eyes off Abha's peaks to contend with Abha's pique. She has finished with the earring and is returning my gaze, her expression an unspoken question.

"You're beautiful," I find myself saying.

She is now less angry than amused. "You haven't come here to flatter me," she replies, but it is obvious she is pleased.

"No, I mean it," I protest sincerely, my eyes straying to the bottle of hair dye she has left inadvertently on the table. "No one would believe you're thirty-five."

"Thirty-six," she corrects me. Even if she joined the movies straight after school, she must be at least forty-two.

"I don't believe it," I retort, striving to keep ambiguity out of my tone. "It seems just yesterday I saw you in *Patthar aur Phool*." In a television rerun, I am tempted to add, but don't.

"So what do you want?" she asks, half smiling, waiting.

"There's much drama going on there," I laugh, with a gesture beyond the door. "I've never seen Mohanlal so upset. Anger made him really articulate."

"Did he send you to me?" she asks, pleasantly enough.

"Yes," I respond in all innocence. "He —"

"You can tell that cowardly son of a *chaprassi* he should have the balls to face me himself," she blazes. "Go on, go and tell him that."

"I will, in just a minute," I concur hastily, cursing my tactical clumsiness. "But I didn't come here only for Mohanlal. I need to talk to you, Abhaji."

"What about?" The situation is still retrievable. She is slowly decelerating from her tigress mode.

I haven't a clue what to say next, so I shift from one foot to the other, looking uncomfortable. My glance lingers on Celestine, who is standing dubiously against the wall like a mouse evaluating a cheese of uncertain provenance. Abha thinks she understands the reason for my silence. She gestures with a tilt of her head, and the dresser scurries noiselessly away.

"Don't come back till I call you," Abha orders, and the door clicks behind me. We are alone: the first time I have been with Abha without an audience, an entire crew looking on.

"Thank you," I say. She nods, slightly impatient. I must think of something to say. I speak without thinking: "Abhaji, I know I'm making a mess of things out there. I'm truly sorry."

Her face lightens visibly. "Sorry? In all my years in Hindi films, I've never heard an actor use that word. Even when it was in the script." She pats the bed, the only other piece of furniture in the dressing room. "I knew you were a decent boy. Come and sit here." Wordlessly, I obey.

She looks at me, smiling. "I accept your apology."

"You must be sick and tired of my incompetence," I say. "I don't blame you for walking off like that."

There is a bright light in her eyes, and it doesn't come from a reflector. "Oh, I didn't walk off just because of you," she says. "I'd had enough of that pair of idiots. When it's obvious you can't do something, when something isn't working, do they try and change it? No, Gopi Master has to have his precious steps just the way he wants them, which is just the way *he* can do them, and that spineless Mohanlal, all he can do is to ask you to try it again. So we do take after take, I wear myself out, you get more and more worried and more and more self-conscious, and that mollusk, that invertebrate, just says 'one more take, we'll get it right now, won't we?' Calls himself a director! He couldn't direct air out of a balloon."

I cannot believe my ears. So it isn't just my fault after all! Abha's words are lifting an incredible weight off my padded shoulders. I feel almost exhilarated. "Abhaji, so what should I do? You know this is my first film. I really want it to work. But the way Mohanlal makes me feel, I wonder why he allowed me to be cast in the first place."

Abha gives me a sidelong look. "Now you disappoint me. I thought you were going to speak honestly with me. None of this false innocent talk. As if you don't know the reason."

I am genuinely taken aback by her words. "What do you mean?" I ask. "I know I hung around the producer's house so much he finally had to sign me. But he wouldn't have done that if he didn't think I really fitted the role. He told me so himself."

Abha sighs. She stands up and walks the two paces to where I sit on the bed. "You really are an innocent, aren't you?" she asks. The question seems to need no reply. "You mean you really don't know." This time it is a statement, not a question. I look up at her, shake my head.

"Who is your father?"

"I thought you were going to say that," I respond hotly. "OK, so he's a minister. But he hasn't lifted a finger to help me. Never has, never will. Hates me being in films. You've got it wrong, I tell you. He didn't get me the role, *wouldn't* get me the role. And in any case, no one signs you just because you're a minister's son. My father isn't even that important a minister. Who'd risk an entire film just to please him?"

"I'll tell you." She stands over me, hand on hip. "Who is the producer?"

This is silly, but I am looking up at her, seeing her face, her bright eyes, through the fabulous twin cones above my forehead, and I feel compelled to respond. "Jagannath Choubey," I reply.

"And who is Jagannath Choubey?"

"A rich man. A producer." She impatiently shakes her head at my replies. "An industrialist."

"Right. What industry?"

"I don't know. Factories of some sort."

"What sort?"

"Clothing, I think."

"Another word for clothing?"

My eyes widen. "Textiles?"

"Got it. And what does a textile magnate need when he wants to make more money out of textiles?" I do not answer. I am too busy looking into the abyss. "Licenses for expansion. Who approves licenses? The minister holding the relevant portfolio. In this case, minor textiles. Last question: who is the Minister for Minor Textiles?"

I groan.

"You really hadn't realized, had you?" Her voice is soft, speculative. Her hand touches my head, rumples my hair. "Poor boy."

I am devastated. I feel an emptiness widening inside me, pushing out all confidence, all pride. I don't know what to say.

Suddenly, she is sitting beside me. She puts a hand to my face, turns it toward her. "Don't be too depressed. Everybody has to get their start somehow. Your way is better than most. You don't know what some people have to do to get their first big roles. You're lucky — you haven't had to do anything."

I push her hand away and get up. I am that emptiness now; nothing else matters.

"Where are you going?"

"To Mohanlal, to quit. I can't do this anymore."

She stands up too. "Don't be silly."

"Look, the only thing that kept me going from one disastrous take to another was the belief that at least the producer had thought me good enough for this role, really suited to it. We've been shooting for weeks, Mohanlal is obviously not happy, nothing is going right, the film is way behind schedule, and now you have just removed the one remaining prop that commits me to this madness. Malini was right: films just aren't my scene. I've got to get out." I make for the door.

Her voice stops me like the lash of a lasso. "Don't you dare!"

I turn around, surprise raising my eyebrows. She is standing near the bed, *both* hands on hips now, and her eyes are blazing. "Now you listen to me, Ashok Banjara. You said you wanted some advice, and you're going to get it. You can wallow as much as you like in your sea of self-pity, but you're not going to get everyone else to drown in it. If you walk out now, this picture is finished. It will be impossible to salvage. Exposed film will be canned, losses written off, contract labor fired. You will be feeling sorry for yourself, and you will go back to your Malini and weep on her shoulder and tell her how right she was. You've got nothing to lose; your career doesn't even exist yet. But the rest of us, Ashok Banjara, *we* have a lot more to lose." She hasn't moved an inch during all this, and I am riveted by the steel of her tongue, held by the magnets of her eyes. Her voice drops a register. "This is my first starrer in two years. They've been saying I'm past it, too old to play the heroine. They're offering me 'parallel' roles now: they think 'parallel' is a politer word than 'supporting.' Six months ago Moolchand Malik asked me to play Rajesh Khanna's mother in his next film. I've got something to prove to these people. If you walk out on this film now, you'll destroy what might be my last chance. I'm not going to let you."

"B–but," I stutter. I've already forgotten how I sparked this outburst, or why. "But it was *you* who walked out, not me," I conclude lamely.

"I walked off, I didn't walk out," comes her riposte. "I'd had enough of that maggot Mohanlal — for today. I'm too tired, Ashok. It all takes too much out of me. I've even swallowed my tranquilizer pill." It couldn't have begun to take effect, I think; Abha has been anything but tranquil. "I'd have been back tomorrow, and it would have done him some good to worry about me for a change. I've been too kind; he was beginning to take me for granted. Let them not forget I'm not some starlet they've elevated from the casting couch. But *you* have no business to throw in the towel. Come here."

I'm not used to women taking that tone with me, but there's something about Abha that eliminates all resistance. I obey.

"Sit down." A firm hand on my shoulder pushes me onto the bed. Just as well. When I'm standing close to Abha I'm inconveniently conscious of how much smaller she is than I am. Having to look up at her magnificent superstructure redresses the balance.

"So you want to quit because you've just discovered they gave you the part for the wrong reasons, and because you don't think you're up to what they're asking you to do. Forget the first thing: most reasons are wrong reasons in this business. Someone gets a part by sleeping with the producer. In the end what matters is that she has the part, the film is made, perhaps it's a hit, and then she's getting offers for lots of other parts she doesn't have to earn on her back. If this film succeeds for you, no one will ask who your father is. One day, Ashok Banjara, he'll be known only as your father. Right?"

I nod humbly. And dumbly.

"Next, you don't think you can do what they want you to do. So you think you'll never make it as an actor. Wrong. Tomorrow you go to the producer, who wants to impress your father so much, and you tell him the film is going down the tubes unless he listens to you. Tell him you can't do Gopi Master's moves. You're too tall, your legs are too long, your back is too straight, whatever. Our two duets can easily be rechoreographed with me doing the dancing around you, while you stand and tilt your head and move your arms — yes, you do that rather well, Ashok Banjara. Then tell him your strengths are being underutilized by that unimaginative twit Mohanlal. Don't look at me like that — don't you know what your own strengths are? For God's sake, child, it's obvious. What are the things you *can* do? You've got long legs, you can leap and jump. Fight scenes, chase scenes, stunt scenes. Tell him to put in lots of these."

I am awestruck. "But will he do all this for me? I mean, change everything? Overrule Mohanlal?"

"Mohanlal's not Jean-Luc Godard," she retorts. "He's an employee, he'll do as he's told. And Jagannath Choubey wants to see his film finished, using the talent he's already got to the best of their ability. He has a lot of money tied up in this film, after all. Not to mention a lot of hopes involving his star's father."

"I'll see him in the morning," I vow. "Abhaji, I don't know how to thank you. I came in here to plead with you to come back to the set, and instead you've shown *me* the light. I'll never forget this, Abhaji. Tell me what I can do for you. Anything at all."

She laughs. It is a relaxed laugh, as if somebody has just called "cut" and she has switched off her overdrive. "If you really want to do something for me . . ."

"Yes? Just name it."

"You've got nice long fingers. Massage my back for me, it's hurting a bit after that last dance routine."

"You bet." Massage her back? I'd have paid for the privilege. "Er — should I say something to Mohanlal?"

"What for?"

"Well, he must be waiting for us."

"Let him wait. It'll be good for his soul."

"And what if someone walks in? While I'm massaging you?"

"Let's see who dares to walk into Abha Patel's dressing room without permission," she says fiercely, adding colloquially, "Mohanlal's dad won't do it."

"OK," I concede, borrowing Mohanlal's copyright on the word. "Shall we start?"

"Use this cream," she says, handing me a bottle. Her fingers move to the silver buttons of her *kameez*. My heart picks up tempo, like the music director's favorite bongo. "Turn around," she commands. My heart reenters adagio. I hear the gentle rustle of silk being slipped off and imagine a lover's notepaper emerging from a fragrant envelope.

"I'm ready now," she says in a low voice. I turn.

She is lying on the dressing room bed, on her front. The *kameez* is the only garment she has taken off: she has folded it onto the solitary chair. Her face is turned toward me, one cheek on the pillow, but her eyes are closed.

Bottle of cream in hand, I sit gingerly on the edge of the bed. I smear some of the cream on her back. The broad strap of her brassiere impedes my hand.

"Are you sure you want to keep this on?" I ask, my voice thickening.

"Yes," she replies shortly. "Let it be."

So much for the romance of the moment. I rub the cream into her skin, which is soft, smooth, devoid of lines: a young woman's.

"Does Celestine do this for you usually?" I ask.

"Yes," she says languorously. "But Celestine has short, stubby fingers. Not like yours." And as I stroke her shoulder blades, she moans in pleasure. The moans are soft, low: the tranquilizer must be working at last.

"Where was it hurting, Abhaji?" I ask a little later. "I'll rub a little more there."

Her voice is sleepy, the words almost a drawl. "Everywhere," she whispers. "Just go on. I'm very tired . . ."

I go on. So she really did want a massage: this was no camouflaged seduction. And I could imagine how tired she must have been, after all that cavorting in the wet, all those takes. And she isn't all that young anymore. My fingers press and smooth and knead, tracing waves and semicircles and military steps on her flesh. She breathes evenly, her small soft back rising and falling as my fingers coax the fatigue out of them. I realize she is asleep.

Damn! Here I am, sent to bring Abha out to film, and all I have succeeded in doing is putting her to sleep. I am annoyed with myself and even slightly with her. Perversely, to release my annoyance, I unhook her bra. It has left a pale discolored swath across her back. She must hardly ever take it off.

I continue stroking her back, the whole of it this time, and find myself unable to resist the obvious temptation. Here I am, a normal, red-blooded sexually deprived twenty-five-year-old Indian male, in intimate proximity to the most famous bosom in India, with only an unhooked bra between me and a vision of paradise. And she is asleep, knocked out; she need never even know.

Gently, I take her by the shoulder and turn her slightly. She does not awake. Emboldened, I turn her onto her back. She breathes sweetly, her nostrils widening slightly at each intake of air. I look at her for a moment: her face is still exquisite, but her skin is beginning to sag, folds are lining her neck, crow's-feet are tiptoeing around her eyes. Abha Patel has built her career on looking cute, but to be cute you have to be young. Her looks are incompatible with middle age, and middle age is creeping up on her like the villain's accomplice waylaying the filmi hero. Except that in the movies the hero could always escape the trap.

She looks so peaceful in sleep. No animal magnetism here, just a woman in repose. Tired, chemically promoted repose, at that. But what a woman.

What a woman. My eyes travel down her neck to the disarranged bra and narrow in puzzlement. I breathe more quickly, my heart pounding like the bongos on the playback track. My fingers, with a will of their own, reach for the cups and lift the brassiere gently off her torso.

I stare in shock. For an instant, the air stops coming into my lungs. My fingers lose their will. The bra drops back into place. My hands are shaking as I turn Abha back and rehook her bra.

I can't believe what I have just seen: breasts so shriveled and empty they are like pockets of desiccated skin, their tips drooping in dismay. Abha's bosom is that of a ninety-year-old. The most famous bust in India is a pair of falsies.

My breathing is still uneven as I get up to leave. She sleeps on, a tranquilized smile playing at the corners of her mouth. She must be dreaming, as millions of her countrymen do in the cinema theaters of our nation. Except that they dream with their eyes open.

Exterior: Day

GODAMBO

The small plane appears at a distance against a clear blue sky. Water shimmers below, the sunlight making patterns of molten gold on the surface of the waves. As the noise of its engines becomes louder, the plane weaves unsteadily. The sound of fist landing on flesh is heard. *Dishoom!*

Interior: a fight is in progress. The pilot lies sprawled across the controls, a vivid red stain across his white-uniformed back. A bald villain is slugging our hero, Ashok. Ashok ducks, kicks. The villain clutches his stomach, the plane bucks, Ashok pushes the pilot aside and seizes the controls. Exterior: the plane dips, straightens itself out. Interior: the villain approaches Ashok from behind, his lips parted in a gruesome snarl. As he raises both hands to bring them down on our hero, Ashok lowers his head and in one sudden jerk smashes it backward into the villain's face. Baldy grunts, clutching a bleeding nose. Ashok half rises, one hand still firmly on the plane's controls, and with scarcely a backward glance sends his free elbow crashing into the villain's solar plexus. Baldy doubles over and falls. Ashok, grim determination on his face, keeps the plane steady. Below, the water continues to shimmer.

The villain, lying on the floor of the cockpit, spots his gun under the pilot's seat. His eyes glint. The gun glints. Ashok, at the controls, has his back to him. Slowly, Baldy inches forward, his bloody hand stretching out toward the gun. Close-up: Ashok, alert eyes scanning the horizon, look of grim determination still on face. Back to villain, inching steadily closer to weapon. Ashok, seemingly oblivious, looks at altimeter, fuel gauge, and assorted other indicators. Baldy's hand nears the weapon. He almost has it! Just as his fingers touch the gun metal, Ashok's foot lands crushingly on his hand. The villain grimaces, yowling in pain. Ashok kicks away the gun, which flies to the door of the plane. The villain gets up, stumbles toward it. He reaches the gun; the plane lurches, the villain trips, falls against the door. His free hand, seeking support, grabs the first thing it can. Alas, it is the handle of the door, which flies open. Villain and gun follow each other into the void.

Long shot, in slow motion, of Baldy plummeting unceremoniously to his wet fate, punctuated by a long, plaintive, despairing scream. A resounding splash is heard; a small fountain mushrooms upward. Shark fins appear ominously in the water. Ashok smiles grimly, brings the aircraft under control. Once again, the plane is seen against the clear blue sky, but now it's flying steadily and purposefully, like its pilot. The water still shimmers.

The credits appear on the screen. The sound track swells with the theme song:

I am the long arm of the law,
I'll always show villains the door
By day or by night
I'll handle any fight
And put all the bad men on the floor!

I am the long arm of the law,
I'll never flinch from blood and gore,
Rapists and muggers,
Car thieves and smugglers,
Will always get it on the jaw!

I am the long arm of the law,
No one is quicker on the draw,
Injustice and corruption,
Forces of disruption,
Will be the losers in this war!

Ashok taxis to a stop. A police Jeep is waiting on the tarmac. A uniformed officer with a thin mustache and fat jowls asks anxiously, "What happened? Where's the villain?"

"He had an urgent appointment," Ashok replies, "with destiny."

Inside the police station more details emerge. "You were right, sir," Ashok tells his senior officer, the ramrod-straight Iftikhar, the only filmi cop whose waistline is as thin as his mustache. "The smugglers have become even more daring. They have taken to using small private planes now." Ashok had hidden on board with the gold biscuits, been discovered, and in the ensuing altercation Baldy had shot his own pilot by mistake. As Iftikhar regrets that neither villain is available for questioning, policemen enter with the boxes recovered from the aircraft, closely packed with the precious yellow metal. The gold glints like sunlight on shimmering water.

"*Shabash,*" says Iftikhar. It is his favorite word of congratulation: he has uttered it, in precisely that tone of rectitude and recognition, in more than two hundred films. Ashok acknowledges the accolade with a manly nod. "But there is much more to do. We must nab the mastermind of this operation — the dreaded Godambo."

Interior: a huge, cavernous hall. Two nervous men walk across a marbled floor. The sound of their shoes on the marble is the only intrusion in the silence. Then the music builds: at first slow, then with mounting tempo, danger in every note. The men pass massive pillars, eerily lit in red and gold, and cast apprehensive glances at the black-clad commandos standing at attention beside each pillar, submachine guns at the ready. Each has a springing animal stitched on a badge on his sleeve, onto which is embroidered the words "Black Cheetah" in gold thread. In the center of the hall ripples a large pool flanked by ornamental fountains whose waters are also illuminated in red and gold. Gradually emerging into view beyond the pool, an imposing figure sits on a jeweled throne. He has a large domed and hairless head: not even a mustache breaks the expanse of solid flesh. He is attired in black, red, and gold; a cape flows behind him, and his feet are encased in gold maharajah shoes, their very points sharp with menace. On his lap is a baby cheetah — a live one this time — which he strokes incessantly.

The men come to a halt at the pool and look across at their master. In the water a fin appears, swirling rapidly, and disappears again. The men swallow, exchanging tense glances.

"Well?" The voice from the throne is deep and gravelly, the voice of a major villain.

The men shift uneasily from foot to foot.

"Where is my *maal?*" the powerful voice asks. In close-up, the villain scratches the cheetah's neck.

"Sir — mighty Godambo, we don't have it," says the thinner of the two men.

"And how can that be? Who dares to deny mighty Godambo his goods?"

"Sir, the plane did not land. The police have captured it."

"What?!" Godambo's voice is raised in fury. The cheetah, its hairs standing on end, sits up on his lap. "You imbeciles have allowed my plane to fall into the hands of the police? Where is the agent who was on board?"

"He is dead, mighty Godambo," the thinner man confesses. (The other man has no lines: it is cheaper that way.) "We believe that this is all the work of that CID inspector, Ashok. He has been on our trail for some time."

"Fools! How dare you allow a mere CID inspector to come in the way of the plans of mighty Godambo!" The voice drops to a whisper, a gravelly one, but a whisper nonetheless. "We will deal with this Inspector Ashok," he adds, each syllable dripping with menace. Pause. "You," he commands the men, "may go now."

Relief floods the pair's nervous faces. "Thank you, mighty Godambo," the thinner one stutters.

They bow, turn to leave. Godambo's brocaded arm reaches out to a button on the armrest of his throne. He jabs his thumb on it, an eloquent gesture of dismissal.

Abruptly, the floor opens up in front of the departing men. They fall in with a short scream, quickly cut short by a glug.

The shark fin appears once more in the pool, circles, dives.

Godambo presses another button in a console beside him. A giant screen emerges: the two men are seen falling vertically into the water, their hair flowing upward, hands thrashing in despair. A dark shadow swims into the screen, lunges straight for them. Close-up:

the thinner man's eyes and mouth widen in a silent scream. The shark attacks again. Godambo watches impassively, then switches off the screen.

The water on the surface of the pool turns red.

"Fools," he says. "For Godambo, failure is betrayal. And the punishment for betrayal is?"

The Black Cheetahs standing at attention reply in a chorus: "Death!"

"Death." Godambo nods approvingly. He continues stroking the cheetah on his lap.

Inspector Ashok comes home to his widowed mother. Amma is of average height, with a round, curiously unlined face and a round, curiously unlined figure. She is draped in the colorlessness of chronic bereavement: white sari, white long-sleeved blouse, white *pallav* covering most of the white hair on her head. Her expression is both kind and long-suffering: Amma has been the hero's widowed mother in so many films that she can no longer imagine herself in a colored sari. (Indeed, she can no longer imagine herself married, and so felt obliged to part from her inoffensive offscreen husband because it was too disorienting to come home to him after a day on the set.)

"Amma!" says Ashok. "Ashok!" says Amma. A heartfelt exchange of domestic pleasantries follows. Mother asks son to wash his mouth and hands quickly because she has made him carrot *halwa*. Son, obeying dutifully, inquires about mother's welfare. Mother responds with her quotidian expression of maternal anxiety about the risks taken by her *beta*. Tearfully she invokes the fate of the father (whose garlanded framed photograph on the peacock-green wall, focused upon in a lingering close-up, reveals him to have been a police officer as well, complete with pencil-line mustache). Ashok, stirred more by the photo than by his mother's entreaties, puts down his *gajar ka halwa* long enough to pledge to fulfill his father's incomplete mission in life: to bring evildoers to justice and to marry off his daughter.

Enter on cue Maya, the daughter in question. She is sixteen and pigtailed and winsomely carries a stack of schoolbooks. Ashok beams with fraternal pride and asks after her studies. More pleasantries are exchanged. To complete the picture of familial unity and bliss, the trio bursts into song:

(Refrain):
We're one small happy family,
We live and love together.
We're one small happy family,
In sunshine and bad weather.

THE MOTHER:

We're one small happy family,
Together we stand and fall.
We're one small happy family,
All for each and each for all.
(Refrain, sung by trio)

ASHOK:

We're one small happy family,
United, good and strong.
We're one small happy family,
So nothing can go wrong.
(Refrain, sung by trio)

MAYA:

We're one small happy family,
Looked after by our mother.
We're one small happy family,
Protected by my brother.
(Refrain, sung by trio)

(Adoring glances are cast at each person as each is mentioned. As they sing the refrain, they link hands and dance around a red plastic sofa. They are, it is clear, one small happy family.)

"Agent Abha. Agent Pranay." The gravelly voice, the cheetah, the pool (its surface again clean): we are back in the headquarters of the evil Godambo.

"Yes, boss." The two step forward.

Abha is petite, pretty; she is in a designer version of the black commando outfit, with black suede boots and a gold lamé chemise over her polo-neck top. But even the talents of the costumier cannot detract from her principal feature: she is built like an hourglass, but an Arab hourglass, perhaps, made by a timekeeper with sand to spare. Pranay is bigger, more strongly built, altogether more proportionate. But even the villagers in the twenty-five-paisa seats can see that he is dissolute; his narrow eyes are flecked with red, as is his narrow mouth, which is busily engaged in chewing *paan*. He sports a thick drooping black mustache, and for no apparent reason carries a whip in his right hand, with which he periodically and arhythmically smacks his left palm.

"I want you to get this Inspector Ashok for me. Agent Abha, you will seek him out. I want you first to find out how much Ashok knows about our operation. Then bring him to me, alive. I want to talk to him." Godambo laughs gutturally, as if the gravel in his throat had been scattered by a passing vehicle. The cheetah, startled, raises its head. Godambo strokes its back. "Pranay, I want you to help Abha. You know what to do."

Pranay chews some more and strikes his palm with the whip, wincing involuntarily. "Yes, boss."

"Good," says Godambo and laughs again. "I want to meet this Ashok. I want to see who is this inspector who dares to thwart the plans of mighty Godambo."

"We will take care of it, Godambo," says Abha.

"Good. And what is the penalty for those who dare to thwart Godambo's plans?"

The commandos answer in chorus: "Death."

Godambo laughs. "Death," he echoes approvingly. The cheetah blinks.

Scene: a nightclub, of the kind found only in Hindi films. A large stage, bedecked with gilt and a dazzling mosaic of multicolored mirrors, faces a valley of white-clothed tables. Seated at these, their expressions bedecked with guilt, is an indeterminate collection of diners, also white-clothed, none of whom look as if they can afford a place like this. (Indeed, they can't; they are all extras, or "Junior Artistes" as the trade prefers they be called, roped in at seventy rupees a day.) They seem remarkably uninterested in the food before them; that is because they are under strict instructions from the executive producer not to consume it. (Their own, somewhat more frugal, repast awaits them in the studio canteen after the shift.) Along one bottle-lined wall is a bar, also surprisingly untenanted: not even a bartender is visible. The reason will soon be apparent — the bar is meant only to serve as a backdrop for our hero, who will lean against it but not drink (one can never be too sure about how well alcohol will go down with our rural moralists). The lights dim; a single spotlight appears on the stage, illuminating a man with a narrow, red-stained mouth and a drooping mustache. Yes, it is none other than Pranay, except that his whip has been replaced by a pair of drumsticks. He is the percussionist of the evening, and apparently the master of ceremonies as well.

"Laddies and genurrmen," he slurs into the mike before him, "the one and only — Abha!"

A roll of drums. The spotlight moves away from him, casting rainbow patterns on the mirror mosaic. As the music builds, red and gold rectangles of stage glass part to admit the star. Hips swiveling in a sheathlike gown slit at the calves, fake diamonds sparkling at her throat and wrists, wireless mike in exquisite hand, Abha twists onto the stage. She smiles at the audience just as Ashok walks in. He is in a tuxedo, complete with black bow tie; not the standard off-duty garb of your average police officer, but the cinema-loving villagers don't know that. (Nor, for that matter, will they ask what on earth an honest middle-class cop is doing in a place like this. The Indian film industry is built on their ignorance and on their willing suspension of disbelief.)

Our hero looks at the girl on the stage, the girl on the stage looks at him, the camera looks at her looking at him, the camera looks at him, too. He leans against the bar, his face framed by a fuzzy background of bottles. The girl swings into song:

> Baby don't leave me —
> You've got to believe me,
> I love you!
> Baby don't leave me —
> Tell me you believe me,
> That I love you . . .

Her hips twist improbably; her mikeless hand, five fingers spread, traces a vivid diagonal across her torso from thigh upward, stopping only at the natural obstruction above. She tosses shoulder-length hair and croons:

> *I'm the kind of woman who takes a lot of loving,*
> *And to get it I may do some shoving,*
> *I know I've been bad*
> *But it makes me sad*
> *To think you don't want me anymore.*

Pranay joins her in the chorus:

> *Baby don't leave me —*
> *You've got to believe me,*
> *I love you!*
> *Baby don't leave me —*
> *Tell me you believe me,*
> *That I love you . . .*

Ashok smiles impassively. The girl is looking at him as she continues:

> *You're the kind of man I want to cling to,*
> *You're the only man I want to sing to,*
> *I'll put all my charms*
> *Into your arms*
> *Don't tell me you don't want me anymore.*

Pranay looks at her, looks at Ashok, then smashes the cymbals attached to his drum set as he joins in:

> *Baby don't leave me —*
> *You've got to believe me,*
> *I love you!*
> *Baby don't leave me —*
> *Tell me you believe me,*
> *That I love you . . .*

Ashok is nodding to the music now, his smile as anodyne as the indeterminable contents of the blurred bottles behind him. Abha, knees bent and leaning backward, vigorously shakes her twin assets,

like a camel removing extra drops of water after a dip in an oasis.
She sings on:

> *For you I'll do just anything,*
> *I want to hold you and wear your ring,*
> *I need to kiss you*
> *Can't bear to miss you*
> *Don't say you don't want me anymore.*

Pranay, looking at her, smashes his drumstick into the palm of his
hand out of sheer force of habit. His pain is drowned in the chorus:

> *Baby don't leave me —*
> *You've got to believe me,*
> *I love you!*
> *Baby don't leave me —*
> *Tell me you believe me,*
> *That I love you . . .*

The Junior Artistes, plates comprehensively neglected, break into
thunderous and synchronized applause.

Exterior: later that night. Ashok steps out of the nightclub. He
stands on the stoop, pulls out a cigarette, places it in his mouth.
(Smoking does not trouble the rural moralists.) A match flares: his
manly profile is lit up as he bends to light the weed.

Suddenly he hears sounds. A woman's voice, raised: "Let me go!"
His head cocked, he listens. Then he shakes out the match and steps
determinedly into the shadows.

Abha is trying to pull herself away from Pranay, who is tugging
at her arm. "Let me go!" she snaps-pleads, outraged virtue combin-
ing with panic in her voice. "No," he snarls, and the audience can
almost smell the whiskey on his breath. "You're coming with me
tonight."

Ashok emerges from the shadows. "Let the lady go," he says, his
voice calm, strong, tough (after three attempts in the dubbing
studio).

"Huh?" Pranay turns bloodshot eyes on the intruder. "And who
the hell are you to tell me what to do?" He pulls a grimacing Abha
closer.

"Never mind who I am," replies Ashok in the same tone of voice. "I don't like repeating myself. Let the lady go."

Pranay scowls. "Try and make me," he says, spitting to one side. He has Abha in his clutches now, leaving only one hand free. Abha struggles (but not too hard).

"As you like." Ashok resignedly slips off his tuxedo jacket, hangs it on the broken branch of a convenient tree. Then, while Pranay is still regarding this process in surprise, he moves forward in a quick-silver maneuver, socks the villain in the solar plexus, wrenches one arm around and liberates Abha. Before Pranay can recover, Ashok has gently moved Abha out of harm's way. The villain's fist comes flying at him, Ashok steps deftly aside, catches Pranay's wrist, and brings him crashing to the ground. The villain shakes his head, staggers to his feet, charges our hero. But without his whip Pranay is not half the man we have seen at Godambo's. Ashok administers a swift lesson in elementary fisticuffs, and Pranay bites the dust. Quite literally: some of the dust gets into his mouth, and he lies there, coughing.

"Get lost," Ashok amiably tells the sprawled villain, as an anxious Abha cowers and hovers behind him. "Or I might *really* get angry." Pranay takes the advice and, with one backward glance, stumbles away into the night, still coughing.

"Oh, thank you," breathes a grateful Abha. "You saved my life."

"It was nothing," Ashok responds modestly. "Let me take you home."

"Thank you," she agrees huskily. "It's only a short walk from here, but I'd feel so much safer with you."

They walk. He tells her she sang very well. She tells him he fought very well. He asks her how she became a singer. "*Majboori,*" she says, a catch in her voice: compulsion. She had no choice. She had wanted nothing more than to finish her studies and lead a normal life, marry someone chosen by her parents, start a family. But her father fell into the hands of bad men. He drank, he gambled, he ran up debts. Her mother wept and told him there was no money for their daughter's school fees, but he would not listen. One day the bad men came and asked for the money. Her father had nothing to give. The men ransacked the house, opened drawers, smashed mirrors, overturned tables, beat her father. But they found nothing of value. "What about your daughter?" asked their leader, an evil man with a narrow red-stained mouth and a drooping mustache. "We hear she can sing. Well, she can sing for the money." Despite her mother's tearful protests, her father agreed. They dragged her away. This was several months ago. She had been singing for them ever since.

"What if you stop? Refuse to go on?" Ashok asks, as the studio stars twinkle overhead, casting slivers of light on the teardrop that trembles on her cheek. "They will kill me." She shivers. "Or my parents. They said they would burn down my parents' house if I even thought of —" Her voice chokes.

Ashok puts an arm around her, delicately wipes the tear off her cheek with his long fingers. "Don't worry," he says, "I'll look after you." She smiles, nestles closer to him. For some reason they are walking by the beach now. Moonbeams play with her hair and shine on her pearly smile, as he introduces himself with the theme song:

> I am the long arm of the law,
> I'll always show villains the door
> By day or by night
> I'll handle any fight
> And put all the bad men on the floor!

As the song continues, the scene keeps changing to depict their evolving courtship. In one verse they are by the beach; in the next, running through a park; in a third, swaying on his motorcycle. Through each change of costume and locale, the song goes on:

> I am the long arm of the law,
> You needn't ask for any more,
> No one will hurt you,
> Nothing can dirt you,
> You are what I'm fighting for!

> I am the long arm of the law,
> No villain will touch you with his paw,
> They'll fall helter-skelter
> When I give you shelter,
> For they know what I've got in store!

I am the long arm of the law,
My skills are the very ones you saw,
Oh, damsel in distress,
Justice is my mistress,
And my heart beats for you at the core!

There are six different shots of Abha running into Ashok's arms in six different parts of town and being clasped in six different tight embraces. When the last note fades away, the camera catches them thus and lingers on Abha's face, the side that is not pressed into the hero's chest. She is smiling: but is it the smile of a woman in love, or of a villainess in victory?

Interior: Godambo's cavern. The cheetah is being scratched, the villainous palm is being struck, the fin is swirling in the pool — we are back in familiar territory.

"Are you making progress, Abha?" The gravel seems to have been troweled on today.

"Yes, mighty Godambo." Abha's eyes are lowered, so it is difficult to read her expression. She has changed from her range of respectable attire in the song — saris, *salwar-kameez* — back into her black-and-gold uniform. "He suspects nothing."

"But what have you found out? How much does he know?"

"I am still trying to win his confidence, mighty Godambo. I haven't been able to ask him that yet."

"It is taking a lot of time," Godambo says. "Pranay here is becoming impatient, aren't you, Pranay?"

Pranay, chewing, grunts affirmatively, bringing the whipstock gingerly down on his palm. He sports a pair of vivid bruises, designed to win the makeup man a *Filmfare* award.

"Poor Pranay had to put up with a lot that night at the club," Godambo chuckles evilly, "just to bring you and Ashok together. He's itching to get his own back now, aren't you, Pranay?"

Pranay chews and grunts even more vigorously. This time the whip handle falls into his palm with a satisfying thwack. Abha winces, but says nothing.

"You're not becoming too fond of this Inspector Ashok yourself, are you, Abha?" Godambo asks conversationally. The cheetah sits up. "Because if any such thought should cross your mind, you know what will happen to your parents, don't you? And to their sad little house?" The cheetah stands up on all fours on Godambo's lap. "Or indeed to you?"

A look of pain, like a fleeting shadow, crosses Abha's face. "I know where my duty lies, mighty Godambo," she says. The gold lamé chemise quivers with suppressed emotion.

"Just as well," responds the domed head on the throne. "But to be safe, I shall ask Pranay here to keep a closer eye on you. Don't want you making any silly mistakes over this Inspector Ashok." He looks at her meaningfully; she averts her gaze at first, looking down, then brings her chin up to return his stare, a strong, confident expression on her face. "Not that I don't trust you, Abha. You're an intelligent girl. You know what's good for you. And if you don't" — he raises his voice to address the pillar-posted commandos — "we all know what the punishment for betrayal is, don't we?"

The expected answer comes, full-throated, uncompromising. "Death!"

"Death," echoes Godambo in confirmation. The cheetah closes its eyes.

"Amma, I have brought someone to meet you."

"*Arré*, Ashok, home so early? And who have . . ." Amma bustles out of the kitchen into the main room with its parrot-green wall and stops short beneath the freshly garlanded photograph of her late and much-lamented husband. She takes in the sight of Abha, demurely clad in a cotton sari, and her eyes widen with surprise and pleasure.

"Ma, this is Abha." Ashok cannot keep the pride out of these simple words, even in the rerecording studio. The heroine–gangster's moll steps forward, hand outstretched, and bends to touch the old lady's feet.

A happy scene follows. Kind words are spoken, embarrassed smiles concealed, shy glances exchanged. Pigtailed Maya enters and, in defiance of all the established patterns of sibling behavior, takes an instant liking to her brother's flame. As Amma produces tea and snacks, the younger women commune in a shared filmi sisterhood. Maya admires the way Abha wears her hair; Abha tells her it is easy to do. Maya giggles a request, and Abha smilingly accompanies her to her room to oblige. In a moment they are back, with Maya's hair done just like Abha's. There is much laughter, but soon it is time for the visitor to leave.

"I've always wanted to have a sister," Maya says artlessly. "Please come back soon."

A troubled look shadows Abha's face. "I'd like to come back soon," she says. She turns away, biting her lip, so that no one can see the tears that have suddenly welled up in her eyes.

It is evening, and Abha is standing alone at some unidentified spot. She sings a slow, high-pitched, haunting lament:

> *I am torn in two,*
> *I am torn in two,*
> *Just like an unwelcome love-letter.*
> *I am torn in two,*
> *I am torn in two,*
> *And I fear I will never be better.*
>
> *How cruel is life,*
> *To bring such strife,*
> *And make me weep and mope;*
> *To have the word "wife"*
> *Strike like a knife*
> *Instead of lighting hope.*
>
> *I am torn in two,*
> *I am torn in two,*
> *I love this precious man.*
> *I am torn in two,*
> *I am torn in two,*
> *For I must fulfill the plan.*
>
> *His every smile*
> *His sense of style*
> *Lights up my wretched heart.*
> *But all the while*
> *With shameful guile*
> *I've been playing my part.*

I am torn in two,
I am torn in two,
My mind quivers with this thought.
I am torn in two,
I am torn in two,
Between the must and the ought.

As the last high note fades into the sound track, it is replaced by the roar of the hero's motorcycle coming down the road. "Abha, why are you looking so sad?" Ashok asks. "Come on, I'll take you for a spin and cheer you up."

"No, thanks, Ashok, I don't really feel like it today. I'm worried about you."

"About me?" asks Ashok. "Why?"

"Your police work. It must be so dangerous. Just today there was an article in the paper about the 'most wanted man in India,' Godambo, and how many people he has killed. What would happen if they assigned you to a case like that, to tackle someone like this horrible killer?"

"Nothing," he responds cheerfully. "As a matter of fact, I'll let you into a secret, I *am* handling the Godambo case. And nothing has happened to me. I shall have that villain behind bars soon enough, and they will give me such a promotion I will be able to afford to marry you."

"Hush," she says. "Don't talk like that."

"Why not?"

"Because you might tempt Providence." She averts her face, swallows, resumes. "Have you — come into contact with this Godambo yet?"

"No. If I had, that would be the end of the story," Ashok boasts. "I have successfully stopped some of his operations, but no one knows where to find the great Godambo himself. Once I can track him down to his hideout, Godambo will be mine."

"Don't do it!" Abha exclaims, then puts her hand to her mouth. "I mean, it might be terribly dangerous. Do you have any leads?"

"Not one," Ashok admits. "I was hoping Godambo would show his hand after we intercepted one of his planes a few weeks ago. But he has been lying low. I must have frightened the fellow." He laughs at Abha's troubled expression. "For God's sake, stop looking so worried," he says. "Remember:

I am the long arm of the law,
No one is quicker on the draw,
Injustice and corruption,
Forces of disruption,
Will be the losers in this war!"

She runs into his arms. "Hold me, Ashok. Hold me so tight I can imagine you'll never leave me."

"But I'll never leave you," he says, holding her. She does not reply, and he strokes her hair. There is a worried expression on his own face.

Interior: lights, throne, pool, cheetah, gravel — the scene is set.

"Yes, Abha? What have you to report?"

Abha is no longer in civvies, but wears a glorious red-and-black pantsuit emblazoned with a gold cheetah springing across her chest. She is clearly in an emotional state because the decorative animal stirs visibly, as if scenting a threat in the jungle. "Sir, you don't need to worry about Inspector Ashok," she says, a ripple moving through her sartorial animal.

"Oh? And why is that?" The voice is smooth now, as if the gravel has been macadamized. Godambo looks remarkably content for a man who has had no costume change in four scenes.

"He doesn't know how to find you. He told me himself he has no leads." Abha's tone is eager, relief mingling with anxiety in her voice. "You are safe, mighty Godambo."

"Safe?" the hairless head on the throne shakes derisively. "I, Godambo, do not seek to be *safe*, like some street corner pickpocket! I seek to eliminate all threats to myself. Must I cower like a fat merchant before a tax man, and try to keep out of Mr. Inspector Ashok's way? No, Abha. Now that I know he cannot surprise us here, I must surprise him instead. I will bring Muhammad to the mountain." He laughs, a deep laugh this time, like gravel being shoveled into a pit. "In a way of my choosing. You have done a good job, Abha. I think

you deserve a rest. For the next part of my plan, I have a more —
passive part in mind for you."

Godambo claps his hands; Pranay emerges, complete with *paan*
and whip, and stands before his master. "Take her with you. You
have followed her closely. You know exactly where to go?" Pranay
chews, nods. "Go then." Godambo laughs.

"Mighty Godambo —" Abha is distraught.

"Yes?"

"I am not feeling well. May I be excused from any further part in
this — this plan?"

"You may not. Why my dear, you are a very necessary part of my
plan." Godambo's expression is almost avuncular. Then it changes.
"You are not" — he leans forward, propping one elbow on a knee —
"you are not refusing an order, are you?"

Abha's voice is very small. "No, Godambo."

"Good. Because refusal is disobedience, you know. And the penalty for disobedience is —"

A hundred black-clad voices oblige him. "Death!"

"Death," Godambo confirms and laughs again. His cheetah, unlike Abha's, continues to sleep.

The black Ambassador car draws up outside Ashok's house. A window is rolled down to reveal Abha in the backseat, her eyes imprisoned behind dark glasses. Inside the car, Pranay is holding a knife
against her side. "Go on," he says. "Call her."

"No," she breathes.

"Godambo was right to warn me you'd gone soft on him,"
Pranay snarls. "Right now two of our Black Cheetah commandos
are in your parents' home. They are just waiting for the signal to act."

"No!"

"Yes. So if you want to see your parents again, do as you're told.
Call her."

Abha stifles a sob. "Maya," she cries out in a choked voice.

"Louder. Clearer. Or else . . ." Pranay places the metal of the
knife on the bared flesh of her midriff, between sari and blouse.

Abha obliges. "Maya!"

There is an answering squeal of recognition, and Sweet Sixteen, back in pigtails, comes running out of the house. She reaches the car; Abha starts to warn her; Pranay savagely pushes Abha aside. The sound of a motorcycle is heard. The car door is flung open. Pranay leaps out, grabs Maya. She screams. Abha's face, frozen in horror and indecision, is visible in the window. The motorcycle enters the street. Ashok sees all three, shouts "Stop!" Pranay leers at him, bundles a screaming Maya into the car. He raises a fist: "Godambo *zindabad!*" he proclaims, disappearing into the car. The Ambassador drives away in a squeal of tires.

Ashok sets off in hot pursuit on his motorcycle.

Chase sequence: the Ambassador roars through the crowded streets, up Marine Drive, heads to the sea. The motorcycle follows, weaving in and out of traffic. The car runs a red light; Ashok mounts a sidewalk to chase it, scattering pedestrians, hawkers, and peanuts from a *moomphali*-wallah's basket. Twice, when Ashok seems to be gaining on the abductors, Pranay leans out and fires a shot from a revolver. Ashok ducks, veers, stays upright but loses ground. As the chase continues, Maya is seen struggling with Pranay inside the car. Pranay slaps her aside and barks to Abha, "Keep her quiet if you know what's good for you." Abha restrains Maya and is rewarded with a look from the young girl that feelingly combines bewilderment and a dawning sense of betrayal.

The car turns off the road, onto a dirt track. It seems to be heading straight for a hillside by the sea, going too fast to avoid crashing into it. Ashok shouts out "Stop!" and slows down himself. The car continues to drive straight on. Just when a crash seems inevitable, the hillside opens up, a huge steel door sliding aside to reveal an entrance for the car. Ashok curses, accelerates. The Ambassador has disappeared inside. The steel door begins to slide back, closing the entrance. The motorcycle roars toward it. The gap narrows. Close-up: Ashok's face, grimly determined, teeth visibly clenched, as he strains every sinew to force his motorbike through the gap in time. The steel door is closing: with a fuel-burning roar, the motorcycle bursts through just as the door clangs shut.

Barely has the applause in the twenty-five-paisa seats died down when the audience and Ashok are both drawn up short. For there is a barrier across the road, guarded by two enormous, half-naked wrestler-types, each wielding a sizable sword. The fatter of the two *pahelwan*s pats his belly, grunts, and moves threateningly toward our hero, sword at the ready. His partner proceeds to do the same. Ashok looks at both of them, begins to dismount. The guards nod to each other in impassive anticipation. Then, suddenly, Ashok swings back into the saddle of the motorcycle, revs up his engine, and makes for a point between the two men. They raise their swords. Ashok roars in, and in a remarkable feat of action (the credit for which stunt man and editor would later dispute), simultaneously he kicks one wrestler in the vitals with an extended left leg and hits another in the gut with an upthrust right fist, while ducking to drive the motorcycle between the raised sword-arms. The two flabby toughs collapse in a heap, and our hero takes his motorcycle crashing through the barrier.

But once more the applause of the twenty-five-paisa wallahs is doomed to die down. For as Ashok rides on in the ill-lit hill tunnel, slowing down to look for the errant Ambassador, a rustle is heard, soon drowned on the sound track by the violins of violence. He looks up in surprise as a gigantic net falls on him, enmeshing him in its chains and bringing hero and motorcycle spinning to the ground.

A light is flashed into his eyes and Ashok blinks, dazzled. Pranay is standing above him, whip triumphantly in hand. "Welcome, Inspector Ashok," the vile villain snarls through red-stained lips. "Mighty Godambo is waiting to meet you."

Ashok is dragged through the cavern by two heavies in black, his hands tied behind him. The audience sees it all again as if for the first time: the marble floor, the eerily illuminated pillars, the Black Cheetahs, the fountain-flanked pool with its darting floating fin, and finally the jeweled throne. On this the bald caped figure sits comfortably, but the pet cheetah is at his feet. It has grown too big for his lap since the film's shooting began.

"So you are Inspector Ashok," the principal villain says gutturally. "Thank you for paying us a visit."

"Where is my sister, *kameenay?*" our hero asks disrespectfully.

"Your sister." Godambo does not seem unduly put out. "Let me show you." He leans back and presses a button on the console beside him. The giant screen again emerges. This time it shows a barred cell, within which Maya weeps, tugging vainly at the bars with handcuffed hands.

Ashok, enraged, struggles to cast off his captors. Godambo laughs. "Why have you brought me here, villain?" our hero asks.

Godambo seems to enjoy this hugely. "Why have we brought him here, he wants to know. But you came here yourself! Uninvited, I might add."

"What do you want with my sister, you castoff from an asylum?"

"Silence!" This is Pranay, accompanying his admonition with a crack of the whip. "No one abuses the mighty Godambo."

"It doesn't matter, Pranay," interjects the most-wanted man in India. "We will tell him what he wants to know. Or perhaps he would prefer to hear it from more familiar lips." The ghost of a smile haunts his impassive, hairless face. He claps his hands. "Agent Abha."

Abha steps forward reluctantly. She is in her most recent Godambo uniform, complete with springing cheetah. Ashok's eyes widen in betrayed realization.

"You know each other, I believe?" Godambo asks.

Outrage and contempt blaze from Ashok's eyes. "I even took you home to meet my mother," he says accusingly, the very thought drenching his voice in self-reproach.

"Forgive me, Ashok," she pleads. "I had no choice."

"No choice! Do you still expect me to believe those lies about your miserable parents?"

"They're not lies —." But she is silenced by a minatory wave of Pranay's whip.

"Can you deny you were working for these thugs all along? Even when we went out together?"

She is silent; she cannot deny it. Ashok looks away bitterly.

"Enough of this love-shove talk," Pranay snaps. "Tell him."

Abha pulls herself together, but the strain shows on her face. "Ashok, mighty Godambo wants you to give up your pursuit of him. And he invites you to join his organization."

"Never!"

"Ashok, if you don't do as he says, he will — kill Maya."

On the screen the concealed camera zooms in on Maya, hands tightly gripping the bars of her cell, tears streaking her pretty face, pigtail dangling by one wet cheek. Ashok grits his teeth, straining to shake off his shackles. He is restrained by the black-clad commandos and a menacing crack of Pranay's whip.

"What kind of man are you, Godambo, to fight your battles through an innocent young girl?" he rails. "Come and face me in hand-to-hand combat, and we will see."

Godambo stiffens in his throne. The hairless visage registers offense. "Don't ever, and I mean *ever,* speak to me like that again," he growls, crunching gravel under every syllable. "What makes you think you are worthy of hand-to-hand combat with mighty Godambo? I could crush you like an ant with one hand tied behind my back, Inspector Ashok, but I won't bother. I have made you an exceedingly generous offer. I can see you need some time to think about it. Very well." He laughs, but there is no amusement on his face. "I shall accommodate you with your sister. But if you want her to see another sunset, Inspector Ashok, you will give me the answer I want by dawn tomorrow."

Ashok's eyes blaze defiance at this ultimatum, but the dialogue writer's imagination has failed him, and he remains silent. A snap of Godambo's fingers, a dismissive gesture, and Ashok is dragged away. But not without casting a bitter parting glance at his erstwhile lady love.

Abha looks away, and this time there are no dark glasses to conceal the despair in her reddening eyes.

Interior: Godambo's dungeons. In the dimly lit cell, Ashok consoles the tearful Maya. She nestles against his chest, and he embraces her as far as the knots on his wrists will allow: elbows and forearms resting on her shoulders, unfree hands clasped behind her head. He looks into her eyes and sings:

> *We're one small happy family,*
> *We live and love together.*
> *We're one small happy family,*
> *In sunshine and bad weather.*
>
> *We're one small happy family,*
> *United, good and strong.*
> *We're one small happy family,*
> *So nothing can go wrong.*

Maya's response is to burst into a fresh torrent of tears.

Outside the cell a Black Cheetah patrols the stone-flagged corridor in hobnailed boots. As Ashok looks up alertly, he hears another pair of footsteps. The commando's boots pause in their stride.

"Who is — oh, it's you, Agent Abha."

"Just checking to see how things are, Ali. All well with the prisoners?"

"They were making a lot of noise, but it's quieter now."

"Could I see them?"

"I'm afraid not, Agent Abha. You know I can't let you in. Strict orders from mighty Godambo himself. No one may disturb the prisoners."

"I won't disturb them."

"Sorry, Agent Abha. I have my orders."

"Good. I was just checking to make sure you were following them. Hey — what's that?"

"What?" The guard whips around, submachine gun at the ready. In a flash Abha brings the butt of her own revolver down on the back of his head. He sinks soundlessly to his knees. She eases him to the floor. Looking around quickly, she pulls his bunch of keys off the belt loop from which they are conveniently dangling and opens the barred gate of Ashok and Maya's cell.

"Come on," she whispers urgently to the astonished prisoners.

"How do I know this isn't a trap?" Ashok asks.

"Of course it isn't," Abha says in an urgent hiss. "I'm risking my life for this. And the lives of my poor parents. Hurry. If Godambo catches us, it'll be certain death."

"What have we got to lose?" Ashok asks rhetorically. He raises his handcuffs. "Do you have the keys for these?"

"I think so." Abha sifts through the bunch, finds a likely key and inserts it. It turns: Ashok is free. He rubs his sore wrists while Abha liberates Maya. The young girl smiles hopefully at her.

"Come on, we've got to get out of here," Ashok says unnecessarily, taking charge. "Do you know the way out of this place?"

"Yes," whispers Abha. "But I'm warning you, it's heavily guarded."

Ashok sets his jaw. "We'll see about that," he snaps, as the three creep out into the corridor.

They advance a few paces. Abha presses herself against a wall and pokes her head round a corner. The coast is clear. She signals, and they run down one more corridor. At the next intersection of pathways, Abha repeats the maneuver. They run — and are drawn up short by the sight of Pranay standing in the middle of the corridor chewing calmly, legs astride, whip at the ready, and a demoniacal gleam of delight in his eyes.

"And where do you think you're going?" he asks sardonically. The red stains on his lips look like blood.

It all happens very quickly. Abha pulls out her revolver. Pranay's whip cracks, and the gun clatters harmlessly to the floor. She cries out, holding her hand in pain. He laughs and again cracks his whip. This time it is Ashok who screams. Pranay is enjoying himself. He advances, the whip snaking out repeatedly, with a noise like a pistol shot. Ashok is hit once more, but then dodges, jumps. Pranay is unperturbed; he enjoys the challenge. "Dance, Inspector Ashok!" he snarls with each flick of his weapon. Ashok sidesteps him nimbly. Pranay strikes, the look of arrogant cruelty on his face turning to one of surprise as Ashok catches the cord of the whip in midlash.

Our hero grips the whip and wraps it around his hand, drawing his tormentor toward him. Pranay tugs at the whip handle, but in vain. Ashok pulls him irresistibly closer. As he nears Ashok, Pranay flings the stock of the whip viciously at our hero. Ashok dodges it. Pranay lunges for the gun on the floor. He is about to reach it when the whip strikes him across the hand. He looks stupidly at a red weal rising on the back of it. Now it is Ashok who has the whip. "Dance, villain!" he barks. The whip descends again, and a streak of red appears on the villain's cheek, competing with the gash of red across his narrow mouth. Pranay dances as the whip swishes repeatedly through the air, catching him on the legs, the arms, the behind. (The moralists in the twenty-five-paisa seats really enjoy this bit. You should hear them laughing and cheering in the aisles.)

Abha picks up the revolver and tosses it to Ashok, who flings the whip aside. "Come on," he says to the whimpering Pranay. "You lead us out." Pranay, clutching his arm, hobbles down the corridor with Ashok's gun pointing at his back. They reach a doorway guarded by two Black Cheetahs. A control panel embedded in the rock next to the doorway glows red. "That's the way out," Abha breathes. "The switch is on that panel."

"Go on," Ashok orders Pranay with an ungentle dig of the gun into his back. "Tell your goons not to obstruct us, or you'll end up with more holes than a Calcutta road."

Pranay hoarsely obliges. "Let them go," he instructs the commandos. "Open the door." Reluctantly the Black Cheetahs move toward the control panel.

"Stop!" There is no mistaking the voice. It contains enough gravel to resurface even Calcutta's roads.

The group spins around. Godambo stands there, huge and hairless, his cape swirling round him. There is no sign of the cheetah. "Don't touch that panel," he instructs his commandos.

"B-boss," Pranay bleats.

"Open that door, or Pranay gets it," Ashok shouts.

"That incompetent? Who let himself be captured this way?" snarls Godambo. "Shoot him. You'd be doing me a favor."

The group is frozen in indecision. Godambo advances.

"If they try to move anywhere near the control panel," he tells his Black Cheetahs, "shoot them. Even if you have to shoot Pranay first." Pranay winces; his master laughs gutturally. "Drop that gun, Inspector Ashok," he says. "Nice try, but it's all over for you."

Ashok tries to look defiant, but the truth of Godambo's conclusion is evident. The gun wavers in his hand.

"Let me do it for you, mighty Godambo." This is Abha! Ashok and Maya stare at her in shock. She pulls the gun out of Ashok's surprised hand. "You didn't really think I'd deserted you, did you, mighty Godambo?" she asks as she walks over to him, the gun in her hand.

Godambo laughs with pleasure. "Agent Abha . . . ," he begins, then stops as the barrel of the revolver presses into his ribs.

"You were saying . . . ?" Abha asks.

(Maya smiles in relief, and the twenty-five-paisa seats erupt in cheers.)

"Don't be silly, Abha," Godambo growls. "Think of your parents. Your home."

"I do," she replies. "And I'm just trying to make sure you will no longer be in any position to harm them."

Godambo's eyes turn round with rage.

"Tell them to drop their guns." She gestures at the Cheetahs and presses her revolver in more deeply.

"Do what she says," grunts Godambo.

The black-clad commandos drop their submachine guns. Ashok picks them up, slings one over his shoulder, and holds the other one. "All right, Godambo," he announces. "You're coming with us." He turns toward the switch on the control panel.

Suddenly, with a swing of his cape, Godambo knocks Abha's hand aside. A swift blow to her wrist and the revolver falls to the ground. Godambo, clutching Abha like a shield, backs away toward the interior. "Now try and shoot me!" he laughs, as Abha flails helplessly in his grip. Ashok raises a gun, realizes it's hopeless: he would hit Abha. Godambo breaks into a run. Ashok follows. "After him!" shouts Pranay, waving on the disarmed commandos in hot pursuit. Maya, alone and neglected, cowers near the doorway, her hands to her mouth. "*Bhaiya!*" she screams in warning. Ashok looks briefly behind him and pauses to release a burst of semiautomatic fire at his pursuers. One of the commandos falls.

Ashok resumes his chase. Godambo is running into his cavernous throne room. This time the pillars are unprotected, but the fountains still play and the pool gleams dully in the neon light. Godambo drags Abha toward his throne. Ashok enters the room and runs across the marbled floor. Pranay and the surviving commando are hot on his heels.

Godambo reaches his throne and stretches a hand toward the armrest.

Abha screams, "Ashok! The floor!"

Godambo jabs a finger on the button. Ashok is still running when the floor opens up beneath him.

He jumps.

In a glorious, fluid leap, immortalized by the camera in poetic slow motion — a leap that would comfortably have won India its first Olympic gold medal in athletics were it reproducible without special effects — Ashok flies over the yawning chasm under his feet, as his weapons fall discarded into the abyss. Ashok's pursuers are not so fortunate. Pranay and the Black Cheetah, with despairing yells, make their fatal splash. The shark fin dives, and as finale the subsidiary villain is accorded only a few glugs of farewell.

Ashok lands on his feet on the other side of the pool. Godambo presses another button, and a loud siren wails through the complex. Red lights flash and blink along the walls. Doors open, corridors fill with the scudding feet of Black Cheetahs.

"You're finished now, Inspector Ashok," Godambo declares emphatically.

As soon as she hears the siren, Maya presses the switch on the control panel. The red indicator on the panel turns to green, and the door slides open. There is the clatter of booted feet from the outside.

"*Shabash,*" says a deep voice. Yes, it is the stern and slim Iftikhar, complete with pencil-line mustache! As a truckload of khaki-uniformed policemen trot into the cavern, assault rifles at the ready, he has a brief word of explanation for Maya. "Your Amma called me," he says. "We followed Ashok's motorcycle tracks here, but were unable to get in."

The policemen take positions and a shoot-out follows, five minutes of meticulously choreographed anarchy. Black Cheetahs emerge on high walkways, spray bullets from their submachine guns, and plunge gorily to their deaths. The celluloid policemen, using weaponry unknown in the armories of their real-life counterparts, shoot indiscriminately, shattering flashing red lights and blasting rock off the rough-hewn walls, but miraculously bring their enemies tumbling down. Grenades are thrown, and little bursts of flame add color to the occasion. The bloodthirsty rural cinemagoers get their twenty-five paise's worth.

Meanwhile, inside the throne room Godambo curses as his henchmen are clearly getting the worst of the raging battle. Ashok stands poised to attack, but he is weaponless now and Godambo holds Abha tightly.

"This is all your doing, Inspector Ashok," he snarls.

"I thought you said you could crush me with one hand tied behind your back, Godambo," Ashok retorts. "But I see you still prefer to shelter behind a woman."

Godambo's pride is stung. Uttering an oath, he viciously flings Abha aside. She falls to the floor with a stifled cry. "Abha!" Ashok shouts.

"Don't worry about me," the heroine breathes. "Get him."

Ashok has no time to express concern as Godambo, eyes horribly wide and teeth horrifyingly bared, leaps on him with both hands. They fall to the floor. Godambo's powerful fingers are at Ashok's throat. Ashok brings his knee up and into Godambo's midriff: that relieves the pressure. Both men rise. Fists encounter flesh: *dishoom! dishoom!* Bodies crash into furniture. A right uppercut from Ashok sends Godambo smashing into the console. A left hook from Godambo puts Ashok head first through the screen. Miraculously unharmed by these calisthenics, the two men expand the locale for their fisticuffs. Godambo leaps over the throne, cape flying. Ashok follows. Godambo reaches a door, kicks Ashok, and opens it. Ashok recovers, follows. The two men are now on an outdoor ledge, overlooking the sea. (Why? Because it would make for a more spectacular climax, that's why. More demanding viewers may assume Godambo was hoping to escape that way.) More *dishoom! dishoom!* follows. Both men fall, pick themselves up, hit again.

A growl is heard. A grrrowl, in fact. Abha screams: "Ashok! The cheetah!" Ashok, his hands at Godambo's throat, looks back in horror. It is Godambo's pet, now grown almost to full size. The villain's wide eyes gleam. "Cheetah, come!" he commands. The animal takes in what is happening and growls menacingly. Then, with a single powerful bound, it leaps toward its master and his attacker.

Ashok steps aside.

"No-o-o-o!" cries Godambo, but it is too late. The animal lands squarely on his chest. Godambo reaches out to try to save himself, then with a last gravelly cry of despair, topples in slow motion into the sea. His confused pet follows him.

The camera lingers lovingly on Godambo's falling torso, the cape swirling around him like a defective parachute. At last he hits the water, with a satisfying splash. The camera stays long enough on the spot to convince the viewer that he does not come up again. Only then does Ashok turn to Abha, a new light in his eyes.

She runs into his arms. He clasps her in their seventh tight embrace.

They are outside now, where a few lugubrious Black Cheetahs are being energetically herded into police vans.

"*Shabash,* Ashok," says Iftikhar. Ashok smiles, hugs Abha, and reaches out an arm to Maya. The sound track swells with the theme song, this time sung by the two women:

48

You are the long arm of the law,
You always show villains the door.
By day or by night
You handle any fight
And put all the bad men on the floor!

They look like one small happy family, smiling for the camera until the words THE END fill up the screen.

[Note: this is an abbreviated version of the story. For reasons of space and stamina, we have omitted one *puja,* two tearful scenes before Ashok's father's photograph, an entire comic subplot featuring a domestic servant in a Gandhi cap and a fat woman in a nightdress, and four songs.]

Monologue: Night

PRANAY

Your first hit. *Godambo.* Your first big hit, in only your second film. You always had it easy, Ashok. Just had to open your mouth sufficiently to move the silver spoon to one side, and producers scrambled to say yes. Actresses too.

Who'd have believed it? None of us took your chances very seriously, not even when Jagannath Choubey cast you in that first film, *Musafir,* with Abha. OK, Abha's was still a name to be reckoned with in the industry, but mainly for those with good memories. She wasn't the hottest property around by any means, no longer ranking beside the likes of Sharmila Tagore and Raakhee as a crowd-puller, but you could have done worse. I mean, you could have ended up with a fresh graduate from the Film Institute, or one of those desperate starlets who've done the unimaginable to get a lead role but who'll never convince anyone, least of all the audience, that she is heroine material. That would have condemned her and you to permanent eclipse. Which, frankly, was what everyone expected. Especially me.

But it worked, or worked well enough to keep you in business. There was that "I shall always chase you" song, which became a hit even before the movie was released, with every street corner *mastaan* and Eve-teaser in India singing it to accompany and justify their un-welcome pursuits. The film itself didn't do as badly as the industry thought it would, so by default it was seen as something of a success. Some of us thought you were pretty wooden, frankly, and your dancing was embarrassing. But it was obvious that the experts had got it wrong. None more so than that harridan Radha Sabnis, the dreaded Cheetah of *Showbiz:*

> Darlings, does the name Ashok Banjara ring a bell with you pus-sycats? [How would it? She'd called you Anil the last time.] That's right, he's the long-legged type with the political connections who came with the tablecloth at Bollywood parties. Can you believe it, darlings, this would-be *abhineta* with the looks of a second-rate ga-rage mechanic actually made it into the passenger seat! Yes, he has a starring role in Jagannath Choubey's latest *masala* movie, *Musafir,* op-posite Daddy's old favorite, Abha Patel. Rumor has it that the ever-green heroine has had more face-lifts than her hero's had dance lessons. Not very promising, pussycats! Choubey seems to have a *maha* flop on his hands. And where will that leave his poor twinkling little stars? Banjara, of course, can always go back to light up the corners of the party circuit, but what will poor dear Abha do? Noth-ing military about the lady, but she should know that dimming stars are like old soldiers — they just fade away. Grrrowl!

Well, it didn't work out quite like that, did it? Cheetah didn't chat-ter too much about you after that. *Musafir* didn't lose money; in fact, I believe it made some. And then Choubey went and cast you with Abha again in *Godambo,* and the rest, as they say, is history. *His* story. Your story.

Lucky bastard. Never again will you need to play the hero in a movie named after the villain.

What do you know, Ashok Banjara, of what it's really like to try and make it as an actor in Hindi films? I'll tell you, I should know. I grew up in the bloody industry. My father was an assistant to a big-name director, but he never graduated beyond being an assistant di-rector. He had work, but never much money. In school I tried to drop names about the stars we knew, but that never impressed the kids for long when it became obvious that there wasn't any money to go with the glamour. I was always the kid who didn't throw a birthday party, because quite simply my parents couldn't afford to pay for one. Ma made rice *kheer* for dessert, sometimes Papa bought a cheap toy in the bazaar or took me for a pony ride at the Bandstand, and that was the extent of the celebration. In my entire childhood I never had a birthday cake. But I was growing up in a world where every other kid I came in contact with got to choose the flavor of the cake and had his name written on it with icing. That became my great aspiration: to have a birthday cake one day, with my name on it. It took me a while to fulfill that ambition. The moment I could afford it, on my twenty-fourth birthday, I ordered the hugest, most expensive chocolate cake I could find and had "Happy Birthday Pranay" inscribed on it in letters an inch high. There were glazed-icing flowers and marzipan rosebuds and little silver balls you could bite into. I had everything put on it, everything. And then I took it home and ate it all by myself. I hated it. I was sick for days afterward. But I really felt I had achieved something, that I had arrived.

I grew up in a two-room flat in Matunga, you know, in the un-fashionable suburbs. Slept on the floor. That wasn't so bad; the real problem was the bathroom. We shared one filthy bathroom with eight other families on the same floor. Everyone wanted it first thing in the morning, so you had to keep getting up earlier and earlier in order to beat your neighbors to it; otherwise you were bound to be late for school or work. By the time I did my matric I was getting up at 4:30 just to be able to use the bathroom. I'll never forget what it was like to grope my way in the dark, stand on that slimy floor, and feel some nameless creature slither across my feet just before I switched on the light. To do that every day, day after day, week after week, with no prospect of anything ever changing. What did you know of that, hanh, Ashok Banjara?

Sometimes, thanks to my father's work, we would be invited to some star's house for a special occasion — Diwali, or a wedding or something. That was the biggest event in our lives. I would spend every day looking forward to the visit. It didn't matter if nobody even noticed my existence there, just stepping into a house like Raj Kapoor's or Sunil Dutt's made life worth living. At the first oppor-tunity I would go into the bathroom — one of the bathrooms, be-cause they all had so many in their homes — and just stand there, on the marble or mosaic-tile floor, just breathing in the reality of being in a bathroom like that. I would run my stubby hands along the chrome towel racks, caress the porcelain sinks, open the shower just to imagine what it might be like not to have to dip stagnant water out of a plastic bucket each time you had a bath. I would sit on the commode even when I didn't need to go, unravel the toilet paper — who in Matunga had even heard of toilet paper? — and roll it back again.

And I would wash my ugly and callused hands. Incessantly, obsessively, wash them. I would make repeated visits to every bathroom in the rich guy's house and wash my hands, running creamy soap over the rough skin, over fingernails I had nervously bitten down to the very edges. I can't remember very much else of what I did at those places, but I would always come home with the cleanest hands in Bombay, the skin of my palms white-dry and wrinkled with all the water I'd poured on them, fragrant with the delicious, unattainable, unplaceable smell of imported soap.

I hate my hands, Ashok. I hate their shortness, their stubbiness, their roughness, their virtual lack of nails. That's probably a genetic trait: I come from a long line of insecure, nail-biting failures. Your long fingers, your hard and gleaming nails — what a thing to envy you for, Ashok Banjara. But I do.

None of this means anything to you, does it, Ashok? Hell, why blame you. You've never stumbled into a big star's closet and found the most incredible collection of ties in the world, a real parade of ties, red and black and blue ties, ties with stripes of every known width and color, plain ties and polka-dotted ties, ties with the badge or shield of an exclusive club on them, ties in silk and rayon and polyester and cotton, broad ties and narrow ties, ties with discreet little designs and ties with psychedelic patterns. The most pointless article of clothing in the world, devoid of purpose, an anachronism even in the climates where it's wearable, a flagrant luxury in our country: what an advertisement for this star's success, that he could afford to throw away so much money on so many useless foreign ties! You wouldn't understand what I felt, Ashok Banjara. You've never reached up, awestruck, to touch these ties and brought the entire rack down on your head so that you sat swathed in a riot of colors, held down by a dharna of textures, trapped in a *gherao* of ties. You've never bent down to pick them up, one by incredible one, and rearranged them lovingly in that remote stranger's closet, knowing the distance that stretches between that stranger's world and your own, even as you touch and feel the dimensions of that distance. You've never vowed, Ashok Banjara, that one day you, too, will possess a collection of ties like that, more ties than you will ever find occasion to wear.

What do you know, Ashok Banjara, you for whom a tie was an object of routine daily wear, something you had to put on to go to the office, not a magical symbol of material success?

What do you know of living in some godforsaken matchbox in a decrepit old building and traveling two hours to make it in time for the nine o'clock shift? What do you know of sitting around the Prithvi Café, drinking oversweet cups of tea because you've got nothing else to do, and drinking them as slowly as possible because you can't afford to keep ordering more, and you can't afford to leave? What do you know of the cut-and-crimp tailors of Linking Road, Bandra, who are the world champions at prolonging the life of your old clothes, lengthening, tightening, reversing, adding, patching them into posterity, and who can imitate any star's costume for you at a sixth the price? What gives you the right, Ashok Banjara, to be one of us?

You've never forgiven me, of course, for knowing Maya before you did. I can understand that. She wasn't the kind of girl I could have expected to meet, let alone be close to. My woman, my only regular woman, really, during those first years in the industry, was Sunita. I know some people called her my wife, but of course we weren't married. I mean, who would marry a vamp? Sure I lived with her for a while, but it was a practical arrangement, you know, and I also lived away from her just as much. I don't want any more of that Pranay-dumped-his-wife stuff being flung at me. Sunita wasn't my wife. And in the circumstances of her life and work, she couldn't be any-one's wife. Really.

I mean, look at her life. Sincerely, would you have married her? OK, not *you*, Ashok Banjara, Esq., but anyone? She comes out of some Gujarati hick town, Jamnagar or Junagadh or somewhere, the kind of town where the biggest thing around is the cinema theater, it's the only place of escape. So what does she do when she's had enough of this backwater? She gets into a train one day with her life's savings tucked into her cleavage to make it in the only other world she can imagine, the fantasyland of Bollywood. Sunita knows that her only assets are those contained in her blouse, and I'm not referring to the grimy notes she has spent within a week of arriving in the city. So she does the round of the producers' offices, and she wears out the hook of her one good bra in a succession of sleazy hotels. Soon she is doing the bump and grind vertically too, for a change, as one of the half dozen sidekicks of the principal vamp in some sizzling dance number. She does it well, she has practiced all the moves, and she is known to be willing to oblige the producer anytime he wants a special favor. Nothing unusual about that — hell, they are *all* equally willing, but they're not all as worthy of crumpling the producers' sheets as Sunita is. So she gets her breaks; she rises from the ranks of the secondary vamps till she is doing her own cabaret numbers. Solo, or in duets with a villain. Like me. Yes, that's how I met her.

She had a heart of gold, Sunita. She took me in, showed me more kindness than I deserved, gave me free run of her flat and her body. She looked on sex as some sort of divine gift to women, a commodity that was easy to offer, cost nothing to give, and brought in great rewards. "It's not much work and it seems to make them so happy," she said innocently to me once. "Imagine if some producer wanted me to sweep his floors instead, or clean out his bathroom. Now *that* would be much more difficult. I'd hate to do that, even for a role. But to give him sex? It's so easy, and sometimes it's even fun."

You think I'm making this up, don't you? You've heard all the stories about how much these women suffer, how they endure the humiliation with teeth clenched and eyes closed, only the thought of their starving babies keeping them on the bed while the raunchy paunchy producer heaves and pants over them. Well, I'm not denying that that does happen, there *are* some women like that, but for the most part, my friend, they know precisely what they're doing and why. Sunita did.

Thing is, once people expect it from you it's kind of difficult to stop. Sunita had been giving herself so readily that the mere fact of my moving in couldn't change the pattern. There was one producer who cast her in his films on one condition: that after the shooting was over, she would repeat the dance number for him in a private performance, this time without any clothes on. He'd set it all up, playback track, lights and all, and she'd repeat exactly the same moves, choreographed by Gopi Master or Sonia Bibi or whoever, minus her costume. Drove him wild, of course. When he called out "Action!" afterward, it was an announcement of his own intent.

What Sunita didn't know was that the camera that stood there, supposedly as a prop — something he could look through and imagine himself directing — actually had film in it. Film which he then screened for his intimates. We found out when I walked in on one of the showings, at the producer's place. Had some sort of errand to run, message to deliver or something, and they let me into his sanctum sanctorum, a bar with mirrored walls and a projection unit. So I walked in and found my wife, sorry I mean the woman I was living with, shaking her bare breasts at me from every reflectable angle and a bunch of old drunks slapping their thighs in delight. I went back and told her, and then I walked out of her life. Well, sort of. I walked out, but not for the last time. Sunita was a girl you kept going back to. Like she said, it didn't cost you anything.

Anyway, that was the nature of my love life during my first few years in films. Whores at Kamathipura, slatterns from the studios, Sunita. Can't say there's much progression there. Till Maya came along.

You barely noticed Maya, of course. You were too full of yourself for that, Ashok. Full of what you thought of as the success of your first film, full of your new hero role in *Godambo,* full of the attentions of the college girls and new generation lady-journalists who had just begun to flock around you in those days. Girls who wore jeans and T-shirts, and cut their hair shoulder-length, and spoke English; girls you could take to the disco and give smarmy interviews to for the new glossy magazines that were outchattering Cheetah. Maya was small, and simple, even somewhat plain. Her hair was so long she could have sat on it. She wore it in plaits; and she favored *salwar-kameez* that clearly hadn't been tailored in a metropolis. She was decidedly unglamorous. She spoke English, but it was a language she'd learned, and she didn't sparkle with the slang and facile abbreviations of Bombay or Delhi. She was the sisterly type, wasn't she, the good little girl next door. You took one look, and you ignored her.

I didn't ignore her. I went up to her on the set. I talked to her. I asked her about her family. Her father was a minor government servant, a railway official I think, then posted in some mofussil town, Bhopal or Bhagalpur or Bhatinda, one of those *Bh*s. She had no one in Bombay. She didn't seem the Sunita-style fortune-seeking type, so I wondered what had brought her to moviedom. Incredible: she was a serious stage actress, she had done a Tendulkar play or something in this *Bh* town, and this guy in the audience came backstage and told her she had to be in the movies. Of course she didn't take him seriously — who does he think she is? Lana Turner? — but no, he was on the level, he came to see her parents, explained he was something of a talent scout, even named two or three actors he'd discovered this way. And he turned out to be Jagannath Choubey's brother.

Didn't think it happened like that, did you? Well, at least you didn't imagine it then, right? Now, of course, you know the whole story. I suppose.

Actually it wasn't that uncommon. Not everybody in movies was born into it, like me and all the Kapoors, or lucked into it, like you. Rajesh Khanna actually won a talent contest. First prize was a screen test. He passed with flying colors.

Maya was so *seedhi-saadhi,* so innocent of any guile. She was the kind of girl any lower-middle-class Indian boy like myself meets all the time, unless he happens to be lower-middle-class in the film world, in which case he only gets to meet starlets and sluts (if that isn't tautological). The moment I met her I realized I'd been waiting and wanting to meet her. Call it love at first sight. No, Ashok, I guess you won't want to call it that. Call it anything.

She was sweet. She was trusting. She didn't respond to me the way other Bombay actresses would, evaluating my unimportance, categorizing me by my role, my accent, my *paan*-stained mouth. She saw someone older, wiser, someone who knew the ropes, who told her where things were, how things should be done, what — and more important, who — should be avoided. For the first time in my life, Ashok, I began to feel I was more than the secondary villain.

And increasingly I became aware that the girl depended on me.

OK, so she had no one else. Except for some distant relatives charged by her parents with keeping an eye on her and whose reaction to the film world was either to gawk or to disapprove. Not much good that could do her. I was far more useful.

Don't look so triumphant! It was also more than that. Inevitably, our contact extended beyond the studio. We started going out together. I gave her lifts home, to the little flat in Bandra where she'd found paying-guest accommodation. The landlady had a strict no-male-visitors rule, not even for relatives, and you can imagine what she would have thought of me. So I dropped her off, and sometimes, when she had the energy and I had the time, I took her out. Once or twice to the Prithvi Café, in fact, just to show her what that was like. I wasn't yet in the five-star-hotel league in those days, though I did give her lunch at the Sun 'n' Sand once, where she stared at the pool-side bikinis in shocked disbelief. But most of the time it was walks at the beach, *pau-bhaji* from a roadside vendor, *bhel-puri* out of folded leaves while we strolled at the edge of the sand and let the seawater trickle through our toes. Neither of us was famous enough to be recognized, let alone mobbed: we were just another of the lower-middle-class couples thronging Chowpatty, getting sand into our sandals and stars into our eyes. I bought her a *paan* once, and because she was so hesitant, I put it into her mouth. She blushed and turned away in such confusion that she made me feel I'd propositioned her.

I hadn't really thought of her that way, you know. There are some women you look at physically, judge them primarily by what you think they'd look like under all those yards of cloth that Indian tradition and Indian tailors conspire to ensure they're swathed in. Then there are women you can't possibly think of that way — older relatives, for instance, or some of the asexual buffalo with hairy moles on their chins you run into at Crawford Market, browbeating the butcher. But somewhere in between there are women whom you relate to quite differently, women who are pleasant and attractive, maybe even beautiful, but whose physicality is not the first thing that strikes you about them, perhaps not even the second thing. These are women with a certain other quality, a grace, a gentleness, an inner radiance that surrounds them when they smile, or speak, or move; women you can love, or worship, or hope to marry. I bet you think that's naive provincial nonsense, don't you, Ashok? You urban sophisticates know that ultimately all women are reducible to what you want out of them. And it's always the same thing.

I didn't buy Maya another *paan,* but I saw a lot more of her afterward, and I began to think of her — well, differently. A day without her seemed to go on forever; I needed her laughter to shorten the hours. I stopped living with Sunita. I shaved more often for Maya; the trademark stubble on my face became a calendar of her absences. I began reading then, reading seriously, acquiring the vocabulary I'm using today and the ideas I haven't yet had a chance to use. I didn't stop chewing *paan,* but I saw Maya didn't like me spitting it out in public, so I found more discreet ways to get rid of the red stuff. She changed me, Ashok Banjara. Or perhaps it is truer to say I changed myself for her.

And how did she react to me? What did she feel about me? I bet you'd like to know. Did you ask her, Ashok, or did you dismiss the subject as being of no consequence? She must have told you something about me, surely? After all, I was the only man in her life between her father and you. She must have wanted to speak about me.

But I suppose you didn't want to hear any of it. Pranay the interlude, an episode best forgotten. Pretend it never happened.

No, I'm sure there is something you wanted to know. I imagined you in those days seething with resentful curiosity about it. How far had we gone? You must have found it difficult to convince yourself that this small-time villain with the red-stained mouth contented himself with walks on the beach. Maya was no schoolgirl, after all, even though she was cast as one. She turned twenty during the shooting of *Godambo,* didn't she? I heard the technicians refer to her once as the Virgin Maya, and I couldn't even blow them up for their irreverence from fear of insulting her by implication. So the Virgin Maya she remained. But after her association with me, you must have wondered, was she still really a virgin? Or was she all *maya,* mere illusion?

What did she tell you? I can't believe you didn't ask. Or was she so offended by the question, you couldn't insist on the reply? I can imagine her, all hurt pride and tears, as you cast implied aspersions on her moral standards. Well, you must have thought, I can always find out on the night. But then she was a bloody good actress, wasn't she? And there can be so many reasons for an absence of blood.

So did you really ever feel sure, Ashok Banjara? Could you easily bear to look at me and wonder whether I'd felt your wife between the sheets before you even realized she existed? Oh, I bet that burned you up.

Or maybe not. After all, you were lucky in the things that really mattered. There had been no publicity: in those days neither Maya nor I was important enough for anyone to write about our relationship. There were no gossip-column stories about us, neither of us gave *Showbiz* interviews in which we could refer to the other as "just good friends," even the industry didn't pay us that much attention. After *Godambo* it might have been different. But by then it was all over between Maya and me.

You won't believe this, but sex was not the important thing with Maya. No, I'm not going to put you out of your misery and admit to — boast about — having taken her to bed. That might matter to you, but I see no reason to oblige. We were close, very close, as close as I could ever have hoped to be to Maya. How close that was is not for me to tell you, Ashok Banjara. It's between your wife and you: whatever she told you, whatever she wants you to believe, is fine with me. What mattered to me was something I couldn't have.

I still remember the evening. It was just after we'd completed *Godambo,* doing the last bit of dubbing. I waited for her to finish her recording with you and Abha — she and I had so few scenes together, after all — and drove her home. Only I didn't go home. I stopped the car at Worli, by the sea-face where that expensive hotel has gone up. It wasn't there then. We stood by the seaside, letting the warm breeze from the Arabian Sea blow specks of spray through our hair. The evening stretched across the horizon like a woman waiting to be embraced. I turned to her, took her in my arms. At first, unresisting in surprise, she allowed herself to be enfolded in them, but she stiffened as I began to speak.

"Maya, I want us to be married. I can't promise you a big house, or lots of money. But I love you, Maya. I'll be good to you."

She pulled herself away, not harshly, but firmly. "Pranay, what are you talking about? What is all this talk of marriage?"

"Why not? You know what you mean to me."

She looked away then, to the streaks of orange and blue that were the sun's farewell testaments for the day. When she spoke her voice was steady, but the steadiness came with effort. "You've been very good to me, Pranay. Very sweet, and very kind. I'll never forget that."

"Thanks, but no thanks," I interjected bitterly. "I'm not standing here looking for gratitude."

"But I *am* grateful."

"Is that all? Are you saying that — everything we've had doesn't mean anything more? Don't you care for me at all?"

"I care for you." Her voice was low.

"And I care for you! Marry me, Maya — I'll make you happy."

"I'm sorry, Pranay." She looked at me for a moment, and I swear I saw a wetness in her eyes, but she turned away again and spoke without looking at me. "But I just don't love you, that's all."

"Why not?" I wanted to rail. But I was shattered, and hurt, and suddenly very desperate. "It doesn't matter," I found myself pleading. "Love will come afterward. It always does. Look at all the arranged marriages that take place in our country. Do you think any of these people love each other? They haven't even seen each other properly, for God's sake! Love comes, in its own time. I'll wait for you to learn to love me. Just like an arranged marriage."

She looked at me directly, and her eyes were as dry as her tone. "No one," she said, and not even her voice could sweeten her bluntness, "would arrange *our* marriage, Pranay."

I gaped at her wide-eyed and understood there was nothing more to say.

I drove her home in silence. As she opened the car door, she turned to me in her seat. "Thank you, Pranay," she said. And she leaned over and gave me the briefest, saddest kiss I have ever had. On my narrow, *paan*-stained mouth.

Then she was gone, and the door of my car clicked faintly closed. She had not pushed it hard enough. I sighed. I would have to open and shut it again, only this time much, much harder.

Godambo was a hit. You were a star after your second film. Maya was noticed — by other producers, by you. They wanted her innocence, as you did.

I didn't do too badly myself out of that film. Offers came for better roles. As a villain, of course, but not just a secondary one. I got scripts in which I survived till the last reel and in the end fell at the hero's hands, not in some bumbling accident like that stupid floor trap. I played all the parts a villain could hope for. The rapacious moneylender, the *seth-sahukar*, preying on the womenfolk of the poor hero's indebted family. The tyrannical landlord, flogging his servants and lusting after his tenants' wives as he canters through his extensive domains on horseback (all this when *zamindari* had long been abolished in the world outside the film studio, but the picture was always set in an undefined, vaguely contemporary period). The city gangster, in checked jackets and ill-fitting sharkskin suits, drinking incessantly, blowing smoke rings at a sequined vamp, and generally having a wonderful time until brought to book by an improbably honest cop for some carefully unspecified crime. I played them all, and as my screen credits grew with my bank balance, I put the money I couldn't legally show the bank into a place of my very own in Juhu. And I watched you and Maya from afar.

Three films, that's all you gave her. Three films, all opposite you, for the actress who was the brightest, freshest talent in the Hindi cinema of her day. Three films to prove her worth, to capture the heart of the Indian public and to break mine. Three films before you obliged her to "retire" so you could marry her.

And I wasn't in any of them. Probably just as well, because I'm not sure I would have been able to bear losing her to you every day, on and off the set. To be obliged to succumb to you on screen, and to watch her succumb to you between takes.

I wonder when it all began. I suppose with *Ganwaari*, just after *Godambo*, when Maya made the transition from sisterly schoolgirl to girlish heroine and Abha from heroine to supporting actress. The famous film about the village girl (Maya was a natural for that part, wasn't she?) who wins a competition to come to the city and spend a week watching her favorite movie star (you, who else?) at work. Surprise, surprise, the worldly-wise Hindi film hero is completely won over by the innocent village belle and spurns his cinematic leading lady (Abha, whose rage seemed genuine) to clinch the *ganwaari* girl at the fade-out. I hated the film, but it was an unexpected success at the box office; it made Maya, and it confirmed you in stardom. Even then, before it was known that your interest in Maya was extending offscreen as well, I saw the movie as symbolic, a portent.

And everywhere I went, on street corners, at wedding receptions, in holiday processions, I kept hearing that wretched song from the film:

> *Is it true? Can it really be?*
> *Is it a dream, or can this be really me?*
> *Standing he-eere, in your embrace . . .*
> *Is it true? Can it really be?*
> *Could it be a mistake, can you really see?*
> *That your lo-ove shines on my face . . .*
>
> *I'm just a little girl from the heart of India,*
> *I know nothing of worldly sin, dear,*
> *I'm just a village girl with stars in her eyes,*
> *And you've taken me by — surprise.*
>
> *Is it true? Can it really be?*
> *Is this life, or a Bombay moo-ovie?*
> *That puts my hand in yours . . .*
> *Is it true? Can it really be?*
> *Are you, my hero, really free?*
> *To give me a joy that endures . . .*
>
> *This doesn't happen in my part of India,*
> *My heart beats so much you can hear the din, dear,*
> *I'm just a village girl who's never told lies,*
> *And you've just made me your — prize.*
>
> *Is it true? Can it really be? . . .*

It was true, of course. And the song was played everywhere, on transistors and record players, over Muzak systems and public-address loudspeakers, by radio disc jockeys responding to importunate requests from Jhumri Tilaiya, by two hundred–rupee per evening hired bands at every imaginable public festivity. And every time I heard it I kept seeing that scene from the film where she looked up at you holding her, and I saw an adoration in her eyes that no amount of nervous direction from Mohanlal could ever have placed there. And I knew you had won her.

The next couple of movies made a star out of her and a prophet out of me. Maya and her makeup men managed to combine her fresh-faced innocence with just enough expert artifice to make her a convincing heroine, without losing the quality that made audiences like her in the first place. She didn't have the figure of Abha or Vyjay-antimala, she couldn't dance like Hema Malini or Saira Banu, but she captivated every cinemagoer in the country. They loved her, Ashok. She was every man's sister or daughter, every woman's ideal. And she could act: she was a true professional.

And then during the shooting of that third film, Radha Sabnis broke the news in *Showbiz:*

> Darlings, brace yourself for a shocker from Bollywood! Your Cheetah has learned that Ashok Banjara, the common man's super-star, the actor whose success gave hope to every garage mechanic in the country, is about to wed! And who is the brave and noble woman prepared to make Saddy Longlegs the happiest ham in Versova? *That's* the shock, little jungle creatures: it's none other than the na-tion's sweetheart, Maya Kumari! Is it true? Can it really be? I'm afraid it is, darlings. When the bombshell bursts, don't say Cheetah didn't warn you! Grrrowl . . .

I grrowled a few times myself, in between tears of impotent rage. I drank myself silly for a week. And then I went back to Sunita, not for the last time, and pushed her against the wall. I closed my eyes and imagined it was Maya. It didn't work, and I wept my drunken-ness and shame into the sink, not knowing who I hated more, myself or you.

What you did was a crime, Ashok Banjara. You deprived India of its most cherished celluloid daughter, you deprived the Hindi film industry of its finest actress, and you deprived me. You deprived me not of hope, because by then I had none for myself, but of that last vestige of pride left to a man who has not been rejected for someone else. Once she agreed to marry you, having refused to marry me, I could no longer take solace in telling myself she had given me up for her career. Instead, she gave up her career for you.

You made her do it, of course. All those interviews about "I wouldn't want my wife to feel she needs to work" — disingenuous bastard. And then you got *her* to tell the press, "I'm giving up films of my own free will because I want to be the ideal wife and daughter-in-law." Did anyone believe those words weren't scripted for her, and rather badly at that? "Ideal wife and daughter-in-law": does anyone ever *talk* like that, outside the movies? Come on, Ashok, you could have done better. Couldn't you for once have had the courage of your characterless convictions and simply announced, "No wife of mine is going to be pawed and chased and hugged in public, not even by me. Maya is being instructed to retire from films to preserve *my* exaggerated sense of self-esteem." But no, you weren't capable of that kind of honesty, were you. I know what you're going to say: how can I blame you — every single Indian actress has "retired" after marriage, from Babita to Mumtaz, from Jaya to Dimple, who only came back to films when her marriage was over. Why these intelligent and resourceful women should all behave as if the acting profession were incompatible with married respectability, I don't know. But they've set the pattern, and that lets the slimy hypocrites like you off the hook.

Even if you'd stopped at that I'd have found it impossible to forgive you. But you then spent the next five years making it much worse.

TAKE
TWO

Interior: Day

I can't believe I'm doing this.

Me, Ashok Banjara, leading superstar of the Indian cinema, commander of fees in the range of several lakhs (can't be too precise, you know how these income tax chaps are), not to mention son of the general secretary of New Delhi's ruling party, wooing an aging gossip columnist over pink champagne, lip-synching the obligatory inanities that an invisible tape in my head plays back to me from a dozen remembered screenplays. But it *is* me, it's my mouth that's saying these improbable things, it's my hand that is placed, with exaggerated lightness, on her gnarled and painted claw. Radha Sabnis, the dreaded Cheetah of *Showbiz* magazine, sits in her lounge, flattered by my attentions, while I pour on the butter that wouldn't normally melt in my mouth. I have come to make peace.

Cheetah sits in an imitation leopard-skin pantsuit on an imitation velvet sofa, guzzling the champagne, for which she is embarrassingly grateful, and eyeing me from under artificial lashes with what some lyricist might call a wild surmise. She is of medium height, thin, *really* thin, like a Bangladesh refugee in costume, and she has a pale death-mask face that seems to have been meticulously disarranged by a malicious undertaker: a hooked nose like the beak of an injured parrot; exaggeratedly shaped eyebrows arched in an expression of perpetual interrogation; a profusion of deep lines that deepen asymmetrically every time she speaks a word; pinched, sallow cheeks; and the whole effect framed by lusterless shoulder-length hair practically dripping with henna. This discredit to the species wields the most powerful pen in Bollywood, and my visit to her is the idea of my new PR agent, Cyrus Sponerwalla.

Cyrus is bespectacled and overweight, but he knows his stuff, and he's got good ideas like the one that contracted his Parsi profession-derived surname from Sodawaterbottleopenerwallah to its current incarnation. Imagine converting a liability like that into an exclusive, distinctive, slightly exotic sounding name that fits on visiting cards, is easy to pronounce, and is a surefire conversation starter. "Icebreaker," Cyrus corrects me. "The ice is what you need the soda-water-bottle-opener-wallah for, party-wise." But Cyrus Sponerwalla is not here to hold my hand, nor the Cheetah's, for that matter. In making love or war, surrogates just aren't good enough.

"This is most generous of you," says Radha Sabnis, the questioning curve of her ridiculous eyebrows suggesting that she doesn't think it's anything of the sort. "Pol Roger Rosé, 1968. A wonderful champagne."

"Orly airport, duty-free," I lie. I have in fact picked it up from my friendly neighborhood smuggler, the real-life equivalent of the Godambos I crush on celluloid. Ah, the wretched dualities of Indian life: the cinemagoer's traitorous villain is the Bombayite's helpful purveyor of necessities unreasonably banned by our protectionist government. "On my way back from shooting *Love in Paris*. It was the best champagne in the shop."

"But how sweet of you," she purrs. "And the Customs must have allowed you only one bottle."

"Just the one." I nod. "But then I had only one person in mind to give it to." I apply slight pressure on her bony hand, resting on the coffee table.

"And what's the occasion, if I may ask?"

"Occasion? Do we need an occasion?" I laugh disarmingly, but she nods, unamused. "Well, let's just say it's our fifth anniversary."

"I don't understand." She seems to be about to move her hand from under mine. The seventy-five-proof gratitude is apparently, like its owner's soul, wearing thin.

"The fifth anniversary of my first mention in your column," I say as lightly as I can. It still rankles, but I've gone too fast: Cyrus had warned me against raising substance too soon.

"Oh, that," she says, unperturbed, but noticeably wary. Damn.

"I thought it was time to bury the hatchet," I plunge in recklessly.

"But there isn't any hatchet to bury." She withdraws her hand and pulls out a cigarette.

I am quick to convert defeat into victory. My newly freed fingers reach for the gold-plated lighter on her coffee table just before she can get to it. Our hands meet briefly over metal and butane. It takes me two attempts to light her cancerous weed, but at last I succeed. As she inhales, I pour more champagne.

"You're right," I respond (Cyrus would be proud of me). "All the more reason to celebrate. Cheers."

We both raise glasses. I gulp; she sips. She still looks wary, but one of her hands has dropped idly back into her lap while the other transfers the cigarette in and out of the red gash that passes for her mouth.

"You can't bribe me, you know," she says archly. "Not even with Pol Roger."

"Bribe you?" I laugh insincerely. "The thought wouldn't cross my mind. No one bribes the dre —, er, the famous Radha Sabnis." Watch it, Banjara, watch it. One more slip like that and you're a garage mechanic for life.

She looks at me speculatively. As so often with those of the female persuasion, I find myself obliged to say something.

"Look," I venture shamelessly, "I've always admired you greatly. . . ."

"Really?" Her eyebrows are most disconcerting, but she is not displeased.

"Really." I am determined now. "Best writer in *Showbiz*" — I quickly see this would not be enough and hastily add an expansive suffix — "-ness. In show business," I repeat for good measure. "Really perceptive, insightful. Everyone thinks so. And I've always said to myself, Ashok, I've said, what a shame it is that you don't know Radhaji better. Why should you condemn yourself perpetually to being on her wrong side?"

"A-ha." That's all she says. Inscrutably, she knocks some ash into a brass bowl.

"So I thought, why not come and see you? Show there are no hard feelings, you know, from my side at least. And really, answer any questions you might have or anything. Just to show you I'm not such a bad chap after all."

"But I have no questions." This sounds tough, but with that extraordinary face it is impossible to be sure she means it to be. The body language is more promising. She has crossed her legs again, and her knees are pointing toward me. Mustn't give up hope.

"Well, maybe I do. You know, perhaps you can tell me what you think I'm doing wrong. Give me some advice."

"Advice?" She uncrosses and crosses her legs again and leans back on the sofa. "What advice could I possibly give you?"

"Tell me" — here I place my hand once more on hers — "how I can become a good enough actor to win the praise of Radha Sabnis."

She gives me a twisted smile, but doesn't move her hand. "Now that would be something, wouldn't it?" she asks, and the lines on her face fall into an indecipherable disarray.

I decipher them my way. I get up from my chair, walk around the coffee table, seat myself next to her on the sofa, and take her hand firmly in mine. "I need your advice, Radhaji," I implore, looking earnestly into her eyes as if emoting for a close-up.

She doesn't flinch. "Are you sure that's all you need?" she asks, stubbing out her cigarette with deliberate care.

Christ, I was afraid of this. I had warned Cyrus: I'll turn on all the charm you want, Sponerwalla, but don't expect me to so much as kiss the witch. To which he'd said, "Look at it this way, man." (Cyrus's American PR slang was always a decade out of date.) "No one knows whether she's thirty-eight or eighty-three. Approach her in the spirit of scientific inquiry, Ashok. Market research, man. Like, we do it all the time. If it comes to that, you might be the first real human being to find out, truth-wise."

Radha's loaded question hangs in the air: "Are you sure that's all you need?" She seems to expect a reply. Despite myself I murmur, "Perhaps not." Let's play along, flatter the hag.

"Hmmm." She puts down the champagne glass. "If you insist." And before I even realize what is happening, she has put an arm around my neck and brought her mouth down on mine.

Kissing is one thing they don't practice in the Hindi cinema: our censors don't like it. But no amount of practice would have prepared me for kissing Radha Sabnis. I am buffeted by a mistral of cigarette fumes, then swept away into alternate waves of asphyxiation and resuscitation. Holding my own in the exchange is like trying to outblow a vacuum cleaner. I am still orally imprisoned, eyes shut in breathless disbelief, when I feel her fingers explore my T-shirt like a skeleton searching for a burial ground. My eyes rounding in horror, I attempt to pull myself away. But I'm obviously not trying hard enough. My lips remain locked on hers and I am aware of the pressure of her teeth: there seem to be about two thousand of them, each as large and strong as a key on Gopi Master's harmonium. She must chew *neem* twigs before breakfast, and unfortunate actors after. As I try to move she half rises, mouth still glued to mine, and pushes me down with a firm hand. Boy, she's strong. The other hand is pulling my T-shirt out of my waistband. Christ, this is *serious!* Eyes closed, I put out a hand to stop her and discover something softer and fuller than I expected upon her anatomy. The appendage seems vaguely familiar, like an old friend encountered in a strange country. Reacting instinctively, I squeeze. Without moving her mouth, Radha Sabnis moans into my throat. I open my eyes in amazement to see what the hell I am up to and close them just as quickly. I must move my hand, the woman might get the wrong idea. But I can't — my arm is pinioned to her chest by the way she has positioned her body.

For a brief moment I contemplate surrender. Isn't that what inevitably happens in our filmi "rape scenes"? But wait a minute, not to me! I'm a hero!

I still have the use of one hand, the one that was holding hers. I release my grip and find she has not released hers. In fact she is squeezing my palm so tightly that I no longer feel any sensation in my fingers — can't do a damned thing with this hand. The improbable contents of my other one are meanwhile pressing and squirming insistently in my palm. I refuse to oblige: nothing will induce me to invite another moan down my esophagus. The female breast, a pedantic biology teacher had once told me, is only a muscle. This one has obviously been flexed so often it could lift weights.

At this moment my own weight is more than I can lift. I am crushed into the sofa: for a woman as thin as she is, Radha Sabnis packs a lot of power. And what's more, she now has one hand free, thanks to my failed sortie. Her fingers are ruthlessly determined, discarding every obstacle in their way like panzers rolling into Poland. One by one, each of my pathetic defenses is dealt with, flung aside: T-shirt, belt, buttons. Unless I fight back, this will be an abject surrender. Air raid sirens wail in my mind: her fingers are tugging at my zip! With a superhuman effort — God, I could have done with a stunt man here — I try to wrench myself away. The result is a pelvic jerk that rolls us both off the sofa, sends us crashing into the coffee table, and deposits us on the floor with Radha still on top, mouth glued to mine and hand safely ensconced where I hadn't wished it to be. A trickle of Pol Roger Rosé, 1968, from the ruins of the coffee table drips stickily into my eyes.

Radha Sabnis lifts her head briefly and smiles at me. "Such passion, Ashok," she says with a winsome shake of the head. "You really must learn to control yourself." Before I can catch enough breath to reply, her teeth have padlocked my tongue again.

I give up. I close my eyes and think of Cyrus.

"Was she amenable, mood-wise?" he asks me later.

I pick lint from her carpet off the sticky champagne on my cheek. "You could say that," I confirm shortly.

"What did she want, man?" he asks insensitively. "A donation to her favorite charity?"

I nod. "You could say that too."

"I hope," says Cyrus solemnly, "that you were in a charitable mood."

Suddenly I find myself laughing. Laughing uncontrollably, in huge, whooping bursts that startle my public relations agent, who looks for all the world like a bewildered owl woken unexpectedly at daytime. I wipe tears and champagne from my eyes. "Cyrus," I announce, "if your bloody idea doesn't get me a better press in Cheetah's column next week — you're fired." I am still laughing as I leave him, but Cyrus Sponerwalla is a very worried PR man indeed.

But I have another associate on my mind: my wife, who is waiting for me. I am supposed to pick up Maya from the beauty salon.

She spends more time being beautified these days than when she used to act.

"You're late," she says as soon as she gets into the car. Maya can never resist an opportunity to restate the obvious.

"I'm sorry," I concede. "I had to stop and see Cyrus on the way, and then all this hassle of coming by the back road, to avoid being mobbed . . . you know how it is."

"I don't, actually," she replies tartly. "I don't know how it is anymore. It's a surprise when anyone recognizes me these days. What on earth have you got on your face?"

"My face?" I reach up to my cheek in alarm. My face is, after all, my fortune. "Where?"

"Near your eye." She reaches across and pulls off a tiny yellow feather. The stuff Radha Sabnis has in her living room! Doesn't a yellow feather symbolize something? "There's all sorts of muck near your temple," she says, handing it to me. I run a finger over the offending spot, which I find coated with cigarette ash in a wine base. "Where have you been?"

"Plying Radha Sabnis with champagne," I reply truthfully. This is difficult, because in the last couple of years I have got used to lying to Maya about my extracurricular activities. But she has seen Radha Sabnis, at least at parties, so the truth is less likely to arouse suspicion than any version of the unconvincing tales she is clearly beginning to see through.

"But how could you get it onto your face?"

"Clumsiness," I sigh. "Opened it badly — it sort of sprayed all over. Didn't have time to clean up properly afterward." Truth again.

Her little face settles into that tight look of disapproval I am becoming accustomed to. "You smell like a brothel," she says. "And it's not only the champagne."

"What are you trying to say, Maya?" I keep my voice low. The chauffeur has heard this kind of conversation before, but there is no reason to make it easier for him. "You can ask the bloody driver where I've been. You're not suggesting I've been having some sort of orgy with Radha Sabnis of all people, are you?"

She is silent. It is not the kind of question you can easily answer.

"Well, go on, are you?"

"No, I'm sorry, Ashok." She doesn't look at me, but at the back of the chauffeur's head. "I guess I'm getting a little irritable these days. You've got your own life, and I hardly see you. I've got nothing to *do*, Ashok. I'm bored."

"I thought, with the house to run, and all the magazines you read, and the visits to the beauty parlor, and all the film functions, you had more than enough to keep you occupied. What more do you want?"

"I don't know." When she is in this mood I can scarcely believe she is the girl I fell in love with, the even-tempered, ever-smiling *beti* of the nation. "I miss my acting."

"Now don't start that again." I am weary of this topic. We have discussed it more times than I have fought screen brawls. "You know we agreed you couldn't go on after marriage. No one does: Babita, Jaya, you know them all. It was difficult enough to get my parents to agree to my marrying an actress. How do you think I'd feel to see my wife being chased around trees? It's just not" — I am about to say "decent," but think better of it — "worth discussing."

"Well, I have to put up with you chasing other women around trees," she retorts hotly. "And God knows where else you chase them." Not that again, oh Lord, I think, but she has weightier matters in mind. "I'm a professional actress, Ashok Banjara, and I'm sick — sick — of not exercising my profession."

I can't take too much intensity in a moving car. Besides, Radha Sabnis has taken much of the fight out of me. "Look," I say earnestly, "I can understand how you feel. Let's wait for the doctor's report on your frog test, OK? If it's clear, I promise we'll work out some sort of role, I mean a *good* role, for you in one of my next films." (This isn't hedging; I'm signed up for eleven films simultaneously at the moment, so I can't talk in the singular.) "If you *are* pregnant, well, of course, that'll be that."

"Oh, Ashok, do you mean it, really? Is that a promise?" She is almost tearful in relief.

"Of course, Maya," I reply expansively. "I don't like seeing you upset like this."

"You promise I can act again if I'm not pregnant?"

"Absolutely." Anything to buy peace. I do not mention that, in a gesture of excitement he would not make for lesser luminaries among his clients, the doctor has already telephoned me this morning with the good news.

"I love you, Ashok," Maya says fervently.

I take her hand in mine. "I love you, too, baby." A small twinge of conscience strikes. "We'll send the driver to pick up the doctor's report in the afternoon."

Back to work. I am no longer entirely sure where or to which film. I now have a secretary who schedules me, thrusts a piece of paper into the chauffeur's hand, and sends me on my way, sometimes to do three films in the two shooting shifts theoretically available. In most Bombay studios, these are 9:30 A.M. to 5:30 P.M. (the day shift), and 6 P.M. to midnight (the evening, or more realistically night, shift). In my early days I would have been lucky to have enough work to shoot every day, but now I am so overcommitted I can't meet my obligations within the two possible shifts. "Gimme dates," scream the producers, sounding like socially starved American teenagers, "gimme dates." So my secretary, the efficient Subramanyam, gives them dates, and sometimes they're the same dates for three different producers. Which means I shuttle back and forth, leaving one shift early and arriving at the next one late, sometimes decamping after one shot and promising to be back for the next, not always keeping the promises. What the hell, the films seem to get made anyway, and as long as they have my name on them they don't do too badly at the box office.

It's not as if I'm being worked to the bone or anything. Any period of film shooting consists of bursts of frenetic activity interspersed with long bouts of hanging around waiting for people to set things up: scenes, lighting, equipment. In one eight-hour shift the director will probably expose anything from one thousand and two hundred to three thousand feet of film, the exact figure depending on how undemanding he is, how competent his crew and cast are, and how many technical things that can go wrong do go wrong. There's about ninety to ninety-five feet of celluloid to every minute of filmed action, so the *most* productive crew actually gets about half an hour's worth of film into the can at the end of an eight-hour shift — and most don't manage half of that. Of that footage no more than one-fifth actually survives the cutting room floor and is included in the movie itself. Which means that each shift actually contributes something like three to six minutes to the movie people pay to see in the cinema theater.

"Have I shot anything for this film already?" I ask the secretary as I am about to leave. The film's name means nothing to me, but then most Hindi film names don't mean anything to anybody.

"Yes, sir," replies my efficient Subramanyam. "You have done two shootings already, sir, last month. One-and-half shifts."

"One-and-*a*-half, Subramanyam," I chide him gently. "You don't know what it's about, do you?"

Subramanyam looks bashful. "No, sir, I am not knowing."

"Well, I guess I'll find out. There'll be plenty more shifts to catch up with the story."

As the star, for a big film I'd have to put in anything from twenty to thirty shifts myself. When I'm doing a half dozen films simultaneously, some of them shot in locations far away from the other directors' studios, "gimme dates" becomes a plaintive cry. I used to think that a movie that took three years to make actually involved people toiling every day for three years. Not a bit of it: all that probably happened was that the producer had too ambitious a cast, and he couldn't get dates. It's worst of all when both the hero and the heroine are stars in great demand. The dates he gives may not coincide with hers, and you can't shoot love scenes on different shifts.

I turn up at Himalaya Studios and am hustled into costume: synthetic sweatshirt, blue baseball cap, unfashionably unfaded jeans and canvas shoes. A dirty white handkerchief is knotted hastily around my neck. I am some sort of local tough, defender of the neighborhood and general all-purpose good guy, who will of course go on to demolish the villains and marry the rich heroine.

"What's supposed to happen here?" I ask the director, as the makeup man puts on the necessary traces of blush to heighten the rosiness of my cheeks. Nearly thirty years since Independence and we still associate pink skin with healthiness.

"We're ready to shoot," he says, trying to sound efficient and in charge. He's a young fellow, some producer's son, known to everybody, even me who's his age, as The Boy.

"Congratulations, but that's not what I meant," I reply. "What are we ready to shoot?" I have long since given up looking at scripts. There are too many of them and they all read alike, and in any case it's too much to keep up with three convoluted plot lines a day.

"Oh. I see what you mean." The Boy is quick to catch on; it's clear he knows his profession. "It's an outdoor shot. Heroine's car breaks down, some rowdies start bothering her, you tell them to buzz off, bash them up when they don't, open the hood and fix the car. Simple."

"Straightforward," I agree. "Any deathless dialogue in this one, or can I make it up as I go along?"

The director looks dubious. There are directors here who make movies without scripts, contenting themselves with story lines on ever-changing scraps of paper, but The Boy is not confident enough for that. He tries to be flexible. "Just the line when you first tell them to buzz off — there's some good stuff in there, I think. Something about haven't they got mothers and sisters. The rest you can ad-lib."

"Good." The makeup man is finished. "Lead me to it."

There is only one outdoor locale at Himalaya, which is not small as Bombay studios go. This is a street that runs past the studio's administration office and canteen into a clump of bushes and flowering trees that could serve, if shot from the right angles, as a low-budget setting for romantic rural interludes. A red Fiat is already parked on the street, and there seems to be a girl in it, though from where I am approaching, most of her face is obscured by a large straw hat. As I step out into the street a ragged cheer goes up from the throng of hangers-on who always seem to manage to get onto the studio grounds. I wave grandly back at them, taking care not to walk close enough to be touched or importuned for autographs.

The director walks up with a closely typed page from the screenplay containing the dialogue he wants me to remember. I dismiss the proferred sheet. "Read it to me," I say. The makeup man, a fat dark chap with a front pocket full of combs and brushes, hovers around, examining me critically in the bright sunlight. The mirror in his hand catches the light and reflects it into my eye as I am listening to The Boy, so I shoo him away with a gesture of irritation. He backs off but continues to examine me from a safer distance, the mirror turned away from my eyes.

The rowdies, in tight-fitting T-shirts and corduroy pants, mill about the car, trying to chat up the straw hat. The inevitable Arriflex camera (every Indian cinematographer uses Arriflex, as if they've never heard of any other brand) stands on a steel tripod, pointing at them. The electrical equipment is now in place, principally a blue wooden box the size of a car battery (for all I know it might well have been a car battery in an earlier incarnation), capped by three fuse boxes and sporting an array of sockets on the side from which sprout a tangle of wires of every color. The technicians, dark dusty men wearing dirty *chappals* and checked shirts that hang out of their trousers, are sitting around on makeshift wooden stools, waiting for me. Let them wait.

They're not the only ones. In one cluster of folding chairs on the other side of the street sit unknown stalwarts of the production team, chatting, reading Hindi newspapers, drinking tea, seemingly disengaged from the day's events. God knows who they are, or what their role is. Every unit I've seen seems to have some fifty people on its payroll at each shift, about twenty of whom are completely idle at any given time. My old friend Tool Dwivedi would have liked nothing better than to be one of them.

I've absorbed the mothers and sisters bit in the dialogue. "Got it," I confirm.

"Ready for action?" The Boy asks.

"Sure. But you're not." I point up the steps we've just descended, where a fading board proclaims Himalaya Studios. "Aren't you going to do anything about that?" My hand sweeps from the camera to the board.

"Salim!" the director yells. A scruffy boy shuffles past, bearing a sign far too large for him that says State Bank of India. The last time I'd been here the Himalaya administration building had masqueraded as a hospital. The lad drags the sign awkwardly up the steps. None of the twenty idle people move to help him.

Salim is a hired hand, slave labor without the slave's security of tenure. The rowdies I shall soon have to bash up are a step higher on the biological scale: they are Junior Artistes, Bollywood's very own term for what the rest of the world knows as extras. Once — just once — in my more naive days and at the prompting of one of the more senior Junior Artistes, I went to Jagannath Choubey to remonstrate mildly with him about the way he was treating them. "What for you asking me this-that?" Choubey retorted in heat. "Why, even the lowest artiste, B-class artiste — why to say artiste, even some poor old toothless man in village scene, some sick grandmother coughing in corner — all getting rupees forty per shift plus rupees seventeen and fifty paise, if you please, for transport and tiffin. Conveyance charge they are calling it. Conveyance charge! And if they say even one single word only on camera, just a *jee-huzoor* even, they are demanding fifty percent additional. And getting; and getting!"

I wondered whether, in the face of his outrage, it would be safe to say that I didn't think this was a lot of money. He cut me off as if he had read my mind. "What-all are these people wanting, then, hanh? They are all unqualified for anything else. Uneducated people. Where else in India will any of them be earning so much?"

He had a point, and I backed away. That was many movies ago; but it occurs to me, as I eye The Boy's rowdies near the red Fiat, that despite these terms there is never any shortage of Junior Artistes. They are produced on demand by "suppliers," like any other commonly available commodity.

"Who's in the straw hat?" I ask the director conversationally while the sign is being switched.

"Your heroine," The Boy responds, as if astonished by the question.

"I gathered that," I reply cuttingly. "But *who* is my heroine in this picture?"

The director looks mortally offended. "Mehnaz Elahi," he tells me.

"Never heard of her," I admit cheerfully. "Have I met her?"

I am not just being crass. There is a flood of new actresses washing up at the feet of producers these days. With the problems they are having getting dates for the handful of recognized big-name females who can still draw crowds at the box office (as poor Abha, falsies notwithstanding, no longer can), one way out for many producers is to cast an established hero against an up-and-coming heroine. I don't mind too much because this new crop of heroines is good-looking, articulate, and largely uninhibited. The periods of enforced idleness at every shooting pass very pleasantly indeed in their company.

"I think she was at the *muhurat,*" the director says, "but I remember you made only a fleeting appearance."

"Ah, yes, that's possible." I am slightly embarrassed. The *muhurat* of any film, the auspicious moment when the opening shot is canned, is not an event its star is supposed to miss. But Subramanyam had, bless him, "given dates." Not that I minded too much. *Muhurats* are packed with oversize individuals in undersize clothes, their eyes and thighs gleaming with a synthetic sheen. When they are not emitting raucous cries of recognition (while looking, in the midst of each embrace, for the next famous face to recognize) their tendency is to drape refulgent garlands on every available tripod, clapper board, or neck. I'm happy to avoid them. In any case, marigolds make me sneeze.

"OK, the sign's up," says The Boy. "Let's go." The cameraman takes up position. So do the rowdies. A sound man crouches behind the car, holding a mike on a fishing rod.

"Start sound! Camera! Action!"

The rowdies start their harassment. The girl in the straw hat looks helpless. I march in, upbraid them. They are not much impressed by my invocation of their mothers and sisters. They are more impressed by my fists. This is not a choreographed stunt scene, merely an impromptu thrashing. One or two of my blows almost make contact, but I manage to stop them just short, knowing from prior carelessness how painful sore hands can be. They turn tail and flee. I turn to the damsel I have rescued from distress.

"That takes care of them," I begin. And then I dry up completely.

For the car door opens, just as it is supposed to, and out steps the most beautiful woman I have ever seen. She takes off her straw hat, and I am at a complete loss for words.

"Cut!" says the director. He strides into the frame. "What happened?" he demands. "You're supposed to say, can I help . . ." He stops, because it is apparent I am not listening to him. Nor is the girl. She is looking directly at the expression on my face, and an intuitive smile is playing at the corners of her mouth.

"Oh," says The Boy, taking this in. "Ashok Banjara, meet Mehnaz Elahi."

"Hello," she says. Her voice reaches deep inside me and strums a responsive chord. An echo emerges: "Hello," I say.

"Well, now that we've got that out of the way," says the director impatiently, "can we try that shot again? Only this time, you're supposed to say . . ."

I get through that shift in a trancelike state. At the first opportunity, when Mehnaz has disappeared for a costume change, I ring Subramanyam.

"Change my dates a bit this month," I instruct him. "I want to give priority to this young director's film. Give him whatever shifts he wants."

"I am doing, sir," Subramanyam confirms disapprovingly, "but many producers not being happy with you. I just warning you, sir."

"Good man. Now give The Boy all the dates he wants, OK? And one more thing — find out all you can for me about Mehnaz Elahi."

Why did I marry Maya? This is probably a hell of a time to ask myself that question, with her expecting our first child in eight months. But as I sit next to her in our living room, answering intimate queries posed by a gushingly sympathetic reporter from *Woman's World* ("Filmdom's Dream Marriage"), I find myself asking it all the time. I look at her, hear myself talking about her to the public, gauge the disarming impression of mutual love and affection we are projecting so effortlessly, and wonder what it would be like to interview myself. Off the record, of course.

What did you see in her? A lovely face, a pretty smile, a gentle vulnerability that made me want to reach out and hold her, protect her against the world. Simplicity, too, of a kind I'd never come across in Delhi. A simple girl, good-natured and kind, with simple tastes, modest, unassuming, soft-spoken. A girl everyone loved.

Everyone loved her, so you thought you did, too? Well, that wouldn't be fair. Everyone loved her, so I began to take more notice of her. And when she returned my attention, I felt terribly flattered that the girl everybody admired, admired me.

And love? Where did that come in? The first time I held her in my arms. It was actually on camera, a scene from *Ganwaari*. She looked up at me, and there was a kind of light in her eyes. I felt all sorts of emotions run through me that I couldn't explain or define. I decided it must be love.

And her? Oh, she loved me. There was no doubt about that.

Did you want to take her to bed? Yes — and, oddly enough, no. I wanted to take her to bed, once. Very badly. I wanted to be the first man in her life, that way. Introduce her to that world, seal my possession of her. Sort of exercise the rights of a husband. But once I had that, once I *was* a husband, the need cooled very rapidly. She's not a very sexy type, really. Small, and thin, and let's face it, not

83

much of a figure. Looks great in a sari, less great in a *salwar-kameez,* awful without either. I can't say I married her to improve my sex life.

So were you the first man in her life? Funnily enough, I don't know. I guess so, I mean it's almost inconceivable that Maya . . . But there was someone she was close to before me, a minor actor, an inconsequential villain type. I can't imagine that she'd have gone to bed with him, but then I can't imagine he'd have not gone to bed with her. The devil of it is, I can't ask her. I can just see her lip trembling and her eyes watering at the very thought of my doubting her. But . . .

And how's it been? Your sex life? With Maya, not terribly good. It didn't take me long to realize I'd married someone who reminded me of my mother. After that it was difficult to summon up much desire for her. I mean, I admire the girl, but how can you feel passion for someone you put on a pedestal? I think we're both relieved she's pregnant now. Production launched, rehearsals can be suspended.

And apart from Maya? What kind of question is that? I'm a married man.

Did that ever stop you? Not really. Well, yes, for a bit. But a man has his needs, you know, and God knows I have the opportunities. Everyone seems to want to bed an actor. You should see some of the fan mail Subramanyam has to process every day. Traditional housewives in Jabalpur write to describe in loving detail what they'd like me to do to them. We just send them a printed postcard in reply, but Subramanyam shows me some of the more extraordinary propositions. And that's long distance. Here in Bombay, it's actually worse. Or better, depending on your point of view. It's always more difficult to turn the girls away than to simply enjoy what comes my way. I mean, come on, no one takes it seriously.

What about Maya? Well, yes, I suppose she'd take it seriously, if she found out. So a certain amount of discretion has been necessary. I'm not sure how effective it's been, though. This industry's full of rumors. Word gets around.

Why don't you tell her, directly? Ah, well, yes. But no, not really. I couldn't do that.

Why not? I couldn't. She has a fiery temper, you know, which I never suspected existed. Shows you how premarital appearances can be deceptive. She would erupt. She might just walk out, leave me.

So what? What do you mean, so what? It was the marriage of the decade, for God's sake. Not just in the film press — we made the front page of the *Times of India*. And I don't want to give her up. It's not as if I want to marry any of these girls, for Christ's sake. My marriage to Maya is important to me. If it ends in disgrace, it'll destroy me.

Nonsense. The public doesn't care all that much. Look, being Maya's husband is part of my image now. People see me not just as Ashok Banjara, but as the guy Maya saw enough in to marry and give up her career for. To go from that to being the guy Maya walked out on — it would finish me, really. And what about my father? He's grudgingly accepted my profession, now that it's made me more famous than he is. But one of the first things he said to me about it was, "Son, you're now a public man. And a public man has public responsibilities. Make sure you live up to yours." How do you think he'll react to having his son the centerpiece of a scandalous divorce? Forget it. The costs are too high.

So you're scared. Perhaps, but it's not just that. Where else would I find a wife like Maya? She's ideal, man, the nation's ideal *bahu*. Half these women I take to the bedroom I wouldn't be caught dead with in a living room. Maya's all right. I just wish she'd ease up a bit, stop complaining so much, be a bit more fun to be with.

And let you sleep with other women. (Silence.)

Well? I have nothing more to say. This off-the-record interview is over.

Naw. It's much easier to deal with *Woman's World*. "I was saying all these romantic things to Maya on screen when I realized I meant every word of the dialogue," I say to the interviewer joshingly, "and which Hindi film actor can afford that? So I had to marry her, before someone changed the script."

The woman journalist laughs. When I see her to the door she presses a piece of paper into my hand. After she has left, I see that it contains her private phone number and two words: "any time."

For a long moment I look at it, recalling the woman's skimpy low-cut blouse and readiness to laugh. I push the piece of paper into a pocket. Perhaps some time.

Cyrus Sponerwalla bursts in while I'm with Subramanyam. His three chins are flapping about as excitedly as the magazine in his hand.

"Listen to this," he declaims.

Darlings, Cheetah is *so* impressed by Ashok Banjara these days. All of you pets know that I haven't always thought very highly of our tall-fair-and-handsome hero. But in his recent films the Hungry Young Man has really polished up his moves. In *Love in Paris* he really brought a certain je ne sais quoi to the hackneyed role of the Indian lover abroad. And reliable sources whisper in my ear that he has a highly developed taste in champagne, Cheetah's favorite drink. No wonder the industry is bubbly over him, eh? Grrrowl . . .

He looks up, breathless from reading. "So how about that, hanh? Should do you some good, faith-wise."

"Sure, Cyrus," I grin. "Faith fully restored. Only, next time there's a bottle to be presented to the lady in question, *you* go. OK?" He turns to leave. "And Cyrus . . ."

"Yes?"

"Before you do, get some exercise, OK? You're in no sort of shape for scientific inquiry."

Exterior: Day/Night

JUDAI

(The Bond)

"What!" The villain's face rises to fill the screen as his voice resounds through the hall.

"Yes, Thakur. It is written in the stars and in the palm leaves handed down for generations that foretell your family's destiny. Your sister's son will bring about your downfall."

"Never!" screams Pranay, a short, angry figure in jodhpurs and black boots, a riding crop in his stubby hand. "This shall not come to pass!" He flicks his whip at the pandit who has brought him the news, scattering the learned man's papers. The Brahmin bends in dismay to pick them up as the feudal Thakur strides purposefully down the immense chandeliered hall, his footsteps echoing on the marble floor.

In a bedroom of considerably less elegance, the Thakur's sister, Abha, in the throes of childbirth, heaves and moans. Her blanket is modestly drawn up to her neck, but a few beads of sweat stand on her forehead like the pearls she has been used to wearing in her earlier films. A kindly midwife, Amma, murmurs encouraging words of solicitude. Soon a cry is heard, a baby's response to the world he has just entered. Amma smiles beatifically.

But something is wrong — Abha is still in pain! Amma's saintly brow creases in puzzlement and worry. Abha moans again, gasps. Her body arches under the blanket. "What is happening, *beti?*" Amma asks anxiously. The answer comes soon, but not from Abha's lips. A second wail is heard, louder than the first; the two wails form an unmusical duet.

"Twins!" exclaims Amma. "Abha, you've become a mother of twin boys!"

Abha smiles exhaustedly. Two babies, miraculously clean and umbilicus-less, are placed on her pillow on either side of her. She turns her head from side to side. The babies (somewhat too large to be convincing, but then where can you get newborns to be Junior Artistes?) gurgle happily.

Outside the bedroom Amma summons a family retainer, Raju, a thin man in a khaki shirt, a brown Nehru cap, and a dustcloth draped over one shoulder. "Abhaji has had twin sons. Go and give the Thakur-sahib the good news." Raju brings raised palms together in an obedient *namaste*.

"Wonderful," says the Thakur insincerely as Raju, hands still folded in supplication, conveys the glad tidings to him in his chandeliered hall. "We shall distribute sweets in the village. Tell my sister I shall come and see my new nephews tomorrow." Raju nods, does *namaste,* and is dismissed.

He has not gone far, however, when he hears the Thakur summon his sidekick, Kalia, an immense black bald-headed man instantly identified by the audience as a villainous sidekick from scores of other films. Raju stands near a convenient window and listens.

"Kalia," Pranay announces, twirling his evil mustache, "the astrologers have forecast my downfall at the hands of my sister's son. I don't know which one of these two is destined to oppose me, but the only way to be safe is to kill them both. See that it is done, Kalia — tonight."

The swell of background music paints an aural exclamation mark on Raju's horrified forehead. He gasps in shock, then sets out at a fast clip for Abha's home.

"No!" screams Abha, clutching her infants to her considerable bosom. "This cannot be!"

"It is true, Abhaji," Raju says sadly, tears in his rheumy eyes.

"There is only one thing to do," Amma opines. "You must flee with the babies, somewhere where they will be safe."

"But where?" asks Abha in desperation. "Where can I go?" She looks directly at the camera. "If only my husband, the boys' father, had not been jailed for a crime he did not commit," she declares for the audience's benefit, "he would never have let my evil brother do this to me."

"What is the use of thinking about him now?" Amma asks impatiently. "You must go soon."

"I have a cousin who works in a factory in Bombay," Raju says. "We can go there. He will get me a job in the factory, and the boys will be safe."

"You have no choice," Amma confirms. "Quick, let me get you ready."

Soon they are prepared to leave. Abha removes from around her neck a black string necklace with two talismans hanging from it.

"Your father gave this to me," she whispers to the babies. "Now you must have it, for luck." She snaps the string in two, then ties each half to a baby's wrist. A close-up reveals a single talisman dangling from each baby's pudgy arm. The two are identical.

Exterior: twilight. Raju and Abha are seen running down a path toward a river. Each carries a basket. Thick foliage abounds on both sides.

"I shall take one basket across," Raju says, "and then come back for you."

He wades across the river, baby and basket aloft. Abha stands at the water's edge, looking helpless, her own basket heavy in her hand. The music on the sound track is dramatic, suspenseful.

"There she is!" a voice cries out as the violins explode in a heart-stopping crescendo. Kalia it is, with another bandit by his side, both on horseback. "The babies must be in the basket. Come on, let's get her!"

"No!" Abha screams as the horses canter down the path. Raju, three-quarters of the way across the river, looks back in uncertainty. "Go on!" she instructs him. "They haven't seen you yet. Go on, quickly! I'll manage on my own somehow."

Raju hesitates, hears the horses' hooves, and wades on. He soon disappears into the foliage on the other side.

Abha steps into the water, trying to hold the basket high. The current swirls relentlessly around her. "Stop!" cries Kalia, charging onward. "Stop!"

Abha takes another step forward, stumbles. A shot rings out, then another. She screams. A red stain appears on her blouse. She falls, and the basket slips out of her grasp. With a last despairing wail, she reaches out for it, but the basket is caught by the current and floats rapidly downriver.

"No!" she screams again (her dialogue was easy to learn). The basket disappears, and Abha sinks under the water as Kalia and his accomplice draw their horses up to the river's edge.

"Too bad," says Kalia as Raju, panting, gapes at them through a gap in the jungle shrubbery that he has hidden in. "All drowned, for certain. Well, that's what the Thakur wanted, wasn't it?" His partner nods: he has a nonspeaking part.

"Well, let's get back to the boss and give him the sad news," Kalia laughs. "He won't be too upset: she was only an adoptive sister anyway." The two wheel their horses around and canter back up the path.

Raju is seen running, the basket in his hand. The camera cuts to the other basket floating safely on the current. Inside the baby cries, waving a pudgy fist with a black string talisman dangling from his wrist. The waters swirl, Raju runs, the basket floats, the baby cries. And the opening credits fill the screen.

As the director's name fades from the screen, the camera pans to a pavement scene in Bombay. A man and a monkey are performing tricks, and they seem to have attracted a larger crowd than such exhibitions usually do in a blasé city. The reason is soon apparent: the man in the lungi, sleeveless shirt, and dirty cap, waving an hourglass-shaped tambouret that clicks rhythmically in tune with his patter, is none other than Ashok Banjara. The crowd that inevitably gathers to watch open-air film shootings is therefore doubling as the monkey-man's audience.

"Performing monkey! Come and see!" Ashok calls out, as if to attract even more custom. "Tricks you've never seen before!" He rattles his tambouret. "Performing monkey!"

The monkey hops about on the hot concrete sidewalk. "Come on, Thakur!" Ashok calls out to him. "Do you like these people?" The monkey nods his head. "Are they bad people?" The monkey shakes his head. "Is this lady pretty?" The monkey nods vigorously, sending titters through the crowd and provoking an embarrassed giggle from the extra playing the lady in the throng. "Would you like to marry her, Thakur?" The animal nods again, its eyes opening lustfully wide and eliciting a louder laugh from the spectators. The lady now looks decidedly uncomfortable. "Do you think she'll marry you?" The monkey slowly, sadly, shakes his head. This time the lady joins in the appreciative laughter.

As the performance continues — the monkey donning absurdly elegant coats and caps, doing cartwheels, responding to Ashok's questions — the monkey-man works the crowd, his fingers dipping deftly into pockets and handbags. The crowd is distracted by the monkey and by Ashok's song:

> *Say hello to the monkey-man, monkey-man, monkey-man,*
> *Say hello to the monkey-man, and give us some rice.*
> *We give more highs than a junkie can, junkie can, junkie can,*
> *We give more highs than a junkie can, at half the price.*

> *Shouldn't we be good to these people?*

(MONKEY NODS)

> *Then try and climb up a steeple!*

(MONKEY RUNS UP A TELEPHONE POLE)

> *Show them how you jump!*

(MONKEY JUMPS DOWN, LANDS SAFELY
ON HIS FEET)

> *Dance, and wiggle your rump!*

(MONKEY DOES SO, LIKE A HINDI FILM
CABARET DANCER)

> *Say hello to the monkey-man, monkey-man, monkey-man,*
> *Say hello to the monkey-man, and give us some rice.*
> *We give more highs than a junkie can, junkie can, junkie can,*
> *We give more highs than a junkie can, at half the price.*

> *Are these ba-a-d folks?*

(MONKEY SHAKES HIS HEAD.)

Shall we show 'em some jokes?

(MONKEY NODS)

OK, do a striptease!

(MONKEY PROCEEDS TO PULL OFF HIS LITTLE
SEQUINED JACKET AND, DANCING,
TUGS AT HIS OUTSIZE SHORTS)

That's enough, at ease!

(MONKEY STOPS, DOFFS HIS LITTLE CAP)

Say hello to the monkey-man, monkey-man, monkey-man,
Say hello to the monkey-man, and give us some rice.
We give more highs than a junkie can, junkie can, junkie can,
We give more highs than a junkie can, at half the price.

So Thakur, it's time to go?

(MONKEY NODS)

Is this the end of the show?

(MONKEY NODS, HEAD DROOPING,
MIMING TIREDNESS)

Time to collect your fee!

(MONKEY LEAPS UP, PICKS UP CAP LARGER
THAN ASHOK'S, AND TAKES IT AROUND
THE CROWD)

Folks, you decide what that should be!

And as people give money, in some cases reaching for their missing wallets in puzzlement, Ashok packs up, singing:

Say hello to the monkey-man, monkey-man, monkey-man,
Say hello to the monkey-man . . .

He is seen whistling the same tune as he enters a slum colony, his monkey perched on his shoulder. Little children run up to greet him, and he dispenses sweets liberally. He is hailed affectionately by passing extras, by shopkeepers, by a tea stall man, and he returns each greeting with a wave and a familiar word. After a while he stops and ducks into a curtained doorway. In a dark little room an old man lies on a string-bed charpoy, coughing piteously, while a beautiful young girl sits at the bedside, looking anxious.

"*Arré* Ashok, is it you?" the sick man rasps.

"Don't strain yourself, Chacha," our hero replies. "Look, I have brought some money for your medicine. You will be well soon." He holds out a sheaf of notes to the girl, who looks embarrassed.

"Go on, take it, Mehnaz," Ashok says. "Your father needs the medicine. If I could read and write I'd have got it myself."

"You're so kind, *Bhaiya*," Mehnaz replies. "I don't know what we'd do without you. But you work so hard for this money — it isn't right, somehow."

"Don't be silly," Ashok retorts. "Isn't Chacha like a father to me? Take it."

The old man coughs again. "What's the use?" he asks wearily. "I am not for this world much longer."

Ashok sits on the bed and takes the old man's hand in his. "Don't talk like that, Chacha," he pleads earnestly. "You will be well soon, once we get the medicines."

"No," the invalid coughs. "Son, I cannot last. There are two things I must tell you before it is too late." His voice weakens, and Ashok has to bend low to hear him. "I know you have always thought you were the son of Pitlu the monkey-man. The truth is he had no son. He found you one day by the riverside, where he had gone to collect twigs for the fire. You were in a little basket, caught up in some brambles at the water's edge. You were a tiny newborn baby, and he took you as a gift from God. Of course everyone in the chawl helped look after the baby, and my wife, your Chachi, God rest her soul, treated you like the son we had never had. You were brought up by all of us, by the entire chawl, though of course you belonged to the monkey-man, who said he needed a little boy to help him. And you seemed so happy with him, and with his monkey, no one was surprised when you took over from him in the end." The old man, exhausted by his effort, stops, coughing. His daughter gives him a sip of water.

"Then who is my real father?" Ashok asks urgently. "How do I find him?"

"I have no idea. There was no name on the blanket you were wrapped in, and the basket has long since gone. But there is one clue."

"Yes?"

"The talisman you wear on your wrist. That was with you the day you were found." Ashok looks at it intensely, his only connection to an unknown world. "When you were little the string went around your wrist several times, but now I see it is as tight as a bracelet. Find out where that came from, and you might learn your origins."

"I always thought it was my father's — Pitlu's," Ashok says. "But whenever I asked him what it meant, he would always say he didn't know, that I had had it since birth and that I should always wear it."

"It is your most precious inheritance, Ashok," the old man gasps.

"Chacha!" Ashok sees the life ebbing out of his mentor, and his voice is almost a cry. "And the second thing you wanted to tell me?"

"Look after Mehnaz," the old man whispers. "She is not of an age to be alone in this world. You are like a brother to her. With her mother and aunt dead, she has no one."

"She will always have me," Ashok vows.

"Good," Chacha says. "Find her — find her a husband just like you." And with this shifting of paternal responsibility, the spark of dialogue that has kept him going so far fades out. His expression slackens, his eyes stare. He has gone to the great rerecording studio in the sky.

"Abba!" wails Mehnaz. "Chacha!" cries Ashok. They fall on the inert form of the extra, who struggles to keep still. Then, in an apocalyptic moment, they look up at each other and fall into a mutually consolatory — and, of course, purely fraternal — embrace.

Ashok — another Ashok, but the audience doesn't know this immediately — walks proudly into a small house in his new uniform. He wears the pale khaki garb and starry epaulettes of an inspector of the Bollywood CID.

"Ashok!" A gray figure rises from a cloth-and-wood easy chair to greet him. Despite the generous application of whitener on his hair, the figure is recognizably Abha's faithful old retainer, Raju. "You have done it! Congratulations!"

"Yes, Father. As of today, you may call me Inspector Ashok."

"This is a proud day for me, son. If only your mother could see you now." Raju wipes a sentimental tear from his eye. "If for all these years I have instilled in you the ambition to become a police officer, it has been only for her." He clasps Ashok in a paternal hug, then stands back, one hand on the young man's shoulder, and looks at him with wet eyes. "Son, the time has at last come when I must tell you something very important. For all these years, I held my tongue, out of fear that the truth could expose you and us to danger at a time when we could do nothing about it. But now, Inspector Ashok, you *can* do something about it."

"Father, I don't understand what you're talking about."

"Sit down, son, and I shall tell you." And he does: in staccato flashback images the story spills out: Thakur, Kalia, talisman, everything. By the end Ashok sits shaken.

"So you are not really my father, Father?"

"No, son. Your father is not a humble lathe operator in a factory who skimped and saved to send you to college and made an officer out of you. Your father is a fine man of good family who was condemned to rot in prison for a murder, a murder for which he was undoubtedly framed by Pranay Thakur's thugs."

"But he might be a free man now! I must find him!"

Raju shakes his head sadly. "In our country, Inspector Ashok, life imprisonment is really for life — unless death comes sooner. If your poor fine father survived the rigors of jail, rigors for which he was completely unsuited, he is probably still in jail now, twenty-two years later. As a police officer, perhaps you can trace him and get justice done."

(The judicial system of India is one about which our filmmakers are blissfully ignorant, which is perhaps why it features so frequently in our cinematic life.)

"Do you know which jail he is in?"

"What does a poor servant know of such things? But you — as a police officer you can probably find out."

"You have been a good father to me, Father — I mean Raju-ji.

Whatever happens, I shall never forget all that you have done for me. But now I must set out to find my real father and avenge the tragic deaths of my mother and brother." Ashok looks at the black string on his wrist. "By this sacred token of my mother's love," he vows, "I swear to avenge her."

"Ashok," cautions the old man, "no hasty actions. Pranay Thakur is a powerful man. An angry youth will prove no match for him. You must use your strengths — your new position, the law — to track him down. That is why I have waited so long to tell you. Do not make me feel I have waited in vain."

Ashok turns to him soberly. "You are right, Father," he says. "I must be patient. I must research the facts, build up a case. And then

> *I shall get him.*
> *He won't escape.*
> *I won't let him*
> *Stay in one shape.*
> *I shall hang and draw and quarter him,*
> *Bury and plough and water him,*
> *Do everything I ought to him —*
> *Then turn him in to the forces of the law.*
>
> *I shall catch him*
> *By surprise.*
> *I shall match him*
> *Size for size.*
> *I shall flog and tar and feather him,*
> *Whip and lash and tether him,*
> *Tie his hands together (hmm!)*
> *And turn him in to the forces of the law.*

Scene: Ashok the monkey-man and Mehnaz the recent orphan scour a bazaar. They go to silversmiths, shopkeepers, jewelers, fakirs, showing the talisman on its string. Each person they approach shakes his head, unable to identify it. One offers to buy it. The monkey perched on Ashok's shoulder turns the offer down on his behalf.

Scene: Ashok the inspector goes from prison to prison, asking in vain about his father. In each frame the prison officials shake their heads too, out of tune with the insistent drumbeat of the sound track. The young policeman walks away, depressed but determined.

During both sequences the sound track swells with a plaintive lament:

> *Seeking —*
> *We must go on seeking.*
> *Must leave no stone unturned,*
> *No candle of hope unburned,*
> *No bit of truth unlearned —*
> *Must go on seeking.*
>
> *Seeking —*
> *We must go on seeking.*
> *Must keep our faith alive,*
> *And never cease to strive,*
> *Whatever we derive —*
> *We must go on seeking.*

Scene: Ashok, Mehnaz, and the monkey Thakur are at a village mela. Amid the colorful bustle of the fairground — painted animals and brightly dressed women, rusty carousels and lusty carousers, turbans and cotton candy in equally startling shades of pink — the trio continue their quest. They are seen receiving yet another negative shake of the head in response to Ashok's extended wrist. Dispirited — indeed, none is more dejected than the monkey, who covers his eyes with his long fingers gloomily — they turn away.

"I'm beginning to think we'll never find out about your amulet, *Bhaiya,*" says a weary Mehnaz, pretty in a yellow *ghagra choli* and pouting most attractively at her costar.

"We will, Mehnaz," Ashok replies. "We must. I cannot rest until I have found out the truth about myself."

Mehnaz looks as if she might be prepared to tell him a few truths herself, but further conversation is thwarted by a commotion in the village square beyond the fairground.

"What's going on here?" asks Ashok.

"It's the Old Woman," says a villager. "Some people are angry with her and want to drive her away."

"What Old Woman?"

"You haven't heard of the Old Woman?" The villager looks at Ashok as a Bombayite might regard someone who thought stars could only be seen in the sky. "She is well known in these parts. She has been wandering around for years. At first she was with a hermit who had helped her in some way. She collected alms for him, fed him, and so on. Then the hermit died and she took to sitting under a banyan tree for days on end, praying. People think she is a holy woman of some sort and they give her food and water. But it never lasts for very long. In village after village she has been driven away because of her madness."

"She is mad, then?"

"You wouldn't think so at first. But every once in a while, when she sees a baby, she starts screaming that it is hers and tries to snatch it away from whoever is carrying it, accusing that person of having stolen her child. As you can imagine, people don't take too kindly to that. So they drive her away, and she wanders off to another banyan tree in another village, until it happens all over again."

"Sad story," says Mehnaz.

"Yes, something terrible must have happened to her in the past," the villager clucks. "It used to be said that she had had some accident and could remember nothing — not even her name or address, who she was, where she came from. So she is just called the Old Woman."

"And a lot of other names, it seems," says Ashok, heeding the voices raised offscreen. "Come, Thakur, let us see what they are doing to this poor Old Woman." The monkey nods agreement, and they set off.

Not a moment too soon. There is a mob gathered near the banyan tree, and the mood is ugly. Voices are raised, and so are fists: one unpleasant extra has a *chappal* in his hand with which he is threatening to beat the old lady if she continues to impugn the parenthood of his baby.

In the center of this throng, her gray hair flowing wild about her, her body clad in shapeless white, her considerable bosom heaving and her face bathed in tears, is — you guessed it, audience! — Abha. Damsel no longer, but evidently in distress.

"Would you raise your filthy footwear against your own mother?" Ashok asks sharply if irrelevantly, shaming the *chappal-*

wielder, and ultimately the crowd, into retreat. (The original screen-play had called for a fight scene here, with Ashok and his monkey bashing up the mob, but this was regretfully deleted by the director in an uncharacteristic burst of sensitivity.) Ashok puts a protective arm around the Old Woman. "Come, Mother," he says, using the term out of respect rather than recognition, but giving the audience their twenty-five paise's worth of irony in the bargain. "Come with us. We shall look after you."

"Who are you, *beta?*" the Old Woman asks as her tormenters melt away, muttering. In the background the tune of "We must go on seeking" plays on, to alert the less attentive members of the audience.

"I am just a humble monkey-man, Mother," admits our hero. "But I cannot bear to see you treated like this. I never had a mother myself, and it galls me to see those who have been able to take their mothers for granted behave in this way. Come with us, Mataji. We have a humble home which is yours as long as you want to stay."

"You are very kind," Abha says gravely. "The blessings of Hanu-man be upon you. And this girl?"

"She is my sister, or rather she is like a sister to me," Ashok explains. "Her father recently passed away and I am looking after her, though a lot of the time I feel she is the one looking after me."

"Bless you both." Then suddenly, as Ashok moves his arm, there is a crash of cymbals on the background track. The camera zooms into a close-up amid the screeching of violins, and Abha's eyes, wide with astonishment, take in the sight of the talisman dangling from her rescuer's wrist.

"Where did you get that?" she screams, lunging for it. "You thief! You stole that! Give it to me."

Ashok catches her raised hand in a firm grip as Mehnaz looks alarmed. "Please, Mother, is this any way to treat someone who has done you no harm? This talisman is mine."

"Liar! How did you get it? Who gave it to you?"

"It has been with me since birth."

(Another smash from the invisible percussionist.) "And who," Abha asks with a catch in her voice, "are your parents?"

Ashok's voice drops. "I don't know, Mother. You see, as a baby I was found in a basket on the river."

"My God!" says Abha and faints, a hand on her heart, as the refrain from "We must go on seeking" deafens the viewers. Before
Ashok can prevent it, Abha has hit her head on the hard ground. The
monkey, wincing, puts shocked hands to his ears as Ashok and
Mehnaz look at each other in mutual bewilderment.

When Abha is revived, the knock on her head has, of course,
affected only her amnesia. She now remembers everything, and at
some cost to the patience of the viewers, remembers it garrulously.
The reunion of mother and son is tearful and heartrending. So is the
background music.

"Raju might still be working somewhere, in some factory in
Bombay, and might know where your brother is," Mehnaz points
out.

"Do you know how many factories there are in Bombay?" Ashok
asks. "That would be impossible. I pray that my brother is alive
and well and that Fate will lead me to him. But first, there are
more urgent things to do. I must find my real father and try to
get him out of jail. And then I must deal with this evil uncle of
mine."

"But how can you get him out of jail?" Abha asks.

"Ma" (the use of the word brings tears to the actress's eyes, not
necessarily for the reasons intended in the script), "in the years that I
have been a humble monkey-man I have made a number of friends
who are on the wrong side of the law. We will find a way."

Abha looks at her newfound son, her eyes brimming with hope
and pride. "Pray that they have not moved him to another jail," she
says.

"Let's go, Ma," says the hero. The monkey hops excitedly about
on Ashok's shoulder as they walk on. The sound track reminds the
audience that they must go on seeking.

"You may visit the prisoner," the jail official tells Inspector Ashok.
The young man, controlling his excitement with difficulty, walks to
the cell. On a rough wooden stool sits Ramkumar, head bowed,
wearing a prison uniform and a thick beard. He is a well-known
character actor, a euphemism for someone who can act but isn't as
good-looking as the (invariably characterless) hero.

"Father," breathes Ashok.

Ramkumar looks up dubiously. "What do you want?" he asks gruffly. "Who are you?"

Ashok grips the bars of the cell. "I am your son," he beams.

"I have no son," Ramkumar replies. "Stop torturing an old man. Go away."

"B-but you have! Your wife, Abha, gave birth to twin sons while you were in jail!" Ashok exclaims. "My revered mother and brother died at the hands of the henchmen of Pranay Thakur, but I survived. Didn't anyone tell you this?" He takes in the expression of growing astonishment and wonder on his father's face and realizes that, of course, no one could have. "I'm sorry, Father." He thrusts out his wrist. "Do you recognize this?"

"I gave it to your mother many years ago." His voice breaking, Ramkumar gets up from his stool and walks warily toward the bars of the cell. "And I thought she had simply decided to abandon a jailbird." He shakes his head, grieving. "How do I know you are telling the truth, that you didn't just pick this talisman up some-where? Why have you come to me only now?"

"Because I have only just found out about you and traced you to this jail," Ashok says. He bends to touch his father's feet through the bars. "If you don't believe me, I'll bring Raju-ji to you tomorrow. You remember Raju?"

"The servant? Yes, of course I do. But" — a blur covers his eyes, and in a single point of light at its center Ramkumar sees his wife, young again, arms outstretched to him as he is dragged away in handcuffs — "it won't be necessary." Ramkumar looks at Ashok still bent, and slowly, as if marveling at the moment, places a hand on his visitor's head. "Bless you," he says, "my son."

"Father!" exclaims Ashok, rising. They embrace, despite the bars between them. (The filmmakers are unaware of prison regulations and they've never heard of the *Jail Manual*, but even if they were and had, they wouldn't let realism come in the way of art. These men from Bombay belong to a purist school of aesthetics.)

"It breaks my heart to discover a son and to know that these bars will always remain between us, while that wretched killer who has reduced me to this goes free."

"Father, I promise you will not have to remain in prison much longer. I will check every rule, explore every legal right you have, to get you out of here. I am a police officer. I can do it."

"You give me hope, my son," says Ramkumar, pride in his voice. "But — do not tell the police I am your father. They will hold it against you, my son, that your father is a convicted criminal. It may even make it more difficult for you to intervene to secure my release. After all these years, I can afford to wait a little longer if need be, but don't take any risks."

"You are right, Father," Ashok agrees. "Very well, I shall keep our relationship a secret. But only until justice has been done and you are a free man again!"

Outside the prison Inspector Ashok walks on air, a starry look in his eyes. He whistles; he does a quick hop, skip, and jump. Startled passersby look at him askance. A lovely girl in a cotton *salwarkameez*, books in her arms, hails him.

"Ashok!" calls Mehnaz. She is wearing outsize sunglasses, apparently to enhance the scholarly look she must sustain for the scene. "What are you doing in this uniform?"

Ashok blinks. "Do I know you?" he asks, though he is clearly not unhappy at being recognized by this exquisite stranger.

"Stop teasing me," she says. "If the police catch you in this, you'll really be in for it."

"But I *am* the police," Ashok protests.

"Very funny," says Mehnaz. "But I must say, it looks good on you, *Bhaiya*. Is it part of the plan?"

"If you say so," agrees Ashok, mystified.

"Anyway, I knew you wouldn't let me walk alone to college," Mehnaz says satisfiedly. "Having forced me to stay out of all your exciting plans and told me I had to finish my studies, I did think the least you could do was accompany me."

"You bet," confirms Ashok, who knows a good thing when he sees it and is, in his elation, game for anything.

"I suppose you think the uniform will frighten all the college *dadas* into behaving themselves," Mehnaz goes on chattily.

"It should, shouldn't it?" Ashok agrees.

"You're talking funnily today, Ashok *Bhaiya*." The girl giggles. They have reached a park that blooms conveniently on their way to the college. "You're really speaking strangely."

"Would you prefer me to sing, instead?" Ashok asks. Mehnaz laughs and runs toward a tree. Ashok bursts into playback:

> *Gulmohars, roses and the iris growing green,*
> *You are more lovely than any flower I've seen;*
> *Take off those glasses and put jasmine in your hair,*
> *And let me watch you just — standing there.*
> *Oooh, standing there.*

(Mehnaz laughs, runs around the tree, then skips lightly over the grass and puts one foot on a park bench. She slips her glasses up her forehead and holds her chin in one hand, surveying Ashok in mock disapproval.)

> *Mountains, oceans, valleys around the tourist scene,*
> *You are a better sight than any place I've been;*
> *Turn off that frowning look and sit upon that chair,*
> *And let me watch you just — sitting there.*
> *Oooh, sitting there.*

(Mehnaz sits on the park bench while Ashok dances around it, singing. He plucks a rose and gives it to her. She inhales its scent, then stretches languorously on the bench, coyly veiling herself and the rose with her thin gauze *dupatta*.)

> *Love-poems, sonnets and the words that I can glean,*
> *You are more to me than any verse could mean;*
> *Slip off that screen of cloth and leave your fragrance bare,*
> *And let me watch you just — lying there.*
> *Oooh, lying there.*

He brings his face amorously close to hers. Mehnaz leaps off the bench and runs to the pathway, laughing. Ashok follows, catches up with her. She is panting: "*Bhaiya*, what has come over you? I've never known you to behave like this."

"But you've never known me," Ashok points out.

"Don't be silly," Mehnaz says. "The joke's gone far enough. Hurry up, or I'll be late for class."

"Wait," says Ashok, catching hold of her hand. She looks at his hand in hers, and the color mounts to her cheeks. "Who am I?"

"You're Ashok, of course," she responds impatiently.

"Fair enough. And how do you know me?"

"You're my *Bhaiya,* aren't you?" She is irritated now and pulls her hand away to walk on. Ashok stands still for a moment, scratching his head in puzzlement. "Am I?" He asks himself. Then he follows her.

"I'll take you to college," he says, "but there's something really peculiar going on."

"I'll say," agrees Mehnaz with spirit. "Are you sure you haven't been drinking or something?"

"I'm beginning," Ashok mutters, "to wonder myself."

"And who are you?" asks the prison officer dubiously.

"I am his wife," replies Abha.

"And I am his son," adds Ashok, monkeyless for the occasion.

The prison officer is not impressed. "He has been in this jail for twenty-two years," he says pointedly, "and there is no record of a wife and son. In fact, it says here" — he picks up a yellowing folder held together with dangling string and leafs through dusty pages — "wife deceased. Next of kin, Pranay Thakur." He looks up at them. "Now you go and get a letter from Pranay Thakur to confirm that you are who you say you are, and I will see what I can do. But I can't promise anything."

They protest, they plead, but the iron wall of prison bureaucracy, at least as interpreted in Bombay, is not moved. "Oh, and one more thing," the official adds. "Even if you get such a letter, please remember that visiting days are Thursdays only. This is not a hotel, that you can come in and see people when you like."

When the devastated pair leaves, the prison official turns to a colleague on an adjoining desk. "Strange, this sudden burst of interest in Ramkumar," he observes. "For twenty-two years not a soul wants to see him, and now suddenly three people this week. Remember the police inspector the other day? I wonder if I shouldn't send word to Pranay Thakur."

Outside, Ashok is grimly determined. "We tried it your way, Ma," he says through gritted teeth, "and you saw how they treated us. If there was any justice my father wouldn't be in prison at all, and now we're not even allowed to see him! Fine, at least we know he's there. Now you leave it to me and my friends. We'll have him out very soon, Ma — and then we'll turn our attention to your adopted brother."

"All right, my son," Abha sighs. "But be careful."

It is dark, but Ashok's face is clearly visible in the moonlight as he stands at the foot of a tree outside the prison walls, a stout length of hemp in his hands. He puts one end of the rope over his monkey's shoulder. "Go, Thakur," he says.

The monkey holds the rope in his thin fingers and leaps onto the tree.

"*Shabash*," says Shahji, one of the two men accompanying Ashok. Both are familiar faces from the first scene at the chawl, people whom Ashok had greeted cheerily as he walked in with his day's pickings.

The monkey scurries along the thin branch that overhangs the prison courtyard. He leaps down and runs to a drainpipe, which he ascends nimbly. Reaching a barred window, the monkey loops his end of the rope around a bar, then proceeds to tie it into a knot. (The audience in the front rows of the movie theater applaud, cheer, and whistle at this: the improbable is far more fun than the credible.)

When the monkey has returned, mission accomplished, to his habitual perch on his master's shoulder, Ashok tugs at the rope to test it. It is firm. Quickly, he ties the other end to the tree trunk. The rope looks taut and strong.

"Let's go, brothers," he breathes.

One by one, the heroes of the chawl clamber up the rope, over the prison wall, and reach the window. Ashok, the first, uses a steel file he has been holding in his teeth to saw rapidly through two of the bars. He jumps in, and the other two follow.

Whispered words are uttered, and the men fan out. The action is swift. A sleepy guard is surprised by Shahji and his friend is knocked out, his bunch of keys taken. Another looks up from his plate to find a knife at his throat and a grinning monkey on his table. Ashok raises a menacing finger to his lips. "One word," he whispers, "let alone a scream, and —" He mimes the act of drawing the knife across the guard's neck. The man chokes. Ashok puts a hand over his mouth and gestures with the knife. "Ramkumar?" he asks. "Don't tell me — just point." The terrified guard, extending a shaking finger, leads Ashok to Ramkumar's cell. The monkey cheerfully helps himself to the abandoned dinner.

"Open it," Ashok commands at the cell door. As the guard fumbles with the purloined keys Shahji gives him, Ramkumar looks up, astonished.

"Ashok!" he exclaims.

"You recognized me?" Ashok asks in disbelief.

"But of course," Ramkumar says. "Though your disguise is pretty good."

"Disguise?" asks Ashok.

"I didn't expect you to do it this way," Ramkumar says.

"It's the only way," Ashok replies as the cell door swings open.

"Thank you," whispers Shahji politely, administering a swift blow with his flashlight to the back of the guard's head. Both guard and hero descend to the floor, Ashok in order to touch his newfound father's feet. (If one were ever in doubt as to the North Indian conservatism of the makers of Hindi films, one need look no further than the number of times the characters touch each other's feet. Some of the producers expect the same of their supplicants, and they don't always stop at the feet, either.)

"Come with us, Father," says Ashok, leading him to the rope at the window. "Do you think you can do this?"

"I have broken rocks for twenty years, my son," Ramkumar replies in a gruff voice. "I can do it."

They clamber out to freedom. Once on the other side of the wall, Ashok unties the rope from the tree trunk, knots the bunch of keys to it, and flings it back in a sweeping parabola through the open window.

"Let them figure that out by themselves," he chuckles, the monkey applauding his efforts. "Come on, Father, let's go. Ma is waiting for you."

"Ma?" Ramkumar's bewilderment is complete. "I thought you told me she was dead."

"When could I have told you that, Father?" Ashok asks in surprise.

They get into a waiting Tempo, with Shahji at the wheel, and drive off into the night. The camera catches a glimpse of Ramkumar.

Hope, fear, confusion, and excitement are reflected simultaneously on the character actor's face.

The sounds of music and the twinkling of lights strung on trees indicate that a party is taking place, but for those in any doubt, outside the entrance there is also a red banner that announces in large, white letters: WOMEN'S COLLEGE. FANCY DRESS PARTY. IN AID OF POLICE-MAN'S BENEVOLENT FUND. (Had anyone suggested to the script-writer that no women's college in its right mind would be associated with such an event, and that even if it were, it would not have called the function a "fancy dress party" or misspelled "policemen's," the objector would have been given a lecture on the creative necessity of artistic license. The misspelling, however, would have been attrib-uted, not to the sign writer at Himalaya Studios, but to a conscious, realistic attention to detail — for which there is always a time and place in the Hindi film.)

Inside the college overdressed extras laugh and whirl with a gaiety rarely seen in any social event at a real women's college in India. Mehnaz is in full evening gown, complete with sash and fake tiara: she makes a convincing beauty queen (her sash proclaims her to be "Miss Alternative Universe 1975"). As she sips a respectably non-alcoholic drink and laughs with a group of girls, a man in a kathakali mask sidles up to her.

"Remember me?" asks Inspector Ashok, lifting his mask briefly to grin at her.

"Ashok!" squeals Mehnaz. "But what are you doing here?"

"This is a policemen's ball, and I'm a policeman," replies the man in the mask.

"Ha-ha, big joke. I thought you were going to prison tonight." In Hindi, one cannot distinguish between "prison" and "the prison" as one might in the language of the banner writer, so Ashok's sur-prise is understandable.

"Me? But what have I done to deserve that?" he asks.

Mehnaz laughs. "Always teasing me, aren't you, Ashok?"

"Am I?" But before Ashok can pursue this line of inquiry much further, a roll of drums indicates the music will be hard to compete against. "Let's dance," he says, and before she can protest he has swept Miss Alternative Universe 1975 onto the floor.

The band establishes the music director's modernity by wielding a number of electric guitars in addition to more traditional, indigenous equipment. The band members also sing the first line of each verse in what they believe to be English:

> *I-I-I-I-I-I luff you,*
> *Don't you know that's really true,*
> *That's why I wanna hold you tight,*
> *Sweetie let's dance tonight.*
>
> *I-I-I-I-I-I luff you,*
> *Don't you feel that I really do,*
> *Can't you see that it feels right,*
> *Sweetie let's dance tonight.*
>
> *I-I-I-I-I-I luff you,*
> *Don't you see it just like new,*
> *It's the moment to see the light,*
> *Sweetie let's dance tonight.*

Ashok and Mehnaz are proficient dancers, although dancing *is* an unusual skill to have acquired in a factory worker's hutment and a *chawl*, respectively; the extras soon gather around them and applaud, just in case the audience itself is not so inclined.

Outside it is dark. Ashok and Mehnaz emerge from under the banner, still masked and gowned.

"How are you going home?" Ashok asks.

"You're taking me, silly," Mehnaz replies. "Except I thought you said you'd come *after* the show and wait for me outside."

"Listen," Ashok begins, "we've got something to sort out here. Look at me properly." He reaches for his mask, but on the way his hands stop at her face, and he cannot resist cupping her chin in his hands.

"Take your hands off my sister," says a voice from the shadows.

Both Ashok and Mehnaz whirl around toward the voice. The face is half hidden in the darkness so Inspector Ashok cannot see it, but Mehnaz recognizes her brother and brings a hand up to her mouth. "Ashok!" she gasps. "But then who is —?"

There is no time to complete the question as her brother, schooled in the rough-and-ready social norms of the *chawl,* which neither permit a stranger to fondle your sister nor encourage you to forgo the advantage of surprise, leaps out of the shadows and administers a swift blow to the inspector's solar plexus. Police training, however, is not to be sneezed at because the cop, while still doubled over in pain, brings his knee up into the advancing assailant's groin. A few more blows are traded, *dishoom, dishoom,* with the man in the kathakali mask getting somewhat the worse of the exchange (for by this point the actor playing him is a double, of course). Then Ashok, whose face has still not been fully visible to his fellow-combatant throughout the encounter, twists the inspector's arm behind him. The kathakali cop groans with pain. Suddenly — just as the *chawl* pugilist, standing behind (and therefore completely outside the view of) his rival, is about to apply the final ounce of pressure that will break his twin's arm — a shaft of moonlight falls on their vein-popping wrists, and Mehnaz sees the two identical talismans glistening in the penumbra.

The background music slams into everyone's deafened consciousness. Mehnaz's look requires no interpretation: at last she understands what has been happening.

"*Bhaiya!*" she screams, running to separate them for now, and to unite them forever. "Stop! Look!"

Ashok heeds these admonitions. He stops. He looks. His eyebrows rise, his jaw drops, and his fingers release their pressure. The inspector takes advantage of this to turn around, fist ready — and then freezes in astonishment as he finally sees the full face of his attacker.

As the two men, immobile, stare at each other, Mehnaz reaches up and slips off the inspector's mask.

"Ashok," she says simply, "meet Ashok."

The brothers stretch a hand to each other, touching the other's talisman and silently comparing it to his own. Then they embrace, and Mehnaz smiles blissfully.

Fortunately, this time the mutual explanations are delivered offscreen.

"Thakur-sahib." Kalia isn't noticeably older now than at the start of the film, but when you have no hair it is difficult to find something to whiten for the desired effect.

"Yes?" Pranay is just as cruel, his eyes just as bloodshot, his mustache just as evil, but paint streaks his temples and more sinister lines have deepened the evil cast of his face.

"Thakur-sahib, we have just heard that Ramkumar has escaped from prison."

"Hmm." Pranay's voice has acquired the richness so necessary in a convincing major villain; even his *hmm*s resonate on the sound track, sending shudders down the spines of the children in the audience. "That is disturbing."

"He is an old man, Thakur," Kalia suggests.

"And a weak one," Pranay laughs. "He was easy meat for us when we wanted him out of the way, wasn't he? I was so shocked when I discovered my father had left everything to Abha and him, rather than me. But when we hung that murder of yours on him, they didn't stay around to claim their inheritance, did they? Heh-heh. No, I don't think we need worry too much about Ramkumar."

"Sir, our contact man at the prison says that a few days before the escape, a woman and a man claiming to be Ramkumar's wife and son came to the prison and asked for him."

"What? How can it be? You told me, Kalia, that you saw them drown with your own eyes."

"I did, Thakur-sahib. But the current carried them away and it is possible, though," he adds hastily, "not very likely, of course, that your sister and one of the babies survived."

"Then why have they waited all these years to reappear? No, I don't believe it." Pranay waves a dismissive whip. "But to be safe, Kalia, we must be a little more careful. At least until the police re-arrest Ramkumar."

"I'm afraid that will not happen, Thakur." Kalia looks down at the floor. "You see, with time off for good behavior, Ramkumar was to have been released two years ago. I had been paying our friend at the prison to — er — misplace the file. I am afraid this omission has now been discovered. No one guesses our involvement, of course, but I believe some inspector established that Ramkumar should not have been in prison at all. Everyone is so embarrassed they have quietly decided to forget the matter of the jailbreak."

"Are you sure no one suspects us?"

"Positive, Thakur."

But neither of them notices, high up on the rafters of the chandeliered hall, that a monkey has been eavesdropping on their conversation. A monkey holding, in its long, firm fingers, a small and powerful miniature tape recorder.

It is evening. Dressed in the brocaded raiments of debauchery, Pranay sprawls comfortably on a dhurrie, leaning against stuffed cotton bolsters and pulling on a hookah. By his side, on a brass tray and beside an elegantly curved brass jug, stands a bottle of Vat 69, the Hindi film villain's favorite tipple. Pranay establishes his villainy by periodically removing the pipe of the hookah from his mouth and inserting the top of the whiskey bottle in its place. He gulps it down as if it were colored water, which of course is precisely what it is.

"Let the nautch commence." Kalia claps his hands, and with a tinkle of anklets the dancer enters the hall, raising a half-cupped palm to her forehead in a courteous *adaab*. Pranay nods appreciatively, as does the bulk of the audience in the theater. It is, of course, Mehnaz, accompanied by one of the Ashoks (complete with false handlebar mustache) and Ramkumar (his beard topped off with the additional disguise of a turban). The girl is covered from neck to ankle in finery, from glittering jewelry to billowing skirt atop calf-hugging silk pantaloons, yet each step she takes radiates more sex appeal than the shimmer of seven veils. The allure of what is left visible is heightened by traditional artifice. Her bare feet are painted red along the sides of the soles and her ankles are caressed by silver *payals*. Her hennaed hands and kohl-lined eyes transmit messages more eloquent than the lyrics of the conventional, euphemism-laden song to which she now performs:

> *Don't tell me to leave, my master,*
> *With you my heart beats faster,*
> *My palms perspire*
> *With nameless desire,*
> *Don't tell me to leave, my master.*
>
> *I am drawn to you like a moth to a candle,*
> *Your heat is more than I can handle,*
> *I am lost, and without shame,*
> *I singe myself in your flame*
> *And fall at your feet like a sandal.*

Don't tell me to leave, my master,
This soul isn't made of plaster,
It throbs with the need
To be strung like a bead —
Don't tell me to leave, my master.

(Unnoticed by the besotted Pranay and the ill-begotten Kalia, Ramkumar has slipped discreetly away on an errand of his own. The cinema audience sees this, but the dance goes on.)

Don't tell me to leave, my master,
If you do it'll be a disaster,
Like a house with no roof,
I'd be warp without woof,
Don't tell me to leave, my master.

Mehnaz dances to these words as so many Indian actresses have done, with a demure grace completely unrelated to the content of the lyrics. At the song's end Pranay, bleary-eyed from many swigs out of his bottle, beckons the girl with a crook of his finger.

"Come here, my dear," he slurs poetically.

Mehnaz looks at Ashok, who nods. She walks to the Thakur, kneels suggestively before him — and in a flash pulls out a gleaming dagger from inside the folds of her skirt and holds it to his throat.

"Don't anybody move," says Ashok, pulling a knife on Kalia. He grins at the goggling Pranay. "Hello, uncle," he says.

Upstairs, Ramkumar rummages through papers in a drawer. At last he finds what he is looking for and holds it up to the light with a gleam of triumph in his eyes. "I've got it," he breathes. "The will!"

He runs into the hall, brandishing the document. "The game is up, Pranay," he declaims, dramatically sweeping off his turban. "You thought you had got rid of me forever. Now I have the proof that this zamindari really belongs to Abha and me."

"Not so fast, Ramkumar," Pranay has regained his evil composure. "Your entitlement only derives from your marriage to my sister. With Abha dead, I am the legal heir. Let me see you fight that in a court of law."

"There will be no need for a court of law," says a quiet voice. Abha has entered the hall! Pranay's consternation is real. "But — I thought —" He staggers to his feet. "Kalia, you told me —" He takes two steps forward, unimpeded. It is a clever maneuver. Before Mehnaz catches on to what is happening, Pranay wheels around, grabs her wrist, and takes possession of the dagger. He now holds it to Mehnaz's throat.

"Drop your knife, nephew," he snarls.

Ashok does as he is told. Kalia, relaxing, bends to pick it up. Suddenly there is a blur of motion as a brown, furry object jumps in through a high window and alights on the chandelier. It is Thakur, the monkey, his tail aloft like a soldier's proud standard. As Pranay cries out in alarm, the monkey loops his tail around the chain of the chandelier and swings from it, rocking the fixture dangerously to and fro.

"Watch out!" cries Ramkumar. He, Ashok, and Abha step back. The monkey swings defiantly one last time and then releases his tail. As he leaps through the air, straight for Pranay, the chandelier comes crashing down on the bald head of the bending Kalia.

The monkey knocks the dagger out of Pranay's hand with an emphatic swipe. Mehnaz runs to the others. Pranay, cursing, lunges at the monkey, who leaps out of harm's way.

"It's all over, Pranay," says Ramkumar. "My sons have all the proof they need of your evil doings. You're going to jail for a long, long time."

"Not without a fight," says Pranay, who knows what the audience wants. He pulls a ceremonial sword off the wall and charges toward them.

Ashok parries his first thrust with a cushion, then sidesteps to the wall and pulls down a sword also. As the others watch helplessly, the two clash and thrust and parry, knocking over furniture and lamps, slashing bolsters and paintings, and considerably reducing the value of Abha's inheritance (while enhancing the producer's tax write-offs).

At last, with neither having the upper hand, Ashok leaps toward a door. "Come and get me, Pranay," he mocks. Pranay steps forward, an evil grin of pursuit on his face, when a voice from the opposite door stops him.

"I'm here, Thakur," says Inspector Ashok, standing at one door. Pranay looks at him aghast, then back to the other Ashok, by the other door.

"No, I'm here, Thakur," says Ashok the monkey-man.

As Pranay remains motionless, disoriented by the twin apparitions, the brothers leap simultaneously at him. This time the fight is an unequal one. Pranay is overpowered, and Ashok the monkey-man stands poised to strike him with the dagger when Ramkumar speaks.

"No, son," he says. "We will not treat him the way he treated us. He must face the full justice of the law, and pay for his crimes in prison."

Ashok looks regretfully at his father. Then, obediently, he lowers his dagger. Inspector Ashok produces handcuffs instead, which are quickly applied to Pranay's wrists.

"In the name of the police," Ashok says solemnly in a procedure unknown to the authorities, "I place you under arrest, Pranay Thakur."

Ramkumar and Abha smile at each other in parental pride. The monkey applauds.

"There is one thing that remains to be done," Ashok the monkey-man says.

"Oh, and what is that?" asks Mehnaz.

"Before Chacha, your father, died, he asked me to do something very important," Ashok recalls.

Mehnaz's pretty brow puckers. "And what was that, *Bhaiya?*" she asks.

Ashok takes her hand. "To marry you," he says mischievously, "to someone just like myself."

He pulls her by the hand to Inspector Ashok, who looks as if, under all that makeup, he just might be blushing. And he joins both their hands together. Laughing, the three embrace. Ramkumar and Abha exchange yet another look of parental pride. And the monkey, not to be outdone, leaps onto the trio and tries to embrace them all in his long thin arms.

The sound track fills with a fast, joyful rendition of "We must go on seeking" as the screen announces THE END.

[The Usual Note: this time we have omitted only two songs in the condensation, but a couple of fight sequences toward the end, three separate scenes of Pranay tyrannizing his tenants on horseback, one rape, a set of flashbacks about the murder for which Ramkumar was framed, and a pair of subplots involving Raju the faithful retainer and Shahji the chawl friend have also been excised in the interests of brevity — which, as we all know, is the soul of It.]

Monologue: Night

KULBHUSHAN BANJARA

Yes, it's true I always disapproved of you. Can you blame me? You were serious about nothing, Ashok, even as a boy. You had a gift for acting as a child, though we really thought of it as pretending — you were a very good pretender. But while you could be anyone you wanted with a few simple props, you never wanted to be what *I* wanted you to be. Oh, I know that sounds like the typical complaint of every father with ambitions for his son, but was I wrong to harbor such ambitions? You were worthy of them: you had the looks, the charm, the style, the glib tongue. And I could have opened doors for you, brought you into the party the right way, got you to move up from the grass roots where only I could have planted you. But you didn't want it. Your brother, Ashwin, with half the natural talent for politics that you had, followed me because I told him I needed a political heir — but not you. First, you preferred that stupid job selling detergent powder to middle-class housewives, and then you went off to Bombay to become, of all things, a film actor. Of course I disapproved.

But even at the height of my disapproval, I never ceased to be your father, Ashok. I know you always accused me of never having lifted a finger to help you. I did not deny the charge. Why should I? You chose this disreputable profession, knowing full well what my views on the matter were. Why should you have expected any help? "My son neither gets any help," I declared to anyone who asked, "nor does he expect any." And I said those last words with pride, though God knows you had not given me much by then to be proud of.

But you didn't know, Ashok, that a father never switches off his fatherhood, whatever his son may do. In those early days in Bombay, when you were still shamefacedly "borrowing" money from your mother to make ends meet — money, incidentally, that you have not remembered to repay her, though she would never mention it — I received the visit of an oily creature named Jagannath Choubey. He did not come to my office at Kapadia Bhawan, where I was then Minister of State for Minor Textiles, but to the house, during the hours I kept for visitors who are not personal friends. In fact, the only reason I gave him an appointment at all was because he said he was calling on me at your suggestion. You never wrote or telephoned much in those days, so I had no way of disproving this, and any contact with you, however indirect, was welcome. So I told him to come.

This Choubey sat corpulently opposite me and presented himself as your great benefactor. "Your poor boy," he said, "has been badly treated"; and he went on to list a long series of disappointments you had had, parts you had sought and been turned down for, petty indignities you had been made to suffer at the hands of producers until he, Choubey, had come by like a porcine knight in shining armor and rescued you by offering you a part in his film. You can imagine, Ashok, the rage I felt building up inside me as this unctuous fellow tried to slip me into his debt for having done you a favor he implied you did not deserve, a favor I would have much preferred him not to do in any case. But I controlled my anger and said nothing. I was waiting for the object of the exercise to make itself known.

Soon enough, Choubey came to the point. It so happened, he said, that he had a few small-scale textile mills, nothing too grand, you understand, just small operations, which unfortunately had been granted licenses up to only half of their real capacity. It would be so much better for him if he could be licensed to expand his production, well, indeed to double it. This required very little effort, just a signature, mine in fact, on a file that had been pending in a subordinate's office for some time. He was sure that once he had explained his position to me I would see my way clear to appending that little, but very useful, signature on that minor little file whose expeditious clearance nobody would particularly notice.

He made it all sound so very simple, Ashok. "And this is why my son sent you to see me?" I asked. I wasn't sure, you see, and I had to know.

"Well, not exactly," he said shiftily, then — "Yes." And I knew immediately that you had done nothing of the kind, that indeed you probably did not even know that Choubey was seeing me. And that intensified and focused my anger, till it became a pure white glow of heat inside me, directed at the overfed, oil-oozing opportunist across the table.

I leaned back in my chair. "And if I were to find myself unable to approve that proposal on the file?" I asked amiably.

He was prepared for this line of questioning. "Then I am very much afraid the financial realities of my business would not be, how you say, permitting me to continue producing my current film," he said. "Most unfortunate this would be. Especially, I am so sad to say, for your elder son's future."

"You presumably have a lot of money tied up in that film already, Mr. Choubey," I observed mildly.

"Tax write-off," he responded smugly. "I have been looking for a few good losses to show."

"Then you do just that, Mr. Choubey," I advised him. "I have no desire to see you, or anyone else, advance my son's prospects in this disgusting film world of yours. If all the inducement you need to put an end to this nonsense is my refusal to sign a file I am not at all sure I should sign anyway, I am happy to give you such an inducement. Good-bye."

The fat little man was a picture of dismay and consternation. He sat squirming miserably in his chair, making little inarticulate noises of supplication, until I cut him short. "And I'd be careful about that tax return you submit when you cancel your film," I added. "I intend to talk to my good friend the Minister of State for Revenue about the circumstances of your proposed write-off. I believe his department would like to look at that return very carefully indeed, as well as your returns for the last few years while they're about it."

"Sir," he whined despairingly, "there seems to have been some misunderstanding. I am not at all threatening to be canceling this film or to be writing it off against taxes, no, no. There is no need at all for your good self to be mentioning anything about it to the Revenue Department."

I agreed that if the film continued to be made and was suitably released, there would be no grounds for suspecting it to be a fraudulent venture to demonstrate losses for tax purposes.

"Oh, yes, sir, I will personally guarantee that this film is being finished most satisfactorily, sir, and given widest possible release," he assured me.

"In that case, *after* that happens and the connections drawn in this unfortunate conversation have ceased to exist," I said, "you may return to discuss the matter of your textile mills. I shall then, but only then, see what I can do."

The little man scurried away in gratitude, his short fat legs practically tripping on his dhoti as he fled. I suspect he had the picture completed in record time thereafter. It was your first film, Ashok, and it did well. I never sought any credit for its successful completion. And when Choubey came back to me later, I did give him something of what he wanted. Not all of it, but some expansion was authorized. He was extremely grateful.

Your mother was, of course, much prouder of your cinematic accomplishments than I could be, and she would drag me off to see your films whenever they came to Delhi. Frankly, they didn't mean much to me. I was embarrassed to see my own son doing some of the ridiculous things you were paid to do, but what astonished me more was that no one else thought any the less of you for it. Indeed, that the adulation you received for doing these absurd things was far greater than, say, I got for an impressive speech in Parliament. I am not sure my disapproval diminished immediately or at all, but it was accompanied by a grudging acknowledgment that perhaps what you were doing counted for something after all. But if you had to acquire fame as a public entertainer, I would still probably have preferred you to have been a classical sitarist or even a test-match cricketer as my colleague Bhagwat's son became, not a fellow who earned his status by wearing drainpipe trousers and shaking his hips before the camera.

And of course you were in another world from us, or perhaps

really two different worlds. What worried me the most was not just the world you *inhabited,* though your poor mother was constantly terrified you were going to come home married to some twice-divorced cabaret artiste, but the world you *portrayed* in your work. I couldn't help feeling that whereas I and your younger brother were functioning in the real India, going out to our constituency, dealing with the real issues of politics, handling the wheelers and dealers who keep the political machinery working, you, my heir and fondest hope, were lost in a never-never land that bore no relation to any accurate perception of the India in which we live.

I'll try and explain myself to you, Ashok, to describe the gulf I felt between our worlds. My India is periodically torn apart in out-bursts of communal and sectarian violence; but communal awareness only enters your films if the producer wants to obtain an entertain-ment-tax waiver for "promoting national integration." Every hero, and for that matter every villain, in your films is casteless and un-placeable, an "Ashok" or a "Ramkumar" or a "Godambo," whereas in my India you will never get anywhere with a man without know-ing who he is, where he comes from, what his caste affiliations are. (In my constituency a man's surname alone can frequently tell you which way he will vote, but in your films hardly anyone of conse-quence in the script has a surname.) In my India poverty means dis-tended bellies and eyes without hope, whereas in your films the poor change costumes for each verse of their songs and always have enough strength to beat up the villains. In your films evil is easily personalized — a wicked zamindar, a cruel smuggler — but in my India I see that evil pervades an entire social and economic system that your films do nothing to challenge, a system that indeed places the likes of your own producers among the grubby cluster at its pyramid.

So smugglers are villains? Fine. Why do they smuggle? Because people, Indians, want goods from abroad that our laws don't allow into India. Why don't our laws allow these goods? Leaving the intri-cacies of foreign exchange balances aside, it is primarily to protect Indian industrialists who make inferior versions of the same goods, often at higher prices, and want to unload them on the hapless Indian consumer without the fear of foreign competition. These worthy na-tionalists safeguard the indefinite continuance of their highly profitable inefficiency by pouring some of their easily gotten gains into the coffers of the leading political parties, which parties, of course, then reaffirm the policy of protection. Can you make a virtue out of that? Yet some of the most stirring patriotic speeches in your films are made against smugglers, who after all are merely meeting a need, helping the common man to beat the vested interests.

But the ironies don't stop there, since in our country even challenging a vested interest becomes a vested interest. So smugglers are antinational? Very well, but Bombay's most successful smuggler is avidly sought after for campaign contributions by every party, including mine, and his endorsement is highly valued for the bloc of votes it delivers from his community. So basically the same class of people pass the protectionist laws, get support from both the beneficiaries and the violators of these laws at election time, buy goods from the smugglers, and denounce them in their films. You sort out the various conflicts of interest there if you want to, but don't tell me it's a simple case of good versus evil.

I told my Prime Minister once that we would solve half the crime in this country by not passing laws that everyone felt it necessary to break. She looked down her patrician nose at me in that way she has, her eyebrows almost meeting in a disapproving exclamation mark just below her streak of white hair. I later learned that she had been thinking of putting me in the Home Ministry, but she concluded my attitude was not the right one for someone who would have to supervise the police.

In politics we are always looking behind and between the lines, tracing hidden agendas, seeing into the motivations for any position that is taken, understanding that what is said is not necessarily what is meant and that what is meant is not necessarily intended to mean the same thing for all time. In your Hindi films there is nothing beyond the surface; everything is meant to be exactly what it is shown to be. There are no hidden meanings, no inner feelings, no second layer to life. All is big, clear, simple, and exaggerated. Life is black and white, in technicolor.

And yet I suppose our worlds are not that far apart after all. You function amid fantasies, playing your assigned role in a make-believe India that has never existed and can never exist. As a politician I too play a role in a world of make-believe, a world in which I pretend that the ideas and principles and values that brought me into politics can still make a difference. Perhaps I too am performing, Ashok, in an India that has never really existed and can never exist.

I joined politics in the days of the nationalist struggle, in the Quit India movement. You know that, I suppose, yet how strange it is that I should be sitting here today and telling you these things that you have never asked me to tell you or never shown much curiosity about. I was a good student, and my teachers had high hopes for me, but like so many others in those heady, futile days of 1942, I felt I had to heed the Mahatma's call to take to the streets to clamor for the British to leave. It was all quite pointless, of course, because the British weren't going to "quit," especially in the middle of a war, just because a few lakhs of us shouted in the streets that they must. So we ended up getting a few bones broken by police lathis and spending our classroom hours in jails. It destroyed a few people, though of course imprisonment during 1942 was a most useful credential for political advancement after Independence. But it changed very little politically. It is interesting how, in so many countries, national myths are built around events of little historical significance — the Boston Tea Party, the evacuation of Dunkirk, the Quit India movement — while the events that really changed the course of a nation's destiny never seem to linger as long in the popular imagination.

Anyway, I was luckier than most, because I spent a few days in jail and then my father used his connections with the British — who had given him the grand title of Rao Bahadur just the previous year for his contributions as a businessman to the war effort — to get me out and send me up to Cambridge. So nationalism got me a British degree instead of the Indian one I had been enrolled for and kept me out of trouble — and the war. I finished my studies in time to come back and join the Congress party in my home district before Independence. There aren't too many of us from that generation with qualifications like that — Shankar Dayal Sharma, some of the Bengal Communists, a mere handful in all, who were always in the right places at the right times and can claim that our academic and nationalist credentials are both impeccable. The Communist fellows, of course, went and blotted their copybook by opposing the Quit India movement, not on the sensible grounds that it wouldn't work, but because they didn't want to weaken the British war effort that was so important to Stalin's survival. They betrayed nationalism in India to protect communism in the Soviet Union, and though they continue to bray that history vindicated their choice, the Indian electorate never forgave them for it.

So I embarked on the only career I've really had, political office, and for the first twenty years I almost didn't have to think about getting elected because we were the party that had won the country its freedom, and in an overwhelming majority of constituencies that was all the voters needed to know. I rose steadily, if unspectacularly, up the political ladder, holding state office, then national portfolios as a deputy minister and a Minister of State. I suppose if I had been just a little more willing to keep some of my more unconventional opinions to myself, if I had shown just a little more patience with the arrant nonsense spouted by our in-house socialist ideologues, I might be a cabinet minister today, or at least have spent some of my Minister of State days in a more important ministry like Home. Instead I have gone from party hack to party elder statesman without the usual intervening phase of senior government responsibility.

But I'm digressing again about myself, like a typical politician, and that won't do at all, will it? The doctor had told us to speak to you about things that would directly interest you, and I can't pretend that my political career has ever been of much interest to you, eh, Ashok? See, your expression hasn't changed at all. When Pranay came out of your room he swore he had seen you react a couple of times, and that's what gave us all hope to go on with this strange hospital experiment. But then I suppose your filmi friends have so much more to tell you about what you want to know.

Even so, I want to finish the point I was trying to make about your world and mine. Which is that we are both involved in pretense. Politicians make speeches in which they pretend that their actions and positions are motivated by policy, principle, ideology, the interests of their constituents, their vision of India, whatever; and they pretend that they expect people to support them, vote for them, give them money, on that basis. But of course issues and values determine little of their actual actions and less of the support they really get: they win on caste calculations, they get money for suborning laws they have enthusiastically passed, they switch parties and abandon platforms at the dangling of a lucrative post or a ministerial berth. And yet why should anyone be surprised? Politics is the art of the expedient: no politician can afford to look beyond the next election and the means that will help him win it. Politics is an end in itself, just like the Hindi film. You cannot judge either by external standards.

And then politics has changed so much since I began my career, just as your motion pictures have. When I used to enjoy seeing Hindi films, the heroes were like Dilip Kumar, intense, sincere, full of dignity, nobility, a willingness to suffer and make sacrifices. Just like the heroes of our national movement, the men inspired by the Mahatma. Look at the men in power today — hustlers, smugglers, fixers, men who can rent a crowd, accept a bribe, threaten or co-opt a rival, do a deal; men who would say that they have risen by dint of their energy, their drive, their refusal to be cowed by the rules. With people like this at the top of our politics, is it any surprise that the heroes of our films are men of the same stamp? And seeing the connection, can I be surprised that this is the kind of hero you've always portrayed?

I'm sorry, Ashok, I'm lecturing you. You never liked that, did you? I often wondered how I had lost you, where my hold on your allegiance, your admiration, had slipped. I was always aware of the risk that with my busy political life I might neglect my children, so I went out of my way to make sure I spent enough time with you — well, "enough" is a subjective word, but certainly a lot more time than I could easily spare. And yet when we were together I constantly felt you would rather be somewhere else, even that my contact with you distanced you from me rather than drew us closer. I asked your mother about that once, and she replied, "You're always lecturing him, KB. How do you expect the boy to enjoy being with you if all the time you're lecturing him?" I had no answer, because what she called lecturing I saw as the essential transmission of paternal wisdom from father to son, and my advice and guidance was always given with love, Ashok. Your brother listened dutifully: you switched off your mind and withdrew yourself from me even before you had left the room.

Once when I took my disappointment and hurt to your mother, she said in that quiet voice of hers, "Why are your surprised, KB? Love, like water, always flows downward." Of course: we can never expect our children to love us as much as we love them. We can't help loving you, the products of ourselves; we have known you when you were tiny and weak and vulnerable and have loved you when there was no real you to love. But your love, every child's love for his parents, is born out of need and dependence. That need decreases with every passing year, while ours, the parents', only grows. It's an uneven emotional balance, Ashok, and always it's the children who enjoy the position of strength in the equation of needs. The pity of it is that you don't see that; you think yourself the weaker and react to my imagined strength, whereas if you only saw how great is my need for your love, you might find loving me so much easier. Ashok, I don't want to believe it's too late for that now.

No, I'm not here to upset you. Though the doctor did say that it could do no harm: "We think he can hear, we believe he can even understand what is being said to him, but he is either unable or unwilling" — can you imagine that, Ashok, *unwilling?* — "to respond. But it is important to keep talking to him, to help him recall things, to provoke and stimulate him, yes, even to make him angry. The important thing is to get a reaction." But I don't seem to have succeeded there, have I, Ashok? You're not reacting to me at all. As usual. I have never been able, all these years, to get you to react to me.

Though sometimes you say or do something that prompts your mother to smile at me and say, "See, he's your son after all, KB." I won't hide what the first of those was, at least after you became an adult. You made us very happy, Ashok, when you decided to marry Maya. Your mother and I could scarcely believe that, after all those years of squiring completely unsuitable girls at college and in Delhi and (we imagine) in your early years in the Bombay film world, you actually brought home the kind of girl we would have been happy to arrange your marriage with. "We can't have done everything wrong," I said to your mother, "if these are the qualities he voluntarily looks for in a wife." And everything since then has, of course, only vindicated our enthusiastic endorsement of your choice. The girl has been a saint, Ashok. To put up with all the things you made her put up with, without complaint, at least without *public* complaint, and to continue being a good wife and mother to your children. Really, you should give thanks to your Maker every day for the good luck He brought your way in the form of that remarkable woman, your wife.

It is strange, isn't it, how so many of the events of your life seemed to parallel your films, and vice versa. Life imitating art, perhaps — if Hindi films can be called art. The most astonishing thing was your doing that film in which you played a pair of twin brothers, precisely when Maya was delivering your own triplets! Your mother and I never stopped marveling about that. And yet it was at that very time, was it not, that you took up with that Mehnaz Elahi of yours. She was with you in that very film — cast opposite you, you later admitted, at your own request. How could you do that, Ashok? When your wife was undergoing a difficult pregnancy and bringing your heirs into the world? Shame on you. Yes, Ashok: shame on you.

We never said a word throughout the whole sordid business, your mother and I. Not one word, in public or in private. Why should we express what we felt when we were the only ones, it seemed, feeling any of it? It appalled me that your whole filmi press took it all for granted: there were knowing references to your affair with this girl, but nothing more. Your liaisons, your activities, were reported without even a hint of raised eyebrows, let alone condemnation, though you had a wife and three children sitting at home, a wife who had given up a lot to be your wife. "Every actor in Bombay has extra-marital affairs, Ma," you had the gall to tell your mother. "It's sort of expected of us. It would be unnatural if I didn't." And what about the values we brought you up with? Was it not unnatural to abandon them?

I shouldn't get angry. It's not *my* emotions the doctor wants to stir up. But it was a shame, really. After that, Ashok, you couldn't very well claim not to understand why I still disapproved of you.

TAKE THREE

Interior: Night

I can't believe I'm doing this.

Me, Ashok Banjara, undisputed Number One at the national box office, the man for whom the filmi press has just invented the term *megastar,* the hero who earns in a day what the president of India makes in a year, not to mention lord and occasional master of the pulchritudinous Mehnaz Elahi, chucking my little triplets under their shapeless one-year-old chins, lip-synching the juvenile inanities that their fond mother addresses them from the other side of the cot. But it *is* me, it's my mouth that's puckering in an inaudible kitchy-koo, it's my finger that Leela, or is it Sheela, or even blue-faced Neela, stretches out to grab in her chortling little grip. Me, Ashok Banjara, proud father, a role that sits uneasily on my expensively padded shoulders. But I am happy to play it, at least for a few takes. I stroke each of my daughters' chubby cheeks in farewell, and they gurgle in response; the Banjara magic appeals to females of every generation. My eyes meet Maya's over the cot, and we exchange a complicitous smile.

"Do you have to go, Ashok?" she asks, as the ayah begins to change the diapers and we move away from the babies.

"You know I do," I reply reasonably. After all, it is my profession.

"You spend so little time with the girls," she says.

What she really means, of course, is that I spend so little time with her. "They've got *you,* my love," I point out. "That's the whole idea, isn't it? One of us must be with them as much as possible. I've got to go out and earn the *daal* and *chawal.*"

"But you don't need to work so hard anymore, Ashok," she says. "We can afford all the *daal* and *chawal* we can possibly want, and more. You told me yourself you didn't know what to do with all the black money that's been pouring in."

What she really means is, you don't have to do so many films with Mehnaz Elahi. She's heard the rumors, like everyone else. But she never asks about her. Never even mentions Mehnaz's name. Proud woman, my wife. I like that about her: her pride.

"Sweetheart, it's a treadmill," I explain, a slight note of impatience entering my voice. "I can't get off it. Not without serious injury. There's a special responsibility to being at the top, you know. I've got to maintain my position. And the only way I can do that is by making more and bigger hits. The best scripts keep being offered to me because I'm Number One. I do them, so I stay Number One. The moment I say no to a sure-fire property, somebody else will snap it up and producers will begin to believe that Ashok Banjara is duplicable. Then no one will want to pay for the original article anymore."

"So what?" she asks. "You've achieved everything there is to achieve in the industry. Why should you have to keep on struggling?"

"I'm not struggling, Maya," I snap. "I'm working. Now you've got to be reasonable. Please." I walk to the door.

"Ashok." There is a catch in her voice. I remember, almost in wonder, how the slightest hint of tears in Maya's tone would melt my heart. Not it is all I can do to control my irritation. "Ashok, don't go today. Please. For my sake."

"Maya, sometimes I don't understand you at all." I do not attempt to dampen the asperity in my response. "People are waiting for me. There is a whole studio gearing up for a shoot. How can I not go?"

"You won't be the first actor who's failed to turn up for a shooting," she says. "You could be ill. I could be ill."

"But you're not," I reply. "And I'm not. Maya, look, if there were a good enough reason, of course I could tell the studio I can't make it. But just like that?"

"So my asking you isn't a good enough reason," she says, averting her face.

I can't take any more of this. "Look, I've got to go," I growl. I shut the door harder than I intended. But I don't have the time to go back and apologize.

What has come over Maya these days? Some postnatal emotional instability, I suppose. It's not as if the triplets are driving her around the bend; with an ayah and two servants, she doesn't have to do much more than occasionally hold the bottle. Maybe it's too easy, maybe she needs a more demanding style of motherhood. She seems happy enough sometimes, but then suddenly she goes all teary and irrational with me, like today. I'm glad her mother is coming next week. That'll take the pressure off me. It would have been even better if she'd gone to her mother for the birth, of course, but then Bhopal's facilities can't match Breach Candy's. So I suggested Maya's mother come here instead for the delivery, but Maya had some sort of silly determination to start parenthood alone, with just me around. She said it would bring us closer together. She even wanted me to be in the delivery room, for Christ's sake. The hospital smartly put a stop to that idea, but it was a reflection of the way in which Maya seems to be grabbing for me all the time these days. Through the triplets she's reminding me all the time that I'm not just Ashok Banjara, megastar; I'm also part — hell, I'm the *head* — of a unit of five. Paternal responsibility's the role, and I guess I know the script.

It's not that I mind all that much. I keep telling Maya I'm happy to see myself that way: Ashok Banjara, husband and father. What the hell, I've certainly not shied away from that image in the media. Cyrus Sponerwalla played the births for all they were worth. *Filmfare* had a double-page spread of Maya and me holding the triplets up to our beaming faces. *Star and Style* did a whole feature entitled "NEW! Ashok Banjara's Favorite Costars." Even Radha Sabnis, whose tone is getting slightly bitchy again since I've failed to make a habit of pouring her champagne and submitting to rape, mentioned it in her Cheetah column: "Darlings, Ashok Banjara may not be able to teach Dustin Hoffman much as an actor, but he has certainly turned out to be a pretty good producer, eh? Triplets, and all girls at that! Well, the Hungry Young Man would never be satisfied with just one woman in his life, would he? Grrrowl . . ."

But now the excitement is fading, and Maya's brief return to the pages of the film magazines seems to be over. I'm getting on with my life, but she doesn't seem to know what she wants. Apart from me, that is. All to herself, all the time. Well, she can't have that. I can't afford to give it to her.

At the studio they want me to do another song picturization, a duet with Mehnaz. Mehnaz is a big name now; it hasn't hurt that she's unusually willing, for a star, to wear what the film industry euphemistically calls "modern dress," garments so skimpy they make obvious what "traditional" dress used to leave to the imagination. "Modern" is the adjective most commonly applied to Mehnaz, but "willing" is the one I prefer. She's always willing: on the set, with the dance director, and (why be coy about it?) in bed. Everyone looks forward to working with her. Especially me.

Old Mohanlal is our director today and he's as anxious as ever, his creased brow revealing nerves as frayed as his cuffs. It looks as if seven has become his standard place on the Mohanlal Scale of High Anxiety. But things have changed. The dance director is a more adventurous soul than was old Gopi Master. He's a Goan called Lawrence who actually has new ideas, in tune with the new music that is sweeping our sound tracks. The traditional techniques of the Gopi Masters have passed away along with the illustrious, semiclassical composer duos who dominated the film world for decades, chubby men with oily hair who thought the violin the last word in modernity. The principles of classical Indian dance don't apply anymore to the snazzy rhythms our popular music directors are now unashamedly plagiarizing from the West. Both the beat and the spirit of the films call for a fresh choreographical approach, and Lawrence is the one who provides the fancy footwork for it. Mohanlal just watches, his face lined in worry and incomprehension.

Lawrence must be fifty if he's a day, a wizened and wiry little man with more energy than Radha Sabnis after champagne. He wears a sleeveless T-shirt, tight corduroy trousers, and smooth-soled dancing shoes specially made for his tiny feet by a Chinese cobbler in Calcutta. Lawrence doesn't just direct, he dances all the routines himself, my bits and Mehnaz's, explaining every step and repeating every action till we've got it right and his T-shirt is soaked in sweat. Through it all Mohanlal pulls threads off his white cotton shirt and gray hairs off his now more sparsely covered head. A feature of Lawrence's dancing style for me is the use of martial gestures: feet kicked high and strong, hands slashing through the air karate-style, assertive thumps of leather boots. Thanks to Lawrence I can dance and still retain my macho image; nor is my lack of fluid *bharata natyam* grace any longer a handicap. But Lawrence also comes up with the hip wiggles and pelvic gyrations that have pushed Mehnaz Elahi so rapidly to stardom. I stand and watch this quinquagenarian gnome, all lean dark skin and sinew, stretch and swivel and grind his nonexistent curves for Mehnaz to imitate, and I resist the urge to laugh. No one else, not even Mohanlal, seems to find anything incongruous in the movements of this fisherman's son, whose style nets him more dance direction assignments than he can have had chicken dinners throughout his entire childhood.

But today's scene is a curious mélange: a traditional, even hackneyed, girl-and-boy-get-amorous-in-the-rain song, with traditional, definitely hackneyed lyrics, being picturized to Lawrence's untraditional, jack-kneed dance movements. While Mehnaz changes into the chiffon sari and skimpy blouse she is supposed to get wet in this scene — the kind of costume that would have made poor Abha's deception impossible, but which heroines have only been called upon to don in these bolder times — Mohanlal spends fifteen anxious minutes discussing the picturization with Lawrence and me. Mehnaz has to be coy and revealing at the same time, and Lawrence has no doubt which he prefers. It is largely thanks to him that this daughter of an aristocratic Hyderabadi family has become the barest exponent of Bollywood's brave new whirl.

Mohanlal no longer speaks to me in Hinglish: I've been mouthing Salim-Javed dialogues for too long now to need that concession to my Anglophone background. Lawrence's Hindi has never been too strong, though, and it is soon apparent that his planned moves for Mehnaz completely contradict the reticence of her lyrics. Mohanlal, his anxiety climbing to a nine, feels the dance has to be altered to conform to the song. Lawrence is volubly outraged. "Change the lyrics," I suggest jokingly. "We can't," Mohanlal replies in all seriousness, his pitch ascending to a ten, "the song's already been recorded." Of course I know that, but my point is that no one is going to care about the lyrics anyway; they're just going to want to see

Mehnaz succumbing to me on screen, and the words she's mouthing will seem incidental. I take Lawrence's side in the debate. Voices are raised. Mohanlal's voice and nerves both threaten to snap, but finally he gives in. Things have changed since *Musafir*. I don't lose too many arguments on the studio floor.

Mehnaz enters at last, a vision in blue georgette on creamy flesh, and Lawrence, appropriately enough, blows a shrill whistle. He is not expressing admiration, merely signaling to the idlers that their time has come to be usefully engaged. The hubbub in the studio dies down. Mohanlal collapses on a chair. We are ready to begin.

"Lights! Camera! Action!"

The tape starts, but the rain doesn't. We try again. This time the rain does, but the tape doesn't. Mehnaz and I are prematurely wet and growing increasingly exasperated. "It doesn't matter," says Mohanlal, uncharacteristically calm. "We'll show it raining before the song starts, so you *can* be wet already. OK? Ready, Ashok?" This last is because I have been staring somewhat obliviously at Mehnaz in the first flush of her wetness. I have seen her without anything on in the privacy of her bedroom, and yet when I watch her fully dressed in public it is as if I am seeing her for the first time.

"Ready," I reply, though I feel anything but. The tape starts, and I pretend to sing:

> Let me shelter you from the rain,
> Keep you safe from all pain,
> Kiss you again and again,
> Let me hide you from the eyes of the world.

Kisses aren't legal yet with our censors, so Mehnaz evades my offered lips and escapes my clutches, dancing away. But I catch hold of one end of her sari *pallav,* which unravels, so as I flamenco toward her she is forced to pirouette back to me, pleading:

> Let me slip away, my dear,
> And overcome my fear,
> Please don't come so very near,
> Let me hide before my modesty's unfurled.

"Cut!" Rarely have I so resented a directorial intrusion. "Now what's the matter?" Mehnaz asks. Mohanlal's anxiety is compounded with embarrassment: it turns out her bra strap's showing. "What do you expect, with this blouse your tailor's given me?" she flashes with spirit. "There's more cloth on one of Ashok's handkerchiefs."

I would have preferred her not to reveal so much familiarity with the contents of my pockets, but the point is taken. There is a hasty consultation: actress, director, costume designer, wardrobe attendant, and (since I have nothing better to do) me. Alternative blouses are brought out for inspection and discarded, for a variety of reasons, as inappropriate. The final solution, I have to admit, comes from me: she could wear the same blouse, but without a bra.

Mehnaz looks at me expressively, and I move my hands in a *Can you think of anything better?* gesture. She retreats to her dressing room while the cameraman calls unnecessarily for a baby — not one of my triplets, thank God, but a small spotlight — and the makeup man powders my glistening nose. When she returns, my heart skips a beat. Little has now been left even to my satiated imagination.

"Go easy on the close-ups," Mohanlal mutters to the cameraman in less-than-chaste Punjabi. "Keep her you-know-whats out of the frame. I don't want the censors cutting the entire bloody song." The cameraman raises a blasé eyebrow and nods elliptically.

We start again. The first couple of verses go without incident.

ME:

> Let me shelter you from the rain,
> Keep you safe from all pain,
> Kiss you again and again,
> Let me hide you from the eyes of the world.

MEHNAZ:

> Let me slip away, my dear,
> And overcome my fear,
> Please don't come so very near,
> Let me hide before my modesty's unfurled.

I pull her to me, drop the end of the *pallav,* and hug her, as we dance in a circle. She has only the thin blue strip of the blouse between her neck and her navel, and I am strongly aroused:

> Let me hold you 'gainst my chest,
> Feel the pressure of your breast,
> Hug, caress you and the rest —

"Cut!" We hear the dance director's whistle before the actual word. This time it is Lawrence who is unhappy. We aren't going around fast enough in the circle and we're holding each other too close (no surprise there). He summons an assistant, a thin, sallow man in glasses, grips him at the elbows, shows us where his heels are, and demonstrates the way he wants us to dance. Mehnaz studies them attentively, but when I stare at these two middle-aged men solemnly going around in circles, I cannot help breaking into a broad grin. Lawrence is not amused. "Let's see you do it now!" he says, blowing his whistle.

We start, but Mehnaz falls headlong into my arms and the whistle is blown almost immediately. In getting her grip and pace right, Mehnaz failed to notice her feet and tripped on an inconvenient plant. Lawrence now decides, much to my resentment, since I have done nothing wrong, to dance with her himself in order to show her how it should feel. I watch Mehnaz, blouse bouncing, in his arms and feel a twinge of possessiveness. A makeup man comes up with a dirty handkerchief to clean the current mixture of rainwater and sweat off my face, but I wave him away angrily.

At last, we continue:

> Let me hold you 'gainst my chest,
> Feel the pressure of your breast,
> Hug, caress you and the rest —
> Let me wrap you up and keep you near my heart.

I wrap the *pallav* around both of us. I can feel Mehnaz's heartbeat through the syncopations of the sound track. I imagine it is her own voice, and not that of the pockmarked fifty-six-year-old playback-singing veteran, that is breathing huskily at me:

> Let me go, dearest, please,
> I must plead for my release,
> Your importunings must cease,
> Let me save myself and hold myself apart.

The whistle sounds again. This time Mehnaz's lips were out of sync with the sound track. She flushes, but I move my lips to indicate, "Don't worry." We resume, and a dhoti-clad delivery man bearing a tiffin-carrier walks into one of the reflectors, sending

Mohanlal's hands skyward and the cameraman into paroxysms of choice Punjabi invective. At last we catch up to the bit where Lawrence gets really bold: I push Mehnaz back from the waist as we dance, my face dangerously close to hers, my hands shimmering on her torso, and intone:

> Let me taste your shining lips,
> Place my hands upon your hips,
> Feel your rises and your dips,
> Let us travel to the heights of paradise.

Mehnaz is obviously aflame. She wants me, she wants me here and now, but the script and the situation leave her no choice:

> Let me be, precious one,
> I am burning like the sun,
> I'm afraid I have to run,
> Let us only speak the language of our eyes.

"Cut it!" Mohanlal shouts in triumph. "Thank you, Ashokji, thank you, Mehnazji. We'll use that one."

"Sorry, boss." The cameraman is lugubrious. "We can't."

"What d'you mean?" Mehnaz, already beginning to turn toward the dressing room, is apoplectic.

"Look, Madam." The cameraman points into the distance. Well in the background, unnoticed by all of us but certain to show up on the screen, a uniformed security guard sits placidly on a stool, surveying the scene with indifference.

"I don't believe it," I say, but secretly I am happy to cavort once more with Mehnaz for the camera. Strange: with Maya, the moment I realized I loved her and wanted her to be mine, I desired nothing so much as to lock her away from prying eyes, to protect her from the cheapening gaze of the public. But with Mehnaz, I can resist no opportunity to flaunt her in front of everyone. I enjoy being with her in public, and I enjoy being watched enjoying her. "Let's do it again," I say decisively.

Mehnaz acquiesces, as she always does with any of my suggestions. I begin to look forward to making a few more suggestions, of a more intimate nature, after the shooting.

The rain falls, my enthusiasm rises, her blouse falls and rises, and we sing-dance to the throbbing climax:

ME:

Let me taste your shining lips,
Place my hands upon your hips,
Feel your rises and your dips,
Let us travel to the heights of paradise.

MEHNAZ:

Let me be, precious one,
I am burning like the sun,
I'm afraid I have to run,
Let us only speak the language of our eyes.

I am still holding her when the whistle blows. As the lights are switched off, I take her face in my hands, and in full view of the entire unit, kiss her full-bloodedly on the mouth. She does not pull away from me; I can feel her nipples harden against my shirt. Her tongue darts between my teeth, and my hands caress the small of her back, pressing her body into mine. Our need is so urgent we might have gone on, but the uncharacteristic silence of the unit, which ought to be busy making dismantling noises, reminds us of our audience. Mohanlal's eyes are almost bulging through his glasses. We laugh and trip and stumble toward her dressing room. The shocked silence follows us, as I imagine its authors would have liked to.

I unhook her blouse even before her startled Chinese dresser has fled the room. Her breasts fill my hands like *prasad* from a generous temple, and I take them in worship, ritually putting them to my mouth, my eyes, my forehead. Her moans are chanted slokas of desire, invoking heavenly pleasures. No man may wear a stitched garment in the sanctum sanctorum of the divine; I bare myself in reverence. In turn, I pull at the coil of her earthly attachment, the knot of her sari. It collapses wetly at her feet, followed by her drenched petticoat. Liberated from these worldly shackles, she circles me seven times, her fingers tracing mystical patterns on my torso. My own hands light the lamp of her womanhood and move in a rite of oblation. She kneels, her mouth closing on the object of her veneration, upright symbol of procreative divinity. Her prayer is bilingual. Our fingers pour ghee on the flames of our need. Rising, the flames unite us with the sacred thread of desire and we are as one in the lower depths of our higher selves.

I have no idea why I'm suddenly turning all religious about Mehnaz. After all, the girl's a Muslim, for Christ's sake. And we usually prefer the missionary position.

Money is becoming a bit of a problem. I don't mean the lack of it, but as Maya pointed out, what to do with what I have.

The problem is, basically, that Subramanyam keeps asking producers for ever more outrageous amounts of money, and the producers then astonish us by paying what we ask for. They come to me in shabby *dhotis* and stained *kurtas,* clutching synthetic briefcases that, when opened, turn out to contain bundles of incredibly crisp notes of whose existence the Department of Revenue is blissfully unaware. These notes change hands, with sometimes the briefcase thrown in as well, and no receipt is ever issued. Over the years I have had to think of increasingly ingenious places to cache the stuff, and it is beginning to — if the verb can be pardoned — tax my imagination.

The small portion of my cinematic remuneration that comes by check is, of course, dutifully banked and the proceeds recorded by Subramanyam in his neat, precise hand in a register that is available for inspection whenever officialdom so desires. Actually, officialdom has never yet so desired, possibly because my father's party has never yet been out of power. Not that my father has consciously tried to protect me. He would never raise a finger to protect me, but he doesn't have to: that is the beauty of being important and influential in India, the number of things you get without having to ask for them. Yet I cannot entirely overlook the possibility that some over-zealous tax official will try to prove his integrity by raiding the son of a senior congressman, and if that happens it is obvious I cannot afford to have my briefcases lying about.

What does one do? At first I made some discreet inquiries of my more successful peers, but I found my colleagues disappointingly closemouthed, perhaps because of my paternal antecedents. The best I could elicit was from Radha Sabnis. "Why, false ceilings, darling, but of course," she said, as if every actor's home came equipped with them. I debated whether to install such a ceiling in my house, despite its actual low ceilings, with the attendant possibility that if Amitabh Bachhan came to visit in the summer he might be decapitated by the ceiling fan. However, even the prospect of eliminating my principal rival in the box office stakes lost its attraction when the next tax raid reported in newspapers involved the unearthing of currency notes and gold bars from an actress's false ceiling.

But I digress. It's true, of course, that there is no shortage of enterprising fellows on the fringes of the film industry anxious to persuade me of ingenious ways to spend my money and enrich themselves in the process. They offer gold mines in Karnataka and liquor distilleries in Kashmir, or quite possibly the other way around. After my first couple of encounters with their ilk, I have given Subramanyam strict instructions that they are not to cast their shady shadows anywhere near me.

It's not that I have just sat on the stuff. I've done the obvious and bought the inevitable bungalow for some outrageous sum, most of which does not figure on the deed of sale. (This is when I discovered that the world of real estate has found innovative use for the language of kindergarten. "How much number two you giving?" asked the unctuous seller when we met to clinch the deal. I was so taken aback I nearly told him my bowel movements were none of his business, but Subramanyam hastily intervened to explain that the term referred to "black" money. Only 35 percent of the already inflated price of the house would be paid in number one, the money you could, so to speak, afford to piss away by check.)

But now that I have my bungalow, and now that Maya has spent several fortunes renovating, equipping, painting, decorating, and furnishing it, what do I do next? I am not attracted by more property I'll never have time to visit. So I turn away offers of farms outside Delhi, cottages in hill stations, my own patch of Himalayan snow in disputed border territory. At least one filmi wife runs a boutique and I ask Maya whether I should buy her one, but she's not overwhelmed by the idea, and then the triplets overwhelm her. In any case it's not so much a new investment I'm after as a safe place to keep the unaccountable surplus cash for the proverbial rainy day. Abha's has come, it's practically a monsoon, but she seems to have weathered it reasonably well. I too must plan for a life after Golden Jubilees.

I cast about for advice hopefully, but in a world where people's most intimate relations are publicized under twenty-four-point headlines in the filmi magazines, the only secrets the denizens of Bollywood are allowed to keep are their financial ones. Money is to be spent as visibly as possible, but never talked about.

So — what to do? It is a measure of my desperation that I actually decide to ask my father. I mean, we haven't exchanged a confidence since the time I told him with boyhood pride that I'd managed to throw a stone through a neighbor's third-story window, which happened, unfortunately, to be closed at the time, and was beaten black-and-blue for my achievement. But who else do I have, right? He is at my home on one of his rare visits to Bombay, clad in his khadi politician's costume and uncomfortably sipping my Scotch in guilty violation of his party's prohibitionist principles. I gulp down my own Macallan and, looking around as much for something to talk about as for his counsel, I broach the subject.

"You know, Dad, you're in politics and all that stuff, so you must know what people do with their money," I suggest obscurely.

"Why, put it in the bank, or spend it, or invest in the stock exchange," says my father, who has a staggering facility for the obvious. "Are you asking, Ashok, for an introduction to a broker?"

"Not really," I admit. "No, I'm sort of asking — generally. You know, there are lots of things people can do with their, uh, white money, but how do your political friends handle the black?"

My father draws himself up to his fullest possible height while still remaining seated and adopts a stern manner. "No political friend of mine *has* what you call black money" — he says the words with distaste — "and if he did, he would cease to be a friend of mine." My father adopts what I have come to recognize as his Cambridge manner: he went to Cambridge as a young man, largely because the only alternative was jail, and he never misses an opportunity to remind me of it. "Ashok, my boy, undeclared revenue is the curse of our country. If the money that is lost every year to the parallel economy could be plowed back into the official one, half our problems of underdevelopment could be solved."

My mind is already beginning to back away from yet another Kulbhushan Banjara lecture, of which I have had many over the years. I knew from the start that it was a mistake to ask him. "If you know anyone who has such unaccounted funds, Ashok, you should urge him to declare it immediately," my father goes on. "The tax authorities are extremely strict about these matters. You know that."

"Yes, you're right, Dad, absolutely." I drain my glass. "Forget I ever asked you."

He sighs, as at some private regret, though I doubt he was regretting his own scrupulous honesty, which had resulted in a considerable slide in the family's standard of living during my own childhood. He was the member of a government that had invented so many taxes that at some levels they actually totaled 101 percent. Obviously no one whose taxes were not deducted at source paid them honestly. Before lecturing me Dad would do well not to support the passage of laws that all reasonable people feel obliged to break. But that's not the kind of thinking my father is capable of, I don't imagine.

We are saved by Maya's entry into the conversation. "Papa," she says brightly — she calls him "Papa" because she finds my use of "Dad" insufficiently Indian — "I've been thinking, and I need your advice."

"Of course, my dear." My father swells with paternal importance. In his view the best thing I ever did, possibly the only good thing I ever did, was to marry Maya. He has been known to say to friends that he couldn't have arranged a more suitable daughter-in-law himself.

"I'm thinking of making a comeback."

"I beg your pardon?"

"A comeback. Returning to films."

I splutter into my Macallan, but my father is even more taken aback. "But why on earth should you want to?" he demands. "You've got the children, a house. . . ."

"The house runs itself, Papa," Maya interrupts. "And now that Leela-Neela-Sheela are on the bottle, they don't even really *need* me all the time. Ashok is away with his shooting and his, his film world social commitments" — I try not to read too much into the phrase — "so much that I hardly ever see him. I thought this would be good for us too, you know, to work together."

My father seems to understand more than I would give him credit for. "I see your point, my dear," he harrumphs, "but really, for you to be running around trees and all that, at this stage . . ."

"Oh, I wouldn't do that, Papa, you're quite right," says Maya. "A more serious sort of film."

"Your husband," my father says pointedly, "doesn't act in serious sorts of films."

Maya laughs, and her laughter is sharp-edged, like the tinkle of broken glass. "Well, this wouldn't be a Satyajit Ray film or even something by one of the New Wave directors, but a slightly more serious commercial film. Songs and maybe a fight or two, but not too much running around the trees for me."

I find my voice at last. "And where do you think you're going to find such a script?" I ask. "People don't write scripts like that, and more to the point they don't film them."

"Oh, I already have the script," Maya says casually. "Subramanyam gave it to me."

I hadn't realized Maya and Subramanyam were such good friends. My secretary, of course, works out of an office in my house, but I had always supposed their contact did not go much beyond Maya sending a servant to ask what he wanted for lunch.

"And why," I ask, my teeth increasingly on edge, "would Subramanyam do that?"

"Because I asked him to," Maya replies matter-of-factly. "We've been talking about things, and I've told him to pass on scripts I might find of interest. So anyway, Papa, .what do you think?"

My father begins to realize he is being set up. "Well," he says, looking more uncomfortable than ever, "what does Ashok think about all this?"

"I don't know," replies Maya, untroubled. "We haven't discussed it yet."

"Well, then, my dear, I think you ought to discuss it with each other," says my father. Good for him! But then he spoils it all by adding, "You know that whatever you do, Maya, you will have my blessing."

"Thank you, Papa," coos my scheming wife. "I knew you'd say that."

My father looks at me looking daggers at her, and diplomatically remembers a prior commitment he has not yet mentioned. I escort him to the waiting official car, which is also to take him to the airport.

"Try and be kind to your wife, Ashok," he says gratuitously.

"I don't need you to tell me that, Dad," I reply.

He looks at me sadly. He is always looking at me sadly. He shakes his head, opens his mouth as if to say something, then closes it. I am about to honk for the driver, who was not expecting to leave quite so soon and is not in the car, when my father opens his mouth again. This time he speaks, but on a different subject.

"Ashok," he says, his expression inscrutably heavy-lidded, "do you know Gangoolie? Our party treasurer?"

I don't really know him, but I know who he is. I nod.

"Well, in his line of work, he knows a fair bit about black money," my father says unexpectedly. "I am not a fool, Ashok, I know there is black money in politics. I have never touched any of it myself, but ever since we idealistically abolished company contributions to political parties, businessmen have found this other way of financing their preferred candidates." Spare me the lecture, Dad, I think. Get to the point. "Anyway, I asked Gangoolie once where people kept their undeclared assets. The small-timers, as he put it, kept their currency in their homes, in safes, in false ceilings, under beds. When necessary, our tax people know where to look. The *big*-timers, however, use Swiss banks."

"Swiss banks," I repeat.

"It seems," my father sighs, "that they find people abroad who need rupees in India, at a favorable rate of exchange of course. The rupees are handed over here, and the equivalent deposited, in Swiss francs, in Geneva or Zurich."

"Isn't that — illegal?" I ask, as the driver, his keys jingling in the pocket of his uniform, runs up to the car.

"Of course it is," my father says. "But because of Swiss banking secrecy, it is difficult for our authorities to do anything about it."

He embraces me in farewell and gets into the back of the car.

"And these people? The ones abroad, who need the rupees? Where do the big-timers find them?"

"The big-timers," my father says, "don't need to look very far." Then he waves sadly and rolls up the window. His car drives away, leaving me more to think about than I had expected.

Strange man, my father. Sometimes I wonder if I have fully figured him out.

Inside the house, I erupt at Maya.

"What was the big idea of bringing this comeback nonsense up with Dad?" I demand.

She is unfazed. "It's not nonsense, Ashok. I'm perfectly serious. And it's not my fault if the only time you are around to be spoken to is when your father has come to visit."

"Maya, we had agreed."

"We had agreed I wouldn't make a comeback if I turned out to be pregnant. I was. Well, now I've had the babies. They're fine, and they're in good hands, which don't necessarily always have to be mine. The agreement is over."

"But there's still a basic agreement. When we got married."

"You're a fine one, Ashok Banjara, to be citing marital commitments to me."

"And what is that supposed to mean?"

"You know perfectly well what that is supposed to mean." Her voice is cold. "Don't make me say it, Ashok."

Guilt rises in me. I try a different tack. "Look, Maya, I understand your need to do something. I really do. But you don't want to rush into a thing like this. Let me look at the script, talk to the producer. Then we can see. What script is this anyway?"

"You mean you really don't know what script I'm talking about? Ashok, you surprise me."

Realization dawns, like the baby spots at the studio. "Not *Dil Ek Qila,* for God's sake?" I ask in horror.

"Why not?" Her voice is calm.

"But . . . but that film is already cast! Subramanyam had no business giving it to you. The only reason the script is here is because the actress who has the principal part specifically wanted me to be offered the male lead. It's not the kind of film I'd usually do. . . ."

"But you're planning to say yes."

"Maybe."

"Not maybe, yes."

"You've been talking to Subramanyam."

"Leave him out of this, Ashok. I'm your *wife,* for God's sake. Don't I count for anything in this? Can't you tell me the truth for once, without beating around the bramble bush?"

Once in a while, Maya's English slips, and I am reminded of how far she has come since her diffident days as a provincial newcomer. But where did she find this rage, this strength?

"OK, I think I'll do it. Choubey, the producer, says it'll enhance my image. Broaden my appeal."

"Bullshit!" Maya's small thin frame is taut with anger. "It's a weak and sentimental script, neither New Wave nor commercial. It's a colossal risk that no actor in your position would normally take. But you want to do it because that slut is in it and she has got Choubey to ask you to."

"Maya," I begin in warning. She rides roughshod over me.

"Don't you see what she wants? Are you so blind, Ashok Banjara, that you really can't see what she's up to? You're going to play a married musician helplessly in love with her, the stunning dancing girl. Do you think the great Indian public isn't going to see that as a statement about your real life? And you want to allow this whore to flaunt her affair with you across the nation while I sit quietly at home. Well, I'm not going to play along with this, Ashok. I am the mother of your children and I'm not going to reduce myself to an object of pity!"

"He stays with his wife in the end," I say lamely.

"Because the slut dies in heroic circumstances to save them both," Maya blazes. "Have you no shame, offering the script as an excuse?"

I can't take any more of this. There are times when the easy way out is the best way out. "I'll tell Choubey I won't do it," I announce.

"You've signed already," she says.

"I have?" This is genuine, because half the time I'm not sure what I'm signing. But it's true that I'd told Subramanyam I would, so he could well have thrust that paper in front of me along with a dozen others.

"You have," Maya confirms. "You could still get out of it, but it wouldn't be worth the grief. And besides, Choubey is probably already selling his territories on the strength of your name."

"It doesn't matter. I'll do him some other favor. He'll want me for another film soon enough, and I'll promise him all the dates he wants."

"No." Maya is firm. "I've thought about it. If you pull out, they'll probably make the film anyway, and that slut will still get the story across the way she wants it. It's better this way."

"What way?" I ask, pouring myself another whiskey. I wave the bottle at her, but she ignores the offer.

"To do it, but to make sure I have control," Maya says grimly.

"Control? How?"

"We're seeing Choubey tomorrow," Maya says. "And we're going to tell him you're laying down three conditions."

"We are?" This is all too much for me. "I am?"

"Yes. One, I shall executive produce." This will be a new one to Choubey, who's never had an executive producer in his life. "Two, I shall be script consultant. The screenplay, you will tell him, needs some minor revisions, and the dialogue wallah will work with me. Three, under these conditions, but only under these conditions, I shall play the wife."

I am totally speechless. I gasp. I gape.

"No one is going to pity me when this film comes out," Maya says determinedly. "I don't know whether it will do anything for you at the box office, Ashok. My comeback may never take off with this part. But everyone who sees it is going to say, *wah, kaisi aurat hai.* What a woman she is. They're going to admire me for having taken this situation into my own hands and confronted it with pride and self-respect." She turns to face me, her eyes bright. "Are you going to be with me in this, Ashok? Are you going to stand up for the dignity of your wife, the mother of your children, or are you going to let that whore walk all over the honor of this house?"

She really knows how to put it, that girl. She should never have left the theater. "Of course I'm with you, Maya," I say. After all, I have a family to maintain. Mehnaz won't like it, but then I've never lost much time worrying about what Mehnaz might like. Thank God there are still women like that.

"Tell me it isn't true, Ashok," begs Cyrus Sponerwalla, all three of his chins wobbling in anxiety.

"What isn't?"

"Like you're going to do a film about adultery," he squeaks. "You, Ashok Banjara, epitome of moral rectitude from Jalpaiguri to Jhumri Tialaiya, are going to play an errant husband on the silver screen."

"I am," I concede.

"The Indian public isn't ready for this, man," Cyrus pleads, blinking behind his glasses like an owl at noontime. "The consumers in the twenty-five-paisa seats won't accept it, idea-wise. Your image will take a dive, man."

"There isn't any explicit adultery in the film, Cyrus. Relax, have a Charminar." I quote the well-known advertising slogan, but offer him an India Kings.

Cyrus turns down the cigarette, and the commercial wisdom behind its marketing. "I can't relax, man, when you're in the process of destroying yourself image-wise," he flaps, dabbing at perspiration with a scented handkerchief. "Look, you're a hero, and a damn good one at that. Why not just stay a hero? Isn't that enough for you?"

"Cyrus, Cyrus." I laugh. "The film magazines have hinted at the looseness of my morals and at that of every other actor and actress in Bollywood for years. It's done me no harm whatsoever. I thought you told me any publicity's good publicity. Speaking of which, take a look at this." I pass him the latest *Showbiz*.

Like all PR pros, Cyrus cannot resist the printed word. And Radha Sabnis is in her element:

Darlings, Cheetah hears the love scenes in our studios are getting more and more torrid. Tongues haven't ceased wagging at Himalaya over a sizzling performance by The Banjara with his leading lady, the ultraliberated Mehnaz Elahi — yes, the very girl who told an interviewer last year that anyone over eighteen claiming to be a virgin was either a liar or a cow. Cheetah learns that the love scene in question continued well after the camera had been switched off, and that the Hungry Young Man's costar turned up for the next shot with a substantial tear in her costume. Well, darlings, perhaps our self-confessed Erich Segal fan thinks that love means never having to sew your sari, eh? Grrrowl . . .

I hear the Sponerwalla chuckle, like an asthmatic chicken gobbling its feed, and then Cyrus is bleating again. "This is a different market altogether, man," he explains. "These things don't matter to those who read them, like, but those who can read anything at all are only fifteen percent, twenty tops, of your overall audience. My PR strategy for you is segmented, man: frequent publicity in the print media, clean image on the screen. The readers of *Showbiz* are thrilled and titillated by all this, and it's fine, so long as the likes of Radha Sabnis don't go on repeating that you're a bad *actor,* which is what can harm you with this segment of the market. Right? But the people I'm concerned about today have never read a film magazine, and they're the core of your mass appeal. Illiterate villagers who go six, seven times to the same film, and who think you *are* the heroes you play. The rural masses don't make fine distinctions between the actor and the part, Ashok. That's why children aren't being named Pranay anymore, or Prem Chopra, because the actors' own real names are so completely identified with their screen villainy. If you were called Chopra, man, would you name your son Prem? He wouldn't be able to introduce himself without women yelling 'rape'! Now you, Ashok, you're clean, image-wise. Not as pure clean as someone like N. T. Rama Rao in Andhra, who has played so many gods in mythological epics that some people have actually built a temple to him. Or MGR in Madras, who has defeated the forces of injustice and evil in so many films that the masses are pleading with him to take over the state government and set everything right. But you're somewhere there yourself, image-wise. You don't go spoiling it by betraying your wife on every cinema screen in the country."

"Point taken, Cyrus," I laugh. "I shall bear it in mind as I look over the screenplay. Look, don't worry. Everything's going to be all right. Maya's going to have the final say on the script."

Sponerwalla looks relieved. "Why didn't you tell me that to begin with?" he asks, putting away his damp handkerchief.

"Because I love to see you earn your fee," I reply heartlessly. "Speaking of which, Cyrus — what do you know about Swiss banks?"

Exterior: Day

DIL EK QILA

(The Heart Is a Fortress)

THE FIRST TREATMENT: THE ORIGINAL VERSION

A hillside in Kashmir. The camera pans across azure sky, verdant slopes, technicolor flowers. Mehnaz Elahi runs laughing across the screen to the strains of an electric mandolin as Ashok Banjara pursues her, singing:

> *You are my sunlight*
> *You brighten my life*
> *You are my sunlight*
> *Come be my wife.*

He finally catches up with her and hugs her from behind: she continues trying to flee and they roll down the hill, locked in an embrace. Close-up: their laughing lips are about to meet when the camera swings skyward and the opening credits fill the screen.

Domestic scene: Ashok with his parents, Godambo and Amma, in their luxurious, indeed palatial, home. Early moments of dialogue establish father's strength (deep, gravelly voice), wealth (luxurious furnishings), and traditionalism (caste mark on forehead). Ashok gets to the point: "Father, I want to get married." "Excellent," says Godambo: he has been thinking along the same lines. It is time

Ashok settled down. It would be good for the family and, provided a suitable match was made, good for the business also.

Ashok looks uncomfortable. "Father, I have already found the girl I wish to marry."

"What!" Outrage on Godambo's face, consternation in his bulging eyes. Amma rolls pupils heavenward and mutters a brief invocation. "And who can this be?" asks the paterfamilias.

"I would like to bring her here to meet you," Ashok suggests.

"Wait!" Godambo is a man of procedure. "Before you bring any such person to our house, let me make some inquiries. Tell me everything you know about her. Who is the girl? What is her name? Is she of good family? Who are her parents? Do we know them, and if not, why not? Where does she live? How did you meet her?" And Amma adds, "Is she fair?"

"Yes, she is," Ashok answers his mother, but one useful response does not get him off the hook. Godambo is not to be diverted. Squirming under his relentless probing, Ashok has to admit that his ladylove is neither rich nor well connected. "But she is a wonderful girl," he says with deep-pupiled intensity. "And I love her."

"Love?" Godambo barks. "What is love?"

"Love," Amma explains maternally, "is something that comes after marriage, Ashok. I love you, I love your father. How can you love a stranger?"

"She's not a stranger, Mother," Ashok begins, then realizes it is hopeless. "Look, if only you both would meet her, you would see immediately what I mean." But his father is reluctant to take matters so far as to welcome this impecunious interloper into his own living room. Then Ashok has an idea. "Come and see her at the Cultural Evening tonight," he pleads.

Godambo is not interested, but Amma, ever the obliging mother, persuades him on behalf of her son.

Scene: an auditorium, every seat full. Ashok and his parents are escorted to a front row. The curtain parts to reveal a stage with the painted backdrop of a flowering garden. Mehnaz enters in a cascade of anklets, covered head to foot in kathak costume of billowing red skirt, long-sleeved red blouse, red head scarf, and red leggings, all spangled with silver. Godambo grunts appreciatively. Mehnaz bursts into song:

My heart beats for you,
I'd perform feats for you,
You are the landlord of my soul;
My eyes light for you,
I'd gladly fight for you,
Without you I don't feel whole.

As she sings and dances, all arched hip and elegant fingertips, she manages to exchange meaningful glances with Ashok, making it clear every word of the playback applies to him. Meanwhile, Godambo, oblivious to this byplay, appears to enjoy himself hugely. When the song is over the audience bursts into well-rehearsed applause, and Ashok rises to his feet to clap vigorously.

At the end of the show, Godambo, in mellow spirits, looks around the hall. "So where is this girl you wanted me to meet?" he asks his son.

"You've seen her, Dad. And I could tell you liked her. Mehnaz Elahi, the kathak dancer. Wasn't she something?"

"What!" Godambo's eyes bulge in horror. "An entertainer! My son wants to marry an entertainer!"

Amma restrains him, but he storms out, wife and son in tow. They are getting into their chauffeur-driven Impala when Mehnaz, now freshly changed into a sari, emerges from the auditorium and walks expectantly toward them. She stops short, though, her pretty face clouded in bewilderment, as Ashok shuts the car door after him with a look of helplessness. Mehnaz is left staring crestfallen into the camera as the Impala drives away in a cloud of dusty intolerance.

Inside the house the scene is Godambo's: rage and outrage alternating with advice about vice. He is furious that his son wants to marry the first plausible hussy who has allowed him to embrace her. Of course young men must sow their wild oats, but marriage has nothing to do with sexual attraction. The girl might be pretty, she might be talented, but she was completely unsuitable for the son of Seth Godambo. When Ashok marries, it will be a social event; his bride will be handpicked from a dazzling array of well-endowed virgins from well-endowed families. There is the business to be considered, the family's standing in the community, the expectations of the society in which they live. If Ashok married—the word makes

Godambo choke—*married* Mehnaz Elahi, he *and* his parents would be laughingstocks. "I understand your needs," Godambo adds in gruff paternalism. "I was a young man myself once. But marriage is another matter altogether."

Yes, Amma explains. Marriage is not just a relationship between individuals, but an arrangement between families. Ashok would not just be marrying one woman, he would be acquiring another family. Can he see Mehnaz's simple father and shrouded mother socializing in Seth Godambo's living room? Ashok has to admit he cannot.

Yet when his parents have finished with him, Ashok is defiant. "Mehnaz is the woman of my heart," he declaims. "I will not let her down."

"Why don't you talk this over with her?" Godambo is surprisingly reasonable. "She may well prove more sensible than you. When are you seeing her next?"

"Tomorrow evening," Ashok replies. "She was supposed to join a show in Bombay, but I persuaded her not to. Dad, I'm not sure I can live without her."

"Don't be so sure she can't live without you," Godambo says meaningfully.

Next scene: Godambo with our heroine, in her lower-middle-class home. Peacock-green walls, peeling ceiling, plastic-covered sofa, garish calendars of androgynous deities. "Miss Mehnaz, I enjoyed your performance at the Cultural Evening last night," he says gutturally. "I would like to engage you for a very special occasion."

Mehnaz is all pretty and obliging.

"You see, my son is getting married," Godambo goes on. "And we are celebrating it in a big way, as befits an alliance between two of the city's biggest families. I would like to have an entertainment show worthy of the occasion. And I would like you to sing and dance for my son's wedding."

"Your son?" Mehnaz asks.

"Ashok Banjara," Godambo says with pride. "Why, do you know him?"

"And he is . . . getting . . . married?"

"Yes, to Lalaji Chhoturmal's daughter, Abha," Godambo replies. "Ashok has liked her for a long time. You see, they were in the same school, and of course we know the family very well."

"Of course." Mehnaz's tone is dull.

"So—will you come for the event? Three weeks from now. I hope you are free, and I would of course be happy to double your fee on this happy occasion."

"No," Mehnaz says quietly. "No, I am afraid I cannot accept your invitation, Sethji. You see, I have a prior commitment in Bombay. In fact, I am leaving tonight."

"I am most disappointed," Godambo says, but he cannot conceal the gleam of triumph in his bulging eyes.

It is later, at dusk; Ashok is waiting at a palm grove near the beach, wearing jeans and a troubled expression. He looks at his watch, then up at the darkening sky. Studio stars twinkle at him. He sings plaintively:

> *Where are you, my love?*
> *I wait for light from the stars above.*
> *You have taken my heart*
> *And hid it from view,*
> *Now no one can start*
> *To rid me of you.*
> *Wh-e-e-re are you, my love?*

There is, of course, no answer.

Song finished, and with one more futile look at his watch, Ashok leaps into his two-seater sports car and drives to Mehnaz's house. "Where is she?" he demands of her poor but dignified parents, as the calendars flap omnisciently on the walls.

"She has gone to Bombay," replies the mother. "And she specifically told me to tell you, if you came by, that she has nothing to say to you. Except to give you this." She puts a crumpled envelope into Ashok's hand. Out of it emerges a silver bracelet, with the image of a dancing goddess on a medallion at its clasp.

"But I gave her this," Ashok protests in dismay.

"And she is giving it back to you," Mehnaz's father, Ramkumar, replies. "She doesn't want it anymore."

"I don't understand." Ashok's eyes are hot with tears. "I don't know what's come over your daughter, but you can tell her I shall always keep this bracelet for her—till the day she comes back to me."

"I shall tell her," replies the kindly mother, "but she isn't coming back, Ashok. She has gone to make her career in Bombay."

Sad, portentous music. The screen intercuts two sets of images: one of Ashok's wedding ceremony, complete with demure bride dripping with gold, sneezy guest dripping with cold, and overweight mother-in-law dripping with tears, the other of elegiac soft-focus shots showing Mehnaz in Bombay, gazing wistfully at the horizon, her sari billowing in the sea breeze, and singing the refrain of Ashok's song:

> *Where are you, my love?*
> *I wait for light from the stars above.*
> *You have taken my heart*
> *And hid it from view,*
> *Now no one can start*
> *To rid me of you.*
> *Wh-e-e-re are you, my love?*

It is some years later. Ashok is seated on a dhurrie on the floor, taking music lessons from a maestro with a harmonium. "Very good," says the maestro, Asrani, an actor seen more often in the role of stock comedian. "Now once again: sa-ri-ga-ma-pa-da-ni-sa." He tosses his head back with a tonal flourish as he runs through ·the scale. "Now you."

Ashok dutifully echoes his guru: "Sa-ri-ga-ma-pa-da-ni-sa."

"Not bad," says the maestro. "But there is something missing." He taps his belly, producing a percussion note like a cork being pulled out of a bottle, and resumes. "Sa-ri-ga-ma-pa-da-ni-sa."

Ashok also tosses his head. "Sa-ri-ga-ma-pa-da-ni-sa."

"You're getting it," says the maestro. "See, it's simple:

> Sa, sambar, *a Southie dish,*
> Ri, *what the Frenchies call our rice;*
> Ga, *gaga, as the Bongs are about fish,*
> Ma, *mother, ain't her cooking nice?*
> Pa, *the man always served first,*
> Da, *daal, the food for healthy chaps,*
> Ni, nimbu pani *for our thirst,*
> *and that brings us back to sa—saag paneer perhaps?*

Ashok's brow unfurrows in comprehension. "You're hungry," he says.

"I thought you'd never get it," sighs the maestro. "Music may be the food of love, but the love of music requires food. Let's eat."

As they wrap themselves around the contents of a *thali* served by uniformed menials, Ashok asks the maestro how good he really is. "Really, not bad at all," replies his instructor, professionally non-committal. "What made you want to take up singing?"

The camera lingers in close-up on Ashok's poignantly inexpressive face. "A friend left me once, some years ago," he says, a faraway gaze in his eyes. "When she left, I felt she had taken the music out of my life. I decided to replace her somehow within myself."

"*Wah, wah,*" responds Asrani heartily. It is not clear whether his appreciation is for the sentiment or the food.

There follow a couple of scenes that establish Ashok in conventional domesticity: scenes involving his dutiful wife and beautiful children. (Note: to be fleshed out if Mr. Banjara accepts the role.) Meanwhile, Mehnaz goes from success to success. She is shown dancing in overflowing halls to standing ovations, receiving prizes and awards, and being featured on posters and in neon lights. (Note: at least one very good song here showing Ms. Elahi dancing, with five costume changes to mark her progress and establish different occasions.)

In some scenes Mehnaz is accompanied by her manager, Pranay, an energetic operator who is seen organizing backstage, berating auditorium managers, arranging for Mehnaz to be garlanded. One day, as Mehnaz emerges fresh from a stage triumph, Pranay clasps her in a joyous embrace. "Wonderful!" he exclaims. "I say, Mehnaz, why don't you and I do something?"

"What?" she asks innocently.

"Get married."

Mehnaz averts her exquisite face so only the camera can see the pain in her eyes. "I am sorry, Pranay, but I cannot."

"Why not? Do you have a better friend than me in the whole world?"

"No, of course not, Pranay," says Mehnaz. "You're a wonderful friend, and a great manager. It's not you. I shall never marry—anybody."

Pranay is bewildered. "But why?" "I gave my heart once to a man, many years ago," she says. "I cannot love anyone else ever again." "Who is this man?" asks Pranay angrily.

Mehnaz does not answer. But in the very next scene the man in question is about to give his first public performance as a singer. And he is introduced fulsomely to a large audience by none other than his own father, Old Mr. Anti-Entertainers himself, Seth Godambo.

"As you know, my son's profession is business," Godambo orates. "And in this domain he has worked with me to create a place for himself in this community as an upstanding citizen. But what is not so widely known is that he also has a musical soul. And he has kindly agreed today, under the able guidance and instruction of Pandit Asrani"—the maestro, his mouth full of *paan,* takes an affable bow—"to sing for you today, all in the cause of charity, of course." Godambo nods, and on cue, the extras break into thunderous applause.

His aesthetic inclinations thus rendered respectable, Ashok launches into his lament:

> *Where are you, my love?*
> *I wait for light from the stars above.*
> *You have taken my heart*
> *And hid it from view,*
> *They have kept us apart*
> *And rid me of you.*
> *Wh-e-e-re are you, my love?*

Where she is, is right there, for, unnoticed by the singer, Mehnaz Elahi has slipped into the audience, and she listens to him sing with tears glistening in her eyes.

The show is over, and Ashok is standing, palms joined in respectful *namaskar,* as a succession of elders and strangers congratulate him on his performance. Abha and Godambo are in another part of the hall, conversing animatedly. Suddenly the look of distant politeness on Ashok's face vanishes as a soft voice cuts through the hubbub near him. "You sang beautifully, Ashok." Our hero looks up in shock at Mehnaz standing among the throng, which considerably melts away.

"You! What are you doing here?"

"I'm supposed to be dancing on this stage tomorrow," she says. (Note: perhaps we ought to give her a stage name as well, to explain why Ashok hasn't heard of her coming.) "I got here early and thought I would look at the auditorium. And I heard you."

Their eyes meet, and it is obvious even to the villagers in the

157

twenty-five-paisa seats that nothing has changed between them. "Why did you leave me that day, without even a word?" he asks urgently. "Because you were getting married to someone your parents had arranged and you didn't even tell me," Mehnaz replies. "Me? But—that's not true!" Ashok exclaims. "You mean you're not married?" she asks. "To Lala Chhoturmal's daughter?" Ashok admits he is, "but only because you left me . . ."

Before they can go much further, Abha calls, "Ashok?" She walks up to them. "Ashok, some people there are waiting to see you, friends of Daddy's," she announces. "Come along now." There is time for the women to exchange a formal *namaskar* before Abha drags her husband away. Mehnaz stares after them for a long moment, then turns and leaves.

The next evening: another Mehnaz dance, another song with a familiar echo:

> *My heart beats for you,*
> *I'd perform feats for you,*
> *You are the landlord of my soul;*
> *My eyes light for you,*
> *I'd gladly fight for you,*
> *Without you I don't feel whole.*

At the end, as the rapturous audience files out, Ashok battles his way backstage. Mehnaz is in her dressing room removing an earring when Ashok enters and shuts the door behind him. "You dropped a piece of jewelry, Mehnazji," he says quietly. He stretches out his hand; in it sparkles the silver bracelet with the dancing goddess rampant at the clasp.

Mehnaz looks at it for a long time, her hands frozen in their earlier position at her earlobe. "So you really did keep it for me," she says at last.

"All these years," breathes Ashok.

She reaches out a hand to take it from him, and his own closes on hers.

"Mehnaz, I have waited so long for you."

She doesn't move. "You haven't waited," she says. "You're a married man."

"That—that was for my parents," Ashok pleads. "For society. Besides, you had left me. What could I do?"

"I only left you when I learned about your marriage," she says.

"That couldn't be," Ashok responds. Then it strikes him. "Who told you I was getting married?"

"Your father, of course," replies Mehnaz. "Wasn't it you who sent him to me . . . ?"

And then, as the enormity of the deception, and of their own mistakes, dawns on them, explanations give way to a clinging embrace. Mehnaz tries to resist, but Ashok is insistent. "So many wasted years to make up for," he says. She succumbs, and as they fall upon the bed the camera focuses on the ceiling fan whirring rhythmically above.

The next few scenes show the progress of the relationship, including one more flowery song in a rose garden. But gardens are public places, and their chlorophyllous clinch is seen by Pranay, who grits his teeth in jealous fury. "Can't give her love to any man, huh?" he snarls. "We'll see about that."

It is evening at Ashok's home. Abha confronts him quietly, with all the deference of the traditional Hindu wife. "You are not home very often these days, my husband," she says. "Daddy says you are not at the office much either. Is something the matter, Ashok?"

"It doesn't concern you," Ashok replies disingenuously.

"I believe it does," Abha insists. "It is that dancing girl, isn't it? You've been seeing her."

"Who told you that?"

"Does it matter? But it *is* true." Abha sobs.

"Look, Abha, I don't mean to hurt you. But this is a woman to whom I gave my heart before I married you."

"I am the woman to whom you gave your vow. What about me and our child? If your heart was already pledged, you had no right to plight it to me."

"I'm sorry," Ashok says, looking it.

"This came for you today." Abha extends a scrap of paper. "Oh, Ashok, please stop what you're doing. I'm frightened."

On the paper, in a minatory scrawl, are the words "KEEP YOUR HANDS OFF MY WOMAN OR YOU'RE A DEAD MAN."

"There must be some mistake," Ashok says. "Mehnaz has no one else."

"Oh, Ashok, please stop it," Abha pleads tearfully. "Promise me you won't see her again."

"I can't." Ashok looks miserable. "I'm sorry." And two faces, one tear-stained, the other anguished, stare devastated into the camera.

Another performance by Mehnaz: this time Abha is in the auditorium, defiantly by her husband's side. Pranay stands in the wings and glowers alternately at his star and her lover. As Mehnaz, *payals* jingling, describes her feelings with fluid, circular motions of her arms, she trills:

> *So we have loved, why be afraid?*
> *We have loved, we haven't robbed a bank.*
> *For our love, we've just ourselves to thank.*
> *It's ours, not for others to trade.*
> *So we have loved, why be afraid?*
>
> *So we have loved, where lies the shame?*
> *We have loved, we haven't hit and run.*
> *Our love's as natural as the sun.*
> *Just the two of us need breathe its name.*
> *So we have loved, where lies the shame?*

Abha, stony-faced, nestles closer to Ashok in her seat. Mehnaz addresses the song directly to him. Pranay takes time off from gritting his teeth to take generous swigs from a bottle of Vat 69 in the wings.

After the show the inevitable occurs. (This is, after all, a Hindi film.) Overruling Abha, Ashok goes to greet Mehnaz. Pranay, his speech slurred, accosts him. Ashok tells him to sleep off his drunkenness. Pranay lashes out. There is a fistfight, the only one in the film. Ashok shows his stuff, and Pranay is left considerably the worse for wear. "Next time," he whispers as the blood dribbles down his chin, "next time I will use a gun."

The following day: Abha goes to Mehnaz, who admits her in courteous surprise. "I am his *dharampatni*," Abha says, his eternal wife. They have a child, Ashok has a future in his father's business. The lives of so many are at stake, above all the happiness of an innocent infant. She earnestly pleads with Mehnaz to relinquish her husband.

Mehnaz is moved. "I have been selfish in seeking to extract a small bit of happiness for myself and Ashok. But I now see that it is at your expense, and that of your child. Never fear, Abha. As a woman

I know what love means. I will do the right thing." (If there are still any dry eyes in the house, the strains of violins on the sound track should be enough to produce tears in them.)

The climactic scene: Ashok and Mehnaz are on stage, performing together. Our hero sits on a dhurrie, singing, while Mehnaz dances around him. The song is familiar, but the lyrics have changed:

ASHOK:

> *Where are you, my love?*
> *Of you I can't have enough.*
> *You have taken my heart*
> *And kept it with you,*
> *Now no one can start*
> *To part me from you.*
> *Wh-e-e-re are you, my love?*

MEHNAZ:

> *Where are you, my love?*
> *You float away like the clouds above.*
> *You have taken my heart*
> *And made my life new,*
> *But now we must part*
> *For I must give you your due.*
> *Wh-e-e-re are you, my love?*

Ashok looks troubled by this departure from the script, but Abha, in the audience, understands the sacrifice Mehnaz will make, and her eyes fill with tears.

But it's not yet over. As the song goes on, Pranay appears in the wings, his eyes bloodshot, his feet unsteady. He is carrying a gun.

The audience of extras cannot see him; the movie audience can. Ashok, his back to the wings, cannot see him either; nor at first can Mehnaz. But as she turns in her dance, she realizes to her horror that Pranay has raised his weapon and is aiming it directly at Ashok. She throws herself directly on her lover as Pranay fires—once, twice, the bark of the revolver punctuating the music and bringing the sound track to a screeching halt.

There are screams, Abha's the loudest. She rushes up onto the stage. Mehnaz lies in Ashok's arms, blood oozing from her wounds. Pranay breaks down, crying, "Oh, Mehnaz, what have I done?" He is promptly handcuffed by two culturally inclined policemen. Ashok cradles our heroine's head in his hands. Abha kneels by her side. "Call a doctor!" Ashok shouts. But Mehnaz smiles poignantly and shakes her head.

"It's too late," she says faintly. "I don't have much longer. Give me your hand." Abha obliges. With difficulty, Mehnaz moves Abha's hand toward Ashok's and joins them. Close-up: husband and wife's hands linked forever, smeared by the blood of the Other Woman.

"Mehnaz," Ashok pleads, "don't leave me." She smiles sadly. "I would have left you anyway," she breathes. "Be good to Abha."

Then the light dies in her eyes, and a drop of red blood drips onto the medallion of the dancing goddess at her wrist. Ashok and Abha look at each other.

"She was," Abha says, "a truly noble woman."

Closing shot: Ashok stands with his arm around Abha, a child by their side, as the flames from Mehnaz's funeral pyre lick up to a bloodred sky. The long notes of "Where are you, my love?" fill the sound track and on the flames appear the words

THE END.

Interval

DARLINGS, nothing can really shock your worldly Cheetah, but shouldn't we draw the line at bigamy? Rumors have reached our scalded ears that one of our more irrepressible shooting stars, who used to be called up-and-*coming* for more reasons than one, has been going around whispering about a secret marriage to a megastar! The libel laws don't allow Cheetah the dubious pleasure of purring their names, sweethearts, but the hitch is, the hero in question is already hitched!! Of course, if you want to give his ladylove the benefit of the doubt, he *could* have converted to Islam for the purpose, since that considerate faith allows a legal escape from the monotony of monogamy, but Cheetah has seen no evidence of that — and believe me, wicked ones, Cheetah knows where to look! Grrowl . . .

MORE, DARLINGS, on the mysterious marital goings-on around Bollywood. Remember Cheetah told you last week about the star who'd allegedly put his light into eclipse by "marrying" one of his satellites? To be honest, little cubs, your Cheetah didn't take it all too seriously, because the uninhibited source of the story isn't exactly famous for needing a wedding ring before making the bedding sing.

Why would anyone, let alone the straying superstar in question, need to marry her? Or so Cheetah thought, and that was fair enough, wouldn't you say, darlings? Well, the lady (and we may as well call her that, until the mystery man says, "that's no lady, that's my wife!") is deeply offended by Cheetah's suggestion that she has been playing fast and loose with (among other things) the truth. The newly respectable Mrs. says she can even name the temple where the ceremony actually occurred! Can you believe it, darlings, a temple! After all, God only knows what goes on in Bollywood, eh? Grrrowl...

PARDON MY BREATHLESSNESS, darlings, but things are really hotting up in Bollywood's Bigamous Boudoirs! Remember the trail your Cheetah has relentlessly sniffed out over the last few weeks? Well, it certainly seems that there's some fire beneath the smoke, after all. The jungle tom-toms tell Cheetah that a garland was indeed draped around one of the screen's more swanlike necks, though it's other portions of her anatomy that usually need draping! The *suhaag* story is only marred by the fact that the man is already married. And that his original *dharampatni* is far from amused. Bollywood's know-it-alls speak in hushed whispers of her righteous fury when the Other Woman's name is even mentioned. Which is more than slightly awkward, since the three of them are actually doing a movie together! What a set of tangled vines for Cheetah's little cubs to figure out, eh? Just put two and two together and you'll come up with a ménage à trois! Grrrrowl...

TO MOVE to more mundane matters, darlings, what is arch-villain Pranay doing making so many trips to the land of Araby? Cheetah's invariably well-informed sources speak of many a flying visit to the modern souks of Dubai, which of course is better spelled "Do-buy." So villainy must be paying! It seems the man with the evil mustache is much seen in the company of an expatriate desi businessman, Nadeem Elahi, who is reported to be in "import-export." Now there's a phrase that conceals a multitude of sins, eh, darlings? But it wouldn't be fair of Cheetah to point out that the principal export of Dubai, at least until oil came along, was gold to our own ill-protected shores, would it? No, Cheetah much prefers some more innocent explanation. Really, with our filmi smuggler's thinning hair, it would be *too too* boring if life imitated art so *baldly!* Grrrowl . . .

REALLY, DARLINGS, what *is* happening on the sets of *Dil Ek Qila,* Jagannath Choubey's much-touted multistarrer that's supposed to mark the comeback of ex–national sweetheart Maya Kumari? Bollywood is rife with stories of flashing tempers and stormy walkouts, script changes and sullen sulks — and that's all offscreen! It's no secret, of course, to Cheetah's well-read little cubs (especially those who read well between the lines!) that the film's two female stars don't exactly see eye-to-contact lens with each other. And neither has to look very far for the cause of their mutual dislike — not much beyond their bedrooms, if Cheetah makes herself clear! Indeed, some of the problems on the set are not entirely unrelated to other matters we've chattered about in recent weeks, but sorry, darlings, the libel lawyers won't let me say more. Meanwhile, producer Jagannath Choubey's bills are mounting every day and director Mohanlal has been seen popping tranquilizers as if they were *golgappas.* Question of the week, darlings: will *Dil Ek Qila* ever get completed, and if it does, will anyone recognize it as the film Choubeyji's enthusiastic PR-wallahs were telling us about months ago? As the costume man said to the actress, I have my doubts on both points! Grrrowl . . .

DARLINGS, whoever heard of a *good* villain? Well, it seems our nasty old Pranay, he of the *paan*-stained mouth and the evil leer, has a heart of gold, and that *isn't* a snide reference to his visits to Dubai, I swear! It seems the man every woman loves to hate has actually set up a fund for Junior Artistes, the long-suffering small-fry we can't bring ourselves to call "extras," *and* he puts in a percentage of his take from every movie he does, as well. Now *there's* an example for some of our *heroes* to follow, eh? Grrowl . . .

NOW ALL YOU faithful little cubs know that Cheetah doesn't waste time on soulful gush, don't you? We only chatter about the sinful and the salacious. But Cheetah heard something soulful today that's too-too interesting to pass up. Remember the unnameable bigamist you've heard all those whispers about? Well, he was in a confiding mood the other day, over a glass of Cheetah's favourite libation, but — alas! — strictly off the record. Which means it's OK to quote him as long as we don't mention his name (or height), eh? So gather round, little cubs, and Cheetah will tell you a slightly longer story than usual!

Well, we asked our friend, why the first marriage, and why the second? He looked intensely into the amber pool in his glass and breathed, almost to himself: "You marry someone. Because she seems right, because everyone else loves her, because you want your father's approval. Even if you've never admitted to yourself, let alone to him, that you want your father's approval. And at first it feels great. Everyone admires her, envies you. Wonderful. Then, after a while, the magic fades. You lose interest in her. Not all of a sudden, but gradually, inevitably. You can't do anything about it. But you don't want to lose her either. It's not as if you dislike her or anything, or are desperate to get rid of her. In any case, it's too late for that: there's the fear of scandal, there are the kids, there's the guilt, and there's the fear of, once more, letting yourself down in your father's eyes. So you go on. You tell yourself it doesn't matter: you'll find your own escapes."

And doesn't *she* notice? "Perhaps. I don't know. Of course she has her own frustrations. But it's different for women." (You can imagine how much self-restraint it took for Cheetah to let *that* pass, darlings.) "Anyway, you're always conscious of your own escapes, your own betrayals, so when you're with her you try to be considerate. You give in to whatever she wants. You avoid quarrels, resentments, anything that'll bring your own duplicity up and into the open. You do and say what's necessary, no more. Out of guilt, yes, and because there's no point in fighting. It's the least you can do for her. It's *all* you can do for her. What you want for yourself you get elsewhere."

And, I can hear you asking, little cubs, what about the Other Woman? "Well, you have no illusions about why you're with *her,* what you want out of her. She's your escape, your pleasure, no more, no less. Problem is, you think you've made that all clear to her, but it's never clear enough. She expects things, things you can't give her, never intended to give her. Attention. Engagement. Commitment. She wants to feel special, too, and however special you make her feel by being with her, there's one thing your wife has that she doesn't: your ring. Your name. A connection to you in the eyes of society and the eyes of God. You keep dismissing it, but in the end the pressure keeps mounting. You've either got to give in or give up — give her up.

"So of course you try to find some sort of compromise. You can't give her any of the public acknowledgment she wants, of course — you can't make her yours in the eyes of the world. So in a moment of weakness, after a sleepless night in her arms and bombed out of your mind anyway, you give her the next best thing — you tell her you'll make her your wife in the eyes of God. Before you quite know what you're doing you get her to pull on her sari and you trot bleary-eyed at dawn to a temple on the rocks with a garland you've bought on the beach, and drop it over her head in front of the idol. No witnesses, not even a priest. Of course you tell her God has blessed your nuptials and that's far better than the blessings of society. But no sooner have you done it than you've got to stagger home and look at yourself in the mirror and confront the enormity of what you've done. And then you find you can't face her again. You can't deal with her on this new footing you've placed yourself on. You did it to preserve the relationship, but in fact you've made the relationship impossible."

So he stops seeing her! Just like that — can you imagine? And what about the fact that the starry-eyed paramour is going around smearing red on her forehead and coyly referring to an anonymous "husband"?

"That's her problem, not mine. I'd tell her to stop it but I can't even bring myself to speak to her."

Sad, stirring stuff, isn't it, darlings? Cheetah was so moved she promptly gave him another drink — by emptying the glass on top of his head! GRRROWL . . . !

DARLINGS, Cheetah was at a Bollywood party with a difference the other day. Seems our villain with a social conscience, Pranay, has political commitments too! The man best known for flogging celluloid peasants and ripping bodices off vamps played host to a Delhi VIP last week while producers and distributors tried to look knowledgeable about national issues. The party was to introduce the well-heeled and high-heeled of filmland to Dr. Sourav Gangoolie, national treasurer of the ruling party and behind-the-scenes confidante of the Prime Minister, no less! Despite some notable absentees (including Bollywood's only ministerial offspring, Ashok "completely-uninterested-in-politics" Banjara), Pranay's bash has to be counted as a success for the *paan*-stained veteran. The dapper Dr. Gangoolie, who is not much seen in the public eye but has a reputation for shrewdness and getting things done, was able to meet an assortment of Bollywood luminaries. He spoke affably to all and sundry, but there was a determined glint in his bespectacled eyes as he squeezed the pudgier hands. After all, there's an election around the corner and Dr. G. is supposed to be the party's principal fund-raiser. And funds are one commodity Bollywood isn't exactly short of, especially of the undeclared variety (but of course Cheetah's just being naughty, little cubs, and the libel lawyers can relax)!! Who'd have thought our Pranay had a top politico up his sleeve, darlings? Mark my words — the best villains always have more to them than meets the eye. Which in Pranay's case is just as well, eh? Grrowl . . .

STOP THE PRESS! Remember the soulful confessions of the straying superstar in these pages a couple of weeks ago? Well, the Wronged Woman (or is she simply the Wrong Woman?) has been pouring her heart out to your Cheetah, darlings, and it's all sizzling stuff! Unfortunately, these lawyers are *such* a bore, my cubs, they just won't let me print it all. Anyway, the burden of her song is that marriage was all *his* idea in the first place — (sorry, *His* idea, she insists I write it with a capital *H*) — and that it's merely set the seal of divine sanction on their holy union. Can you believe such a thing, darlings? But what amazed Cheetah even more was how she went on about Him and what a great influence He is on her life and how she wouldn't let anyone speak a word against Him because He is her Force, her be-all and end-all. Now Cheetah knows this is usually how actresses sound when their ends no longer justify their jeans and the time comes to discover religion, but the lady in question is in her prime and her hero's no one's idea of an idol. Wonders will never cease! Stay tuned, darlings — the lady's nothing if not "revealing," and there may be more revelations to come! Grrowl . . .

TUT, TUT, DARLINGS, all is not well between Bollywood's hottest screen twosome, at least not after the spectacular fiasco of their *Dil Ek Qila,* which is finding it difficult to survive its initial week in most theaters! When Ashok Banjara walked into producer Jagannath Choubey's glittering Diwali bash the other evening (and what a bash it was, my little cubs, more sparkle than a mineful of diamonds, and fireworks to put Venice to shame) guess who should make a beeline for him, slinky in a silvery *salwar-kameez,* but his recent costar Mehnaz Elahi! And guess who walked past without a greeting, as if he could see right through her!! The poor little itch girl stood helplessly in the middle of the room, her seductive smile turning into a strained simper. Of course this was for all of six seconds, before she was surrounded by her usual sea of admirers and swept away to another shore, but six seconds is long enough for your Cheetah to notice, my cubs! It was not long before the room was abuzz with speculation, much of it asking what Bollywood was coming to if one flop, even such a *maha* flop, could do this to relations between two friends and colleagues. Some people were already renaming the film *Dil Ek Killer*! Cheetah, as always, knew more than she was prepared to say — but as The Banjara knows so well, some things are better done than said, eh? Think about that, my little cubs! Grrrrowl . . .

END OF INTERVAL
BACK TO MAIN FEATURE

Exterior: Night

DIL EK QILA
(The Heart Is a Fortress)

THE SECOND TREATMENT: THE REVISED VERSION

A hillside in Kashmir. The camera pans across azure sky, verdant slopes, technicolor flowers. Maya runs laughing across the screen to the strains of a dozen violins as Ashok Banjara pursues her, singing:

> *You are my sunlight*
> *You brighten my life*
> *You are my sunlight*
> *Come be my wife.*

He finally catches up with her and hugs her from behind: she continues trying to flee and they roll down the hill, locked in an embrace. Close-up: their laughing lips are about to meet when the camera swings skyward and the opening credits fill the screen.

Domestic scene: Maya with her parents, Godambo and Abha, in their luxurious, indeed palatial, home. Early moments of dialogue establish father's strength (deep, gravelly voice), wealth (expensive rings on fingers), and traditionalism (caste mark on forehead). Maya gets to the point: "Father, I would like to get married." "Excellent," says Godambo: he has been thinking along the same lines. It is time Maya settled down. It would be good for her and, provided a suitable son-in-law was found, good for the business also.

Maya looks uncomfortable. "Father, there is already a man whom I wish to marry."

"What!" Outrage on Godambo's face, consternation in his bulging eyes. Abha rolls her own pupils heavenward and mutters a brief invocation. "And who can this be?" asks the paterfamilias.

"It's someone I met at the music class," Maya says nervously. "He's a very fine person and a wonderful singer. Let me bring him home to meet you. I'm sure you'd like him."

"Wait!" Godambo is a man of procedure. "Before you bring any such person to our house, let me make some inquiries. Tell me everything you know about him. Who is the man? What is his name? Is he of good family? Who are his parents? Do we know them, and if not, why not? Where does he live? What is his profession?" And Abha adds, "Is he tall?"

"Yes, he is," Maya answers her mother, but one useful response does not get her off the hook. Godambo is not to be diverted. Squirming under his relentless probing, Maya has to admit that her beau is neither rich nor well connected. "But he is a great musician," she says with deep-pupiled intensity. "And I love him."

"Love?" Godambo barks. "What is love?"

"Love," Abha explains maternally," is something that comes after marriage, Maya. I love you, I love your father. How can you love a stranger?"

"He's not a stranger, Mother," Maya begins, then realizes it is hopeless. "Look, if only you both would meet him, you would see immediately what I mean." But her father is reluctant to take matters so far as to welcome this impecunious interloper into his own living room. Then Maya has an idea. "Come and see him at the Cultural Evening tonight," she pleads.

Godambo is not interested, but Abha, ever the obliging mother, persuades him on behalf of her daughter.

Scene: an auditorium, every seat full. Maya and her parents are escorted to a front row. The curtain parts to reveal a stage with the painted backdrop of twin snow-covered mountain peaks. The symbolism is made even more obvious as Mehnaz enters in a cascade of anklets, covered head to foot in kathak costume of billowing blue skirt, peak-hugging blue blouse, blue head scarf, and blue leggings, all spangled with silver. Godambo grunts appreciatively. Ashok, seated on a dhurrie on the stage, bursts into song:

My heart beats for you,
I'd perform feats for you,
You are the landlord of my soul;
My eyes light for you,
I'd gladly fight for you,
Without you I don't feel whole.

As he sings and Mehnaz dances, all arched hip and elegant finger-tips, Ashok manages to exchange meaningful glances with Maya in the audience, making it clear every word of the playback applies to her. Meanwhile, Godambo, oblivious to this byplay, appears to enjoy himself hugely. When the song is over the audience bursts into well-rehearsed applause, and Godambo rises to his feet to clap vigorously.

At the end of the show, Godambo, in mellow spirits, looks around the hall. "So shall we meet your young man now?" he asks.

"Oh, yes, thank you, Papa!" Maya exclaims, bright-eyed. "Did you like him?"

"That boy," Godambo's eyes bulge with pleasure, "has the making of a very great singer indeed."

Backstage Mehnaz is cooing to Ashok. "Wasn't that wonderful, darling?" she asks, placing her hands on Ashok's shoulder. "You and I," she adds huskily, "can make beautiful music together."

Ashok disengages himself. "Excuse me, Mehnaz," he says. "I have an important appointment."

Mehnaz tosses her hair in displeasure and flounces out of the dressing room.

Ashok emerges from the auditorium, looking handsome and poised. After he deferentially greets Maya's parents, they get into Godambo's chauffeur-driven Impala.

When Mehnaz, now freshly changed into a slinky *salwar-kameez*, emerges from the auditorium, she sees Ashok — a look of eager expectation on his face — shutting the car door behind him. Mehnaz is left staring crestfallen and resentful into the camera as the Impala drives away into the future with an optimistic squeal of its white-walled tires.

Next scene: Ashok with his parents, in their lower-middle-class home. The decor is conventional: pale-green walls, peeling ceiling, plastic-covered sofa, garish calendars of androgynous deities. His father, Ramkumar, is poor but dignified, and anxious about his son's

choice. Marriage, he points out, has to do with more than mere attraction. Could Ashok cope with the stresses of being married to the
daughter of Seth Godambo, of having a wife wealthier and more important than himself? And what about them? Marriage is not just a
relationship between individuals, but an arrangement between families. Ashok would not just be marrying one woman, he would be
acquiring another family. Could he see his own simple father and
sari-swathed mother socializing in Seth Godambo's living room?
Ashok has to admit he cannot.

Yet when his parents finally meet Maya, they are charmed by her
sweetness and simplicity, her modesty and manners. "But she's wonderful!" Ramkumar beams. "She's just the kind of girl we would have
wanted to arrange for you to marry," he adds. "Despite your obsession
with music, you must still have something of me in you if you look
for the same qualities in a wife that we would in a daughter-in-law."

Maya blushes modestly, her smile dimpling her slim cheeks.

It is later, at dusk; Ashok and Maya are running through a palm
grove near the beach. Maya wears a sari and a joyous expression. The
flow of the tide caresses the shore, sending up froth that seems to
gurgle happily in celebration of our heroine's love. The sun's rays
bathe her beauty in a golden radiance as she runs through the grove,
and Ashok, losing sight of her among the trees, sings with feeling:

> *Where are you, my love?*
> *I wait for light from the sun above.*
> *You have taken my heart*
> *And hid it from view,*
> *Now the trees will not part*
> *To bring me to you.*
> *Wh-e-e-re are you, my love?*

And Maya's answer comes echoing through the palm fronds: "I-I-
I'm he-e-re." Ashok grins in delight and resumes the chase.

Five verses later, he has caught her. They embrace, and her last answer is a lilting whisper: "I-I-I'm here." Ashok's head moves toward
hers, and the camera caresses the waves as they wash the shore. . . .

Afterward, Maya and Ashok walk by the sea, now calm in ama-
tory contentment. Ashok buys a small garland of white flowers for
Maya to wear in her hair. Impulsively, she slips off her necklace and
gives it to Ashok. "Keep this," she says, "as a memento of my love."

It is a thin chain, strung through a medallion of a dancing goddess. Ashok kisses the medallion, then gives it back to her. "How can I wear a necklace?" he asks with a laugh. "Wear it on your wrist," Maya suggests, "like a bracelet." Ashok loops the chain three times around his wrist, the medallion resting on it like a watch. "Don't try and tell the time with it," Maya giggles. "Any time is a good time," Ashok responds, "to think of how much I love you."

Scene: Godambo with Mehnaz Elahi. "I enjoyed your performance at the Cultural Evening last night," he says gutturally. "I would like to engage you for a very special occasion."

Mehnaz is shrewdly obliging.

"You see, my daughter is getting married," Godambo goes on. "And we are celebrating it in a big way, as befits an alliance involving one of the city's biggest families. I would like to have an entertainment show worthy of the occasion. And I would like you to dance at the wedding. Especially since the bridegroom is an associate of yours."

"An associate?" Mehnaz clearly hasn't heard about Ashok's plans.

"Ashok Banjara," Godambo says with pride. "Why, hasn't he told you?"

"There is a lot," Mehnaz replies with a set expression, "that Ashok doesn't tell me."

"Well," Godambo says, looking uncomfortable, "will you perform at the occasion anyway?"

"Of course." Mehnaz's tone is dull.

"Good. So you will come for the event? Three weeks from now. I hope you are free."

"Oh — three weeks from today." Mehnaz is quick to make the most of a bad job. "I am afraid I cannot accept your invitation, Sethji. You see, I have a prior commitment in Bombay. Of course, I could try to change it. . . ."

"You must," Godambo insists, "or I would be most disappointed. And," he says, looking at her with the eye of an experienced businessman, "I would of course be happy to double your fee on this happy occasion."

"In that case," says Mehnaz happily, "how can I let you down for such an important event?"

And so to the wedding. As the ceremony progresses, complete with demure bride dripping with gold, catered food dripping with ghee, and overladen bar dripping with Scotch, Mehnaz, gazing wistfully at the bridegroom, dances for her supper as a temporary accompanist sings a variant of Ashok's song:

> *Where are you, my love?*
> *I wait for light from the neon above.*
> *You have taken my heart*
> *And hid it from view,*
> *Now the marriage mart*
> *Has deprived me of you.*
> *Wh-e-e-re are you, my love?*

But this time there is no answer.

It is some years later. Maya is seated on a dhurrie on the floor, taking music lessons from a maestro with a harmonium. "Very good," says the maestro, Asrani, an actor more usually seen in the role of stock comedian. "Now once again: sa-ri-ga-ma-pa-da-ni-sa." He tosses his head back with a tonal flourish as he runs through the scale. "Now you."

Maya dutifully echoes her guru: "Sa-ri-ga-ma-pa-da-ni-sa."

"Not bad," says the maestro. "But there is something missing." He taps his belly, producing a percussion note like the glug of a drowning diver, and resumes. "Sa-ri-ga-ma-pa-da-ni-sa."

Maya smiles prettily and in turn tosses her head. "Sa-ri-ga-ma-pa-da-ni-sa."

"You're getting it," says the maestro. "See, it's simple:

> Sa, *salary, monthly cash flow,*
> Ri, *receipt for getting same;*
> Ga, *garment, when bank is working slow,*
> Ma, *materialism's no shame;*
> Pa, *paupers can't teach a thing,*
> Da, daal-bhat *costs a lot,*
> Ni, *needs are what make me sing —*
> *and that brings us back to sa — something you forgot?"*

Maya's brow unfurrows in comprehension. "You haven't been paid," she says in contrition. "I'm so sorry, Panditji."

"An able pupil," exclaims the maestro. "Music may be the riches of the soul, but the soul of music requires riches. Or at least a humble pittance."

As Maya hurries to her safe to pay her teacher, the maestro remarks on how good she has become. "Very good indeed," he pronounces, nodding in satisfaction at the notes she is deferentially offering him. "What made you want to take up singing?"

The camera lingers in close-up on Maya's poignantly inexpressive face. "I used to take lessons, years ago," she says, a faraway gaze in her eyes. "That's how I met my husband. I gave up singing when I married him. But now, my husband spends more and more time on his music. When he leaves, I feel he is taking the music out of my life. I decided the only thing I could do was to learn it myself so that I could join his world."

"*Wah, wah,*" responds Asrani heartily. It is not clear whether his appreciation is for the sentiment or the money he has just finished counting.

There follow a couple of scenes that establish Ashok in affectionate domesticity: scenes involving his beautiful wife and dutiful children. Intercut with these are scenes of his professional relationship with Mehnaz: he sings as she dances, her sighs in his direction completely unrequited.

Scene: Maya is about to give her first public performance as a singer. And she is introduced fulsomely to a large audience by none other than her own father, Seth Godambo.

"As you know, my son-in-law is a very good singer," Godambo orates. "And in this domain he is now joined by the not inconsiderable talents of his wife, my daughter, Maya." (Applause.) "She is a good wife, but what is not so widely known is that she also has a musical soul. And she has kindly agreed today, under the able guidance and instruction of Pandit Asrani" — the maestro, his mouth full of *paan,* takes an affable bow — "to sing for you today, all in the cause of charity, of course." Godambo nods, but even without this cue the extras in their seats applaud the winsome debutant with rare enthusiasm.

Her aesthetic inclinations thus rendered socially respectable, Maya launches into song:

> *All I want is to sing for you*
> *Because, you know, I've this thing for you,*
> *That throbs in every note;*
> *All I want is to be with you*
> *Because, you know, I can't be free with you,*
> *If music sticks in my throat.*

Her diffidence slips away with every verse, and at the end the audience is on its feet, applauding, all except Mehnaz, who gets up from her seat at the back of the hall, her mouth set in a thin line of resentment, and slips out.

Maya goes from success to success. In a series of quick cuts, she is shown performing in overflowing halls to standing ovations, receiving prizes and awards, and being featured on posters and in neon lights. Meanwhile, Ashok's career fades. He and Mehnaz are seen in nondescript theaters before dwindling crowds, his name set in increasingly smaller print on shabby notices, while Maya's name and face glow in every newspaper. His expression becomes increasingly lugubrious as Maya continues to receive accolades. And after one performance, as everyone else claps, Ashok is seen turning away and walking out of the hall.

"Depressing, isn't it?" Mehnaz, her curves enhanced by a slinky dress, is by his side in a nearby garden; she is carrying a snakeskin handbag. "To see all this adulation, when true talent like yours goes unrecognized?"

Ashok sees no hint of sarcasm in the question. "I'm happy for Maya," he says, sounding far from it. "But sometimes . . ."

"Sometimes you wish this hobby of hers would leave some room for the professionals like us," Mehnaz says shrewdly, her pectorals heaving in sympathy. "People don't applaud her singing, Ashok. They're in love with her, the simple girl-next-door with the looks and manners of a housewife, a woman who looks as if she'd sooner offer you a cup of tea than charge you admission to hear her sing. The crowds love it: they go and sit there, and they look at her, and it doesn't matter how well she sings or how much better we — I mean you — do. Style and glamour are passé, Ashok." Mehnaz undulates with regret as she turns toward him. "No one wants excitement any more. Simplicity is in."

Ashok looks at her. "I rather like style and glamour myself," he says, in a tone that suggests he does not admit his other meaning, even to himself. "Not everyone rejects excitement."

"It took you a long time to recognize it, Ashok," Mehnaz responds huskily. "Come to my place, I'll give you a drink."

"But . . . Maya . . ." Ashok's protest is feeble.

"She's so busy being felicitated, she won't even notice," says Mehnaz. "Her manager can take her home. Come on."

And with only a brief, hesitant glance toward the hall where his faithful wife is receiving her due, Ashok is led from the garden by the temptress with the snakeskin bag. An apple litters the path, and Mehnaz kicks it aside with the tip of a high-heeled shoe.

Inside the hall Maya turns to her manager, Pranay, an energetic operator who has been seen earlier organizing backstage, berating auditorium factotums, arranging for Maya to be garlanded. Maya's gentle features are clouded in apprehension.

"Ashok doesn't seem to be anywhere," she says. "What do you think could have happened?"

"He must have got tired of waiting," Pranay says. "Don't worry, I'll take you home."

"It's not like Ashok," Maya says, her dark eyes troubled. "I hope he's all right. He hasn't seemed himself of late. I hope he isn't sick."

"He'll be all right," Pranay retorts unsympathetically. "If you want my opinion, the only thing he's sick of is your success."

"How dare you say that!" Maya blazes at him loyally. "How dare you!"

"Take it easy." Pranay backs off. "No offense meant. But the fact is that he's less and less happy with your good fortune. I've been watching him closely, Maya. You and I have been together too long for me to hide these things from you."

"If you go on saying these things, Pranay" — Maya's delicate nostrils flare with rage — "you and I won't be together much longer. Ashok's my husband. He doesn't even *think* like that."

"Fine." Pranay concedes. "He's *your* husband. Just forget I said anything."

But the seed of doubt has been planted in Maya's furrowed mind. "Where do you think he is now?" she asks.

"I don't know," Pranay says guardedly. "Seeking consolation of some sort, I suppose."

"You mean sitting in some bar drinking himself silly in self-pity?" snorts Maya derisively. "Huh — that shows how much you know Ashok. He's not like that at all. Take me home. I'm sure I'll find him there."

"I'll take you," says Pranay. "But remember, drink isn't the only consolation there is."

The audience knows that, because Ashok and Mehnaz are in a

warm room with a log fire. (Note: this is Kashmir, remember?) Each sports a glass and a smoldering look. They circle each other, the glow from the fire reflected in the heat on their faces. Mehnaz sings:

> *You and me, locked in a room,*
> *And I have lost the key.*
> *You and me, locked in a room,*
> *And I know you want me.*

ASHOK JOINS IN:

> *You and me, locked in a room,*
> *And I have shut the door.*
> *You and me, locked in a room,*
> *With a rug upon the floor.*

MEHNAZ:

> *The look in your eyes*
> *Is really no surprise*

(SHE LIES DOWN)

> *And I'm not prone to argue.*

ASHOK:

> *There's nothing shoddy*
> *About your body*

(HE BENDS TOWARD HER)

> *And I've only seen the far view.*

TOGETHER:

> *You and me, locked in a room,*
> *With only each other for comfort.*
> *You and me, locked in a room . . .*

Ashok is almost upon her. The camera shows two logs burning, the flames licking toward each other. Then suddenly the logs fuse, and the fire spurts upward in a searing triangle.

Maya is still awake when Ashok returns home. They are both red-eyed, for different reasons.

"Where have you been?" she asks.

"Out."

"I can see that. But where? Have you been drinking?"

"Yes."

"And?"

"And what?"

"Don't you have anything to tell me?"

"No. Do you?"

In the face of his belligerence, Maya bites her lip in silence.

"Well? Do you?"

She says nothing, but the tears well up in her limpid eyes.

"No? Good. In that case, good night." And Ashok throws himself on the bed, while Maya, sitting with her knees drawn up against her chest, sinks her chin into her folded arms and weeps through the night.

It is the next day. "I'm sorry, Pranay. I don't feel like singing this evening. Please cancel the show."

"What has happened? You sound terrible, Maya." Pranay takes her chin in his hands and removes the dark glasses with which she has covered the evidence of her tears. "My God, you've been crying. What's the matter?" She does not answer. "Is it Ashok?"

Maya averts her gentle face so that only the camera can see the pain in her eyes. "Please don't ask me, Pranay."

"Why not? Do you have a better friend than me in the whole world?"

"No, of course not, Pranay," sobs Maya. "You're a wonderful friend, and a great manager. It's not you. It's just that I can't talk about this . . . to anybody."

Pranay is bewildered. "But why? Did he beat you?"

"No," she sniffs, shaking her head for emphasis. "It's worse."

Comprehension dawns on Pranay. "So I was right, wasn't I?" he asks. "He was out seeking consolation" — she nods miserably — "with a woman. My God, I even know which woman."

"Witch-woman," echos Maya.

"Mehnaz," breathes Pranay, "of course." He turns to her with a sudden onrush of passion. "Maya, that man is not worthy of you. Leave him, Maya. Come with me. I shall look after you the way I have looked after your singing."

"Stop!" Maya's face is again awash with her sorrow. "Pranay, how can you even speak like that! Ashok is my husband, my *dharampati*. I can never think of leaving him."

"But Maya, stop thinking only of your duty to him! What about your duty to yourself?"

"My duty to my husband *is* to myself," Maya says slowly, as portentous music fills the sound track. "When I married Ashok I gave my heart to him, and my life. I cannot love anyone else ever again."

"But look at the way he is treating you," says Pranay angrily.

Maya does not answer.

"Don't waste your life like this, Maya," Pranay pleads.

"My life is committed," Maya says nobly. "There is no waste in fulfilling my dharma as a wife. But I do not intend to sit idly and let my husband drift away from me. I must have done something wrong. I shall undo it now and win my husband back."

(Respectful applause from the twenty-five-paisa seats.)

Ashok is on stage, singing as Mehnaz dances. But his eyes are not on her: he has a sad, wistful expression on his face as he gazes soulfully at the dress circle and sings:

> *Where are you, my love?*
> *I wait for light from the stars above.*
> *You have taken my heart*
> *And hid it from view,*
> *Life has kept us apart*
> *And rid me of you.*
> *Wh-e-e-re are you, my love?*

Where she is, is right there — for, unnoticed by Ashok, Maya has slipped into the audience, and she listens to him sing with tears glistening in her eyes.

The show is over, and Ashok is standing, palms joined in respectful *namaskar,* as a thin trickle of decrepit well-wishers congratulate him on his performance. Suddenly the look of distant politeness on Ashok's face vanishes as a soft voice cuts through the hubbub near him. "You sang beautifully, Ashok." Our hero looks up in shock at Maya standing among the debris on the stage.

"You! What are you doing here?"

"I just thought I'd come and watch you sing," she says softly. "Do you mind?"

"Mind? Of course not. It's just that — you haven't done this in a long time." Their eyes meet, and it is obvious even to the villagers in the twenty-five-paisa seats that nothing has changed between them.

"Why did you leave me that night, without even a word?" she asks intensely.

"Because I didn't think you cared whether I stayed or not," Ashok says miserably. "I wanted — oh, I don't know, attention, perhaps."

Attention is just what he's going to get, for Pranay suddenly appears, his eyes bloodshot, his feet unsteady. He is carrying a gun, which he points directly at Ashok.

Maya turns, sees him, and throws herself on the assailant. But she can only deflect the shot. Pranay fires — once, twice, the bark of the revolver punctuating the music and bringing the sound track to a screeching halt. Maya screams. Ashok collapses, bleeding profusely in Eastman color.

Scene: a hospital. Ashok lies swathed in an improbable array of bandages that carefully leave his face made-up and visible. Bottles drip assorted fluids into his veins. A worried Dr. Iftikhar tells Ashok's parents, "I am sorry, but the situation is serious. We cannot save your son without a rare type of blood. And yours," he tells the stricken Ramkumar, "does not match."

"But I have the same blood type as my husband's," Maya exclaims. "Please take whatever is necessary to save my *dharampati*'s life." Cymbals clash on the sound track as symbols flash on the screen.

"*Shabash*," says Dr. Iftikhar. (He has been waiting a long time to say it.)

After a few quick cuts (both cinematic and surgical), Ashok and Maya lie on adjoining cots, smiling wanly at each other. The precious red fluid drips into him from a large bottle suspended above his bed.

"You saved my life," Ashok declaims. She smiles in satisfied response.

Ashok, remarkably restored, goes on. "Oh, Maya, I've done a terrible thing. I've been untrue to you and to myself. I'm miserable, Maya. Won't you forgive me?"

"There is nothing to forgive, Ashok," Maya says, rising from her

bed to embrace her husband and placing her head against his chest. "I want to tell you something. I have decided to give up singing."

"What?" In his astonishment Ashok almost sits up, but he is drawn short by his tubes. "Give up singing! But why?"

"I only took it up to become closer to you, my husband," says Maya, as treacly notes drip through the sound track. "Instead it has only driven us apart. I don't need it. You give me all the music I need in my life."

"You're doing this for me," Ashok says in wonder. "What a noble woman you are, Maya! How could I ever have dreamed of betraying you?"

They look at each other in wordless communion.

A knock sounds at the door. It is Mehnaz. "I am leaving town, Ashok," she announces, to catcalls from the audience. She says to Maya, "I took something I had no right to. I must now return it to its true owner." And she drops a chain into Maya's palm. The medallion of the dancing goddess shines back at him as the dancing godless turns on her heel and walks out of their lives.

Scene: another Ashok performance, but this time there is no Mehnaz, no dance to accompany. Ashok is on center stage himself, having taken over the spot of the woman who now sits in the front row smiling adoringly at him, as he dedicates his impassioned and familiar melody to her:

> My heart beats for you,
> I'd perform feats for you,
> You are the mistress of my soul;
> My eyes light for you,
> I'd gladly fight for you,
> Without you I don't feel whole.

At the end of the song, as the rapturous audience exclaims their admiration, Ashok steps to the front of the stage. "As you know, I am singing to you today because my wife, Maya, has announced her decision to give up the stage," he declares. The crowd expresses its disappointment. "But I too do not wish her to abandon something that gives so many of you so much pleasure." Shouts of enthusiasm from the crowd. "Maya is determined not to pursue a single career.

So today I am proud to announce the birth of a new singing duo —
Maya and Ashok!"

The crowd erupts. Maya, taken aback, blushes bashfully in her
seat. Then, urged on by the crowd and by her own husband, she
walks up to the stage to stand by Ashok's side. Together, smiling,
they sing:

ASHOK:

Where are you, my love?
Of you I can't have enough.
You have taken my heart
And kept it with you,
Now no one can start
To part me from you.
Whe-e-e-re are you, my love?

MAYA:

Where are you, my love?
You shelter me like the roof above.
You have taken my heart
And made my life new,
We shan't ever part.
I'll always give you your due.
Whe-e-e-re are you, my love?

As they sing, Ashok's arm wound protectively around his wife,
Pranay smiling fraternally in the wings, the camera moves back, taking a long shot of them, the stage, the crowd. The long notes of
"Where are you, my love?" fill the sound track, and on the now-
distant image of the happy couple appear the words

THE BEGINNING.

Monologue: Day

MEHNAZ ELAHI

They wouldn't let me in, would you believe that? "Sorry, moddom," that lousy little Bong at the entrance to the intensive care unit said, "strict instructions. Doctor's orders." Doctor's orders my foot. I bet it was that shrewish little wife of yours. Honestly, what you saw in that woman is beyond me. I know, I know, I shouldn't be saying these things against your wonderful, saintly Maya. But as long as you're going to lie there and not tell me what I can and can't say, I'm going to say what I think. And what I think is that that precious Maya of yours is an absolutely insufferable little prig. There's nothing she wouldn't do to put me down, to humiliate me. Me! The only woman who's been a real woman to you.

"You mean you won't let *me* see Him?" I asked incredulously, and the Bong shivered, in this Bombay heat he shivered, I tell you. "If you don't let me through," I said, "I'll kick up such a fuss that this hospital will find itself torn to shreds in every film magazine in the country." Do you know how many film journalists are waiting outside? I'm asking you, Ashokji, not the Bong. At least twenty-five, I swear. "Do you want your name in all the papers, Mr. Bannerji, for being the banner-ji who banned Mehnaz Elahi from visiting her own husband?" That really shook him up, I can tell you. He looked around nervously, up and down the antiseptic corridors, and whispered through his crooked teeth. "Family all gone to lunch, moddom," he admitted. "You go in quickly now." So here I am.

I suppose I shouldn't have used the husband bit, since you seem to hate it so much now. But you didn't once, did you? When you took me to that temple and put a garland of marigolds around my neck and gave me your ring and said, "In the eyes of God we're man and wife"? Oh, I was so moved then, Ashokji. I thought you really meant it. Only afterward Salma said to me, "In the eyes of which God, hanh? If he really wanted to marry you, why did he take you to a temple, instead of converting to Islam and marrying you proper?" And I had no answer. I mean, I never expected you to leave your prissy little malnourished wife, but if you were a Muslim you could legally have two wives, know what I mean? Instead of doing this temple thing like all those other actors just to make the woman feel respectable while knowing full well that it hasn't any validity in anybody's eyes but God's. *If* He's looking. "Maybe *his* God was, but Allah certainly wasn't," Salma sniffed. OK, so I know she was just trying to make me feel bad, no film star is going to marry poor pimply Salma even as a third wife, poor thing, so she has to get her own back. But even then, I've got to admit she has a point, hasn't she? Go on, tell me, hasn't she?

But of course you can't. Look at you lying there, not saying a word, Ashokji, oh, it's enough to make me cry. Not that you said many a word when you were with me. Always desperately anxious to rip off my clothes you were. And the rest of the time, the real strong-and-silent type. But then you always said I did enough talking for the two of us.

And why not? My mind opened up when I was with you, Ashokji. Really opened up. All sorts of ideas filled my head. And not just the wicked ones you always accused me of! I mean, ideas about *really* important things. Like life, and love, and philosophy, and things. If I hadn't known what it was to be loved by you, I'd never have turned to the Guru.

Look at that — I've never even told you about the Guru. And whose fault is that, hanh? Ever since you entered politics, you've avoided me. Everyone's going to the Guru these days, simply everyone, except you. And God knows you need him more than most. I wanted to take you to him myself, but could I even get you on the phone? Only that wretched Subramanyam, saying "Sorry, miss, I not knowing." And you, you don't know what you're missing, I tell you. The way that Guru found me, even that was a miracle. The man is really incredible.

But as if you want to know anything about me these days. Me, your wife, Ashokji! OK, not your lawfully wedded wife, but what was it that witch Radha Sabnis called me — your "awfully bedded wife." I know you were angry when that temple marriage got into the magazines. What could I do? I was so lonely, so hurt when you stopped seeing me, Ashokji, my dearest, and I was simply pining for you, so I *had* to give those interviews. Will you ever forgive me? Will you? Well, why shouldn't you? After all, I never used your name. I always said "Him." With a capital *H* — I always told them to write it that way. Some young journalist-shernalist said we only write it that way when we write about God. And I said, so what, He was God to me.

I know some people laughed at me. And that you were angry, so angry you snubbed me in public by turning away from me at Jagan-nath Choubey's Diwali party. I bet your little shrew put you up to it. Why were you angry, darling? I hadn't broken my promise to you never to discuss our relationship in the press. I hadn't broken my promise because I never confirmed it was you I was talking about. Oh, I had to talk about the relationship, about the influence you had on my life, the Force you represented in my existence — did you like that at least, "the Force"? That was a word my Guru gave me. I had to, Ashokji, or it would have driven me crazy. All alone, knowing I was your wife and yet having none of the prerogatives, isn't that the word, of wifehood. Sometimes I wonder, why did you do it? I didn't ask for it. It was all your idea, this whole temple *chakkar*. You took me there, you bought the *mala,* you put it round my Muslim neck and pronounced me your Hindu wife. And ever since then you've tried to pretend it never happened. Oh, Ashokji, I'd have loved you with or without your *mala*. I want your love, not your name or your money. Why have you turned away from me, my life?

My Guru tells me I should learn to accept this. Learn detachment, he says. Take life as it comes. So I'm supposed to enjoy your atten-tion when you give it to me, ignore your slights, and don't let either touch — what does he call it? — the essential core of my being. Oh, it sounds so easy when the Guru says it. But when I'm sitting here, looking at you all silent and bandaged up, Ashokji, it's not easy at all. I want to weep, you know that? Weep. Even if I've got a shift to go to straight from here and it'll really mess me up.

I can imagine you saying, "Don't be melodramatic, Mehnaz." You were always saying things like that. What melodrama-shama did I inflict on you, hanh? OK, OK, the one time that I cut my wrist. But that was just a little cut, really, a skin cut, just to frighten you, just to make you stay. I saw in your eyes then that you didn't want me to die. That's all I wanted to see. I knew you'd have to go back to your little pocket edition of a wife afterward, anyway. But I wanted to see you wanting me, you know? Not just my body. Wanting me to live. That's why I did it. I know I shouldn't have. Don't mind, promise? It won't happen again. My Guru has told me never ever to do anything like that again. He saw it in my eyes, he said, that once I had tried to take my life. Can you imagine it? After that, I'd do anything for him. And I won't try suicide again, really I won't. I just wish you'd show me sometimes you need me. Show me that you're not only committed to that dried-up little minx, and I'll be as good as gold. Better, even, because gold isn't going up much these days. I wish you could see this necklace I'm — oh, never mind.

That's all I wanted, Ashokji, to matter to you. That's all I ever asked of you. Not just bang away at me when you needed me and then pretend in public I don't exist. Oh, I know you never promised you'd be anything else. Remember that first time, when I was practically melting in your arms, and I said, as a feeble last attempt at resistance, "But you're a married man"? And you said, in that voice of yours, God, that voice, "A married man is still a man." That was all I needed, that line, in that voice of yours, and with that look in your blazing eyes so bright it set me on fire. Of course I succumbed, I practically collapsed around you there and then, so I can't blame you, you know I never have. But later, when I told Salma what you'd said, she retorted, "A married man doesn't have to stay married — if he's a man."

Oh, you know Salma, I didn't take her words to heart or anything, not really. But deep down inside, I can't help feeling there just might be something to what she said. You were just trying to have it both ways, weren't you, Ashokji? You never intended to acknowledge me in any way, except with that hypocritical temple garlanding of yours, with no witnesses. No witnesses — yes, Salma pointed that out too, and I said that it just shows how spontaneous the whole thing was. And all she could say was, "Mehnaz, you poor sap, when are you going to stop fooling yourself? He knew exactly what he was doing. That man of yours, or rather *not* of yours, is a selfish, calculating bastard and the sooner you realize it the better." You know what I did? I told her to get out of my house. I screamed at her: "Out! Out! You jealous, pimply housewife, just because your husband can't get it up doesn't mean you've got to get me down! Get out!" And I really pushed her out of the house, you know. All for you. The things I did because of my love for you, Ashokji. Sometimes when I think about them I can't even believe it myself.

And what did you give me in exchange? Torment, neglect, humiliation. No, I'm not just being melodramatic, Mr. Ashok Banjara. Really, the things you made me put up with for you! I mean, how could you do to me what you did over *Dil Ek Qila?* A perfect script, tailor-made for me, a great Mehnaz Elahi part, and because I'm silly enough to be besotted with you, I ask them to cast you opposite me. Of course they were thrilled by the idea, everybody knew what was really going on between us, even if you pretended they didn't. Dream casting, they said, slobbering over the gossip columns. Dream casting.

So you get the script, and what do you do to it? You let that wife of yours take it over, change the story, destroy my part, control the film and drive it to ruin! Did you even try to protest, Ashokji? A perfectly good plot destroyed, all the thrill and suspense taken out, dollops of sacchariney sentimentality added that was bound to turn away the crowds. And I tried to tell you — but would you listen? No huzoor! Heaven forbid! I tell you, if it weren't for you and my contract, and not even in that order, I would have walked off that film on the first day. I could see what she was up to, the minx! But you, you were so blinded by your guilt, or whatever it was, you couldn't see anything but her tight little behind. Well, if she was such a loyal and noble little soul, Ashokji, what was Pranay doing in that film, once all the villainy had been cut out of the story? What was the need for him to be there at all? You tell me that, Mr. Devoted Husband. Go on. Tell me. Just try.

Not even that worked, hanh? Poor thing, you must be really bad.

The doctor says he can't understand it. Did I tell you I telephoned the doctor? He was absolutely thrilled to be speaking with me, I tell you. "Miss Mehnaz Yelahi, yis it yactually?" He was practically gurgling with pleasure. But when I asked him what was the problem he sounded really troubled. "There yis no yapparent medical reason why He cannot talk," the doctor said in that all-knowing Tamil way. They're all very concerned about you, Ashokji. Not just me. But look, isn't being India's Number One Superstar enough for you? Must you try to be India's Number One Medical Mystery as well?

I'm sorry if I'm sounding so flippant. It's not easy for me, really. When I first heard about the accident I thought I would kill myself. "Why Him, O Lord?" I asked the heavens. "Why not me?" I've been simply frantic with worry ever since, Ashokji, really I have. But my Guru tells me to be calm. He says there is no use worrying about what has happened and what might happen, because it is already willed. "Why shed tears about the workings of destiny?" he asked. "Does the river weep because it must flow to the sea?" I was really impressed by that. But I don't find it all that easy to be calm about destiny when there is a chance it might take you away from me. Even more completely than you've taken yourself away.

Stupid of me to say that, I'm sorry. You'll be all right, everyone says so. The whole country is praying for you, Ashokji. Really. There are open-air prayers in mosques and temples and *gurudwaras* and churches and fire temples and *jamaatkhanas* and wherever else it is that people get together to ask their Maker for favors. I even hear the Prime Minister is planning to break an official journey tomorrow to visit you in the hospital. I know your father is a politician and all, and you were even in Parliament for a while, but the Prime Minister just doesn't do that for everyone, you know. You're special. Not just to me — you're special to the whole country, to India. You'll be all right. Everyone wants you to be well.

Even my Guru. You must meet Guruji one day. I think you'll really like him, Ashokji. He's got this marvelous smile: suddenly his lips part wide, revealing two rows of brilliant white teeth lighting up a gap in his brilliant white beard. And his eyes, Ashokji — you ought to appreciate them. Where yours are so clear and transparent, his pupils are black and deep, so deep they contain the wisdom of the world and you feel you could drown in them. He speaks in a quiet voice, not a particularly remarkable one, but what he says, Ashokji, what he says! I'll try to bring him here sometime. Actually people go to him, you know, he doesn't come anywhere, but perhaps for you, in your condition — I'm sorry, I'm making you sound as if you were pregnant or something, isn't it? No, I think he'll come. If I can get Mr. Horatio Bannerji to let us in.

Aren't you going to ask me what I'm doing with a Guru? Me, a good, convent-educated Muslim girl from a nawabi family? No, I don't suppose you are going to ask me anything today. Salma did. At her most pompous. "You're betraying both your religion and your class," she said stuffily. "Not to mention your education. But then *that's* never mattered to you, has it?" And the truth is, it hasn't. Nothing has. The only thing that's mattered to me since I joined Hindi films is you.

My joining the movies was a betrayal too. My parents had forbidden me even to *see* Hindi films. They were only made, they said, for the servant class. So of course I had to go. And I loved them! The glamour, the clothes, the dazzle — I wanted so much to be a part of that world, to escape the boring old prison my parents kept me in. I didn't think of acting first. I mean, how could I, I hadn't even acted in kindergarten. And if I had even tried to get a role in a local play, my parents would have flipped. When I entered the Miss India contest, just to spite them, and I won, they practically disowned me. Their daughter, being stared at by strangers! But what really made them go bananas was when I stayed on in Bombay after the contest and accepted all those modeling offers. I mean, what else does a Miss India do, right? And I enjoyed it. I think I particularly enjoyed their hysterics about it. My father even came to Bombay to take me home. But I've told you about all that, I think. Anyway, when I did the soap ad, the one that showed me in the shower, they *really* disowned me. My father said, "I have no daughter," and he went into mourning. Just like that! My uncle sent me a telegram telling me not to come back home, ever. Can you imagine?

I still remember my first day as an actress. My crash course at Roshan Taneja's acting school didn't count. I was the beauty queen who'd done the soap and towel ads; that's all the producer knew or cared about when he signed me. I had visions of stardom, fame, glamour. The movie was about, what else, a beauty queen who sold herself on the side. It was called *Call Girl*. Really subtle stuff, hanh? Lots of bikinis and leather microskirts that none of the established actresses would wear. Or *could* wear.

They sent a car for me, I remember, and that was my first disappointment. I'd expected a swank foreign car like the ones the stars drive around in Malabar Hill, but it wasn't even an Impala, let alone a Cadillac convertible. Just a scratched, black, rattling Ambassador with holes in the upholstery and rusty springs poking through. We drove into a ramshackle shed in some grimy suburb, which turned out to be the studio. I got out, still expecting air-conditioning and gloss. What I got was a bunch of stinky studio sidekicks pushing me this way and that, change this, wear that, wiping their brows and their noses and shouting at each other and at me, with an occasional "ji" thrown in as an afterthought. This went on for hours and hours and then I found myself stumbling into a dingy room. "Makeup, madam," they said, and a thin, slimy man with the hands of a skeleton plastered all sorts of evil-smelling white and pink muck on my face, neck and, most enthusiastically, my cleavage. His nails were black and chipped; a cockroach ran out of his powder case. After all this they wanted me to stand before the shining spotlights and smile seductively.

"Ya Khuda," I groaned to the director, "*this* is supposed to be glamorous?"

"No, madam," he replied, pawing me with his eyes. "*You* are."

And you know what? I was. Because none of that mattered.

What matters to you, Ashokji? Anything? Me? No, I'd only be fooling myself. Your wife? I don't think so. As a woman I can say that if she mattered to you, you couldn't treat her the way you do. Or treat *me* the way you did. Your children? You hardly talk about them. I think that what matters to you is your image. The way you see yourself is the way others see you. It doesn't matter what kind of husband or father you are, the important thing is that you're seen as a husband and father. You *are* all those roles you play on the screen, aren't you, Ashokji? Because there's nothing else, is there, nothing else underneath — no other character competing with the character of the role. Maybe that's what makes you so good: you *are* the role each time, or maybe the role is you. But what that "you" is nobody knows. I wonder sometimes about those scriptwriters who write roles "for" you — what "you" do they base it on? The screen "you," or course; they write a part that is as much as possible like the other parts they've seen you play. And so you are what you've been on the screen, and the screen continues to let you be you, and no one knows the difference, if there is one.

Have I ever told you how alike you are to everyone? Because you are, you know. With everyone you behave in the same sort of way, the relaxed, confident pose, the smooth voice, the effortless charm. It always works best the first time, or when the other person is alone with you. But when they meet you again, and they see you're exactly like that once more, or worse still, when they meet you in a larger group or with other people, and they see you treat all the others the same way, they feel terribly distanced from you, Ashokji. The same people whom you've won over the first time feel cheated, because they feel they are no different to you from anyone you might meet the next day or the next year. And indeed they aren't, are they, Ashokji? No one makes the slightest difference to you — all that matters is how you relate to them. In the process you offer them this perfect exterior, but people are terribly inconvenient, Ashokji, they don't stick to the script, they don't confine themselves to their quota of dialogue, their interactions don't cease when the hero has no further use for them in the plot, their feelings aren't switched off when the director says "Cut!" And so they walk away from you, and they find other friends, and you're left without friends in the world. Even those who'd normally be happy to be a supporting actor to a hero, because this hero makes it plain, without ever saying a word, that he doesn't need their support and won't notice it when it is taken away.

OK, OK, I know what you're going to say, or what you would say if you could. You'd say, "Don't be silly, *paglee,* am I the same with you as I am with Cyrus Sponerwalla? You see a different me than other people see, or most other people, anyway." I suppose that's true, you *are* different, but only just. With women you're different not because you want to reveal any more of yourself to them but because you want them to reveal themselves to you. Physically, of course. I don't think you've ever cared very much what goes on inside our heads. So with women you switch on an extra bulb in those eyes of yours, Ashokji, but it doesn't cast any light on you. And if you do treat a woman who attracts you differently from the way in which you treat a man, you treat most women alike as well, whether they're sleeping with you, costarring with you, or merely writing gossip columns about you. Except when we're actually in bed together, for instance, is there much difference between the way you behave toward me and the way you behave toward Radha Sabnis? The casual observer would find it difficult to tell from your conduct which woman is actually your lover and which is the bitchy columnist you're trying desperately to avoid, without showing it, of course. Though actually, the thought of anyone being Radha Sabnis's lover is hysterical — I bet you'd never do it for all the black money in Bombay.

Hai, what a fate, to be able to talk like this to you at last, for the first time sitting down and fully dressed, and not even to know whether you've heard a word I said! Whenever I tried to talk to you before, you know, after we — don't make me shy — afterward, I knew you weren't listening. Don't try and protest your innocence, I knew. All along I knew. Well, almost. I became suspicious at first because you would seem so attentive as I talked, lying there with my head on your shoulder, and you'd grunt every time I paused, which would only encourage me to go on. But whenever I asked a question you answered with a kiss, and the kiss led on to other things, and then my questions never got answered. This was fun for a while until I began to think it odd that your affection for me always rose whenever I wanted an answer from you. So I started putting in odd things, outrageous things, into the middle of what I was saying but without any change of tone at all, and you never reacted to any of them. I'd talk about a sari I'd seen, or about this aunt of mine whose husband used to beat her, or about the latest things Salma said, and I'd casually add a phrase like "this was the time I was selling myself for a hundred rupees an hour" or "you know the aunt I mean, the one who was sleeping with your father," and you wouldn't bat one of your droopy eyelids, you'd just continue grunting at all the right places.

So then I realized that your mind was somewhere else entirely, once your body had spent itself in me, and that you weren't listening to a word I was saying. All those precious, intimate little secrets and thoughts and anxieties and family events that mattered so intensely to me and that I wanted to pour out of myself to share with you, the things that I wanted to give you to make myself truly and completely yours, the private doors I was opening to let you into my world and not just into my body, none of these things had made the slightest dent in your consciousness. And you know something, Ashokji? It didn't matter. I was so happy lying there with the hairs on your chest tickling my cheek and your arms around me caressing the hollow of my hip, that I chattered cheerfully on, knowing you weren't listening and yet feeling the joy of saying all these things to you that were a more precious gift from me than the ones you valued. I thought, it doesn't matter that he isn't listening, maybe he too is enveloped by the soft intimacy of my voice, maybe the actual words don't matter as much as the fact of my saying them, maybe the sound of my words is enough to tie me to him more securely than the fleeting union of our pelvises. Maybe — and maybe he just can't be bothered. But I don't want to know. I love him.

Can any woman have loved you more unselfishly, Ashokji? And yet, when you'd had enough, when you'd tried every position you wanted to try and got bored with the familiarity of me beside you, you just spurned me, Ashokji, you garlanded me at your temple and you let me go, you pretended not only that I didn't exist but that I had never existed. And now I cannot even get you to say, for once, for the first and last time, that you loved me.

Oh, Ashokji, I so wanted to be cheerful, but how can I? See, I'm wiping a tear with the corner of my sari *pallav* — how you used to hate me doing that! But I can't bear it just to look at you lying there. In a way it's just like old times, isn't it, with you lying there and me talking away into the void. Except that you don't even grunt now.

You know what I think, I think you really got angry with me over that business of the Swiss money. Really, how was I to know it would be such a *jhamela?* You said, "Listen, Mehnaz, this brother of yours in the Gulf, can he help?" and I said, "If I ask him to, I'm sure he will." And then you met him and the two of you worked it all out, why blame me? The whole thing was your idea anyway. I remember how it happened; see, even if you remember nothing that I ever said to you, I always remember every word that you spoke to me, even how you said it and what you were wearing, if anything, when you said it. On this occasion you were wearing only a wristwatch, and it wasn't Swiss — see, I made a joke — and you said how unhelpful Cyrus Sponerwalla had been about helping you stash away your black money. You did a perfect imitation of him squealing in horror, "Like, man, that's *illegal!*" You did it so well I could practically imagine Sponerwalla's chins quivering and eyes popping, even though I hadn't met the man yet. And so I said, not even half seriously, "He should meet my smuggler brother from Dubai, Nadeem'll really give him an education." And you suddenly sat up, practically spraining my neck, and said, with that look in your eyes that means you really want something, "Are you serious? Can I meet Nadeem? What does he do? When is he next coming to India?" I sort of rubbed the side of my neck a bit and sat up too and said, "Of course I was half joking. He's not really a smuggler — can you imagine? — but he does know about these things, he's a businessman," and you were so interested you didn't even ask me how my neck was feeling. I told you, I remember everything.

So one thing led to another and when my brother came down to India you sat with him and asked earnest questions about Swiss bank accounts. At least so he told me, I wasn't even there, but I don't see why he would lie. So Nadeem said, "Sure I have a Swiss bank account, many of us in the trading business have to, and I can help you open one." And he took a lot of trouble too, explaining how it could be in any name or number, and you thought of using your birth date as the number and Nadeem explained how easily that could be traced back to you, and finally you settled on Gypsy as a translation of Banjara. Remember how you forced poor Choubey to switch a whole sequence from Kashmir to Switzerland in that film, *Himalay ke Peeche,* so that you could tie this up in Geneva yourself?

I didn't mind, because it meant boating on the Lake of Geneva with you, the Alps rising white and majestic behind like the cover on a box of chocolates, and letting the spray from the Jet d'Eau blow onto our new parkas as we laughed at the absurdity of the Swiss manufacturing a tourist attraction in the midst of all this natural splendor. And how you chased me into St. Pierre's Cathedral, saying you wanted to make love to me in a confessional, and the look on your face when you discovered it was a Protestant church and they either didn't sin or wouldn't confess to it! And your shock on discovering that the casino wouldn't permit bets above ten francs and that a box of chocolates cost twice that much. And the Piaget watch you bought me, even though I told you I never wanted to know the time, never wanted to see it passing when I was with you. And how I dragged you off to the hotel where Professor Calculus had stayed in my favourite Tintin adventure, and you said stuffily, "Is that all you read, comic books?" but you still photographed me near that life-size cutout of Tintin they had in the hotel lobby. Are you amazed at how much I remember? But what I remember most of all about that visit to Geneva was how disbelieving you were that you could walk anywhere without being instantly mobbed and asked for autographs — and the tone of regret in which you said, "It must be this parka, I could be any cold tourist." Oh, Ashokji, how much I loved you then, and how much I love you now.

My Guru says I must stop looking back. The past is always there with me anyway, he says; what I am is the result of the past as it shapes itself into the future, which in turn immediately becomes the past. The present, he says, is an illusion: each moment has either already happened or has not yet happened, it is either past or future. The problem with Westerners, he says, is their obsession with the present, which means they are living for something that does not exist. Does that make any sense to you? It didn't entirely to me, but the Guru is obviously a great man and I cannot always expect to understand everything he says.

I'll tell you something that he should have said to you when you were getting mixed up in all those Swiss bank accounts. It's something he said to me when he was explaining why I should renounce my worldly goods to his ashram. "In our legends and our shastras," he explained, "there has always been a conflict between Lakshmi and Sarasvati, that is, between the goddess of wealth and the goddess of the arts. In other words, my dear, wealth and art are not compatible: one constantly destroys the other. It is better, in the natural order of things, for the wealthy to have no taste, and for the artistic to have no wealth." If you had only realized that, Ashokji, you wouldn't have got into that whole mess.

But you didn't really do *too* badly, did you? I mean, considering. After all, you're not in jail or anything. How you got it so screwed up I don't know. It was a simple enough arrangement. Whenever my brother and his associates needed money here, they got it from you, and Swiss francs went into your account — for your family holidays abroad and Maya's selfish little shopping trips to Harrod's. No one asked any questions and no one need have, if you hadn't gone and got mixed up in politics. Now who asked you to do that? That dried-up little minx of yours wanted to be a minister's wife, I bet. I mean, what else could she be after *Dil Ek Qila,* hanh? I wouldn't have been able to show my face to a producer after that disaster, let alone to a camera. But she gave you more guilt by "sacrificing" her career again, as if she had any career left to sacrifice. Great comeback that was. More a go-away than a come-back, if you ask me.

I was very angry with you then, Ashokji, and with the way you just stopped seeing me. But Guruji counseled me again, quoting Manu this time — you know, the ancient lawgiver. From time immemorial women have had different roles at different times. The same woman who is treated as a chattel in domestic matters is an essential and equal partner in rituals, religious sacrifices, the offering of homage to ancestors. An Indian woman's consolation, the Guru said, is that she knows where she is irreplaceable, in what she is indispensable, and when she is irrelevant. And that applies not just to me, but to that minx Maya as well.

Who's that? What . . . ?

Oh, it's you. Hello. What do you mean what am I doing here? I'm visiting our husband.

OK, baba, don't scream, I'm going now. All right, all right, there's no need to make a fuss. I was going anyway. Oh, and I suppose you should know, for the doctor, that I didn't get a peep out of him. But then I couldn't see the part of him that usually responds to my presence.

Have a nice day, *Mrs. Banjara.*

TAKE FOUR

Interior: Day

I can't believe I'm doing this.

Me, Ashok Banjara, product of the finest public school in independent India, winner of its English Elocution Prize, best-dressed undergraduate at St. Francis' College, drinker of eighteen-year-old Macallan, standing up on a rickety platform in *churidar* and *kurta,* declaiming the virtues of the Prime Minister's party in chaste Hindi to a rural throng that look like they couldn't even afford the proverbial twenty-five paise for their cinema seats. But it *is* me, it's my mouth that's moving in political recitation, it's my arms that are gesticulating under the shawl that's draped toga-style over my khadi *kurta,* it's my voice calling for social justice, rural development, and votes. Me, Ashok Banjara, political campaigner and aspiring member of Parliament. Now there's an unlikely turnabout. I carefully enunciate the idiomatic *muhavrein* that a Bollywood lyricist has scripted for me, I fling my right hand skyward and pause for acclaim; and as the acclaim comes, I tell myself, you can't be serious, old son — or can you?

It's all happened so suddenly. OK, I can't pretend the thought hadn't entirely occurred to me. After all, it's in my genes. I *am* my father's son, even if I've tried to deny it all my life. And I've never really been able to shake off the underlying desire (again, repeatedly denied) to win his approval. I couldn't at school, in my choice of job, in my plunge into films; I could, and did, when I picked a wife. Somewhere at the back of my mind lay the thought that I might one day do something that would make him truly proud of me. And politics was the only possibility: it was his world, he'd always wanted me to join him, I'd refused — and now I confronted the wonderful paradox that my nonpolitical fame had actually improved my prospects of being able to enter his world successfully.

But I never really tried to do anything about it. Even when Cyrus, as nonpolitical an adman as ever violated Bombay's prohibition laws, mentioned it once. "Have you ever thought, man," he fantasized over his third whiskey one hot, "dry day" evening, "of entering politics?" I looked at him as if he had suggested I put on a loincloth and a tin helmet and do a mythological film. "Really, Cyrus," my look said.

He reacted instantly to my disdain. "Hey, it's not such a bad scene, man," he protested. "Opportunity-wise. I mean, look at these Southie guys, MGR, NTR, you know. Big-time Tamil, Telugu movie stars, and when they entered politics they were, like, unstoppable everywhere their movies played. Now you, man, your movies play everywhere. You're not a regional actor, like. Only real handicap's your initials. Kinda inconsiderate of your parents to be so *kanjoos* at the naming ceremony when they coulda, like, spread themselves around. AB lacks something, ya know? Kinda like a kid trying to remember the alphabet. Call yourself ABR and you could be bloody Prime Minister one day, big guy."

"AB-*yaar*, you mean," I joked. "Me and MGR? Come on, Sponerwalla, I'd look awful in dark glasses and a Gandhi cap."

Cyrus was easily distracted. "Wonder why they call it, like, a *Gandhi* cap," he mused bibulously, turning the melting ice speculatively around in his forbidden liquid, "when the old Mahatma didn't wear one himself. Or very much else," he observed irrelevantly, "clothes-wise."

So we moved on, topic-wise; and Sponerwalla never raised the idea again. But the thought lingered at the back of my mind, in the recesses we subconsciously reserve for the vaguest of our aspirations. I never did find a moment to pull it out of that obscure mental corner, dust it off, and hold it up to close examination. There was too much else to do: Subramanyam kept giving dates, Mehnaz kept clamoring for them, there were too many shootings and parties and interviews and trysts to think about anything else, let alone politics. Which, in any case, was my father's world and my brother's, emphatically not mine.

Oh, once in a while the thought slipped in by itself, like a shaft of light through half open blinds, when I was feeling particularly jaded by my fourth interchangeable role of the week or worn out by the insatiability of Mehnaz's appetite for me. Then I would briefly indulge it, playing with the idea the way I played with one of the triplets' plastic ducks found unexpectedly in the bath, squeezing the toy idly with soapy fingers till it slipped out of my grasp. Wouldn't it be great, I would think on these occasions, to abandon everything, the dance sequences and the love scenes, the Masters and the mistress, and surprise Dad with my engagement in *his* cause? But then I would think of how exactly I'd have to go about getting involved in politics, what it would imply my actually *doing,* and my half-risen enthusiasm would fade rapidly. I didn't fancy myself squatting with the slum-dwellers in a dharna against their proposed eviction or leading clamorous demonstrations against petrol prices, like the few politically active Bollywood stars I knew. That wasn't my scene, man, as even Cyrus would admit. And so the idea would float away as casually as it came, quickly supplanted by the more important bath toys of the real world.

And then suddenly, without my doing anything to plan, it took over my life. I realize now that Cyrus and I weren't the only people to have had this particular thought, but I'm still a little bewildered by the speed with which it all worked itself out. I was at some function to be felicitated on my thirty-fourth (or possibly forty-third, I've lost count) straight silver jubilee film when some joker with a paper flower in his lapel suggests before a microphone that I am the most popular man in India. No political leader, he says, not even the fellow with his name in *The Guinness Book of World Records* for the globe's largest electoral plurality, can come close to my popularity anywhere in the country. Someone in the crowd shouts out "Ashokji for Parliament!" and pandemonium breaks loose; soon the assembly have taken up the cry in a chant and will not subside till I stand up with folded hands and promise to consider their demand. This is just to buy some peace, not because I have the slightest interest in following my dear dad's ponderous footsteps, but startlingly the news is all over the papers the next day: "Banjara thinking of joining politics." Within a day a bigwig from my father's party is on the phone: could I come to Delhi, the Prime Minister wants to meet me.

Well, of course I go, and after the inevitably delayed flight I am met at the tarmac and whisked off directly to the prime ministerial presence. Dad is nowhere in sight. Just as well, as it happens, because it turns out they're offering me his seat.

It's going to be a tight election, the PM says. The Opposition thinks, rightly, that Dad's seat is vulnerable, and they are planning to field one of their stalwarts, a recent defector from the ruling party — Pandit Sugriva Sharma, Mr. Turncoat himself, who has changed parties more often than Mehnaz has changed costumes and probably for more money as well. The learned Pandit is a man of much erudition and little scruple who has therefore acquired a reputation for great political principle: each time he quits a party he makes it sound like an act of self-sacrifice in pursuance of a noble cause. In the process he has assembled a handy coalition of interest groups whom he has persuaded at some point or another that he is their ablest defender: slum-dwellers, untouchables, Muslims, and the left. In the present climate, poor old Dad doesn't stand a chance against him. The party is deeply anxious; defeat would not only mean the loss of a seat that the party has held since Independence, but would also show that the Pandit is more popular than the party he left. That could be fatal for the party — losing this one seat to Pandit Sugriva Sharma might give the Opposition a boost that could well threaten the government nationally. In short, the PM wants him beaten. But how?

Enter, on a white charger, Ashok Banjara: popular, especially among the underprivileged, whose fantasies he embodies; potentially as effective a campaigner as the experienced Pandit, and demonstrably a better speaker; and, as a bonus, heir to the family's long connection to the constituency. I couldn't have been more ideal as the choice for assuming my father's drooping mantle. The PM's measured eloquence wins the day. I agree before I have entirely realized what I am agreeing to.

On the drive to my father's, though, just one thought suffuses my mind: at last I am doing what he had wanted me to. For years he has been berating me for having chosen films rather than politics. Now finally I can give him something to be proud of: not just a son who walks in his father's footsteps, but one who is actually invited to do so by the leading politicians of the country. I can already imagine our reconciliation: I shall bend to touch his feet and ritually seek his blessing, and he will embrace me, tears — who knows? — pouring down his usually stony cheeks.

My brother, Ashwin, opens the door for me. Something is not right: he looks positively funereal. I burst past Ashwin to my father's study, and find him sitting in his armchair, looking as still as death. Oh, no! I begin to wail inside myself, but he looks up at the interruption and my heart calms down. Thank God you're alive, Dad, my mind says, thank God you're alive today.

"Dad, you'll never believe what's just happened!" I exclaim.

"I have no choice but to believe it," my father says heavily, and my excitement freezes like a horse shot in midgallop.

"He knows," my brother says quietly, blinking behind his glasses. "The Prime Minister's office just called."

Now I understand the gloom. "You mean you've only just been told they weren't going to give you the ticket? I'm so sorry, Dad. I naturally assumed you were behind — all this. I had no idea."

I sit down gently in the chair next to my father's. Dust rises from it: he has been alone in that room too often. "I'm really sorry about the way they've handled this, Dad," I say. "But the PM seemed in no doubt that you would have lost to Sugriva Sharma. At least they're not giving your seat to someone else. It's in the family — and it's me, your son and heir, doing what you'd always wanted me to do. Aren't you happy about that?"

"Why are you doing it?" my father asks abruptly.

"Because they asked me to. The *Prime Minister* asked me to."

"And why do you think the PM asked you?"

This is hardly the way I had expected the conversation to go, but I humor him. "Because I can win."

"Correct." My father's face shows no signs of pleasure at my answer. "And why do you want to win?"

I stare at him nonplussed, unable to comprehend the question.

"I can understand the party's motives," says my father. "I can't understand yours."

"But Dad, you've been telling me for years I was wasting my time in films! Here's a chance now to put my years in films to good use, in an area you wanted me to!" My voice is rising.

"I can see that, Ashok, I'm not a fool. But *why* do you want to do it? The party wants to retain the seat. Why do you want to win it?"

I am again wordless with incomprehension. My father tries a different tack.

"What will you do with your victory? What will you do once you've won?"

I get what he's driving at. After all, I've seen Robert Redford in *The Candidate*. "I'll do," I say firmly, "what the party and the government want me to do."

"What do you believe in?" My father is relentless today.

"What do you mean?"

"You've just been adopted as the prospective parliamentary candidate of the country's ruling party," my father snaps. "What are your beliefs? What do you believe in?"

I try a conciliatory tone. "Come on, give me a break, Dad," I say. "I believe in what you believe in."

"And what's that?"

"Oh, you know, democracy, nonalignment, socialism."

"I don't believe in socialism. I've tried to tell you that for fifteen years. If I did, or was prepared to pretend I did, I'd still have the party ticket today."

"Well, whether you believe in it or not," I snap back, "the party does. It's part of the officially adopted platform you would have been sworn to uphold if you had been a candidate."

"So you believe what the party tells you to believe."

"How does it matter?" I am really exasperated now, and I'm shouting. "When has any of this ever mattered to anybody? Does anyone vote because of what a politician believes? Does he then conduct himself in office according to what he believes? The name of the game, Dad, is winning elections. That's what the party has taken me on board to do, and I thought you'd at least be happy about it, for Chrissake."

"Why should I be happy? For nearly twenty years now I have been urging you to join me, to take an interest in my work, to involve yourself in the constituency. You have done none of these things, you have not heeded a single request. Now, when you do, it is at the behest of my enemies in the party — and it is at my expense."

"Dad, they would have taken the ticket away from you anyway. I heard the way they talked about your chances."

"You don't understand a thing, do you?" My father's voice is already hoarse, his face tired and weak. I realize with a shock that he has become what I had never thought of him as becoming — an old man. "It was *I* who told the PM I would not be a candidate at these elections against Pandit Sugriva Sharma. I know precisely the reasons why I am vulnerable, foremost among them my age and the sense that I have exhausted my capacity to do anything for the constituency. Especially since it is clear they will never make me a full minister. But I *also* told the PM who should get the ticket in my place. And till a few minutes ago, I thought the party had concurred with my judgment."

"Who?" I stand up from the chair and demand belligerently. "Who would you rather have had the ticket than me, your own son?"

"My own son," he says, and I realize he is not echoing my question but answering it. "Your brother. He has worked long and hard to deserve this opportunity. He has involved himself in the problems of my constituents. He knows the names of hundreds of them, their difficulties, their hopes. He has walked the roads and tramped through the fields; he knows each village by sight. The people recognize him, trust him, and love him — and he does not suffer from my handicaps of age, unrealized ambitions, and unfashionable beliefs. Pandit Sugriva Sharma would not have beaten him."

I turn around to look at my brother, who stands near the doorway, looking deprived. Christ, I'd had no idea what was going on. "All the more reason," I say quickly, "why I need you to be my campaign manager, Ashwin. I can't win without you." I walk up to him and look him in the eye. "Ashwin — will you help me?"

His eyes drop behind his spectacles. "Of course, Ashok-bhai," he mumbles.

I turn to my father, who is sitting hollowly in his chair, embittered in defeat. I realize he is waiting for me to ask him the same question. He will then, graciously but grudgingly, extend to me his blessings.

I look at him, slouched sullenly in his chair, his face set in that look of disapprobation I have seen on his face all my life, and decide I am not going to give him the satisfaction.

"You'll never be able to stop disapproving of me, will you, Dad?" I ask.

Then I walk out of the study, and out — as far as I can help it — of his life.

I am tired. The speeches are all right; that's like acting a particularly undemanding part. It's the trudging through the countryside that kills me. In the *chappals* that are part of my nationalist attire, my feet take a pounding from the hard, unrelenting soil, from the slushy muck of the fields, from the grimy dust in the streets. Once in a while some villager runs up with a lota and washes my feet in ritual welcome. But before the water dries, I am off again, and wet feet seem to suffer much more the depredations of rural pedestrian travel. I am getting increasingly anxious to shake the dust of the Hindi heartland off my toes.

As I walk through villages, trailing behind me the curious crowd of idlers, party workers, and fans (many, alas, too young to vote), as I smile and engage in the rituals of campaigning — talking, questioning, ducking into thatched huts to solicit the peasantry, sitting on charpoys with hookah-puffing farmers to seek their wisdom, standing on the back of the flatbed Tempo to harangue the bazaar through a megaphone — I cannot escape the unworthy suspicion that Ashwin is deliberately putting me through this punishing schedule to get back at me. But when I ask if all this is really necessary, he has a reasonable answer: with an opponent like the Pandit, I can't leave anything to chance. I need to make myself known to the voters as someone who is not just jetting in from Bombay and expecting to win on my stardom alone.

Maya has come down to help and she is a great hit, wearing simple cotton saris and greeting the women with great respect, not just with folded hands but, in the case of the maternal figures, with an attempt to touch their feet (she rarely has to go through with the whole gesture because the toothless old ladies lift her up in, well, touched gratitude). I watch her in action, ever the dutiful housewife, and realize once more what an asset she is as a wife. To think, for instance, of Mehnaz in this role, with her exquisitely painted face and nails, her silks and her urban chatter, is inconceivable: she would lose me ten votes for every one her glamour obtained. Whereas Maya is, as always in public, perfect in the role.

The fact that she abandoned her brief filmi comeback after the disastrous *Dil Ek Qila* has only helped. Rural voters don't think too highly of young actresses, though they like to watch them: in their lexicon the term *actress* equals something between "brazen hussy" and "fallen woman." They see Maya, though, as a wife and mother; she doesn't look or behave like an actress and the few who know she was one also know she gave it up to be the wife and mother she now so plainly is. So she is welcomed into their homes, where she asks knowledgeably about babies' colic and the availability of sugar. Between her and me, we've sewn up the female vote in the constituency, and, as everywhere in India, men are merely a minority. When Maya goes back to Bombay to rejoin the kids, promising to return in a week's time for the concluding stages of the campaign, I am feeling extremely confident.

Ashwin is not.

Much against my better judgment I have agreed, at his request, to attend a strategy session with the main campaign workers one night. It has been a particularly exhausting day, and I am not fully attentive as he introduces a number of disquieting trends and a larger number of unquiet party men in terms that fail to register clearly in my bleary consciousness. To my uninitiated mind, earnest Rams merge with voluble Shyams, caste calculations fuse confusingly with the arithmetic of the campaign accounts. As the conversation wears on, though, my confidence fades. The details may still be fuzzy in my mind, but the overall picture is depressingly clear.

The consensus of the professionals seems to be that the Pandit has too many groups committed to him: the Brahmins because he is a Brahmin, the minorities because he is known as a champion of the minorities, the poor because he can always blame the party in power for their poverty. The latest blow is that, after a national deal between their parties, the official Communist party candidate has just withdrawn in his favor. The traditional mistrust of the outsider is also being assiduously cultivated by Sugriva Sharma's campaigners. Although we are both first-time contenders in this constituency, the

Pandit is a former Chief Minister in this same state, and he can trace his roots — as he never fails to remind his audiences in the broad local dialect — to the hills a hundred kilometers away. Whereas I don't look or sound like a local, and I haven't a fraction of his political experience to offer. The Pandit, I learn, has taken to referring to me patronizingly as "the boy," a term that is gaining circulation; his side-kicks more disparagingly call me *naachnewala,* the fellow who dances. The Rams and Shyams shift uneasily in their steel folding chairs, shaking their heads grimly and drowning their despair in endless cups of oversugared tea.

I cannot believe this. "What about my crowds?" I ask. "What about the way people follow me about? What about Maya?"

"We can't afford to read too much into all that," Ashwin says. "It might just be the Madurai effect."

"The what?"

"The Madurai effect. Sorry, political shorthand." Is it my imagination, or does Ashwin seem to revel in reminding me of my ignorance at every opportunity? "In the 1967 elections, the biggest crowd in the history of Indian elections turned up at Madurai to listen to Mrs. Gandhi, the new Prime Minister, campaign for the local Congress candidate. They stayed four hours in the heat and applauded her to a man. When the voting actually took place, the Congress candidate lost his deposit."

"In other words," I interpret the lesson, "they came out of curiosity, not out of support?"

"Exactly," Ashwin nods. "In our country, elections are a popular *tamasha* every five years, a spectacle, an entertainment for the bored masses. People will gather to watch an unusual candidate in much the same spirit as they might stand around to watch a monkey-man performing tricks." I look at him sharply, but the simile seems to have been chosen at random. I don't know how faithfully Ashwin has watched my films. In fact, I realize with a twinge of guilt, I don't know very much about Ashwin at all. I spent very little time with him after going to college and entering my own world. I have no real image of my brother since the days we played cricket outside the house as schoolboys. I recall with a fond smile that I used to bully him into long spells of bowling.

"So what do you think we should do?"

"Keep at it," Ashwin replies shortly. "That's all we *can* do. There are no public opinion polls, no way we can really be certain if Sugriva Sharma has the votes he thinks he does. It's always possible that the endorsements of the leaders of each of these communities and factions may not, in this case, translate into votes at the booths. That's one hope: your appeal as a film star may reach deeper into people's personal voting intentions than their leaders' instructions. And then there's the idea of Ganeshji's here. I think we should pursue that."

"What idea was that?" As usual, I seem to have missed something. I look at Ganeshji, the idea man Ashwin indicates, a dark and pudgy campaign worker with more oil in his hair than you need to run a Jeep. He has been chain-smoking *beedis* throughout the conference; any suggestions he may have made were occluded by struggling to emerge from behind a smelly miasma of fumes, which were occasionally cleared by a gust of air from his rasping cough. Really, it's not *always* my fault I don't catch what's going on.

Ashwin is patient with me. "As Ganeshji points out," he says, with a perfunctory nod to the innovative smoker, who beams in creative pride, "the Pandit is taking his own community for granted — the Brahmins and the rather sizable 'Hindu vote' that, in this constituency, comes with them. That may yet prove a tactical mistake, because there are quite a few Brahmins who probably consider Sugriva Sharma something of a traitor to their caste. We must step up our appeals to that community and to the Hindu-inclined element generally. There's one particular suggestion Ganeshji has that we can act on tomorrow."

The thought of tomorrow is already exhausting me. "What's that?"

"There's a local sage here, a sort of guru who runs an ashram on the banks of the river. He has only been in the district for eight or nine years, but he's already something of a legend. People are beginning to come from all over the country and even from abroad to listen to him. The villagers hold him in awe, the Brahmins particularly, since he is said to know more about the scriptures than the priests at the temple. You should pay him a visit."

I groan. "Now I've got to get the blessings of a godman?"

"We don't know whether he'll bless you," Ashwin says, "but even if he just sees you, it could have a positive effect. Every little bit counts, Ashok."

Of course I agree; not that I have a choice. Plans are duly made for a pilgrimage to the ashram in the morning. Apparently the Guru's fame has spread so far and wide that he is attracting a growing number of foreigners, some of whom are acquiring prominence in his entourage. This has inevitably fueled the usual resentments, and the Guru has had to keep his local and expatriate followers apart as much as possible. For both linguistic and factional reasons, therefore, he has taken to holding two public sessions a day, one in English and one in Hindi.

"I suppose you'd like me to go to the Hindi one," I say brightly. "To be seen to be there by the local yokels."

"Wrong," says Ashwin. "I think you ought to go to the English one. If things go wrong there, the damage can more easily be contained than if you suffer some sort of public indignity in front of your own electorate."

There is some discussion, but the party hacks all come down on Ashwin's side. It has been a long time since I've found myself in a collective enterprise where I can't always get my own way.

The visit to the Guru settled, my sturdy supporters file out, leaving behind their *beedi* stubs and tea glasses and scraps of paper, the residue of political cogitation in India. Ashwin's eyes are closing behind his glasses. I feel the time has come to tell him how much I appreciate what he is doing.

"Ash," I say, recalling a nickname I haven't used since our school days, "I want to tell you how much I appreciate what you are doing." And since that doesn't sound fraternal enough, I gratuitously add, "So all those days I spent playing cricket with you in the backyard are finally paying off for me, hanh?"

He stares at me for a long time, as if debating in his mind whether to say something or not. His better instincts lose the debate. "Ashok," he says at last, looking me directly in the eye, "you know what my most abiding recollection is of playing cricket with you, my elder brother, role model, and hero? It was you, five years older than me, deciding to bat first, making me bowl for what seemed like hours in the hot sun, and then, just before it became my turn to bat, hitting the ball into the neighbor's estate so *you* wouldn't have to bowl to me. It happened," he adds levelly as he sees me about to react, "more than once."

What can you say to a thing like that? I had no idea that my brother had stored up these petty resentments. But my tongue has done enough damage already. I choose to be sensible; for once I say nothing.

The Guru sits cross-legged on a raised dais, his posterior resting on a mattress covered with a dingy white sheet, his back leaning against a pair of lumpy bolsters. He is dressed in a white robe of uncertain provenance, part Arab djellaba and part costumier's fantasy from *Hadrian VII*. His balding head is decorated by a cap of even obscurer antecedents, a velvet circle that might have been an Orthodox Jew's shower cap. The lack of hair on his scalp is more than amply compensated for by the rest of his face, which drips with a lush gray beard that flows in immaculately groomed profusion down his chest. Rings gleam on his fingers, enlightenment in his dark eyes. These are at last open: they have been closed for the last half hour as the Guru meditated, arms stretched out and thumbs tucked into fingers, while Ashwin and I and a host of saffron-clad devotees (themselves, like their master's attire, of varying and unplaceable origins) sat on the floor and waited reverentially.

The Guru surveys the assemblage, gently lifts a berobed haunch, and breaks wind. An echo seems to follow, but it is only the devotees letting out a collective sigh.

"So, who have we here today?" he asks, casting his gleam in our direction.

"Sir, zese peepul 'ave come to pay zeir rhespects," says a Frenchwoman in saffron who seems to be the Guru's principal assistant. "Chri Ashok Banzhara, 'oo his a film hactor from Bombay, and 'is brozer. Chri Banzhara," she adds disapprovingly, "his also a political candidate in ze helections 'ere." Some curious heads turn in my direction.

The sage's beady eyes light up, their black pupils luminescent with interest. "Ah, friends from the cinema world," he announces. "A most interesting domain, and how like our religion, is it not?" He seems to expect no answer, and I wonder if it is now my turn to make social chitchat. As I prepare to rise to my feet to greet him, I feel Ashwin's restraining hand. "Wait till after the discourse," he whispers. That's right, of course: the Guru has to address the assembled faithful, as he does at this hour every morning, and then we might find it possible to present ourselves. It is said that the Guru chooses the subjects for his sermons upon opening his eyes after meditation. That certainly seems to be the case today.

"Indian cinema has many remarkable affinities to Indian religion," he intones to my astonishment, gazing into the distance as if at some great TelePrompTer in the sky. "Hinduism, as I have explained before, is agglomerative and eclectic: it embraces and absorbs the beliefs and practices of other faiths and rival movements. It co-opts native dissenters — Buddha, Mahavira — and plagiarizes foreign heresies, finding the Protestant work ethic, for instance, in the karma-yoga of the Bhagavad Gita. The Hindi film is much the same: it borrows its formulas from Hollywood, its music from Liverpool, and its plot lines from every bad film that Hong Kong has ever produced. The moment an Indian director, a Mrinal Sen or a Benegal, makes a well-regarded serious film, he is promptly seduced into the industry before he can constitute a threat to it from outside — rather as Buddhism and Jainism were reabsorbed into Hinduism in our country. But the underlying philosophical premise is even more absolute. For just as the Hindu notion of time runs cyclically, repeating itself endlessly, so also Hindi cinema consists of endlessly repeated variations on a few basic themes. The Indian film is the idealized representation of the Indian attitude to the world."

"Outrageous nonsense," I whisper to Ashwin. He shushes me with a warning finger to his pursed lips. The Frenchwoman looks disapprovingly back toward us. I notice that she is uncommonly pretty and that under her thin cotton robe she is braless.

"I have described to you in an earlier discourse the challenge that Hindu philosophy offers to the notion of a duality between God and man, between the Creator and His creations. In the *Upanishads,* the ultimate goal of the believer is the realization of his Oneness with the Absolute. All of us, all of you, are one with God; God is within you, and you are within Him, or It.

"Aha, you might say, then how is God portrayed in so many different forms, as blue-skinned Krishna, as bow-carrying Rama, as elephant-tusked Ganapati, even as female, in the forms of so many divine goddesses? There is a simple answer. The Supreme Being, the essential First Cause of our creation, is visualized in a variety of forms because of *our* weakness — our inability to worship the divine without personifying it. It is our avidya, our ignorance, that prevents us from grasping the essence of divinity, hence the need to depict the First Principle in forms more comprehensible to humans. This became particularly important in spreading religious belief to the masses, the ordinary people who wanted to worship specific divine qualities such as the ability to make rain, the power to destroy evil, the conferring of good fortune. Instead of bestowing all these functions on one Supreme Being, Hinduism ascribes different names to different manifestations of God, each with his or her own characteristics, duties, and, shall we say, heavenly talents, all just to make divinity more accessible. Thus we have Sarasvati the goddess of learning, Kali the goddess of destruction, Rama the warrior-king of righteousness and justice, and so on.

"Now is this not also what the Hindi film does? In all Hindi films there is only one theme: the triumph of good over evil. The actual nature of the evil, the precise characteristics of the agent of good, may vary from film to film. The circumstances may also change, as do the stories in our *Puranas*. The songs vary, as do our religious *bhajan*s. But there is no duality between the actor and the heroes he portrays. He is all of them, and all of them are manifestations of the Essential Hero. Therein lies the subconscious appeal of the Hindi film to the Indian imagination and the appeal, along with it, of the Hindi film hero."

I can scarcely believe how raptly the devotees are taking in this twaddle. Some of them have their eyes closed, in order, I assume, to better experience the ecstasy of the Guru's words. Other eyes are wide open, as if to admit as much as possible of the sage's radiance. "This can help us," Ashwin whispers into my ear, and when the Frenchwoman looks back, I sense a softer expression on her face, and I hope it is because she is beginning to identify me with her Guru's Essential Hero.

"And what about the heroine, do I hear you ask?" There is unctuous laughter, I am not sure why. "I shall tell you. Do you know why Brahma, the divine Creator in the Hindu trinity, is always depicted with four heads? There is a story that goes back to the time when he created woman — yes, the female human. He carved her out of his own body, not from a spare rib; you see, we are a vegetarian people." (More appreciative laughter. The devotees obviously found this rib-tickling.) "Now in those days Brahma had only one head, that's all he had need of at the time. But he admired his own creation, this First Woman, so much, and looked at her so ardently, that she felt obliged to hide in embarrassment from his desire. This she tried to do by running away from his line of vision, but if Brahma could create a woman, he could certainly create an extra pair of eyes. So in order to be able to see her wherever she hid, he grew a head on each side, another one behind, and even one on top, to complement his original single head. Is this not like the ubiquitous camera of the Hindi film?

"But to return to Brahma. Inevitably the woman could not escape him, and she succumbed to his desire. Out of this consummation came the birth of our original ancestors, the founders of the human race. Wait a minute, I hear the accountants among you saying, That story gives Brahma five heads — why is he portrayed only with four? Well, there is a postscript to the story. The other members of the divine trinity did not entirely approve of Brahma being able to look up into the heavens as well as keeping an eye on earth. So Siva, a god of action if ever there was one, took his sword and cut off the top head, leaving Brahma with four. Like the Hindi filmmaker, Brahma can look around and beneath him, but not rest his gaze on higher things."

The devotees nod, while I wonder what on earth any of this has to do with his main point. Or indeed whether he has a main point at all.

"But I digress. We have talked about the creation of woman, but not about her role as heroine. Here I must turn a little to Vedanta; I hope my foreign brothers and sisters will be patient with me. The universe is made from, and made up of, two simultaneous Causes, or principles — a spiritual Cause called purusha, the male principle, and a nonspiritual Cause called prakriti, nature, seen as female. I am sorry, dear ladies, that you are not seen as spiritual: perhaps too many of our ancient philosophers were men. But the mutual interdependence of these two principles is fundamental — the male principle cannot create anything without the female nor can prakriti produce the natural universe without purusha. Now what is this prakriti, this female principle? It is made up of three gunas, three basic qualities: the shining; the dark, or passive; and the dynamic. This is the tradition from which the Hindi film heroine is unconsciously drawn. She shines, she is resplendent, she is fair (and this is important, because it is said that the goddess Parvati, criticized by her husband, Siva, for her dark complexion, had to perform austerities and penances in the forest before Brahma granted her the fair skin for which she is now famed. No Indian actress can succeed without reminding audiences of the postpenance Parvati.) She is also passive, the object of the hero's adoration and the villain's lust. But these two gunas remain in uneasy equilibrium; it is the third, her dynamism, that unsettles this equilibrium and makes the Indian film heroine a heroine."

This is going right over my head, a direction in which no real Hindi film heroine has yet traveled. I shift my weight uncomfortably from one thigh to the other and try to admire the curve of the Frenchwoman's unhaltered breast, which pushes against her saffron shift like prakriti looking for a purusha.

"You would be right, my dears, in tracing the modern Hindi film to the epics and myths of our ancient times," the Guru goes on. "Each character fulfills the role assigned to him or her in the film as each of us fulfills the role assigned to us by our destiny on this earth, our dharma. The Hindi film hero's dharma is to be a hero, the villain's is to be a villain. It is the same, after all, in the *Mahabharata,* whose personages act out their roles without being able to deviate in the slightest from the script of destiny. Their dharma determines their character, and their character determines their destiny; yet even this dharma is the result of their actions in their past lives. There is nothing they can do about it: they do what they do because they are who they are, and they are who they are because they have done what they did. This is a concept you can apply in toto to the Hindi film hero.

"A prime example of this species is now sitting among us. He has come to seek the benefits of my wisdom, and this pleases me. So for his sake, I shall conclude this discourse with a story from the *Maha-bharata* — not, alas, a story like the delectable episode of Brahma and his lady — but the story of an argument, a debate, shall we say, among the five Pandava brothers, the 'heroes,' if you must, of the great epic. The topic they were debating was a typically Hindu question of hierarchies. Which, they argued, was the highest of human pursuits —*kama,* pleasure; *artha,* wealth; or *dharma,* righteousness?

Their uncle and counselor, Vidura, thought the matter was self-evident: the answer was obviously dharma. Arjuna, the most intelligent of the Pandavas, was not so sure: he put artha first, regarding pleasure and righteousness as merely two adjuncts of wealth. (He would obviously have made a very successful merchant-banker today.) Bhima, the glutton and strong man, disagreed. In his view, the satisfaction of desire, in other words kama, was obviously man's first duty, since without the desire to achieve, any achievement would be impossible. The twin brothers, Nakula and Sahadeva, wanted it both ways: man, they declared, should go for all three — first pursue righteousness, then wealth, and lastly, pleasure. (I am beginning to think they had a point there, but not necessarily in that order.) Finally, the oldest brother, Yudhisthira, paragon of virtue, surveyed the options and sadly rejected all of them. The only thing for a man to do, he concluded, was to sidestep the debate altogether and submit himself to Fate.

"I will not draw the lessons from this argument for you. It is yours to interpret as you see fit. But today we have with us a man who has sampled kama, accumulated artha, and seeks to fulfill a dharma of service to the people. He has my benediction."

And with that the Guru closes his eyes and resumes his posture of meditation. The devotees rise silently and begin to shuffle out soundlessly on bare feet.

I stand up, delighted by the unexpectedly positive conclusion to the Guru's rambling discourse, but uncertain what happens next. Ashwin, satisfied, is already heading for the door. I stop the Frenchwoman as she walks toward it.

"Don't I get to see him now?" I ask. "Privately?"

"Can't you see? Ze Guru his meditating," she replies.

"But I've come all this way just to talk to him," I say.

"What you 'ave to say, ze Guru already knows," she declares sententiously. "Ze Guru alone decides hif 'e needs to talk to you."

Ashwin beckons. He doesn't want me to make a fuss.

"Wait." The Frenchwoman looks at her master. The Guru has opened one eye owlishly and is raising a hand. Slowly, he points at me and beckons. When Ashwin and the devotee try to follow me, he stops them with upraised palm. A long finger opens out and points exclusively to me. It folds back, a peremptory summons. I ought to

218

feel insulted, but I find myself enjoying the privilege. "Private audience," I say, shrugging at the Frenchwoman. She folds her hands to the Guru and walks out with Ashwin, shutting the door. I am alone with the man of God.

As I walk toward him, I see that he is laughing. Great waves of silent mirth convulse him in his cross-legged pose, so that his be-robed body literally quakes on the mattress. Strands of gray beard disappear into his closed mouth, his sparkling eyes dance with merriment, his hands helplessly hold his sides. I don't see what is so funny, unless, while he was meditating, some higher consciousness cracked a joke on the astral plane.

"AB!" the Guru says at last. "So you really didn't recognize me!"

Incredulous, I advance closer to the august presence, trying to visualize a face behind the beard. "Tool!" I exclaim. "What on earth are you doing behind all that shrubbery?"

"Shh," Atul ("Tool") Dwivedi, fellow Fransiscan and Coffee House habitué of collegiate notoriety, raises a long-nailed finger to his lips. "Not so loud, or you'll have the entire ashram down on us." He pats a place next to him on the mattress. "Try and look reverential, in case anyone looks in," he says. "God, it's good to see you."

"It's good to see you, god," I respond irreverently. "How did all this happen? Didn't you go off to BHU to study philosophy or something? No one's heard a thing out of you since."

"I did go to the Benares Hindu University," Tool confirms, his eyes now droll rather than divine. "To study philosophy. And — other things."

"And what happened to your hair? And this beard — almost white already?"

"Don't you remember my father? Premature baldness runs in the family. And the things I have thought about over the years," Tool says, "have grayed me. But we're not young anymore, Ashok, you and I. You must be over forty."

"Forty-one next week." I had not really imagined that that disqualified me from thinking of myself as young. Tool has sobered me.

"How do you stay like this? You must have a picture in the attic." We had both seen *The Picture of Dorian Gray* in preference to reading the book.

"Fifty pictures," I joke. "Almost all of them hits."

"Yes, I've been reading about you." Tool adopts the distant gaze of his scriptural discourse and quotes from memory. "Darlings, national politics will never be the same again, at least not for our ruling party. Cheetah has learned that a funny thing happened on the way to the quorum: the Prime Minister has decided to offer a party ticket to Bollywood's reigning box office monarch, your very own Ashok Banjara. Of course, it can only be the kind of coincidence so beloved of our scriptwriters that the constituency from which the PM wants to make this MCP an MP has belonged for goodness knows how many years to the Banjara Daddy! Who would ever suggest that our hero hasn't got everything on his own merit? Not Cheetah, my little cubs. After all, with so much talk these days of more women candidates being nominated, our Hungry Not-So-Young Man could make an excellent Minister for Parliamentary *Affairs,* eh? Grrrowl!" The Guru's eyes twinkle at my evident astonishment. "So you see, I've been expecting your visit."

"I can't believe you read that stuff, let alone know it by heart," I say.

"But I used to be a filmi fanatic in college! How quickly you forget," Tool reproaches me. "Besides, theology can be trying. A Guru must have his little pleasures."

"Time for kama, hanh?" I joke. "By the way, thanks for the endorsement."

"My pleasure," he responds, and I imagine the weak pun is intended. That's how we all were at St. Francis'. "But it wasn't entirely unmotivated. I need your help."

"You? Mine? I thought you had it made here. Women, prestige, adulation — what more could any Franciscan want?"

The Guru scratches his bottom through the robe. "I'll answer that philosophically some other time," he replies. "But the short answer is, I'm getting rather tired of the rural life. Too many mosquitoes and not enough electricity. I'm thinking of making a move."

"And what can I do to help?"

"Well, I need your advice, and some contacts," the spiritual guide says matter-of-factly. "What would you say to my trying to set myself up in Bombay, as a sort of resident Guru to the stars?"

"Why not? I admired your patter this morning."

"That's nothing." The Guru waved a dismissive hand, as if swatting one of his troublesome mosquitoes. "Bollywood doesn't want abstruse comparisons between cinema and advaita. What it wants is a philosophy to justify itself by."

"Go on." I am intrigued.

"Your cinema world is full of mendacity, imitation, corruption, exploitation, and adultery," he says in the briskly bored tone of a schoolteacher taking a roll call. "It's endemic, it's ingrained, it's part of reality. In fact, all these things are part of the daily assumptions of the Hindi film industry and of those involved with it."

"And you think you can change that," I suggest helpfully. "Reform it. Reintroduce spiritual values."

"On the contrary," Tool retorts. "It can't be changed. No one wants to change it, and the system wouldn't work any other way. After all, despite these things, or more probably because of them, India now has the world's largest film industry. And it's one that flourishes with great efficiency and financial viability in the face of some appalling infrastructural, logistical, and technical drawbacks. It's little short of a miracle that it works as well as it does. Not even a godman wants to mess with a miracle."

"So what *do* you want to do there?" I ask, puzzled.

The Guru sighs. "I've done my stint of dharma," he says. "I've spent the best years of my life learning, meditating, and now running an ashram. I've begun to enjoy a bit of kama at last, especially now that these foreign women have discovered me. The time has come, I think, for artha. I want to live well."

"Whatever happened to nonattachment?" I ask jocularly.

"Oh, it's very important," Tool says. "I want my followers to be completely unattached to their material possessions. The best way of achieving this is, of course, to give it all to the ashram. As for myself, I will own nothing: everything will be in the name of the ashram, for the greater good of its members. But I will have the use of such things as the ashram sees fit to give me, and I intend to have so many that I can afford to be nonattached to any of them."

This sounds more jesuitical than Vedantic, but I listen keenly as the Guru abandons the digression and returns to my original question. "What I will give Bollywood," he explains, "is a philosophical framework for its ills. I'm thinking of calling it Hindu Hedonism. Like the sound of that? No? Well, maybe I need to think about that some more. But labels don't matter, so perhaps I won't need one. The idea is to let people continue doing all the venal things that they are so successful doing, but to teach them to feel good about them rather than guilty. Done something you feel bad about? You were only fulfilling your dharma. Was it something really terrible? Well, you'll pay for it in your next life, so continue enjoying this one. Guilt? Guilt is a Western emotion, a Judeo-Christian construct we only feel because we are still the victims of moral colonialism. The very notion of 'sin' as some sort of transgression against God's divine will does not exist in the Hindu soul and should be eradicated from the Indian soil."

I stare at him in bemusement, unsure whether he is serious. He carries on unperturbed. "Moksha, salvation, is the thing — the idea is not to seek forgiveness for sin and liberation from guilt, but ultimately to escape the entire human condition, to be liberated from space and time and the endless cycle of birth and rebirth. The only sin is violation of your dharma, which means not doing what your situation obliges you to do: Arjuna having moral scruples about killing on the battlefield was in danger of violating his dharma, whereas when he fought and killed he was upholding it — not the kind of thing your Westerner with his Judeo-Christian moral code can easily live with, eh? The Occidental wants to die with no sins in this life to pay for; the Indian should look on death as an opportunity to experience immortality, with the sins of this and previous lives rendered irrelevant."

The Guru pauses for breath. "*Shabash,*" I say, feeling like Iftikhar. "And adultery? What do you say to the chap who's cheated on his wife, lied to her, kept a mistress? What do you say to the mistress?"

Tool looks at me like a lynx at midnight, seeing into my darkness. "Monogamy is a Western imposition," he says shortly. "It didn't exist in India before the British came. But that would be too easy." He sounds sententious again. "The scriptures are full of examples of the noble heroes of our epics sleeping with more than one woman," he intones. "Krishna is the obvious example — he loved sixteen thousand women, it is reliably recorded, and fathered, less reliably, eighty thousand sons. His greatest consort, his affair with whom is immortalized in painting and sculpture and dance all over India, was a married woman, Radha. Deception was therefore essential, though it was easier for a god than for other adulterers; once when Krishna

222

spotted Radha's husband shadowing her to one of their nocturnal trysts, he adopted the form of Kali, so that the spying cuckold saw his wife busy in adoration of his own favorite deity!"

"Krishna was a god," I demur. "His rules were different. What about humans?"

"Arjuna embarked on one of the great erotic sagas of our history, traveling the length and breadth of India to expand his mind and expend his body. Even righteous Yudhisthira had at least three wives, and no one's really counting. In fact, it is difficult to think of one hero from our *Puranas,* of one man who remained faithful to a single woman. My own contribution to national integration is that I have had congress with at least one woman from each of the twenty-two states and six Union Territories, including the Andamans — but then they went and annexed Sikkim." He sighed. "So much to do. But I digress. The precedents are considerable, yes, even human ones. But," he adds, anticipating my objection, "the postcolonial laws, regrettably, have enshrined this barbarism, what the cheerful Cheetah calls the monotony of monogamy, so lying and cheating become mandatory. Not to worry: the *Puranas* have an answer for that too. As Krishna explains to Yudhisthira in the *Mahabharata:*

> *In the matter of truth and deception,*
> *There's room for many an exception;*
> *It's all right to lie*
> *In dharma, provi —*
> *-Ded it's in areas enjoined since Inception:*
> > *the protection of cows;*
> > *the fulfillment of vows;*
> > *defending either a marriage*
> > *or a Brahmin's carriage;*
> > *but the most merit is earned,*
> > *where women are concerned.*
> *In these cases above, be ambivalent,*
> *For our theology's quite polyvalent;*
> *In every season*
> *There can be a good reason*
> *For a lie and Truth to be equivalent.*

"You made that up," I accuse him admiringly.

"The verse, yes, but every idea in it is gospel," he swears. "Look it up. But in any case, AB, the Indian people never judged their gods by mortal standards. That's why Krishna was worshiped for acting in ways his followers wouldn't dream of tolerating in their own lives. Adultery, gluttony, theft, all came easily to the favorite deity of the Indian middle classes. But we're not judgmental about our gods." He smiled, more wickedly than wisely. "It's much the same with you movie stars. You make the modern myths, so the same double standard applies to you. Your fans adore you for doing things they'd find shocking if their neighbors did them." He looks at me searchingly. "So how do you like my Hindu hedonism? Will it play at the Prithvi?"

"They'll lap it up," I agree. "Especially the actresses."

"Ah, the actresses." A purply-pink tongue emerges from the midst of his graying foliage and licks a pair of dry mauve lips that briefly come into view. "I intend to explore with them the belief of the Alvar school twelve centuries ago that the soul, in its longing for God, must make itself female in order to receive divine penetration. The soul of an actress, I shall explain, starts off with a considerable advantage in this respect."

"And you, I take it, will provide the divine penetration?"

"A mere mortal substitute, old soul. In anticipation of the sublimity of the spiritual process to follow."

I shake my head in admiration. "You've come a long way, Tool, since the days when we used to chat up the co-eds by saying that we would live up to the ideals of St. Francis, who was kind to birds."

"Who used to *caress* the birds." Tool Dwivedi corrects me, shaking his head in turn. "You've obviously come a longer way, Ashok, if you started off being kind to them. But tell me, what can you do for me?"

"I'll happily introduce you to my friends and producers," I respond without hesitation.

"Good, but not directly," the Guru says. "I don't want too many awkward questions arising about our connection. St. Francis' College is not a good background for a Hindu holy man who wants to be taken seriously in the West. Officially, I grew up on the mountainside at Rishikesh and the riverside in Benares." The beard parts again in a smile.

"And I'm not sure," he adds, sounding anything but unsure,

"that it'll do either of us any good to be publicly associated with each other. No, Ashok, I want to keep you up my sleeve. In fact, I don't mind at all if you conspicuously keep your distance from me. Could be useful later on. But give me a few names and unlisted phone numbers. Tell me a few inside stories. Help me know in advance what's likely to be bothering some of these people. Straying husbands. Suicide attempts. Family secrets. There's nothing more impressive than surprising a prospective disciple with some startling piece of information you couldn't possibly have had in the normal course of things."

"You need Radha Sabnis, not me," I reply. "But sure, I can give you some of that stuff. Just tell me when, and how."

"We shall arrange an even more private audience in due course to exchange that information," the Guru chortles. "In the meantime, tell me how I can help you."

"You can repeat your endorsement in your Hindi session," I suggest. "And —"

"Consider it done," he cuts in. "They are probably already exchanging amazed whispers about your having the longest audience the Guru has ever granted. But I shall find a way of making it more explicit for the villagers."

"Thanks. And in Bollywood you can help take someone off my hands who is getting just a little too awkward for me right now. She's ripe for a religious experience. It's just what she needs to take her mind off me."

"I understand fully," says the Guru. "I shall expect Ms. Elahi's private phone number from you shortly."

I shake my head again, in wonder and relief. This guy could end up solving *all* my problems.

Exterior: Day

MECHANIC

SYNOPSIS

Ashok is an automobile mechanic in Bombay, working in a garage repairing the big cars of the powerful (and the powerful cars of the big). One of the garage's clients is an important politician, Pranay, whose pretty but spoiled daughter Mehnaz regularly drives in to get her red sports car serviced. Ashok's attitude to her is an uneasy compound of gender attraction and class incivility. But one day (with smartly choreographed *dishoom-dishoom*), he rescues her from assailants — and turns down the cash reward her father offers him. Mehnaz is smitten, Pranay resentful.

Ashok lives in a slum where, as the theme song makes clear, he is the popular solver of everyone's problems:

> (ASHOK DANCES AROUND A CAR,
> WRENCH IN HAND)
>
> > *I'm just a good mechanic*
> > *If your car breaks down, don't panic —*
> > *I'll fix it;*
> > *If your engine starts to sputter*
> > *Or your oil flows in the gutter*
> > *Don't allow your heart to flutter,*
> > *I'll fix it.*

I'm just a good mechanic
If you have a problem, don't panic —
I'll fix it;
If your rickshaw needs repair,
If your roof lets in the air,
Don't worry, don't despair,
I'll fix it.

But the slum is to be razed to make way for a development, and Pranay, the local legislator, is in league with the developers. Mehnaz, now Ashok's devoted admirer, is present when Ashok leads a demonstration against the demolitions. She follows him on a protest march to her father's house. Pranay is outraged, but she refuses to reenter his home until he agrees to receive the protesters as well. He does so with ill grace, but after a bitter quarrel in which Pranay rejects their demands, Ashok storms out, Mehnaz by his side. Pranay's hired goons give chase, but they fail to restore either their boss's daughter or his dignity, and Ashok, aided by his slum friends (principally by his sidekick, the comedian Ashwin), routs them in style.

That night Mehnaz, newly homeless, has to share Ashok's slum hut, and finds it difficult to stay on her side of the thin cotton sheet he has strung up as a partition. As the sound track pants in rhythm with the hero's heartbeat, Mehnaz softly sings:

Don't go too far —
It frightens me.
Don't come too near —
It frightens me.
Don't go too far, don't come too near,
Be like a star, shine on my fear,
Enlighten me.

Don't go too far —
It frightens me.
Don't come too near —
It frightens me.
I want you in, I want you out,
If you go or come, I want to shout,
It's night in me.

[*At this point the film skips and jumps, scratches and crosses of light appearing in the upper corners of the frames. The censors have added to their archives of forbidden pleasures, leaving their symbol — an isosceles triangle, the inverse of the national symbol for contraception — on the certificate that precedes the movie.*]

The next morning the inhabitants of the slum, Ashok, Ashwin, and Mehnaz at their head, block the bulldozers with their own bodies. Destruction and development are briefly held at bay. But then Ashok is arrested by a corrupt policeman, Kalia, and though a court soon sets him free, he loses his job and home (to the tune of a lugubrious version of the title song).

But all is not gloom and despair. Mehnaz (who, it turns out, is only Pranay's adopted daughter) and Ashok have a simple slum wedding. This takes place in a suspiciously spotless temple that only a studio could have devised. Their exchange of garlands is blessed by Ashwin and assorted extras.

When the audience returns from intermission, it is election time. The Indian public is to enjoy its five-year privilege of choosing the agents of the country's recurring misrule. Ashok is to challenge Pranay in his own constituency.

The election campaign has all the effervescence of a Bollywood cabaret. Montage: Pranay's men declaim his virtues from loudspeaker-equipped vehicles and distribute rupee notes to the trucked-in crowds at his rallies; Ashok's neighbors accost individuals in the street with palm-folded sincerity. Pranay has glossy posters and gigantic hoardings of himself expensively displayed on every convenient site (and some inconvenient ones), while little urchins with charcoal scrawl Ashok's electoral symbol — what else but a simple wrench? — on every available wall, sometimes ripping down a picture of his rival to make space.

At the height of the race, Pranay challenges Ashok to a public debate at a sports stadium. Pranay confidently predicts that Ashok will not accept the challenge. Ashok, the villain declares, is scared, knowing his ignorance makes him a very poor match indeed for Pranay's greater experience. Despite his misgivings Ashok has no choice but to accept the challenge. Pranay declares that his rival really has no intention of turning up for the debate. If Ashok does not come to the stadium, Pranay says, it will confirm once and for all that he is not up to the job.

On the day of the debate, with the campaign reaching its climax, Ashok is abducted by Pranay's thugs. The villain's scheme is to demonstrate Ashok's cowardice before tens of thousands of people. Our hero is left tied to the back of a chair in an old warehouse, a gag across his mouth.

At the stadium, where huge red banners advertise Pranay's challenge to his rival, people are filing in. "Where could Ashok be?" Ashwin asks Mehnaz. "This is not like him at all."

She suspects foul play and tells Ashwin about the warehouse where her father hides smuggled goods. As the sidekick sets out to rescue the hero, Mehnaz, rapidly transformed by colorful folk attire and accompanied by a half dozen pretty women from the slum, keeps the restive crowd entertained with an impromptu harvest dance. The song to which they undulate went to Number One in the Binaca Geet Mala, Radio Ceylon's hit parade, for six long weeks:

> *Our message is the message of the earth,*
> *Hope for those who're wretched from their birth,*
> *We want to give a break*
> *To the little folks who make*
> *Chapati, not cake*
> *And have everything at stake*
> *To prove they are humans of great worth!*
> *Rise and shine with a smile of joy and mirth!*

As the women sing and sway, clicking little sticks together and kicking up their legs, Ashok struggles with his bonds, but he cannot free himself. Ashwin arrives at the warehouse and finds it guarded by a solitary *chowkidar*. "What's that?" he asks, pointing at the man's foot; when the hapless extra looks down, Ashwin knocks him out. "The oldest trick in the script," the comedian sighs, before smashing a window and leaping in to free Ashok.

In the stadium the dance comes to an end.

"We'll never make it," Ashok pants; it's too far to run, the bus is too slow, and they can't afford a taxi. They step out into the middle of the road, forcing a black and yellow auto-rickshaw to screech to a stop, its driver shouting imprecations. Ashok and Ashwin leap in. "To the stadium, quick!" they exclaim. "It's a matter of life and death!" The three-wheeler's scooter engine bursts loudly into life and they careen down the street.

At the stadium, Pranay declares that his opponent has conceded his unfitness by his absence. As Mehnaz tries to contain the restlessness of the crowd, the camera cuts back and forth between the mounting tension at the stadium and the hero's desperate dash to get there in time.

A traffic jam! The auto-rickshaw phut-phuts to a halt before a confusion of trucks, cars, cycles, and bullock carts, horns (and horned creatures) bleating. But the driver now knows his passengers' cause; the auto-rickshaw mounts the curb, scattering hawkers and passersby, and races exhilaratingly down the sidewalk, its driver tooting a warning with repeated squeezes of the rubber bulb that serves as his only siren.

Scene shift: goaded by a triumphant Pranay, sections of the crowd start chanting, "We want Ashok, we want Ashok." Pranay smiles hugely as the chants intensify and the crowd begins to rise to its feet. "Enough is enough," declares Pranay. "I cannot be expected to wait forever for someone who does not want to face the real issues in this election. I suggest we give Ashok a count of ten, and then cancel this meeting." Mehnaz gasps in dismay, but can do nothing. "All together now," says Pranay, and the crowd joins him in shouting, "Ten!"

The auto-rickshaw squeezes between two buses, as Ashwin comically presses himself into Ashok's side in fear.

"Nine!"

The auto-rickshaw brakes to avoid a beggar child, spilling Ashwin in the process. As he clambers back on, Ashok throws the child all the coins in his pocket.

"Eight!"

The auto-rickshaw weaves to avoid a car and grazes a fire hydrant, which gushes forth brown water. A family of parched pavement-dwellers gratefully stretches out their hands toward the liquid.

"Seven!"

Inspector Kalia is in the act of accepting a bribe from a shady character sporting an underworld mustache, trademark stubble, and dirty white bandanna when he sees the auto-rickshaw bearing down on them. With a scream he and his accomplice move aside just in time, in opposite directions. The villain promptly flees, bribe unpaid. Kalia calls after him in vain, then pursues the auto-rickshaw.

"Six!"

The auto-rickshaw causes a car to brake sharply, sending a sheet of canvas floating from the car roof into the air. The canvas lands on a poor woman with two babies who is huddling against a wall and covers them like a blanket. The woman looks up at the auto-rickshaw in gratitude.

"Five!" Pranay's smile has become triumphant; Mehnaz is in despair. The faces of Ashok's supporters reveal both puzzlement and anxiety.

"Stop!" Kalia shouts from his police Jeep, drawing alongside the auto-rickshaw. Our heroes grin at him and roar on. Kalia is shaking a fist at Ashok when the three-wheeler turns sharply left, and Kalia and his Jeep, caught unawares, continue straight on, plunging into the sea with a splash. The crooked cop surfaces spluttering, seaweed replacing the habitual betel leaf in his mouth.

"Four!"

The scooter reaches the stadium. "Here, sahib?" asks the driver. "No," says Ashok, "drive in!"

"Three!"

Ashwin hastily reties the gag on Ashok and loosely knots the ropes on the hero's wrist. The auto-rickshaw bursts through the entrance, past a startled gate attendant, and phut-phuts down the center aisle of the stadium. The crowd turns in amazement. Mehnaz's eyes light up in hope.

"Two!" Pranay shouts, but he is the only one still counting.

The auto-rickshaw squeals to a stop in front of the stage. Ashwin clambers out, helping a bound and gagged Ashok into view. Ashok raises his tied wrists in the air. The crowd erupts.

"One," Pranay says feebly, looking around him wild-eyed. Ashok ascends the stage and stands before the mike. A delighted Mehnaz, beckoned by Ashwin, comes up and unties the gag. "Brothers and sisters, this is how they tried to silence me!" announces Ashok as Mehnaz waves the gag with a flourish. "But they cannot silence the voice of the people!" The crowd roars its enthusiastic approval. "This man" — Ashok points at Pranay — "thought he could humble me in your eyes by preventing my voice from being heard by all of you today. I was tied and gagged and thrown into a godown. But the people do not go down so easily." There is good-natured laughter mixed with sounds of outrage toward Pranay. "It is this crook, this smuggler, this kidnapper, this razer of your homes, who claims to represent you today and asks for your votes. What answer will you give him?"

The crowd roars its reply with one voice, which is echoed in the pounding of angry feet swarming toward the stage. His eyes widening in panic, Pranay screams a futile plea for mercy, then turns and flees, the throng at his heels. A long shot shows him running into the distance, the cries of his pursuers fading into the dust kicked up by their feet.

The final shot: a *kurta*-clad Ashok, newly elected, is being garlanded in triumph. He folds his palms in a *namaste,* then raises them above his head in a gesture to the crowd. "The people's court has given its verdict," he declares. "Together, we shall march on to a new dawn."

The camera pans to a poster of Ashok's election symbol, the wrench, behind him, and the theme song returns to the sound track:

> *I'm just a good mechanic*
> *If your car breaks down, don't panic —*
> *I'll fix it. . . .*

And the screen fills with the portentous words THIS IS NOT THE END, ONLY THE BEGINNING.

The camera lingers in close-up on Ashok's garlanded face, the adulatory crowd, and the words on the screen before the picture fades to the strains of the national anthem and the lights come up in the cinema hall.

Monologue: Night

ASHWIN BANJARA

Maya tells me she hasn't been able to speak a word to you so far in the hospital. She just sits here and looks at you, she says, till the thoughts well up in a surge that drowns the words. "There was so much I wanted to say to him earlier, and couldn't," she told me today. "What is the point of trying to find the words now?"

Of course I tell her how useful it might be to you, how it might help to bring you back to normal, and she just smiles sadly. I don't suppose the "normal you" gave her much joy, did you? No, that's cruel — and I don't want to be cruel to you. Not now.

It's strange about Maya, that you should have married someone like her. I suppose everyone at home keeps telling you that. I pictured you with someone beautiful and brittle and glamorously Westernized, like smuggled bone china. Instead she's stainless steel, Ashokbhai, like the *thalis* Ma used to serve dinner on when we were little. Always there, clean, safe, durable.

I don't think you know how close I've become to her, Ashokbhai. Closer, certainly, than I am to you. It's not as if she tells me her secrets or anything like that. Maya wouldn't; if she has secrets, they'd remain secret. And she has too much pride and too much loyalty to you to discuss her feelings about you with me. What she said just now was as revealing as she has ever been.

And yet what companionship there is in her silences! When I am with her I feel instantly secure, caught up in her strength, her determination, her fierce sense of what is hers to protect. I become part of her defenses, not a stranger to them. With us there is so much that need not be spoken. Especially in relation to you. We understand each other instinctively because we are both your — no, forget it.

What was I going to say — "victims"? That wouldn't be fair. Let's just say we both have gone through certain experiences with you, as brother, as wife, that have defined us and helped us define each other. Experiences of which you, the catalyst, are blissfully unaware. That's the incredible thing about you, Ashok-bhai: you sail through life with such grand style, the breeze in your hair and the surface of the water all placid, without the slightest idea of the churning of the currents beneath, the torment of the smaller fish, the fate of the creatures caught up in your propellers. In fact, you wouldn't even notice if it was seaweed you were cutting up in your swath, or sardines, or dolphins bleating for help. OK, OK, I'm getting carried away. But I have not met another human being as completely unconscious of the effect he has on people as you. It must be wonderful, that perfect self-absorption, that remarkable degree of self-contentment. I, who find myself constantly anxious about what others might think of me, envy you in this as well, as in so many things.

But, to be fair, you demand so little of people. Perhaps because you never see what you *can* demand of them; you have no idea of the potential of any human being, not even their potential to give. So you see people in specific little frames, playing a part in a particular situation — fulfilling your needs in bed, directing you in a film, helping you win an election — and you are completely indifferent to them outside those frames. If someone encroaches upon your life in a way that's beyond the role you've subconsciously assigned him or her, you don't know how to handle that person, any more than if an actor had walked in front of the camera and spoken someone else's lines. Everyone has a place in your screenplay, but that place is well defined. When they have played their part, you have no use for them, at least not until their part comes up again.

Once at a party in Delhi I met a girl called Malini who said she knew you before you joined the movies. Rather nice girl, really —

she's involved in some sort of street theater movement, bringing culture to the masses, but not pretentious at all about it, very committed in fact. She gave me the impression that she'd been close to you; she said wryly that she'd tried to dissuade you from going to Bombay because she was afraid you wouldn't make it there. (She laughed about that so charmingly that I caught a glimpse of the kind of person she must be — passionately caring but modest — and I marveled at your luck in finding them every time.) It was clear, as much from what she *didn't* say as what she did, that you meant a lot to her — and that you had at least given her the impression at one time that she meant a lot to you.

Anyway, you know what she said? Mildly, not complaining, but with a tone of regret that I thought masked some stronger feeling. She said that once you left Delhi you made not the slightest effort to contact her ever again. She said she was so sure you would that she kept making excuses for you — that you were having a very rough time in the early days, that you were waiting to be a success before you got back in touch, et cetera. Of course, you didn't write or call, and she realized, as so many before and since have realized, that she wasn't as important to you as she thought she'd been. But it took some time for this to sink in — how much we all like to deceive ourselves, Ashok-bhai, about you!

She decided to take the initiative herself. At first she had no idea how or where to contact you, and then you had a couple of hits and your Bombay address started popping up in the magazines, at least the name of your bungalow and the rough area it was in. So she wrote to you — a simple, direct, personal letter saying how happy she was about your success, bringing you up to date on her own life, and expressing hope that you could meet on your next visit to Delhi. She got in return, three months later, a printed postcard with your picture on the back, a standard fan mail response typed on the other side, and an autograph she knew wasn't really yours — because she *has* your real signature, you see, on the program or brochure of a play you had done together. You can imagine how she felt. I could: she didn't have to tell me, and to her credit, she didn't even try.

I told her about your Sponerwalla and your Subramanyam, and how her letter probably never even got to you, but what excuses can you make for such a thing? The very fact that you hire and keep a secretary who can do something like that shows how little you care, how unimportant these things are to you. How unimportant *people* are to you. People don't really matter to you, Ashok-bhai; they never have. With no exceptions: not Dad, not Ma, not me, not even your kids, and certainly not Maya. Least of all, I'm sure, these Mehnaz Elahis of yours or the Malinis of the past. It wouldn't surprise me if you ended every relationship the way you ended the one with Malini, without a good-bye. Why bother to take the trouble to say farewell when you don't really care if the other person fares well or not?

I'm sorry, Ashok-bhai. I suppose everyone who comes in here and talks to you says all sorts of pleasant and cheerful and affectionate things to buck you up and help you reemerge into our world, whereas here I am, needlessly wounding you. And yet who has better right than me, after growing up in your shadow all these years, doing all the things you rejected, and finally watching the biggest prize of my life fall easily into your lap when it was at last within my reach? Don't get me wrong, Ashok-bhai, I'm not bitter. I've never been bitter about you, just accepting. You were there from the day I was born, you were part of my firmament, like the sun and the moon and the stars, and the things you did or that happened to you were as ineffable, as unsusceptible to change, as the movement of the planets. I reacted to you, but I never presumed to think I could do anything about you. You simply were, and I adjusted my life accordingly. So you hit the ball into the neighbor's when you didn't feel like bowling to me, and yet a few weeks later there I'd be, bowling to you again. I discovered early that, in relation to you, free will was always an illusion.

Why am I sounding so negative? You know I hero-worshiped you, Ashok-bhai. How could I not have? You were such an admirable figure in my eyes: tall and handsome, good at sports, a very public personality from an early age with your theater and your speech contests and your girls on either arm. I derived so much of my identity from being your brother, it was inevitable that you could do no wrong in my eyes. All this — this criticism came much later, when, after years of being out of your shadow's reach, I saw you again at close quarters and realized what you were. Saw also that you couldn't help being what you are, but that didn't make it any easier to live with.

What a waste your political career was, Ashok-bhai. Why did you do it? Dad understood all along, of course: you stood with no other thought than that you could win. Very useful for the party: by winning in your constituency you helped them deflect the threat of Sugriva Sharma. You served a very specific purpose. But did you think for a minute that they might have another purpose in mind? Did you even think who the "they" were, what the forces were within the party, how the factions stacked up, who had it in for whom, whose interests you might have served by winning, who wanted you out of the way the moment you'd fulfilled your purpose? Did you bother to do any of your homework, make political alliances, pay homage to the mentor you needed, or even acquire an adviser? No, Ashok-bhai. You thought you could go through the political world the way you did the film world, picking up scripts designed for you, doing what came naturally and reaping the benefits. It didn't work that way, after all, did it? And if you had only asked me, I could have told you it wouldn't; I would have saved you all the frustration, the humiliation, the waste. And in the process I could have prevented you from destroying Dad's political legacy and my political hopes.

It was that Swiss bank thing that really pissed me off. Why? Why did you need it? You wandered into politics and assumed the prevailing mores, but just as you did in films, you assumed the worst of them. There are actors in Bollywood who pay their taxes, surely, and there are, even if it sounds like an oxymoron, honest politicians. But you, Ashok-bhai, with your languid eye on the main chance, you would never have sought to be either. How was it that you never learned anything from Dad?

I'm sorry. I'll change the topic, promise. But what can we talk about, Ashok-bhai? *You're* about all we have in common. Politics? No, I've said too much already. Films? What do I know about films? I took Dad to see that film you made in the first flush of political enthusiasm, *Mechanic*. Your first real failure after *Dil Ek Qila*. There it was, your statement of purpose, your cinematic attempt to promote your political image with the masses. And what crap it was, Ashok-bhai! Dad squirmed in embarrassment throughout, and I, your ex–campaign manager, didn't know which way to look.

Of course, Dad kept objecting to all the wrong things. A real-life Pranay would never support slum demolitions, he pointed out. In fact, he argued, the slums exist because of the Pranays, who give these areas political protection by making populist speeches about squatters' rights and who thereby assure themselves of both the votes of the grateful slum-dwellers and the financial support of the mafia dons who really run the slums and who collect extortionate rents for a few square feet of public property. Not only that, no politician would conduct himself in an election year the way your Pranay does: even if he stood to gain from slum demolition, he would surely pretend otherwise rather than lose such an enormous bloc of votes. When the slum delegation goes to him, he would at least promise to "look into it" or "see what I can do" — utter some such time-honored insincerity. But your movie has him behaving with all the overweening arrogance of the Hindi film villain.

"But it's only a film, Dad!" I whispered. And he would say, "But even in a film, things have got to make sense. Why aren't there other candidates in this election, in a country with two hundred and fifty-seven registered political parties and no shortage of aspiring Independents? How is it that the field is left to a thug and an upstart?" Or again, at the ridiculous climax, "Which idiot politician would provide an unknown rival with a free platform like that?" Pranay's strategy in a race like this would obviously be to ignore his rival rather than give him such a major buildup and have to kidnap him — I mean, really, Ashok-bhai, how ridiculous can you get. But again, there you are, Hindi films. Only in Hindi films would a politician choose such a roundabout way to eliminate an ill-equipped rival and then choose to leave him locked up with one decrepit guard at a predictable address. Where do people leave their brains when they go to see this nonsense?

Forget the political stuff for a moment: how about the rest? Can you imagine for a second a real Indian mechanic in a romantic entanglement with a real Mehnaz Elahi? It's impossible: all these rich girl–poor boy fantasies the Hindi films churn out fly in the face of every single class, caste, and social consideration of the real India. "Just giving the lower classes the wrong ideas," Dad growled, not entirely in jest. After all, the dramatic rise in what the papers call Eve-teasing, which is really nothing less than the sexual harassment of women in the street, isn't entirely unconnected with Hindi films. Where else could all these lower-class Romeos have picked up the idea that the well-dressed women they once wouldn't have dared to look at are suddenly accessible to them?

So, thanks to the kind of roles you play, the lout thinks he'll get the rich girl just as you do in the movies. Except that in real life, the rich girl won't look at him, let alone sing duets with him. In real life, there isn't a lout who looks, talks, or for that matter smells like Ashok Banjara. These louts are a different species, dear brother, and yet you play them as if they were just like us. They aren't just like us, even if it might suit you to make your living pretending that they are.

There, too, I guess one can say, "It's only a film." But even by the standards of your films, *Mechanic* was a bust, and not just at the box office. If Pranay was going to take the trouble to send thugs to bash up Ashok in the garage the first time, why wouldn't he send them back to finish the job they didn't complete? And when Mehnaz goes off to the slum with Ashok — who could believe she doesn't have other friends to stay with? Maybe even a boyfriend? Why is it necessary to make her an adopted daughter suddenly, toward the end? Some of the great Greek myths are about daughters who betray their fathers because of their love for the resplendent hero: you could have been the Theseus to Pranay's Minos. But no, our audiences can swallow any amount of improbable crap in the plot, but not the idea that blood can possibly betray blood. No wonder even our Prime Ministers believe the only people in politics they can trust are their sons.

And why, while we're about it, did your sidekick have to have my name? A comically frightened Sancho Panza–type buffoon who gets Ashok out of trouble — is that what "Ashwin" conjures up in your mind, Ashok-bhai? Don't tell me you didn't write the script — you were vain enough to add yourself to the story credits. What would it have cost you to at least change the name of this sidey, for God's sake?

I know, I know: you didn't mean to offend me. In fact, you might even have intended, with typical sensitivity, to be paying me a tribute of some sort. Thanks, but no thanks, brother. The only tribute I ever wanted from you was your withdrawal from the seat that was rightfully mine. Instead of which you took it from me and made it impossible for me ever to have it again.

Will you, to whom nothing much matters, ever understand what my political life meant to me? All those years spent in the constituency, all those elections fought, petitions received, complaints heard, problems solved or sympathized with, homes visited, calculations worked out, promises made and largely kept — what were they for? I was building up a life, Ashok-bhai, I was creating a sense of what I was that had nothing to do with you, but would do everything for me. I was doing it first of all for Dad, to help him, and then I realized I was doing it to show him that I could be what he'd hoped you'd be, his true son and heir. And then, slowly, I began doing it for myself. I became not just a son, not just a brother, but Ashwin Banjara, political worker — and almost certain inheritor of the constituency when Dad finally decided he'd had enough. I even spurned all thought of marriage because I wanted nothing to distract me from pursuing my cause and my ambition. Wedded to politics: that's what I was. With a worm's-eye view of the political world, crawling toward my own little morsel. Till you swooped down from the heavens and carried it away just as I was reaching out to touch it.

Even then, Ashok-bhai, though not without difficulty, I accepted reality, learned to live with my role. I sort of told myself that being right-hand man to Ashok Banjara was probably just as good a way to matter in national politics. And in due course, with your prominence and your exalted connections, you would ensure I was well looked after — an adjoining constituency, perhaps, or a *Rajya Sabha* seat, or perhaps even your own when you moved on to bigger and better things. But you destroyed all that, Ashok-bhai, destroyed your career and mine, and now you've all but destroyed yourself.

I'm sorry, I didn't mean to be cruel. I'm dreadfully upset about your accident, you know that, don't you? I want you to get well soon. The whole nation is praying for your recovery.

Isn't that incredible? After everything, when all seemed lost, just as you seemed to have embarked on a long and inevitable decline, to become again the focus of national attention through an accident? If you surv—— when you come out of this, Ashok-bhai, you'll again be the hottest property in the history of Bollywood. There are prayer meetings at street corners, Ashok-bhai; the louts are taking time off from Eve-teasing to pray for your health; little boys are neglecting their homework to ask Heaven to intercede on your behalf. Your old films, even *Dil Ek Qila,* are being rereleased to bumper crowds. You're Number One again, Ashok-bhai, not just at the box office but in India's hearts. Maybe this is when you should have joined politics.

It's sort of like what happened in Madras, in 1967, when the fading screen hero MGR, swashbuckling star of a hundred Tamil films, was shot, really shot, by the established film villain — and a former mentor — M. R. Radha. He was taken to the hospital and the Tamil-speaking world stopped turning. Men and women wept openly in the streets, commerce came to a standstill as shops closed, crowds of more than half a lakh waited patiently outside the hospital for hourly bulletins as the great man fought for his life. A delegation of rickshawallahs, who were the epitome of the common man as portrayed by MGR in his films, pulled their vehicles all the way to Madras to be by his bedside. Poor people from the streets came to pay their respects; so did VIPs from their air-conditioned homes. The only difference from what's happening with you today is that MGR's fans didn't pray for his recovery, since, like all members of his anti-Brahmin DMK party, he was a declared atheist. However, some folks who found it hard to shake off their old habits prayed to portraits of MGR himself. *You* try and figure that one out. On second thought, in your condition, don't.

For six weeks the cinemagoers of Tamil Nadu held their breath. MGR survived; what is more, he conducted his campaign for the Legislative Assembly from his hospital bed. He had been given an unwinnable seat by a party chief jealous of his popularity; he went on to win by the largest majority in the electoral history of the state. What is more, he carried the state for his party as well. Photographs of the bandaged actor were splashed across the papers, with captions of him declaring: "I wanted to come to your homes to seek your votes, but I was prevented from doing so. Now I must ask for your hearts."

He got them, of course. And their votes as well. Then he went on to split the party, unseat his chief rival, and win a state election at the head of his own version of the DMK, organized entirely around his fan associations. He was Chief Minister of Tamil Nadu for almost a decade, and such was the magic of his name that he continued to rule the state from a hospital bed, this time after a stroke, though he was so badly crippled he couldn't even speak. When it was suggested that the people of Tamil Nadu were being ruled by a vegetable, his handlers put him up on a high stage before a massive crowd and ran a brief tape of one of his utterances through the sound system. Another notable first for India: the country that invented the playback singer had now come up with the played-back politician.

So you can do pretty well politically out of this accident, Ashok-bhai. They say the PM is coming to see you. Who knows, perhaps the party'd be willing to rehabilitate you. After all, the massive outpouring of grief must suggest that the people have forgiven your little peccadilloes — if they ever mattered to them. The party isn't going to treat you as an embarrassment it's relieved to be rid of when the great Indian public obviously holds you in such regard. This accident could actually be the rebirth of your political life. Think about it! Just uttering the words makes me feel much better. It isn't all over yet, after all, for us. For you. The moment you can speak and respond, we must start planning your comeback.

I'm sorry about all the things I said earlier. You know how sometimes things look so bleak that one says more than one intends to. But now the political blood is tingling again in my veins. We can show them yet, Ashok-bhai. It'll be the greatest comeback since Indira Gandhi.

Look at the bright side. Before all this happened, let's face it, you were heading downhill like an Indian Railways train — faster than anyone would have thought possible on the way up. People were used to you; they were tired of you. The accident, the grave risk to your survival, has been a great shock, the kind of shock that galvanizes the system. It was no longer possible to be bored by you.

Of course, it's been a shock to everyone, Ashok-bhai. And perhaps most of all to the public, whose property you've really been. The girls, your triplets, have taken it all rather well. Rather too well, perhaps: I've seen Sheela preening into a hand mirror before walking past the anxious throng into the hospital, Neela puts so much makeup on her dark face that she only looks human under flashbulbs, and Leela seems to emerge from every visit to your room with the air of someone walking out of a movie theater. None of this is more real to her than any other scene you've starred in, Ashok-bhai. And why should it be? You're hardly real yourself: they've seen more of you on the screen than in the flesh. You haven't spent much time with them at home or anywhere else. You even went on family holidays with a servant-maid in tow. You were, you *are,* a larger-than-life figure to millions, but to the few around you, you weren't quite as large as life.

Except perhaps for the little one. Little Aashish looks so sad and bewildered by it all, standing there with his short stubby thumb in his mouth and his big black eyes round in incomprehension, nibbling at his nonexistent nails, wondering why everyone is behaving like this. It's when I see him, your son, that I feel the greatest pain.

Sorry — hearing all this, if indeed you can, many of the things I've said must only make you feel worse. But you mustn't, Ashok-bhai. Just take it as one more incentive to get well again: to win back people; to win back your political place. I'm sure it'll gladden you to know how spontaneous the outpouring of good wishes is. People have really rallied around after the accident. You won't believe how kind everyone's been. Even people who've had their problems with you in recent years. Old Jagannath Choubey showed up with an enormous bouquet of flowers. Mohanlal came and fretted anxiously, pulling so much string off his fraying cuffs that I thought he'd unravel his entire shirt before he left. Pranay has been very solicitous, asking Maya how he could help, taking the girls out for an afternoon at the beach, commiserating with Dad and Ma. He's not really my type, but Dad thinks Pranay's too good a man to be associated with the Hindi film industry, and he's a villain! Even canny Sugriva Sharma, fresh from his recapture of what used to be your seat, sent a cable. I have it here somewhere — I'll read it to you: WISHING MOST SPEEDY RECOVERY STOP INDIA'S HEART BEATS FOR YOU STOP NATION'S SCREENS NEED YOU STOP SUGRIVA SHARMA. He released it to the press, of course, before it even got here: Parliament isn't the place for you, but the nation's screens are. Wily bastard.

In fact, Pranay's really been the best of the lot. I don't particularly like to admit it, because something about the fellow makes me uncomfortable, but he's really taken an awful lot of trouble. He's come every day; he must have had to cancel a shift or two to do it. And I hadn't imagined you two were so close, though I guess you *have* done a lot of films together. When the doctor wanted us to talk to you like this it was Pranay who volunteered to try it first. He's the only one who really seems to be able to console Aashish: in no time the boy climbs onto Pranay's lap and tugs at his absurd ties and for a moment forgets his bewilderment. One day Pranay rather ostentatiously took off a florid tie and looped it around Aashish's neck. He was delighted and wouldn't give it back. "It's yours, my boy," Pranay said, "a present." And I could have sworn I saw tears in his chronically red eyes.

Everyone is overcome by the occasion, Ashok-bhai. Your occasion.

Even that harridan Radha Sabnis. Look what she wrote in the latest *Showbiz:*

> Darlings, isn't it terrible what has happened to our precious Hungry Young-No-Longer Man? Cheetah hasn't always been nice about The Banjara, but we all love him, don't we? I'm praying and waiting for his recovery so that we can celebrate it together in a glass of Pol Roger 1969, his favorite champagne. [Funny, I didn't even know you *had* a favorite champagne.] In his meteoric career Ashok Banjara has come to personify the Hindi cinema as we know it — the style, the razzle-dazzle, the energy, the charisma. As they say in the ads for runaway prodigals, come back, Ashok — all is forgiven. We need you, lover-boy. Grrrrowl . . .

Lover-boy? Well, she might have chosen a more appropriate epithet, but as I said to Pranay, it proves her heart is in the right place. "Who'd have thought she even had a heart?" was his rejoinder. "Perhaps Ashok was one of the very few who dug deep enough to find it." Odd remark, that, but I suppose he was just trying to be nice about you.

I've talked a lot with him myself, actually, somewhat to my own surprise. Not that there's much choice, when you're sitting together in the waiting room. Did you know that Pranay's some sort of closet Commie? Oh, very restrained and reflective and all that, but overflowing with conviction and jargon. "I was not surprised when Ashok entered bourgeois politics," he said to me, well out of Dad's hearing, thank God. *Bourgeois* politics — can you imagine? "After all, every Hindi film hero is ontologically a counterrevolutionary." He said that, really, "ontologically." I had to look it up in the dictionary afterward. And I don't think he's even been to college. Where do these guys pick this crap up from?

"A counterrevolutionary?" I asked incredulously. "How?" He acquired this terribly intense expression, all beetle brows and outthrust jaw. "Because they serve, unconsciously or otherwise, to dissipate the revolutionary energies of the masses," he replied. "The frustrations and aspirations that would fuel the masses' struggle for justice is sidetracked by being focused on the screen success of a movie star. The proletariat's natural urge to overthrow injustice is vicariously fulfilled in the hero's defeat of the straw villain — me." I swear the guy didn't even smile. "Films in India are truly the opiate of the people; by providing an outlet to their pent-up urges, the Bombay films make them forget the injustice of the oppressive social order. Evil is personalized as the villain, rather than as the system that makes victims, not heroes, of us all. A false solution is found when the villain is vanquished, and the masses go home happy. The ownership and control of the means of production remain unchanged."

Absurd, of course, but can you believe words like these coming out of the mouth of a Bollywood type? Especially this fellow, with his white shoes and ridiculous ties? And there was more, believe it or not. To make conversation more than anything else, I found myself saying something about the melting of class and caste barriers in Hindi movies, you know, along the lines of what I said to you just now about *Mechanic*. He objected quite strongly. "It is just the opposite. Romantic love across caste and class lines," he declared solemnly, "is used to cast a veil over the classic contradictions inherent in these situations. It is an exploitative device to blur the reality of class struggle by promoting an illusion of class mobility. Instead of making the revolutionary youth want to overthrow the landlord, the Hindi film promises him he can marry the landlord's daughter. The classless cuddle," he concluded, "is capitalist camouflage."

"You ought to enter politics yourself," I suggested half jokingly, only to receive an earful about the bourgeois parliamentary system.

Speaking about the proletariat, though, you know we've kept them out of here. I'm afraid a combination of hospital rules, security considerations, and Maya's preferences have left the great unwashed in the courtyard even as we troop into the intensive care unit for these measured monologues. I can't imagine Cyrus Sponerwalla is any too

245

happy about that, but then we haven't let him in yet either. Anyway, what I wanted to tell you was that on my way in I spoke to one of the fellows waiting outside. He was, would you believe it, a rickshawallah, condemned to a short and brutish life pulling human loads far too heavy for him through rough and pitted streets in rain and heat wave alike. He had spent all his savings to take a train from Calcutta to come and watch anxiously for your recovery. Somebody presented him to me and I stopped and talked, not just because I felt I had to, but because I was genuinely curious about what you meant to this man — a man who had, in effect, abandoned his livelihood to be by your bedside, or as close to it as he could get. Why did he like your pictures, I asked him.

He liked the action, he replied in Darbhanga-accented Hindi. Ashokji was a master of action, stunts, fights. He didn't like pictures without action; if there is no action, he asked, what is there to see?

And this action, what did it represent for him?

The triumph of right over wrong, he said. The victory of dharma. The reassertion of the moral order of the universe. Ashokji was the upholder of Right: for this reason, he was like an avatar of God. The other avatars, Rama, Krishna, maybe even Buddha and Gandhi, are all worshiped, but they lived a long time ago and it was difficult to really identify with any of them. Ashok Banjara, though, lived today: his deeds could be seen on the silver screen for the price of a day's earnings. And it was as if God had come down to earth to make himself visible to ordinary men. For me, sahib, he said, Ashokji *is* a god.

I left him, strangely humbled by the purity of his devotion to you, and trudged up the stairs into the hospital. I'm afraid I forgot to ask him his name.

Interior: Night

I can't believe I'm doing this.

Me, Ashok Banjara, superstar of the silver screen, heartthrob of the misty-eyed masses, unchallenged hero of every scene in which I have been called upon to play a part, languishing in the back rows of the House of the People, the Lok Sabha, while cretinous *neta*s in crumpled khadi, their eyes and their waistlines bulging, hold forth inarticulately on the irrelevant. But it *is* me, it's my chin that's resting on my despairingly cupped palm, it's my elbow that's weighing heavily on the polished wood of the parliamentary desk in front of me, it's my lids that are drooping resignedly over my disbelieving eyes as I take in the spectacle of representative democracy in action and yawn. Ashok Banjara, parliamentary acolyte, ignored and condescended to by people who wouldn't be cast as second villains in Bollywood: what is life coming to?

I thought they'd at least make me a minister. After all, not only was I better known and more widely recognized than everyone bar the Prime Minister, but I had, after all, conquered the dreaded Sugriva Sharma for them. I thought I'd get to pick my reward — "so what is it to be, Banjara-sahib, Foreign Affairs or Information and Broadcasting?" Perhaps, modestly discounting my extensive travels, I would pronounce myself insufficiently qualified to run the country's external relations and graciously accept I and B instead, where

I could take care of the film industry. I even had a humble speech planned, expressing gratitude for the opportunity to serve.

But none of it. When the Cabinet list was announced, I scoured it in vain for the most famous name in India. "What's this?" I asked Maya in astonishment. "Where am I?" She thought that the jealous time-servers in the upper echelons of the party had prevailed upon the Prime Minister to name me as only a Minister of State or a deputy minister. "After all, Ashok, you *are* new to government." I bridled at this, but she pointed out the names of other friends and allies of the PM (including a genuine political heavyweight) whom the chief also had felt obliged to relegate. So I waited.

But when the second tier of appointments to the Council of Ministers was announced, I did not figure among them either. And the Prime Minister wouldn't return my calls. "I am leaving message, sir," Subramanyam assured me. "Yevery time I am leaving message, but they are simply not phoning." It is an unusual situation for him, and he is even unhappier than I am at this reversal of his standing.

"What did they bring me here for?" I asked Maya incredulously, "if they don't want to give me anything to do?"

"I suppose," she suggested ruminatively, "I suppose until they put you in the government, you should do what people in Parliament are supposed to do."

"Make speeches?"

"You're good at that, aren't you?"

Well, there was no need to answer that. So here I am, immaculate in *kurta-pajama* of the purest white silk, the cynosure of most of the eyes in the visitors' gallery. But down here in the well of the House they won't let me get a word in. Whenever I raise my hand someone more senior is recognized ahead of me; by the time the queue thins, the debate is over. Whenever I raise my voice, I am shouted down. Half of the subjects discussed are obscure to the point of absurdity, and my flagging interest is not stirred by having to follow them through the speeches of a bunch of semieducated morons who would sound incomprehensible in any language. The other half of the subjects are hardly discussed at all: either they feature long ministerial monologues after which the party MPs are roused from their slumbers to vote dutifully for the government, or they degenerate into shouting matches with the stalwarts of the Opposition, who make up in volubility what they lack in numbers. Occasionally, both monologue and shouting match are punctuated by noisy walkouts by the other side, the Opposition protesting against a government bill it's numerically powerless to overturn.

"After all the trouble they took to be elected to Parliament," I innocently ask a pair of fellow MPs once, "why do they walk out of it so often?" An Opposition MP gives me a lecture on the importance of the symbolic gesture of protest, but the effect is rather ruined by a cynical colleague who asks why walkouts only occur *after* the exiting MPs have signed the attendance register that ensures their daily fee.

I'm out of place in this world. I clap my hands to applaud the PM; the other MPs thump their desks. I patiently wait for a speaker to finish; the others heckle and jeer and interrupt anything I try to say. I don't know the difference between a starred question and an un-starred one or how to go about asking either; the others (those who count, anyway) can cite thirty years of precedents and use *Robert's Rules of Order* the way a makeup man uses a handkerchief. I've been assigned to the Consultative Committee to the Ministry of Infor-mation and Broadcasting, but it's never convened; the other MPs are bringing officialdom to book in the Public Accounts Committee or wangling foreign trips to inspect the use of Hindi — the national lan-guage, after all, not to mention the vehicle of my fame — in India's diplomatic missions abroad. I can't cope; and what's more, I've come to realize I don't care.

I look around me at my fellow-backbenchers in this teak-paneled sanctum of national legislation. Some snore sonorously, undisturbed in the innocence of their ignorance. Others are awake, but equally immune to contamination by ideas. The most knowledgeable are the most powerless: the members of the Opposition, one of whom said to the PM in frustration the other day, "We have the arguments, but you have the votes." That is the ultimate clincher in parliamentary democracy: the irrefutable logic of numbers. How does the quality of the debate matter, if you can win by the simple issue of a three-line whip? The MPs are herded in to vote: what they do before and after is of little concern to the party bosses. The air around me is heavy with lugubrious inattention. I get up, unnoticed except by teenagers in the gallery whose *dupattas* rustle in dismay at my depar-ture. I leave and wish I did not have to return.

"I'm bored," I confess to Cyrus Sponerwalla, who has come to

Delhi in the line of duty to see me. "I don't know how long I can stand this life."

Cyrus perspires less in the dry heat of the capital, and his bulk seems to take up less space in the larger, airier rooms here. His tone is correspondingly milder, his ideas more ingenuous. "If you can't do much in Parliament, man," my PR man advises me, "use your position there to do something outside it, like. This is a great public relations opportunity, man."

"Oh, yeah?" I ask. His dated Americanisms are infectious. "Like what?"

"Well, when MGR was elected to the Tamil Nadu State Assembly and didn't have much to do, like, he distributed free raincoats to all the rickshawallahs of Madras during the monsoon, so they could go about their business without fear of getting wet. And," he ends lamely on seeing my expression, "without catching a chill."

"Well, thanks very much for the helpful suggestion," I reply, making no effort to keep the sarcasm out of my tone. "My district happens to be in its third year of drought. I'm sure they could think of all sorts of useful things to do with a raincoat."

"It's just an idea, like," Cyrus says defensively. "You could do something else, sorta situation-specific. We could come up with another gimmick, something different, idea-wise."

"Yeah," I respond heavily. "Like an umbrella, perhaps?"

"Yeah," Cyrus is enthusiastic. "Free umbrellas. With your picture on 'em. Or maybe the party symbol. Let's see, man . . ."

"Sponerwalla." My tone is warning. "You're getting carried away. Umbrellas? In a drought?"

His three faces fall simultaneously. "They could keep the sun off their heads," he suggests weakly.

"Or they could be applied with force to the posteriors of anyone who tries to distribute them. Talk sense, Cyrus. That's what I pay you to do. And speaking of payment, who'd pay for all this? A few lakh raincoats or umbrellas or for that matter plastic buckets don't come cheap."

Cyrus ponders this. "The party?" he suggests. I shake my head. "Some rich businessman?"

"In exchange for what?"

"Surely there are some favors you could do a businessman? Putting in a word with a minister?"

"I can't do myself any favors here, let alone anyone else," I retort. "Even if I can put in a word, why should a minister pay any heed?"

"Because you're Ashok Banjara," the Bombay man says confidently.

"That, Cyrus," I sadly tell him, "is no longer enough."

In fact, it's actually better these days to be Abha Patel. She has given up the films, traded backless cholis and slinky dresses for heavy silk saris, let her hair run to gray (and tied it up in a businesslike chignon), and been elected to Parliament in a landslide. She hasn't got a portfolio either, but she is heading so many committees and forums on women's issues and doing it all so visibly that no one dare embark on anything that relates even tangentially to women without consulting her first. Under her high-necked and long-sleeved blouses she still sports her falsies, if only for consistency, but it's her voice people are interested in these days. There are moments when I'm tempted to go to her for advice again. But too much water has flowed under too many bridges since the last time.

Cyrus leaves, but not before asking me to help a nephew get into the Planning Commission Secretariat. I tell him I didn't even know there *was* a Planning Commission, let alone a Secretariat for it. He assures me there is, and that it would benefit immeasurably from the talents of a Darius, or possibly Xerxes, Sponerwalla. Wearily I tell him I will see what I can do. I am learning the vocabulary of political Delhi.

But I am still not at home here. Quite literally, in fact: they have yet to allot me a house because the previous occupants of official residences, usually defeated MPs, are traditionally slow to vacate them. So I am based — having refused to live at my father's — in something called a hostel. It is only marginally better appointed than the dressing rooms at Himalaya Studios, and I have resolutely resisted getting used to it. Not that I need to. Subramanyam has found me a posh farmhouse in the suburbs, complete with air-conditioners, swimming pool, and more Italian marble than Michelangelo would have known what to do with. It's called a farmhouse to get around the zoning restrictions, but there isn't a cow in sight and the only agriculture practiced in the vicinity is landscaping. I was pleased, but Ashwin threw up his hands in horror at the thought of my living there. "The occasional Sunday brunch with intimate friends, perhaps," he said, "but live there? You'll destroy everything we've said about you in the constituency and confirm Sugriva Sharma's worst exaggerations. You've got to live somewhere more fitting, Ashok-bhai. A standard government bungalow like any other MP. Or stay with us." He was careful not to say "with Dad."

"I guess you're right about the farmhouse," I conceded reluctantly, "but I'm not staying with Dad. I'll wait it out in the hostel. I'm hardly here anyway."

This is true. Whatever my political importance or relative lack thereof, I am still in great demand at receptions and parties of every sort and return to my TOA ("temporary official accommodation") only to sleep. Maya is in Bombay most of the time anyway; she thinks it would be too disruptive to pull the kids out of their school. In any case I have the parliamentary fringe benefit of free domestic air travel and can always use it to meet my domestic obligations. Frankly, I don't mind the separation too much. I can be away from Maya without feeling guilty about it: after all, I'm sacrificing family life in the national cause. As the triplets grow (without somehow managing to grow *up*), it is a sacrifice I am increasingly willing to make. They are all of ten or thereabouts, and the house is already littered with cassette tapes, love comics, costume jewelry, and pinup posters of British pop stars and Pakistani cricketers. God knows who or what they will seize on when they enter their teens.

The only traditional home comfort I have brought with me is Subramanyam. He is disconsolately ensconced in a temporary office and clearly prefers dealing with producers to dialing politicians, a task at which he is conspicuously less successful. But having him around to take care of the big little things in life is the one positive element in my current existence. Well, not always positive. The biggest little thing he has to contend with these days is the flood of social invitations that have deluged me since my arrival in Delhi, and he hasn't quite mastered the knack of wading through them.

Every time I leave Parliament feeling like the hero's friend who doesn't get the girl, I am consoled by the Delhi party circuit. This is a vast industry, probably the single largest contributor to the capital's GDP and certainly to my now expanding waistline. I am invited to diplomatic receptions and ministerial inaugurations, spiritless launches of spiritual books, endless seminars on such appropriate topics as India's Timeless Traditions, teetotal cocktails hosted by alcoholic party men, dinners to celebrate everything from a wedding to a new government contract. At these events I rub shoulders (and occasionally other anatomical parts) with journalists, party workers, bureaucrats, more journalists, middlemen, wives of middlemen, editors, itinerant intellectuals, foreign correspondents, diplomats, students, chronic partygoers, chronic party givers, yet more journalists. Subramanyam's complete ignorance of the social pecking order outside Bollywood means that I attend far too many functions, none of them of the slightest political value to me. I am fed, lionized, photographed with, and generally (as the French ambassadress innocently trilled) "very solicited." Some of the solicitations are more welcome than others. Few are turned down.

"Subramanyam," I explode one morning, "I can't believe you sent me to a reception to celebrate the National Day of Outer Mongolia."

"But wery important I am thinking," he replies defensively. "Diplomatic and all."

"There were about two thousand people there, almost entirely gate-crashers from the university looking for free drinks," I tell him feelingly. "The ambassador hadn't the slightest idea who I was. I was pinned to a corner by a Chinese woman interpreter in glasses who kept telling me how much cleaner Beijing was than Ulan Bator. The gate-crashers all recognized me, though, and kept pestering me for autographs. I was so busy signing napkins that I couldn't even take a sip from my drink. At the end of the evening the interpreter said it was most interesting that Indian students couldn't drink alcohol at a foreign embassy without a signed permit from a member of Parliament. She was going to report it as a rule they would do well to apply back home in China."

Subramanyam looks suitably chagrined, though I think he has rather missed the point. I resume my attack, brandishing a slip of paper. "And what was this?"

He looks at the note he had neatly written out for me, on the basis of a telephone message. "Evening with Mrs. Sippy group, sir," he enunciates, as if I can't read.

"I know what it says, you idiot, but what did you think it meant?"

"Mrs. Sippy, sir, you are knowing Mrs. Sippy, wife of wee-eye-pee producer in Bombay. Many big movies, sir. I thought you be happy, sir, to be accepting Mrs. Sippy invitation. Wery correct it was done, sir. Secretary called and all, said no time to be sending card. Real style, sir, no?"

I take a deep breath. "Subramanyam," I explain with more patience than I possess. "It turned out to be Mississippi. A group from Mississippi. American visitors, Subramanyam. They wanted to know about Indian culture and customs. They spoke very slowly and clearly and loudly because they knew they were talking to a foreigner. They asked about sacred cows and whether I was from the acting caste. They wondered if Indian women were branded on their foreheads at birth. How can I ever forgive you, Subramanyam?"

"I am sorry, sir," he says miserably. "I am not understanding all this new-new names. You better be getting someone better, sir."

"Don't be silly, Subramanyam," I respond in some alarm. What would I do without him? "You'll learn. These social engagements don't matter very much anyway. I have more than enough of them to attend. My real problem is during working hours. I've really got nothing to do."

A wary gleam lights up in Subramanyam's beady eyes. Intimate awareness of my political unimportance has helped make him chronically homesick and, sometimes, presumptuously familiar.

"Why not you going back to films, sir?" he asks. "Though *Mechanic* not doing wery well, many producers are wanting, sir."

"I'm afraid they'll just have to want some more, Subramanyam," I advise him. "I've only been an MP a few months, after all. It's hardly time to give up."

"Oh no, sir, you are misunderstanding," Subramanyam assures me. "I am not saying you should be giving up political life, no sir. But you can be doing both films and politics, sir, like MGR he was doing."

I wish everyone wouldn't keep throwing MGR at me. Ashwin, Cyrus, now even Subramanyam. The fellow went on to become a Chief Minister, of course, which has rather stolen my thunder. I'm just a backbench MP, the political equivalent of the fat-arsed females with tree-trunk thighs who dance behind the heroine.

"I don't know how the PM would react to that, Subramanyam. Let me see. I'll think about it."

Ashwin, who lives where he always has, with our parents, is categorical. "The party wouldn't like it at all, Ashok," he says firmly. "It wouldn't fit well with the new image they want you to build, and it would give Sugriva Sharma and his ilk a chance to say I told you so. Remember how the good Pandit used to declare during the campaign that you'd be too busy chasing actresses for the cameras to do anything for the common people of the constituency? Our people's line always was that you'd achieved all you wanted to in Hindi films and that you now wanted to turn your energies to serving the district. When you announced after the election that you would wind up the film projects that were in hand and cancel the ones on which shooting hadn't yet begun, it got very favorable play. You can't go back on that now."

"But I'm not doing very much here, Ash," I say. "And I — I'm bored."

He gives me a look of withering contempt, like a makeup man asked to powder the arms of a too-dark actress. "You should have thought of that earlier, shouldn't you?" it seems to say. But Ashwin's only words are: "Then it's about time you took up my suggestion, Ashok-bhai."

"No." My reaction is not as strong as usual, because his look has shaken me; but the word comes out instinctively. His suggestion was that I start receiving the inevitable flock of visitors and supplicants from the constituency — and, because I didn't have an acceptable house of my own, that I do so where they were still coming, in other words, at my father's house.

Ashwin shrugs, but it is not a gesture of indifference. He cares: there are really people in politics who care. "Look, they're not coming all this way just to see Dad, or to hear me tell them you're tied up in Parliament. The handful I send you there get little more than a *namaste* and a smile from you, in some open space like the Lok Sabha courtyard. That's not enough, Ashok. They want to sit properly and talk to you, tell you their problems, seek your help. You've got to start doing this."

"Fat lot of good it'd do," I cut in. "What little we can deliver by way of favors, you're already doing in my name."

"You know it's not the same thing," he said, visibly curbing his evident impatience. "Ashok, why won't you do this?" No "Ashok-bhai" here. I notice that the suffix always slips when he can't summon even ritual respect for me.

I go on the offensive for once. "You know perfectly well why I won't set myself up at Dad's place. He never issued one word of support for me during the election — no endorsement, no campaign appearance, nothing. When I won, he couldn't find it in his heart to congratulate me. Not even when I came home in triumph."

"Ashok-bhai, you're overreacting." He's trying.

"You know what he said? Within my hearing, to you? He said, 'Ashwin, well done.' Just that. And then he turned to me, I was standing there looking at him, and the words just stuck in his throat."

"Words, words — why do the words matter so much to you, Ashok-bhai? Everyone knows how he must have felt. Does everything have to be a line of dialogue from a script before you can see it?"

Despite myself, I decide to let that pass. "What would you say he felt at the time?"

"Pride, satisfaction, the obvious things."

"Well, he didn't exactly make them obvious."

"Oh, Ashok-bhai, you're being childish. What gesture did you make to him? Did you go and touch his feet and seek his blessings?"

I take a deep breath and expel it very slowly. "Ashwin," I say calmly, "I don't care to discuss this any further. And I am not coming to hold court in my father's house. That's final." He eyes me evenly, and I realize with a pang that he doesn't like me at all. It is a half-formed suspicion that has nestled at the base of my consciousness for a long time, like a coiled serpent waiting to spring. I recoil from its hiss now and turn away from my brother. "If these people want to sit and talk to me, send them here," I say, waving my hand to take in the drab white walls of the hostel room.

"Are you serious?" Ashwin asks, his eyes narrowing.

"Every morning, from nine to ten," I confirm expansively. "Oh — and don't feel obliged to be here yourself, if you'd rather not."

I want him to turn to me, to take me in his arms and say, "Brother, I know you need me, I know my resentment has hurt you, I am sorry, I shall always be by your side." But of course he does not.

"If you think you can manage on your own," he says stiffly, "I'll be happy to direct them here and leave it all to you." And this is the same Ashwin who has told me for weeks that I need a political mentor, a political handler, and a political secretary — none of which I have yet acquired.

I nod. "Do that," I say. "I've asked too much of you already."

He leaves, and I watch him go, noticing him really as if for the first time: the walk, the movement of his arms, the shape of his narrow hips under the *kurta-pajamas*. He is so much like me.

"Ashokji." Dr. Sourav Gangoolie, party treasurer and Minister of State in the Prime Minister's Secretariat, rises from a plush chair in his air-conditioned office and waves his unlit pipe in my general direction. "So glad you could come."

His warmth is as unreal as the frigidity of the air in the room. I sit gingerly in the chair he offers me and find myself sinking with uneasy comfort into its leather-upholstered welcome. On the wall a lurid Husain print portrays Indira Gandhi as Durga, all-conquering goddess of South Block.

"Some tea?" Dr. Gangoolie — the honorific is of as uncertain provenance as the spelling of his surname, but that is what everyone calls him — blinks at me behind thick horn-rimmed glasses. He wears, unusually for a politician, safari suits rather than more indigenous garb and tries to conceal buck teeth behind a trimmed beard and a rarely lit pipe, whose function, it has long been rumored, is primarily to prompt him to keep his lips sealed. With his short hair, beaky nose, and prominent ears he looks like a subspecies of owl, but a more knowing and less corpulent variety than the genus Sponerwalla. Fittingly, Dr. Gangoolie has a reputation for both erudition and discretion, which has only increased with his appointment to the Prime Minister's Secretariat while still holding his party post. Behind his desk is a framed caricature of Dr. Gangoolie himself by the cartoonist Kutty, but where smoke curls out of the pictorial pipe, the real one is, as far as I can make out, unlit.

"Oh — no, thank you. I'll wait," I reply. I expect I'll get another cup when I'm with the PM, and few liquids are as undrinkable as government-issue tea.

Dr. Gangoolie seems somewhat put out by my reply, for he opens his mouth and closes it again on the mouthpiece of his pipe. I feel impelled to ease the strain. "As you know, I've been trying to see the Prime Minister for some time now," I say defensively.

"Yes, yes." He looks uncomfortable, like a producer reminded of a promise. "The PM has been really, so to say, busy. So many meetings, visitors, overseas trips, you know how it has been."

"Yes, of course," I reply graciously. "I can well imagine. But I am glad the summons has come at last."

"Oh, dear." The resemblance to an owl becomes even more pronounced as Dr. Gangoolie tilts his head sideways and examines me in dismay through his glasses. "I fear there has been, so to say, a misunderstanding."

"There has?" Dr. Gangoolie's habit of lapsing into a sibilant "so to say" is beginning to grate.

"I am afraid so." Dr. Gangoolie takes his pipe out of his mouth and smiles ingratiatingly, but the eyes behind the glasses are stern. "You see, it is not the Prime Minister who wishes to see you today, but, so to say, me."

"You?" I flush with embarrassment. "But my secretary said the Prime Minister's office had called — I'm sorry," I mutter, cursing Subramanyam for taking so long to get the hang of this place.

"That's all right," Dr. Gangoolie says in a tone that almost sounds cheerful. But he does not offer me another cup of tea. "How are you, so to say, getting on here in Delhi, Ashokji?"

"It's a different world for me, Dr. Gangoolie," I reply candidly. "And there's still a lot I have to learn. But I do wish I could be of some greater use to the party and the government than adorning the back benches and casting the occasional parliamentary vote."

"Indeed you can, Ashokji." Dr. Gangoolie looks delighted at the turn of the conversation. "That is precisely why I have, so to say, called you here today. It is — uh — a rather delicate matter."

"I'm all ears." I sit up. This is the first time the powers-that-be have taken any interest in me.

"Of course, what I am about to say must not, so to say, go beyond these four walls." He indicates them with a sweep of his pipe, as if to leave me in no doubt about which four walls he means.

"Of course." I am at my professional best; my voice reflects a man who is firm, clear, dependable.

He looks suitably gratified. Then his expression changes. "How

260

much did the party contribute to your election expenses, Ashokji?" he asks abruptly.

I am somewhat taken aback by the question. "I don't really know," I say tentatively. "My brother, Ashwin, handled that kind of thing."

"But would you hazard, so to say, a guess, perhaps?"

"Oh, seven, eight lakhs?"

Dr. Gangoolie gets up, walks over to his desk, pulls a file out of a drawer, consults it. "Seventeen lakhs, three hundred and four rupees," he says, slipping the file back and closing the drawer with the turn of a key, "and sixty-two paise."

I raise my eyebrows, impressed.

"One of our higher subventions," he says smugly, "but then it was, so to say, an important race. Some of our other first-time candidates got only eight-nine lakhs."

"I'm grateful," I say.

"Not at all, not at all," Dr. Gangoolie waves his pipe dismissively. "It was our duty as a party. Posters, Jeeps, megaphones, speaking arrangements, so to say, tea and coffee for party workers, petrol, garlands, transport for older voters — there are so many things that cost money in winning an election. And do you know how much the Election Commission allows us to spend? In total?"

"No," I confess.

"One lakh exactly," Dr. Gangoolie says. "And that is what our accounts officially, so to say, show — perhaps even a few rupees less."

It is my turn to blink. "But that's absurd," I say. "How can *any*one run a campaign on so little?"

"Well, some candidates don't even have that much," Dr. Gangoolie responds contentedly. "But the bigger parties, and certainly ours, are left with no choice, so to say, but to violate the laws."

"You mean my campaign was illegal?"

"No more so than most, so to say, of the other victors. If not, indeed, all of them." The pipe describes a large circle, taking in the entire rotunda of Parliament.

"But our party" — I use the possessive pronoun with self-conscious pride — "has been in power for so many years. Why didn't we change the law?"

"We didn't need to." Dr. Gangoolie assumes the professorial air for which he is especially respected by the dropouts and dunderheads who dominate our party. "Some laws exist, so to say, to codify an ideal, a desirable, not to mention politically salable, state of affairs. It is widely recognized that their fulfillment may not, so to say, always be realizable in practice."

"In other words, everyone knows the law is there to be broken?"

"Ignored, my dear boy, not broken." Dr. Gangoolie taps the bowl of his pipe on an ashtray, but nothing emerges. "You ask why we don't, so to say, change it. Why bother to when it poses no difficulties in practice? Whom would it help? In fact, the present restrictions imply certain, so to say, advantages for a party in power. To spend above the legal limit, one needs illegal money, or perhaps I should say money that has not been accounted for." I nod. "Who has the easiest access, so to say, to such sources of funds?"

"A party in a position to do favors?" I suggest.

"Precisely. You are, so to say, a quick learner." Dr. Gangoolie beams, yellowing teeth parting his black beard. "So in fact a low legal limit is of some benefit to us, because we are usually in a position to do better than others once the account books are closed. In fact, raising such funds has been among my, so to say, principal functions for the party."

"I've heard."

Dr. Gangoolie acknowledges his repute with a nod. "But these days things are not, so to say, so easy."

"Why?"

"Well, the Prime Minister and the people around him are anxious, so to say, to clean up the party. The government is launched on a full frontal assault against corruption — a term much misused in our public life, incidentally, but that is, er, another matter. The Finance Minister is busy conducting raids against businessmen whose books are not, so to say, as clear as the complexions of your leading ladies." He allows himself a little laugh at this witticism. "It is not a good time to be asking them for unaccounted donations on the side."

"I see." I am not at all sure how far I can see, or where all this is leading. But something tells me I will not have long to wait to find out.

"But elections still have to be fought, our democratic processes, so to say, defended," Dr. Gangoolie adds without irony. "So our minds have turned to alternatives. Instead of getting our funds, so to say, in small quantities from large numbers of Indians, why not get them in large amounts from one or two foreigners? It is easier, much less messier, altogether simpler. For myself, too, I must admit to a certain sense, so to say, of relief at not having to repeatedly stretch my hands out to some of the grubby little men with whom we are obliged to do business. Meet a foreign businessman, strike a deal (in the national interest, of course), agree on a certain, so to say, commission — nothing corrupt here, it is, so to say, a standard practice — and a generous amount of foreign exchange goes directly to a bank account in Liechtenstein or Switzerland."

"Ah." I am beginning to feel distinctly uneasy.

"And this, Ashokji, is, so to say, where you come in."

I am taken aback. "But why me?" I ask in a mixture of genuine surprise and feigned innocence.

"Come, come, Ashokji, you are, so to say, a man of the world," Dr. Gangoolie says affably, making it sound like a postgraduate degree. "We all know that your eminence in the film industry is not fully reflected in your tax returns. We have no real objection, of course, but we are confident, so to say, that you are in a better position to help us in Switzerland than most."

I look at him in some alarm. "I don't understand," I say carefully. "Even assuming that I know, that I can find out, about such things, why would the party need me? I mean, in your position, with your authority and connections, and given the kinds of people you're dealing with abroad, nothing should be easier than having the money put discreetly into an account, or accounts, for you."

"How true," Dr. Gangoolie agrees with an emphatic bobbing of his pipe. "That is indeed how it should be. But we are, so to say, a divided government." He jabs his pipe at me to make his point. "Times are bad. There are people in Revenue Intelligence who are taking their instructions too seriously. With encouragement from certain elements in the Cabinet." He looks suitably mournful. "It is a sorry state of affairs. No one knows whom to trust any more. There are, so to say, wheels within wheels." On his Bengali tongue that comes out as "heels within heels," and I have a mental image of rapidly scurrying feet. "I am told that the minister concerned has even ordered external surveillance, by a foreign detective agency if you please, of all pending and current transactions. So it is actually *more* difficult these days to obtain a commission from a government contract than, so to say, from a private one."

He sucks briefly on his pipe, his eyes narrowing as at some private reflection. "We shall do something about this," Dr. Gangoolie adds darkly, looking like an owl who has smelled a rat. "But that will take some time. For now, we cannot open a new account or involve anyone connected with the transaction who might be monitored. We need the convenience of a private account, and so to say, rather quickly."

"Let me see if I've got this," I say. "You want to have a large sum of money paid into a preexisting account abroad that has nothing to do with the government. And you thought of me."

Dr. Gangoolie nods. "There are others known to us, of course, Indian businessmen based abroad, even in Switzerland. But we think you would be safer. And, of course, the party would be suitably grateful."

I do not reflect long. When in Delhi, play by Delhi rules. I am just at the beginning of a political career and could do worse than get into the good books of the bosses when they need a favor. I nod. "Anything to help the party," I say.

Dr. Gangoolie exhales his delight. "Excellent," he replies, pulling out a pouch of imported tobacco. He must be relieved, because now it seems he is really going to fill his pipe. "Now, so to say, listen carefully. Here are the details."

How was I to know? This is what I find myself saying to Ashwin when the dung hit the punkah. It's not as if you were there to advise me either, brother. How could I judge with what authority Dr. Gangoolie was really, so to say, speaking? I thought I was doing what anyone in my position would have done.

Not anyone, he retorts, looking exasperated. Only you.

It happens so fast I can barely see the blur. Like one of Mohanlal's simpleminded directional techniques that shows the passage of time by the pages on a wall calendar flipping rapidly through the dates. One moment I am basking in my newfound regular access to the Prime Minister's office, the next an enterprising newspaper has found (or been leaked) evidence of a commission that was never supposed to have been paid. Documents start being circulated in Parliament. Dr. Gangoolie is expelled from the party and denounces its ideological direction to explain his departure. The investigation is stepped up by a self-righteous minister; Switzerland starts being mentioned. An account labeled Gypsy is unearthed, to the delight of amateur translators and travel agents. Maya's shopping trips to Harrod's are alluded to on the front pages. The PM's supporters in the party attack the investigation. The minister threatens to resign rather than drop his inquiries. Fingers are pointed at me; two-bit journalists start compiling dossiers on my visits to Geneva. MPs step aside as I walk toward them in the Central Hall of Parliament. The whispers mount. The Prime Minister truthfully denies ever having met me since my election. Voters in my constituency are interviewed and quoted as saying that they have not seen my face there since the voting tallies were declared. (True, but dammit, wasn't I *supposed* to be in Delhi?) A syndicated columnist suggests that I was brought into the party because of my film world connections with smugglers, black marketeers, and foreign exchange violators. No Hindi film hero has been more rapidly reduced to unproven villainy.

I am still in shock from these attacks, but what really breaks me is the defense. I know the government will not expose my involvement, because they cannot do so without betraying themselves. But the way they choose to protect me! The Prime Minister lets it be known he has not so much as spoken to me in months. An anonymous, highly placed government source tells another columnist that if I were of any importance to the party I would have been better employed than on the back benches; therefore I am obviously a politician of no consequence who couldn't possibly have any connection to a major national transaction. "Ashok Banjara was brought into politics to win a seat, not to run the affairs of government," a party spokesman with hair coming out of his ears bluntly tells a journalist with steam coming out of hers. A government-appointed inquiry fails to establish any connection between me (or anyone else in the party, not even, so to say, Dr. Gangoolie) and the published documents. The recalcitrant minister, who has meanwhile been kicked upstairs to a more prestigious portfolio, denounces the inquiry as "a whitewash of black money" and leaves to set up his own party.

Legally I am in the clear; my exoneration, though, is based upon the absolute reiteration of my irrelevance. There will be no criminal charges against me, but politically I am as finished as a cabaret dancer on crutches.

There really is only one thing to do. I quit.

No one has to ask me to do it. All it takes is one conversation with my brother. "It's all gone, Ashok," he says with finality. "All gone. And you don't even know why. You don't even understand what the game was, whose interests you were serving, who set you up, who rode you to a fall, why. It was just another part in a story you thought you didn't need to understand. But on this shift, Ashokbhai, somebody gave you the wrong lines."

"I know, Ashwin," I admit glumly. "Tell me what it was about."

"What is there to tell?" Ashwin is both depressed and dismissive. "You were taken for a ride, that's all."

"But what about all the stuff Dr. Gangoolie told me? What did it mean?"

"That? Oh, that," Ashwin says. "That was done with the political equivalent of reflectors, playback, dubbing. That was all show business."

What can I say to that? I resign from Parliament and announce that, for personal reasons, primarily that of being saddened and disgusted by the vilification to which I have been unjustly subjected, I am also leaving politics for good. Because I ask Ashwin to look over the text of the statement, he puts in a sentence of thanks to the voters of my constituency for having elected me. Before my announcement reaches the newspapers, Pandit Sugriva Sharma declares his renewed candidacy for the seat.

In their relief at being spared the embarrassment of having to defend me, the party tries to negotiate a deal with the Pandit. They will put up a weak candidate, in effect letting him have the seat, provided he confines his electoral attacks to me rather than the party. Confidently, he spurns them. Our ex-minister endorses Sugriva Sharma's candidacy. His victory is a foregone conclusion. Even then, Dad and Ashwin are asked to stay away from the constituency during the by-election.

I have, as our Hindi film dialogists say, rubbed the honor of the Banjaras in the mud. I decide to leave Delhi. But I have to say good-bye to my brother. Good-bye, and farewell: I want him to fare well.

I walk into the house on the way to the airport. My mother's face is impossible to read when I tell her of my decision. "*Jeeté raho, bété*" is all she can say. May you go on living, my son. The same traditional blessing she had given me when I first set out for Bollywood. I had not found the words encouraging then; I do not find them discouraging now.

Ashwin isn't home. She doesn't know when he'll be back. "I'm sorry I can't wait, Ma," I say. "Tell him I wanted to say good-bye. I'll telephone him from Bombay." I hear the clatter of a cane and the shuffle of tired feet at the entrance to the room. Even before I look I know who it is, though I hadn't known Dad had started using a cane. I want to reach out to him. He stands in the doorway a shrunken man, his face gaunt and lined, a shambling figure far removed from the towering personality I have always sought to escape.

"So you're leaving," he says. His voice is hoarse, echoing a fraying hollowness within. I nod soundlessly. I would like to say something more — "sorry," perhaps, "sorry, Dad." I haven't called him "Dad" in ages. But no words come.

"Leaving. Escaping. Running away. As always." He leans on his cane, each utterance emerging in an angry rasp. "Why?" He spits out the question.

"There's nothing left for me to do here." I am shaken, made defensive by the unexpectedness of his rage.

"There never was anything for you to do here." The bitterness flies out of his mouth like spittle. "And once I had such high hopes for you. My—*son*." His voice breaks slightly at the lost possibilities of the word. "Why?" he resumes, his cane smashing at the doorjamb. "What for? What was the point of it all?"

"KB," Ma says, "you're shouting."

"I know I'm shouting!" He turns to me and I realize that not even in my childhood have I seen him so angry. "Go! Go to your films and your sluts and your dancing and kicking! Go — go and destroy something else!"

"Dad —"

"Don't say another word!" And I see, to my horror and disbelief, that he has raised his cane and is holding it as if he is about to strike.

"KB!" My mother's alarm is genuine. Quickly she goes to him

and gently lowers his arm. They both look at me, and I am lacerated by the jagged edges of pain in their eyes.

There is nothing I can say to them. I leave the house without another word.

"I wasn't enjoying it anyway," I say to Cyrus, whose nephew has been turned down by the Planning Commission. "But one thing I'll never forgive the bastards for: they froze the Gypsy account, into which the commission had been paid, without warning me to get my own money out first. Cyrus, I'm practically broke."

To his credit, Sponerwalla doesn't remind me he'd argued against my foray into the land of the cuckoo clock. "That should be easily remedied," he says, looking like a chocolate lover who's just found the soft center. "Let the producers know you're back in business, and they'll come flocking to you again."

But they aren't. Subramanyam's face registers even lower levels of disappointment than it did in Delhi: producers aren't available when he calls them. The one or two offers that are made are at figures I would have turned down five years ago.

"What I am to be telling them, sir? When I told that sir would not be interested at that price, Choubey-sahib saying you tell him anyway, it is more than anyone else will be giving him these days." He averted his eyes, like a Brahmin before a shish-kebab. "Sorry, sir."

"Don't be sorry, Subramanyam, it's only a phase." I reassure him with a confidence I never felt in the political world. "These people only know the box office, where they have only heard of up and down, and because of what has happened they think I'm down. What they don't realize is that I may be down in politics, but as an actor, I'm as good as I ever was, and the people love me."

"Yes, sir," says Subramanyam dubiously.

"You don't seem convinced," I laugh. "Well, don't worry. You tell Choubey-sahib I said no to his offer, but that I want to see him. Ask him to come here, let's say, at teatime tomorrow."

Fifteen minutes later he is back. "I am not getting Choubey-sahib, sir," he confesses. "Only his secretary I am getting. He is making me hold on for quite some time, then he is saying, 'If Ashokji wanting to meet Choubey-sahib, tell him to come here.' I starting to say something, sir, but then line going dead."

"Hmm." I digest this pieces of news; it's worse than I thought. I suppose the balance sheet of the last few years is none too good: *Dil Ek Qila,* a few middling hits, the failure of *Mechanic.* And now a bad name in the press, though for reasons that have nothing to do with my acting. The reek of defeat still clings to my aura. "Well, Subramanyam, perhaps it's time I paid a visit to Choubey-sahib after all."

Choubey-sahib lives in a bungalow, of the kind that few producers can afford today: set back from the road, big gate, even a little stretch of grass in front. I am ushered in by a deferential manservant and shown to an overstuffed sofa.

I look around me with interest. It is years since I have been here, years since the producers started coming to me. Continued success has added to Choubey's prosperity and his furnishings. Sofas, chairs, and a divan are upholstered in red raw silk and generously laden with cushions and bolsters clad in varying hues of the same material. The walls are not spared: I touch one and find it has been papered in raw silk. Yet little of it is visible under a scattering of modern art, all acquired since it became the fashionable thing to buy: a couple of Husains from his mass-production period, an intricate Charan Sharma (mounds of stones seen through a half-open window, the producer's view of his extras), and a gigantic Anjolie Ela Menon catch my eye. So do the photographs Choubey has placed on every available surface, all depicting the greater glory of Choubey: Choubey with the Prime Minister, Choubey with the dynastic scion who nearly became Prime Minister, Choubey being garlanded by some overdressed woman with a smile as false as her pearls, Choubey with wife and offspring in a studio pose, Choubey with (I am pleased to note) me. Some of these (but not mine) are signed. There are also solitary Choubeys in evidence, from a youthful, chubby-faced Choubey to a more contemporary Choubey, still chubby-faced but no longer youthful, the fat cheeks set in the sullenness of success. Many replica Choubeys, but no original: of the real thing, there is no sign.

"Is Choubey-sahib in?" I ask the manservant.

"Yes, sahib, he is in," the man confirms. "Sahib, *chai,* sahib?"

"Coffee, I think," I demur, just to assert myself. "Have you told Choubey-sahib I am here?"

The man shifts uneasily from foot to foot, his eyes evading mine. "Sahib, I'll go get the tea," he says in Hindi, backing away toward the kitchen.

"Not so fast," I say. "You haven't answered my question."

He stands on one leg and cocks his head, as if trying to recall it. "Have you told Choubey-sahib I'm here?" I repeat.

"Sahib, Choubey-sahib is sleeping," the man informs me sheepishly.

"Well, go and wake him up then," I demand. "He said eleven o'clock, it's almost quarter past already."

"I'll go get the tea, sahib," says the servant and disappears before I can catch him again.

I resume, in silence but not tranquillity, my inspection of the Choubey living room. There are three *Filmfare* statuettes on a sideboard, Best Picture Awards for God knows what, perhaps even something starring me. A brass hookah stands on a corner table, an outsize Nataraj on another. Choubey clearly hasn't left his interior decor to the kind of people who do the sets of his films. There are wooden elephants, a clay Bankura horse, a bejeweled Rajasthani camel. Glossy coffee table books of photographs by Raghu Rai and Raghubir Singh jostle for space with well-thumbed issues of *Showbiz, Stardust,* and *TV and Video World.* Choubey has certainly acquired culture with a vengeance.

The tea arrives, accompanied by thick milky *peda*s on a plate. "Have you told Choubey-sahib?" I ask ungratefully as the servant sets the tray down.

"Sahib, I — sahib, Choubey-sahib is just coming, sahib."

I am not mollified. "Did he say that himself?"

"Sahib, Choubey-sahib is sleeping. He has given me strict instructions not to disturb him. But he will wake up soon, I am sure. I am sorry, sahib. I am sure it will not be long, sahib."

"Well, what time does Choubey-sahib normally wake up?"

The servant shifts uneasily again. "Sir, about this time."

"About? What time exactly? When did he wake up yesterday?"

"Sahib, yesterday he woke up at noon."

"And the day before?"

"At noon."

"So have you ever seen him wake up at eleven and keep an appointment?"

"Yes, sahib, many times."

"And when was the last time?"

"Sahib, I — I don't remember."

So Choubey had called me for an appointment in the morning with every intention of keeping me waiting till he had woken up. That's the way you treat aspiring actresses and perspiring journalists, not superstars. I feel a deep surge of anger and humiliation well up within me.

I rise.

"Sahib, you haven't had your tea."

"Give it to Choubey-sahib," I say brutally, "with my compliments."

And I walk out, with as much dignity as I can muster. It is not a lot. After all, I had asked for coffee.

"So what do I do, Tool?"

I am sitting with my erstwhile classmate and current Guru at his new ashram in Worli. I know the compound well: it used to be the old Himalaya Studios. The video revolution, spiraling studio costs, and skyrocketing property prices have changed the economics of the film studios: the owners of the Himalaya got far more from the Guru's expatriate backers than they could have hoped to earn in decades of rentals to film production units. Where once the studio was the fantasyland in which any world could be conjured up with canvas, paint, and a box of nails for next to nothing, filmmakers are finding it cheaper today to hire actual locales. When I began my movie career there must have been thirty film studios in Bombay, and nine-tenths of each film was shot entirely in a studio. Today there are hardly seven or eight, and some of them — like S. T. Studios, in which I shot my first film — are said to be on their last legs. If they could sell, Cyrus tells me, they would; but not all are as lucky, or adept, at getting the necessary bureaucratic permissions as Himalaya. Because of the land-use laws not every studio can sell its property to the highest bidder, so large studio lots, for which a developer would cheerfully pay a fortune, rot underused in prime locations. Rather like me.

"You're sure no one saw you come in?"

"Yes, Tool, I told you. Blinds down in the car, side gate, back way into the building. As we'd agreed. Come on, Tool, give me a break, will you?"

"And don't call me Tool. It's undignified."

"It's your name, for Chrissake. I didn't invent it."

"Guruji sounds better."

"Not to me. What's all this, Tool? Are you going to abandon me, too?"

"Only if you persist in calling me by that abominable college nickname."

I've never seen him so tetchy before. "OK, OK, Guruji it is," I say. "Now act like one and give me some advice. I need it badly."

"I know." Tool scratches himself in an intimate place and scowls into his beard. The jolly bright-eyed sage of our last encounter seems a world away from the irritable figure picking his toenails in front of me. Actually, he should have much more to be jolly about: thanks at least initially to my advice and guidance, he has become the rage of Bollywood, whereas his blessings have only brought me back where I started — in fact, *behind* where I started.

"As I see it," he says, "your situation is this. By going away to Parliament you lost momentum; the pictures you canceled were given to other actors, some of whom did rather well. Your last hit was more than two years ago. The *Mechanic* flop still lingers in producers' minds, and since then your public image has taken a beating thanks to your Swiss shenanigans. Whatever political popularity you had has been dissipated by your resignation. You are not returning to films triumphant on another field of battle, but vanquished or, at least, disillusioned. So it's no surprise you're no longer the obvious choice for the role of antiestablishment hero, gloriously conquering injustice and tyranny. If anything you're seen as somehow part of the corrupt system you used to beat as a hero. In the circumstances, producers are no longer clamoring for your signature at extortionate rates; they've found other actors who'd do just as well for less. Right so far?"

"Thanks for cheering me up, Guruji," I confirm bitterly.

Tool goes on, oblivious, his fingers caressing between his toes.

"Dilemma: if you say yes to one of these producers, you go down in their eyes, you become one of many, affordable, dispensable. If you keep saying no, you starve." He smiles for the first time. "In a manner of speaking. That *is* how you see your choice, isn't it?"

"You could say that," I concede reluctantly. "So what do I do?"

"There is a third way." Some of the jolliness returns to Tool's face, like lights slowly coming on before a take. "A man came to see me yesterday, a fat fellow called Murthy. You don't know him, but he's a producer. In the South. And he's very, very, wealthy."

"Never heard of him."

"He makes movies that don't feature in the *Filmfare* awards and whose stars don't get space in *Showbiz*, but that do extremely well with the masses. His last film grossed over a crore."

"I can't believe I've never heard of this chap. Murthy? Are you sure you've got the name right?"

"I've got the name right." Tool tucks a foot under his thigh and blinks at me. "He makes mythologicals."

I look at him like a tea-drinker waiting for the infusion to brew. "And?"

"That's why you haven't heard of him. He makes movies that people go to see as if they were going to a temple. When you go to see a reincarnation of God you don't care who's acting the part. So Murthy hasn't had to look for big names in Bombay. He's got his own regulars, and he does well with unknowns."

"So now he wants to break in to normal Hindi films and is looking for a superstar? Me."

"No." Tool looks too self-satisfied as he registers my disappointment. "No, he believes in sticking to what he's already doing well. He'll continue doing mythologicals."

"So why did he come to see you?"

The Guru looks at me disapprovingly beneath bushy eyebrows. "The relations between a guru and a client are always confidential," he intones with a solemnity that, in happier times, would have made me laugh. Instead, I nod in contrite acknowledgment.

"All right," I mumble, chastened, "but where do I come in?"

Tool raises one hand, with forefinger upright. "That's the interesting part. Murthy is planning a new film — the mythological to end all mythologicals. A film about the end of the world. *Kalki*."

I look at him, still unsure. "And?"

"You'd be perfect for the part!" the Guru beams. "The last avatar — a divine figure of grace and strength who comes into the world riding a white stallion, with a flaming sword in his hand. He sees that dharma has been violated and mocked, and he launches on his divine dance of death because he must destroy a corrupt world. What a role! What a part!"

"You've got to be joking, Tool. Me? Do a mythological? I'd be a laughingstock."

"N. T. Rama Rao isn't. That's about all he's done, and he's a Chief Minister. Think about it, AB. I have some influence with Murthy. I can convince him to offer you the part."

"Convince *him?* Since when have I been reduced to this, Tool? In the old days a maker of mythologicals wouldn't get in to see me. Convince *him?*"

"If you can do better yourself," says Tool, affronted, into his beard, "you needn't ask my advice."

"I'm sorry. Go on. Let me hear the rest of it."

"Murthy gets a big name, the biggest name he's ever used. In turn, he delivers a massive publicity blitz, making *Kalki* your vehicle. You use it to restore your image — to identify yourself forever as the destroyer of corruption, not the begetter of it."

I'm beginning to get the point. "I'm intrigued, Tool," I admit. "I mean Guruji."

"This," he says with the sudden enthusiasm of a Sponerwalla, "could mark the beginning of your renaissance. A brave step to redefine yourself in the eyes of the masses. An opportunity to play the religious chord in the hearts of the Indian public. The formula wallahs don't want you? To *naraka* with them! You will turn to God."

I am swept up by his fervor, by the messianic light in his eyes. "I'll do it, Guruji," I breathe.

I don't even ask him what he's getting out of it. Or how much.

Exterior: Night

KALKI

The camera pans over a vast, arid plain, taking in an opulent city dotted with poor people. Down its narrow streets, thin dark men in loincloths carry heavy gold-handled palanquins under whose lace canopies recline sleek women adorned with glittering jewelry. They pass a sad-eyed child wailing in the gutter, an old man lying sick and helpless on the side of the road, a cow dead or dying, flies swarming around its lank head. A beggar woman, infant at her hip, hand outstretched, asks piteously for alms. The women in the palanquins avert their imperious gazes, and the beggar stares after them as their bearers trot past, her hand still reaching out in futile hope.

Ahead, a sumptuous chariot, its gleaming carriage pulled by a healthy, impeccably white horse, comes to a halt. Its way is blocked by the broken-down cart of a ragpicker. As the mournful buffalo yoked to the cart chews ruminatively on a dry stalk, the ragpicker, his torn and dirty bundles slipping off the cart's open back, examines his wooden wheel, which has come off entirely and tilted the cart to an acute angle.

"Out of my way!" snarls the mustachioed man in the chariot. He wears a silk tunic with a gold breastplate; bands of gold encircle his fingers, wrists, triceps and hang from his ears. He cracks his whip to lend emphasis to his command.

The ragpicker cowers and points helplessly to the broken wheel.

"Sahib," he says anachronistically, for the usage was to be a legacy of colonialism, "my wheel is broken."

"That's not my problem," the man in the chariot snaps. "Get your cart off the road."

"Sahib, I ca-. . . cannot. The wheel will have to be repaired first."

"Do you expect me to wait, imbecile? Push it out of my way." This time the whip comes down on the ragpicker's shoulders.

"Ye-e-s, sahib." The ragpicker tries to lift the collapsed end of his cart, but it is too much for him. Sweat breaks out in beads on his face, he grunts with the strain, but the cart will not budge. He goes to the front and tries to coax his buffalo to move. It does not. He prods the animal with a stick. The buffalo starts up, but the cart only creaks and collapses further, one corner now touching the dusty ground.

"Sahib . . . you see—"

The man in the chariot leaps down, red eyes blazing, and hits the ragpicker with his whip. His victim raises his arms across his face in a gesture of self-protection and abasement, but still the blows rain down. Hearing the disturbance, four men, clad in simpler versions of the whip-wielder's costume, and with copper bracelets rather than gold, run in. A command is barked: the four push aside the ragpicker, seize his cart and bodily turn it over, and send the cart and its contents crashing and splintering against the wall. The buffalo, lowing, falls; the ragpicker's worldly goods lie shattered and scattered at his feet; one of the four men cuffs him soundly for good measure as he sprawls on the ground. But the way is now free for the chariot.

An old blind woman with flowing white hair bends down to take the ragpicker's head in her hands. "What have they done to you, my son?" she asks, sightless eyes staring into the camera.

He says nothing. She looks into a distance beyond the vision of the seeing and says in a terrible voice, "It will all be over soon, my son. Justice will come to this world. This evil will be destroyed."

The ragpicker utters a disbelieving sound, half moan, half laugh. "How, Ma? Who will do it?"

"Don't worry," she replies in the same tone. "He will come."

"Who, Ma?"

She does not need to answer, for the sound track thunders and flaming titles fill the screen like flashes of lightning:

ASHOK BANJARA
as
K A L K I

As the credits continue, the theme song is heard, sung by a chorus of voices *bhajan*-style to the accompaniment of a wheezing harmonium and clashing castanets:

> *In the darkness of the world*
> *dharma's banner is unfurled*
> *as the evil and the sickness must be fought;*
> *when all good is crushed and curled*
> *and insults to God are hurled,*
> *it's time for action to take the place of thought.*

> *Kalki! Kalki!*
> *arise, o lord, your noble time has come;*
> *Kalki! Kalki!*
> *descend to earth and strike* adharma *dumb.*

> *The poor can eat no rice,*
> *the rich indulge in every vice,*
> *the awful time of Kaliyug is here;*
> *men are trampled just like mice*
> *as oppression claims its price,*
> *but now the time for deliverance is near.*

> *Kalki! Kalki!*
> *Hope dawns at last upon your glorious birth!*
> *Kalki! Kalki!*
> *Our salvation comes when you destroy the earth.*

[*"Now wait a minute," the superstar said to the producer. "I thought Kaliyug was* now. *I thought Kalki was yet to come, that Kalki would come at the end of our modern era to destroy the present-day world, which has lapsed into immorality, et cetera, et cetera. Why then have you conceived this as a costume drama, set in the age of chariots and palanquins?"*

[*And the producer replied, "Mythologicals in modern dress? What you are saying? You are wanting me to lose all my money or what? No, my dear Thiru Banjara, when the Indian public is coming to see mythological, it is coming to see chariot, and palanquin, and costumes with much gold. How it matters what time story is being set? When our noble ancestors were thinking of Kaliyug, were they imagining motorcars and suit-pant, if you please? And kindly be thinking also of something else. If this filmistory taking place today, without palanquins and all, in independent India, and Kalki is to come down to destroy that, how will be reacting our friends the censors? You think they will be liking? You think they will be saying, 'Please show wickedness of our politicians, and police, and corruption and all, we will give U certificate and recommend entertainment-tax exemption'? No, my friend, they will be going cut-cut with scissors, they will be banning on grounds of likely to incite disaffection and public disturbance. And then where I will be? And not to forget: where you will be?"*

[*"You're right, Murthy-ji," said the superstar. "Forget I ever asked."*]

Vignettes of Kaliyug, when the moral order of the world is turned upside down: in a luxurious palace rules an evil queen, with a hooked nose and white-streaked hair, seated on a throne of burnished gold. She is surrounded by courtiers with ingratiating smiles who bend deeply from their copious waists. A young man is dragged into her audience hall and flung at her feet. "He is from the stables," says an oily courtier. "He wants more. He has been saying that the horses eat better than the stablehands."

"Take him away and flog him," says the queen. "Then send him away. We can hire two new stablehands on the wages this ungrateful men is being paid." The man shouts his defiance as he is led out, but his eyes bear the haunted look of one who acknowledges his own defeat.

Next comes a young woman clad in a coarse black-and-white print. She has been going from pipal tree to pipal tree, telling stories about evil and injustice across the land. "Have her tongue torn out," says the queen. The woman is too numbed with shock to protest as courtiers leap gleefully to execute the command.

An old Brahmin sage is then brought in, a former counselor to the late king. At first the queen is respectful; the old Brahmin has helped the throne in the past, he has persuaded bandits to lay down their weapons and embrace dharma, he is a man of learning and wisdom. But his message now is unwelcome: he wants the queen to retire, clad only in bark, to the forest to commune with the trees and the animals and to contemplate the Absolute.

"But I am not ready for such an exile," says the queen.

"The people want it," replies the Brahmin, "and I demand it of you. Otherwise I fear Nature herself will revolt against your rule, rivers will flow backward toward their source, clouds will drop blood rather than rain, the very earth will crack and blacken in its shame." The queen trembles in rage. "Lock him up and starve him," she screams as her courtiers scurry to obey. "I do not want to hear his voice again." The Brahmin is led unprotestingly away, his face serene in its knowledge of the inevitable.

More vignettes: the poor and the wretched huddle in the streets, unshaded from the blistering sun, their pitiful bodies covered in soot-blackened rags, while the debauched rich cavort in sumptuous homes, partying at perpetually groaning tables on mounds of grain and flesh borne by flocks of occasionally groaning servants. As liquor flows from stone jars and animal bones are flung to the floor, skimpily clad women dance for the amusement of the revelers, shaking their pelvises to suggestive lyrics in a rhythm unlikely to have been heard in India much before A.D. 1960. When the song ends, they fall into the arms and laps of their laughing patrons from whose embraces the camera cuts to shots of temple sculpture that render explicit in stone what the lyrics have already hinted at in words.

Yet more vignettes: Brahmins are abused and beaten by muscular men in chariots, their womenfolk used without fear of consequence. In one scene a laughing officer of the court rips the clothes off a protesting woman and takes her by force. [*"Wonly mythological story with rape scene,"* said the happy producer to the superstar. *"But yit is all in the* Puranas. *Guruji was confirming."*] Moral collapse falls both ways. Slatterns seduce strangers in temples before the shocked but unblinking gaze of the deities. Servants become masters and claim their former mistresses; men of nobility and breeding are forced into the streets. The social order has broken down; the world is in chaos.

The land is scorched dry in dismay. Cracks and fissures open up in the earth; not a blade of grass grows. Plants and flowers wither into ashes, leafless trees raise skeletal branches in surrender. In the barren fields men and women begin to drop dead, their knees buckling in exhaustion. Seven suns appear in the scorching sky, each burning with the fury of heavenly rage. Their rays shoot down to earth like lasers, sucking the world drier still: wells crumble into dust, rivers are drunk up by the insatiable rays, the seas churn skyward and evaporate. Into this desolate land, in a little hut in the midst of a dying forest, a little boy is born to a Brahmin hermit and his dutiful wife. A boy who emerges in the shape of a well-known child artiste, with a halo shining round his head.

"The Lord has blessed your womb," the saffron-clad hermit says to his wife, as he prostrates himself before his own son. "Vishnu has come to us." And as she does likewise, throwing herself at the child's pudgy feet, the boy is transformed by a cinematographic miracle into Ashok Banjara, clad in resplendent white, a bow in his hand and a quiver of divine arrows on his bare shoulder.

"Rise, Mother," he says. "You have given me birth; you shall not bow before me." He lifts her to her feet and turns to offer a respectful *namaskar* to the hermit, who takes the dust of the superstar's feet onto his forehead before rising, his long white locks now lustrous with divine benediction.

"The world is no longer a fit place for the likes of you," Ashok says sadly. "The natural order of the universe has been turned on its head; injustice and depravity reign; dharma is in disarray. The time has come to end it all."

The hermit nods. "Kaliyug has reached its nadir."

"See," says his wife, "I do not even have water with which to wash our Lord's feet."

"There is no need," Ashok says, compassion battling smugness on his visage. "Your tears of joy as you bent to receive me have already bathed my feet." His surrogate mother looks suitably gratified at this hyperbole.

"What will you do, my Lord?" the hermit asks.

"What is necessary." Ashok looks around him. "For everywhere I see that dharma has been violated and mocked. Betake yourselves to pray for the next world, because this one is coming to an end." And even as he speaks the skies appear aflame. Gigantic clouds, garlanded with fire, appear between the suns; thunder roars. "A mighty conflagration is building up," Ashok says, "which shall reach from the bowels of hell to the thrones of the gods. And then the rains shall come, a mighty crushing flow that will dissolve what the fire has burned, till the dry riverbeds become surging torrents, and the seas swell up to invade the sandy coasts; then mountains shall tremble and crumble into the dust, and the earth sink under the cleansing flood. For twelve years this rain shall last, and through it all, I shall dance the dance of destruction, till no one of this cursed earth remains upon it. When it is all over, the fire spent, the waters calmed, then, once again, will peace and dharma return to the world. But for now, my blessed parents, you who have been chosen to bring me, as a son of Brahmins, upon this earth to fulfill my divine mission — I must bid you farewell."

Ashok raises folded palms to them, the halo shining ever brighter around his head. He raises one hand, and instantly a white stallion appears by his side; his robes are transformed into the short battle dress of a warrior horseman; and in his right hand has sprung a brilliant sword, its sharp edges aflame with sulfur and righteousness.

"Kalki," his parents breathe.

And then he is off, fiery weapon in hand, to show the forces of evil that he has come to put out their faithlessness with a great conflagration.

[*This is how it happened.*

[*The crowds outside the studio were enormous; inside, the massed ranks of actors, extras, technicians, production executives, delivery boys, hangers-on pressed around the equipment for the shooting of the great horseback sequence. People were milling about; somebody shouted "close the doors," and somebody did.*

[*Proud of his record of not having employed a double for most of his stunts ("They'd never find one who could really look like me," he used to say), Ashok, flaming sword in hand, began his canter on the white stallion. For a moment it was as glorious as it was meant to be, the resplendent figure of righteousness charging onward to bring retribution to a faithless world. Then a flame seemed to spurt from the sword, singeing the horse, which bolted out of its rider's control. The rest was a blur. The stallion ran wild, through the studio set, into the technicians and their equipment. Amid the screams Ashok Banjara fell, thrown by his mount; his sword fell with him, plunging into some carelessly strewn cloth, which promptly ignited; and with a whoosh the flames leaped to the ceiling.*

[*Tongues of flame licked scripts, sets, and sidekicks. Accompanying the screams of panic, cast and crew and hangers-on ran everywhere they could; someone got to the door but found it shut, the tumblers of the lock having fused in the heat. The blaze voraciously devoured wood, canvas, drapes,*

metal, and human flesh. Smoke choked the lungs of those who were screaming for help, acridly scarring the throats of dialogists, sapping the sinews of
stuntmen, obscuring the eyes of actresses.

[When it was all over, the destruction was complete. The smoldering
remnants of the set turned up twenty-seven bodies, including that of the producer, Murthy. Another twenty-three were admitted to the hospital, where
four died in intensive care and one, an actress who had been burned beyond
recognition, committed suicide with her mother's help.

[Ashok Banjara had contusions, concussions, broken bones, and burns.
But he survived.]

Monologues: Night / Day

PRANAY

So they tell me it doesn't look too good. Vital signs in decline, the doctor said. I can't say I'll grieve for you, Ashok Banjara. In fact, your departure should make a lot of things easier. But still, I don't really want you to go.

Now that's a lot, coming from me. You've never liked me, but I've hated you. Right from the moment you took Maya away—but much more in the years since, for all you've done to her. When I came to the hospital first, befriended your parents, talked to your brother, it was all for Maya's sake. To establish myself here where I could do her some good. But after all these weeks, Ashok, and I admit this grudgingly, I've developed a bit of an interest in you and your welfare. Especially after the doctor initiated these talking sessions, and I found myself the only one who was willing to volunteer for the first one. There's a strange sort of bond that's sprung up in the process. I don't suppose you feel it. I don't suppose you feel anything, for that matter. Not that feelings were exactly your strongest suit before the accident either, hanh?

Enough of that. I haven't come here to be nasty to you. What I've had to do I've done already. Something tells me you even know it. And it's really begun to take effect on you.

Poor Ashok Banjara. You'd have really enjoyed the adulation you're getting at this time. This accident has really been the remaking of you. The crowds, the banners, the prayer meetings! OK, so the Prime Minister's visit couldn't take place as scheduled, but they say it's only a postponement, pressing business of state or something. In any case, it's not the bigwigs who matter. Take it from me. It's the little guys, the ones who've had to give up something to hold this vigil for you outside the hospital, their love is the love that counts. I should know: I was one of them. Before I acquired my silk shirts and four hundred ties, I was like those chaps out there, the petty clerks and the youths without jobs. I was one of them, in spirit and in class origin.

Class origin. What's the point of mentioning that to you? You probably think "class origin" refers to who you studied with at school. I'm the only one among you clods who reads. But it's people like me who are the vanguard of revolution — we, the frustrated lower-middle-class whom your lot have squeezed to the point where we have to worry every day where our next meal is coming from. OK, not me personally, but I haven't forgotten what it was like. I'm still from the underclass, and it never leaves you. I don't have to force myself to remember.

Did you ever wonder why you were so much more popular a filmi hero than a politician? Why the mass adulation you enjoyed as an actor failed to translate into mass political support when you needed it? Elementary, my dear hot-son. Your screen image was that of the angry young man, the righter of wrongs, the rebel against injustice, the enemy of the establishment. But when you became a politician, you were revealed as what you are — the polar opposite of your screen image. A part of the establishment. The son of a politician. The Prime Minister's man. The people who cared for you as a hero couldn't care for you as a leader. You no longer meant anything to them.

Ironic, hanh? And even more ironic — when you ceased to be a politician and *this* happened to you, they forgot the political stuff and remembered you only as their hero. Look at them outside this hospital. You can see why I despair of the Indian proletariat. Sometimes I wonder if they are even capable of revolution.

I tried to talk to your brother about all this the other day. Nice fellow, your brother, as unlike you as it is possible for a brother to be. A decent chap, and seems to like me, though I say so myself. But the poor fellow was aghast at my politics. I could imagine him thinking how hypocritical it all seemed — successful screen villain emerging from the blast of air-conditioners to speak up for the proletariat. "Bathtub socialism," somebody called it the other day. I see no contradiction. I was lucky enough to join the system and make it work for me. I know how to make myself useful to the Choubeys and the Gangoolies, useful enough to get what I want from them. But that doesn't mean I can't see the system for what it is. The film world is the one place where these class distinctions don't matter. You can take a street corner tough and make him into a star and even have the convent-educated daughters of millionaires pining for him, a man they wouldn't have spoken to in the street or admitted into their living rooms. You can also have a rich man's daughter, classy English accent and all, reduced to stripping for the roles she can get. Ability, public popularity, these are still the clinchers. Hindi filmland is India's only true meritocracy.

Except — there's always an except — except for all these filmi dynasties that have suddenly sprung up. Can you imagine it — spoiled, overfed kids whose only qualification is that Daddy was a star, leaping onto the screens and demanding star billing! And it's actually working, that's the unbelievable thing. The public is lapping up these tyros as if their being there was the most natural thing in the world. After all, we are a country that still believes in handing professions down from father to son, the same way the caste system came into being. If you are a doctor, your son must be a doctor. If you are a Prime Minister, your son must be a Prime Minister. If you are a movie star, your son must also be a movie star.

So I must qualify my earlier assertion. Bollywood may still be a meritocracy, but it is a meritocracy tempered by genes. And by looks. I'm not a bad actor. I know my limitations, but I grew up with the medium, I know what I can do. And yet, with a face like mine, who'd cast me as a hero? I might be able to act the pants off the idiots who call themselves the stars of the screen, but villain I am, villain I'll always remain.

Except to Maya.

All those years that you were neglecting her, I remained the one person she could talk to. You didn't know that, did you? But then you knew so little about her, you had so little time to devote even to thinking about her. You were so busy pursuing your own agenda, you never thought of finding out about hers. Like who she spoke to. Or what she spoke about. Or whether, finally, she felt she had to do something about it.

At the beginning it was just her needing to talk to someone. She rang me out of the blue one night. It was late, nearly eleven. You weren't home; it wasn't clear when you would be. She just wanted to talk. I had a woman with me, but I turned away from her and gave my full attention to Maya. Just the opposite of you: you had Maya but turned your attention to other women. As on the screen, so in real life: I had to be your antithesis.

The phone conversations increased in frequency and in length. She got from me, the man she didn't — she had said couldn't — love, the things that you, the man she did love, couldn't, or wouldn't, give her. Patience. Caring. Understanding. Support. Occasionally, but only when she asked for it, friendly advice. Which she never took, because mainly my advice was "Maya, leave him. Walk out." She couldn't do that, or she wouldn't — and I suppose I always understood why.

But then she came to need more than telephonic communion. The first time she asked me to meet her it was for a cup of coffee at an expensive hotel, the kind of place you'd expect to find movie stars. When we went there at three the place was deserted, and even a passing journalist would have found nothing to remark about in the sight of the two of us drinking coffee in a public place. But when she suggested it again I worried about the risk of being seen — worried for her sake, not yours. And so she asked me to come to your home instead, the one place you were unlikely to be found.

I've been wanting to get this off my chest, but when I came here the first time I couldn't bring myself to do it. Even now, if I really believed you could hear all this, register it, react, I might not have the courage to speak so openly. But it's important for me to make a clean breast to you. Before it's too late.

I want you to understand something, Ashok. With Maya it was never just gender attraction, sex, call it what you like. It was, for me, very much more than that. We've abased the word "love" so completely in our business that it has come to mean much less than I intend it to, but I do love her. And always have. Even when she was completely yours and I had no contact with her beyond the occasional greeting at the sets when she came to visit you, which she still did, poor innocent, in those early days of your marriage. My feelings for her lay dormant during the years that had nothing to sustain them, but they were always there, like a current waiting to be switched on again. That kind of love doesn't die, Ashok. It was always there for her, and on that our subsequent relationship was built. Not because I wanted to hop into bed with her or she with me.

I don't suppose you could really understand that, because I don't imagine you've felt anything for any woman beyond the desire to possess her. You must have agonized over whether you were the first to possess Maya, or whether I, insignificant villain that I was, had beaten you to it. Let me put you out of your misery. I hadn't. Maya would not have slept with someone she didn't love, and at that time she didn't love me.

I'm saying this to help you come to terms with what I'm going to tell you now. In the last few years Maya was tormented by your treatment of her, torn between her duty to you and the triplets on the one hand and her need for love on the other. She thought she could find consolation in conversation with me, but it was soon obvious I had much more than my silences to offer her. Before she made that leap of faith she gave you so many chances, Ashok, to claim her back. You never seized any of them. One small gesture from you would have been enough, one sign that she mattered, that her loyalty was reciprocated by your love. You didn't bother. In the end you whittled away her resistance with your indifference as surely as I did by my sheer constancy.

And so it happened. We loved, and we loved while unable to acknowledge our love. The fact that I gave her my love made her, ironically, a better wife to you: not out of guilt so much as because she was fulfilled in a way she had not been before and could turn to the other things you wanted out of her without the emptiness and bitterness she had choked on before. She became a diligent daughter-in-law, a dedicated mother, a loyal political wife on the campaign trail. And from wherever she was, she always returned from her duty with you to Bombay, and to me.

As long as you survive, Ashok, in any condition, she will never leave you. I don't think you'll survive, but if you do, I won't mind. I have what I want, which is more than I had dared hope for.

And yes, I suppose you should know, though a husband less self-obsessed than you would have guessed it a long time ago. Aashish is not a Banjara. For in the course of discovering her love, Maya, our Maya, bore you my son.

KULBHUSHAN BANJARA

My son. My son, I cannot bear to see you lying there, bandaged and still, the life ebbing out of you. Why did this have to happen, Ashok? I expected one day to have you come and light my pyre, send my soul to another world. I cannot, I will not, imagine you going there before me.

There is so much to say, my son. So much I should have said earlier, before all this. But you would not have listened. And I was too proud to speak. That is what came between us, my pride and yours.

I will not make the mistake of lecturing you again. I — I'm sorry. The words do not come out easily, Ashok. They trip over lumps I did not know I had in my throat. They hurt.

You hurt me, but I took too long to realize how much I had hurt you too. Why could we never talk directly about these things, about our expectations, hopes, fears? You never saw beyond my disapproval, and I never looked beyond your resentment. Even though my disapproval has always turned out to be justified, because every time I disapproved of something you did it was for *your* sake. I knew it would be wrong for you, that it would hurt you. When you entered politics, how bitter you were about my disapproval! And yet I knew from the first day that the way it was happening, the way you were going into it, you were doomed to failure. Even I could not predict the scale of the disaster that would overtake you. But you would not listen, my son. You never did.

Ashok, stay on. Fight this — whatever this is that is taking its toll on you. Come back, and make a fresh start. You have all of us with you, and so many friends and well-wishers from the film industry, even the political world. And of course you have the people, the great ordinary masses of India. They all, we all, love you, Ashok. Come back to us. Don't give up.

That friend of yours, that fine young man, Pranay, was telling us what this trag—— this accident has revealed about the place of films in our country. The experts, he says, were all predicting that as in other countries, television and video would sound the death knell of the film industry; that once people had alternative sources of entertainment, they wouldn't turn to the cinema any more. There were visions of theaters closing down, film people being thrown out of work, stars reduced to the twenty-inch mediocrity of the TV screen. It hasn't happened. And it hasn't happened, Pranay says, because, in addition to the economic realities that restrict the number of people who can have access to TV and video, the magic of the cinema has not faded in India. This is something that the vast, nationwide outpouring of grief and support for you has proved again, beyond doubt.

Ashok, my son, there are rickshawallahs who have walked hundreds of miles to be by your side, beggars who have given their pitiful alms to temples in offerings for your recovery, housewives who have refused to eat until you are discharged from the hospital. You have incarnated the hopes and dreams of all these people and of all India. You cannot let them down now.

And you cannot leave me, Ashok. In all these years, I have made my disapproval clear, but I have not directly asked you for anything. I am asking you now, Ashok. Do not go away from me, my son. Let me take you in my arms and ask for your forgiveness.

I . . . I've said it at last. Forgive me, Ashok, for everything. For the lectures. For the disapproval. For the sin of always having been right, and of having known it, and of having shown I know it. Forgive me, Ashok, and come back to me. I want to hear you call me "Dad" again.

Ashok . . . my son . . . I can't go on.

ASHWIN

I have a message for you, Ashok-bhai. The Guruji rang. You remember him, from the election? He's here now, a sort of resident seer to the stars. I had no idea you had maintained contact with him, but then I have no idea about lots of things involving you. I told him there was no indication you'd be able to hear or understand what anyone had to say. He said, "He'll understand." So I'll read you his message.

It's in Sanskrit, a verse from the Valmiki *Ramayana:*

> *dharmadarthaha prabhavati*
> *dharmath prabhavate sukham,*
> *dharmen labhate sarvam,*
> *dharma saarabinda jagat.*

Hope I've said it right. The Guruji also supplied a translation: "From dharma comes success, from dharma comes happiness, everything emerges from dharma, dharma is the essence of the world."

Is that all? I asked him. Is that the message? And he said, "Tell him that dharma is what life is all about, the upholding of the natural order. Tell him that whatever he did was in fulfillment of his dharma. Tell him to have no regrets."

I'm passing it on, Ashok-bhai, but for what it's worth, I think it's too easy. One has to have regrets. I have regrets. A life without regrets is a life lived without introspection, without inquiry. That's not a life worth living.

MAYA

It's too late, Ashok. There was so much to say, so much I wanted to tell you, so much you never had time to listen to. Now I see you lying there, and I have no words for you anymore. You wrote me out of your script, Ashok. You left me nothing to say.

TAKE SIX

Interior: Night / Day

I can't believe I'm doing this.

Me, Ashok Banjara, best-educated actor in the Hindi film world, former member of Parliament, man of action who gave both "man" and "action" new definitions, Bollywood's first megastar and most articulate of interviewees, lying in a hospital bed festooned in tubes and drips and bandages, listening to the hate and frustration and regret of a motley cast of characters from my life. But it *is* me, it's my ears that are taking in this drivel, it's my lips that refuse to move in response to my command, it's my tongue that does not so much as flicker when I painfully demand of it the shout that will deliver me from these voices. What is the matter with me? The doctors of Bombay's best hospital do not know. What is going to happen to me? Who tampered with the script?

The voices echo and resonate in my mind, the only part of me that Kalki's act of destruction has left untouched. My mind, grown large enough to occupy the useless rest of me, is huge, cavernous, full of shadows and empty spaces, airless and vast, a prison for pain. My mind sees shades of light and degrees of darkness, feels the warming lick of a million tongues of flame, hears the hollow percussion of a lifetime's listening. My mind does not sleep.

The voices fill it, merge, rise, withdraw, return; they do not leave me alone. They are the sum of all the voices I have ever heard, from the harsh Hindi of the ayah of my infancy to the Tamil lilt of my secretary, Subramanyam, and they swell to fill the spaces between my ears, between my ears and my heart, between my heart and my head. Through them I try to interpose my own clamorous, insistent, screaming, voice. But they do not hear me.

I hear them. Through the encroaching mists of pain that now shroud my senses, I hear them. They sit on that chair facing me, they look intently at the mask of my face for any sign of recognition or reaction, they avert their gaze or bury their face in their hands or blow their nose or weep, and it is as if I am a screen at which they are looking, something to which they respond but that cannot change what has already been said. They sit there, and sometimes they get up and walk about the room, and then they leave my line of vision. But I can always hear them.

The doctors are the worst. They come in, they consult their clipboards and they talk to the nurses as if I didn't exist, didn't need to be lied to. They cluck and frown and mutter phrases like "no progress" or "very disturbing" without heed to the effect they are having on my morale. They think I can't hear! One of them even sat here and said, "If you can hear me, cough." As if I could raise a cough in my present state. Another tried "Blink." Blink! If they only knew how hard it is for me to open my eyes once they are closed; it is easier for me to keep my eyes always shut or always open than to shut *and* open them to blink for their satisfaction. But I confront my pain and try. My eyes close. And they refuse to open again! I try, but the strength ebbs away from my lids, and they remain resolutely shut. "He blinked," says a nurse, without conviction. "He closed his eyes," retorts the doctor. And they label the experiment "inconclusive."

Like my life. I don't know what they can do to give that back to me; I feel it slipping away, like the wet sari of a dancing actress. For the moment that I hold her sari in my hands, I can feel its texture and its wetness and sense the shape of the body to which it is attached, but I know that with each twist of her hips, each choreographed shake of her bust, she is taking the sari out of my outstretched grasp. And that in the end the rain will still keep coming down, the music will continue playing, but I will be left holding nothing but my own emptiness.

I don't want to die. I'm too young; I was having a good time; I'm not prepared for this. And yet the longer I lie here, stabbed by pain, the less I want to cling to life. The things I have heard — the things they all think of me! My God, is this what I have really been all these years?

But what about the others? The masses, the great public whom no one would let into this hospital? They came from everywhere and nowhere to see me, from the six thousand cinemas of our land they walked and trudged and took trains and rode to see me, from huts and hovels and *dhabas* and hotels they traveled to see me, and no one let them in. Instead access to me has been restricted to an intimate handful who care much less for me than those waiting outside. *They* are my true intimates, I want to shout to the doctors. It is in their lives, their hearts, that my legacy lies. Allow them in, they will numb my pain, they will revive me.

For doctor, there is much I have given them, huddled as they are in a world of little work and low wages, cramped space and closed prospects, social tyranny and perpetual struggle. I embodied their alternative, their other life. To invent something that is beyond reality, to incarnate escape and by so doing to make it true, as true as anything else they have ever known and infinitely more pleasurable: that is what I have done and done better than anybody else. I bestrode the cinema screen and I reified the dreams of millions, saying to them, Look, in me, Ashok Banjara, you can see your dreams come alive while you are awake, you can take my fate in your hands and we can triumph together. I have kept India awake by telling the nation it can dream with its eyes open. I have given each Indian the chance to reinvent his life, to thrill to the adventurous chase, to chase the unattainable girl, to attain the most glorious victory, to glory in the sheer joy of living. I have brought dignity to innumerable lives, doctor; more, I have brought hope.

The same hope that they are now holding out for me in their vigils outside this hospital. Let them touch me with it, doctor. Allow them to heal me with the truth of their devotion, as I have lifted them with my own truth. Yes, truth. For what I have done is take a part, a situation, a line of dialogue, an expression, a gesture and make it more than that: I have carved a space with each, made a shape, broken a shackle, freed a bird that has soared in countless imaginations.

In my acting as in my life, I rode the stallion of time with the free rein of opportunity; and in so doing, I gave the ordinary people, the ones in the twenty-five-paisa seats, a truth more valuable than the tattered truths of their tawdry lives.

The pain is becoming unbearable. What is the truth of my life, doctor? Does it lie in the words of these mealymouthed intimates you have dragged in to see me, spouting their fears and their wishes and their self-justifications in the hope of eliciting the relief of a reaction? Is it hidden in the words my *dharampatni,* my wife of fifteen years, cannot bring herself to say? Is it visible in the innocence of round-eyed little Aashish, whose short stubby fingernails betray a parentage I know isn't mine? Or can it be found, doctor, in the movement of the original of those fingernails, as Pranay turns knobs and dials he isn't supposed to touch — Pranay, whom everyone thinks of as kind, smiling, decent, pulling tubes and wires and switches while I lie here helplessly and scream silently into the void?

He did it, doctor, and you don't even notice! Through my pain I demand of you: how intensive is your care? Your nurses come in and take readings off machines that are no longer connected. Another nurse adjusts a drip hours later and does not try to find out how long it has been askew. I feel the pain and the desperation in equal measure, the dying and the rage at the cause of the dying, undetected in the bright lights of your hospital. The villain has done it — he has killed the hero. And you, the production crew, don't even notice.

I feel reality leaving me. I feel it all flow out of me through the deep ravine of my mind, the reality I have known and held dissolving in the flames that envelop my being. In my pain Abha's augmented bust bounces away from my grasp, Subramanyam's soft syllables hiss in dissonance, Cyrus Sponerwalla's three chins wobble precariously around my face, Gangoolie's "so to say" echoes cavernously in my ears, Tool's beard catches fire and the flames curl up between Mehnaz Elahi's parted thighs, for I am the flame and I am in her. You are all coming in now because that infernal machine is beeping and I can see the golden outlines of your faces, Ma don't weep I have never seen you weeping, Maya stony-eyed after fifteen years how could you be, Dad so pale and gasping I know I shall see you soon again somewhere else, Ashwin really shattered for at heart you always loved me and I knew you did, Pranay the bastard whose face I do not want to see. Dear doctor, please take him away, please take my pain away.

You are not real. None of you is real. This is not real. Only the pain is real. And me, I am not real either, and I will never be real again.

I am seeing you all now in flash forward, and you are out of focus, the print is overexposed, the celluloid has caught fire, for God's sake do something, do something about this pain. Your shadows interweave with the flames in my mind, your silhouettes shift on the walls in a spectral dance, the flames flicker in your eyes and garlands of fire encircle my brain, I am falling now endlessly through the flames, in their illumination I see you all again, a funeral procession of fluttering shadows, the pain is gone now, in its place there is the limpid clarity of darkness and glowing and shadow and fire, always the fire, the final fire that will shoot me to the sky.

But not yet. Someone will find out how to stop the pain, someone will find out who did it, someone will arrest the villain for the crime, someone will find the lyrics to the theme song, someone will gather the crowds for a joyous celebration, and then, only then, as the flames flicker and the shadows dance and the people in the twenty-five-paisa seats applaud and whistle and the stories merge and melt and dissolve in the heat, only then will it be, only then can it be,

THE END.

Glossary

While the meanings of most of the Indian words used in the text should be apparent from their context, a glossary may be of interest to some readers. The words defined below are, unless otherwise specified, from Hindi, the language of the Bollywood films featured in the novel.

abhineta—actor
adharma—unrighteousness; opposite of *dharma*
advaita—a system of Hindu philosophy
arré—[slang] "hey!"
bachcha—child
bahu—bride, daughter-in-law
beedis—small Indian leaf cigarettes
bété—son
beti—daughter
bhai, bhaiya—brother
bhajan—devotional song
bharata natyam—a popular system of South Indian classical dance
Bong—[Indian-English slang] Bengali
chakkar—[Hindi slang usage] business
chamcha—sycophant, hanger-on
chappals—slippers

chaprassi—peon, gofer

chawal—rice

chawl—slum settlement

chowkidar—gatekeeper

churidar—tight pajamas

churidar-kameez—outfit of tight pajamas and loose shirt

daal—lentils (an Indian staple). *Daal-chawal* is the Indian equivalent of bread and butter.

dada—[slang] tough guy

desi—domestic (in the national sense), indigenous

dhaba—roadside tea-and-snack stall

dharampati [formal usage] husband

dharampatni [formal usage] wife

Diwali—the Indian festival of lights

dry day—[Indian-English usage] a day when the sale and public consumption of liquor is forbidden

dupatta—a long scarf worn by women with the *salwar-kameez* and similar outfits

ganwaari—village girl

ghagra—Indian skirt

gherao—a form of protest picketing that imprisons the target, who is surrounded by demonstrators

godown—warehouse

gunas—good qualities

gurudwara—Sikh temple

jamaatkhana—place of meeting and worship for some Muslim sects

jee-huzoor—"yes, sir"

jhamela—mix-up

judai—a bond, a twinning

Kalki—Indian mythological figure, the tenth avatar of Vishnu, who will be incarnated on earth at the end of Kaliyug to destroy the world

kameenay—[an insult] third-rate fellow; scoundrel

kameez—loose shirt

kanjoos—miserly

karma-yoga—the yoga of action; one of the principal ethics derived from the Bhagavad Gita

khadi—homespun (worn by Indian politicians as a symbol of nationalist simplicity) *lakh*—100,000

lathis—staves, usually of bamboo, used by Indian police in crowd control

maal—[slang] goods

maha—big, great

Mahabharata—ancient Indian verse epic

masala—spice

mastaan—hood, thug

mela—fair

moomphali-wallah—peanut seller

muhavrein—idiomatic expressions, proverbs

musafir—traveler

naraka—hell

neem—margosa tree, whose twigs are used to clean teeth

neta—leader

paan—Indian digestive of leaf and spices, chewed usually after meals

paglee—madwoman

pahelwans—wrestlers, tough guys

paisa—the smallest Indian coin (100 paise = 1 rupee, about 4 U.S. cents today)

pallav—the loose end of the sari, draped over the wearer's shoulder

Patthar aur Phool—[imaginary film title] "The Stone and the Flower"

pau-bhaji—Indian snack

payal—anklet

Puranas—ancient Sanskrit texts

salwar-kameez—outfit of loose pajamas and loose shirt

seedhi-saadhi—[slang] straightforward, innocent

shabash—"congratulations," "well done"

shastras—ancient religious texts

slokas—ancient religious verses in Sanskrit

Valmiki Ramayana—sacred Indian epic of the god Rama, as told by Valmiki

yaar—[slang] pal, friend

Ya Khuda—"Oh, God!"

zamindari—a feudal system of land tenure in which tenants tilled land for a *zamindar,* or big landowner

zindabad—"long live"

Acknowledgments

My research into the Bombay film world was made possible in great measure by Mr. P. K. Ravindranath, Press Adviser to the Chief Minister of Maharashtra, to whom I am most grateful. My thanks, too, to the able and cooperative officials of Film City, Bombay, who gave me detailed access to their sets, studios, and locales, and to the film crews who allowed me to intrude upon their work. My research would not have been possible without the help and hospitality of the Parameshwars of Bombay: thank you, Valiachan and Valiamma, Viju and Anita. I should also like to acknowledge the filmi magazines of India for providing much grist for my fictional mill and to pay particular tribute to Malavika Rajbans Sanghvi for her witty and perceptive feature articles on Bollywood in the nonfilmi media. Of course, I remain solely responsible for what I have made of the material.

"Ashok Banjara" was invented in 1972 by a subeditor at *JS* magazine in Calcutta, Narayan Ojha, who thought my too-frank campus journalism warranted a pseudonym. Tragically, Narayan did not live to see his creation acquire new life in these pages, but the name of my protagonist is a small tribute to this fine journalist and greathearted human being.

My thanks, too, to Jeannette Seaver, David Davidar, Ann Rittenberg, and Nandita Agarwal for valuable editorial advice and invaluable positive reinforcement; to Deborah Rogers, for her faith and support; and to Professor P. Lal, for a verse from the Valmiki *Ramayana*.

My parents, Chandran and Lily Tharoor, were, as always, a precious source of inspiration and encouragement: to them I shall always be grateful. My wife, Minu, read the manuscript with her usual care and insight; I cannot thank her enough for her patience and understanding. As I wrote the book my sons, Ishan and Kanishk, were constantly in my thoughts, but not in my vicinity; otherwise, as the old saw goes, this book would have been finished in twice the time.